PRAISE FOR

"One of the worst writers of our generation."

—Rabbi Zachary

"Stop giving me his books! Seriously, it's not funny and will never be funny. I want to know which one of you got ahold of my address."

—Mark Damon

"I said, *'get me out of here!'*"

—Anonymous at publisher's request

"That was seriously incomprehensible [. . .] Can you repeat your question but a little slower and in actual English?"

—Katherine from the bar

"I saw him naked once."

—Nigel from Mr. Lee's PR Team

"That guy's an asshole."

—Theodore Lee in a poor disguise

PUBLISHED WORKS BY THEODORE LEE

Smokin' Mirrors Trilogy

Ace of Shades

Black Is the Night

Smokin' Mirrors (Spring of 2025)

Impermanence

The Bounty

THE BOUNTY

THE
BOUNTY

THEODORE LEE

This book is a work of fiction. Names, characters, places, and incidents either are the product of the author's imagination or are used fictitiously. Any resemblance to actual persons, living or dead, events, or locales is entirely coincidental.

ISBN: 9798345129128

For posterity

Contents

| 1 |

WHAT BECOMES OF THE BROKENHEARTED

You're not good enough. Those four words often returned to Edwin Dorset, resonating in his mind as if from anywhere other than himself; at times, those four words were all that he could think about, all that he could hear when spoken to: "*You're not good enough.*" Four words (or were they *five* words?) hammered into him as a child, having followed him into adulthood. Nagging and ever constant—his own existence, filtered through all the experiences he had in life—reaffirmed, *conditioned* by all that the world tossed his way, without him being aware of it. "*You're not good enough,*" the world told him—voices from the past, voices from his own mind.

"*You're not good enough*"—oh, such a blanket statement. . . .

Sometimes, Edwin wondered whether he was supposed to have been born at all. He had never belonged, truly, nor did he feel there was any purpose to his being. Could there be such a thing as purpose, after all, or destiny? If anything, he felt that his life until then had been nothing more than an inconvenience, nearing its expiration date. Though such thoughts were unfounded, though they did not have any base to hold onto, they latched onto him like parasites, refusing to let go. He was only twenty-three, and already he felt as if his life had passed him by, as if all that he could ever achieve, all that he could ever accomplish, had come and gone—as if he weren't good enough for anything better.

Edwin had an inkling, however unwarranted, that he would die any day soon. Sometimes, a part of him desired death, that sweet lust for relief, and no matter how hard he tried to break away from that desire, he couldn't get rid of it entirely—didn't know *how* to get rid of that desire—because that desire, whether or not he liked it, was a part of him now, that inclination for self-destruction, as much as he was a part of it.

Edwin had no family, kin, or legacy to call his own; there was no one around to notice his absence—or at least, no one he could think of at that moment, trapped as he was in a mindset that kept him from thinking such clear thoughts. He felt too much inside, and he couldn't understand why others didn't. He was an outsider looking in and perhaps always had been. A drifter, searching for purpose, an excuse to live, a reason to exist in a world without purpose, without reason.

But there was still a desire within him—a desire for life, for better things. And he yearned for new memories—for a world outside his own, for a world where he mattered and where his actions had consequences. For a world where he could alleviate others' suffering, a world where no one had to suffer at all.

And yet, what was stopping him from making such a change?

What was keeping him from the path that lay ahead?

Was it only himself . . . ?

Grief had followed him all these years, and as much as he tried to escape it, it always caught up to him. Hadn't enough time passed since his brother's death? Since his foster parents had come and gone, ever so quickly, hardly taking even a brief span in his life? If it was grief that he constantly felt—if it was grief that had followed him all these years—then the losses of Lamar and Mr. and Mrs. Kemp couldn't have been the sole reason that he felt so crippled by despair. He had known this sorrow before those losses; it had been with him ever since he could remember, ever since his first memory. The anguish, that empty yearning for more, for something greater than what was given. This feeling had been with him from the very beginning.

But how could he feel such a loss for a life he had never had? A life that he might never have. It was seldom he could entertain any thoughts of a life outside his own, outside his present circumstances and the invisible box enclosing him, those emblematic walls of his own creation separating him from his full potential.

He wanted more.

An unseen future loomed ahead—a future he couldn't see just yet.

But those four words (maybe *five* words) always returned to him: *You're not good enough*. Such a baseless indictment, without the courtesy of any constructive criticism. Who was it in his mind that was saying he wasn't good enough? And who the hell were *they* to say what was "good enough"? Everyone had a different definition for what was good enough; hell, everyone had a different definition for what was "good." And good enough for what? What was the criteria for being "good enough"? Was there a goal in existing to meet such a requirement? Why should anyone ever feel the need to apologize for their own existence, let alone for their lack of luck in life? Yet, those four stupid words (probably *five* stupid words) wouldn't go away—they were ever internal, silent to all but the bearer. Edwin tried desperately to ignore them, but as of late, he was losing the battle. Again, he sometimes entertained the thought of putting it all to rest—of doing the unspeakable.

Such thoughts made him feel uneasy.

And with such thoughts came the images of those he would leave behind. He pictured the reaction of his unlucky roommates, Tommy and Marco, the moment that they found his body rotting away in his bedroom, its early stages of decomposition and deterioration in progress. He sometimes wondered how many days it would take them to realize he was dead were they not to stumble upon his carcass right away. Would it be a week before they smelled it from outside the room before deciding to investigate? He imagined the look of horror on their faces as they stepped into the room. (And would he have locked the door? He didn't know, didn't want to know, and didn't even want to think about it.) No, he couldn't do that to his roommates—offing himself in his apartment like that, leaving his body behind, only to force them to take care of it, all the while leaving them behind with that sick feeling of guilt for something they hadn't been able to stop, had they just known how he was feeling, if only he had just reached out to them. . . .

Perhaps it was an inconsiderate thing to dwell on his own death—to sometimes want it. However involuntary it was, Edwin couldn't let the desire for that sick lust for relief overtake him. He made an effort to war against such self-destructive ideation. He had made a promise long ago, and he couldn't forget it: He would never end his own life, at least not willingly. And it was his goal to live up to that promise. No matter how much pain he had to endure. No matter how many times those four words (and, really, were they four words or were they five? perhaps if he were "good enough" he would know) kept returning, unwanted. Even though sometimes, no matter how much time or effort he put into fighting such self-destructive thoughts, he couldn't get rid of that desire, not entirely. Because those four words (or five words, depending on how you looked at it) always came back to him. Those thoughts were a part of him now, a part of his DNA, and he was tired of the battle, that uphill climb that got only steeper with every year—the battle against his internal demon, as it was—that constant fight as of late to press onward, to not despair.

Edwin's earliest memory in life, the first memory that he could pinpoint ever having (rather vividly, as well), had been one of pain. *Suffering.* He couldn't remember how young he was. He could have been three, four, or maybe even five. It was a seemingly insignificant event among the many other events to enter his life, and yet this one event, this one seemingly insignificant memory in time, stuck with him for dear life, holding him captive even after all those years. And though he may not have realized it at the time, this one little memory, the first of many such memories, would dictate how he viewed things for the rest of his life (or, at least, a good part of his life)—a bit ironic that the experiences of a child could affect an adult's perception of the known world around him. But perhaps, like any genuine work of art, or anything that moves you and keeps you alive, memory too cannot be judged rightly by a single glance;

as with all experiences of existence, only a slight shift in perspective can change everything.

Before falling into the foster system, the child Edwin would explore the tracks behind his neighborhood on the outskirts of Oakland. He often went alone, not always out of choice but rather out of necessity; in fact, Vicky had *always* let Edwin roam on his own without questioning where he was or where he had been; the little guy often wondered if she even knew that he was gone at all. He usually left in a hurry whenever Vicky's friends came over. He hated the putrid smell that surrounded them: cheap cigarettes and rancid sweat. He felt invisible when they were around, as if he were never there. They were strung out in the living room, Vicky among them, with needles in their arms and lobotomized looks. Whenever Vicky's eyes were on him while she was strung out, he could never tell if she recognized him or not. Did she even know who he was? Who *she* was . . . ? Had she ever considered him her son? To this day, he still wondered what had become of her.

But on that day, just like the others, Edwin had nimbly climbed out of Vicky's bedroom window and scampered across an alley. Wooden fences aligned a narrow pathway, following alongside the apartments. The cluster of buildings were small and each identical, save for the lawns, which were strewn with litter. (No one seemed to bother, of course, and certainly not the landlords.) Edwin followed the scattered patches of grass rooting out along the broken pavement, and he imagined the grass coming to life, rushing forward before him, moving toward an unknown destination, an unknown adventure awaiting him. In those times, adventure followed Edwin wherever he went; the world was still new to him, every color bright, every emotion raw and unfiltered. But most of all, there was freedom to a life unburdened by an adult's years of hardship, of an adult's having to worry about tomorrow. For Edwin, there was only the *now*.

In his right hand, Edwin held a Superman toy, outstretched in a flying pose (albeit missing one arm). The Man of Steel donned his classic red and blue costume—the one with the red undies *over* the pants rather than under them. The toy had been a gift from Lamar the previous Christmas, and Edwin brought it with him everywhere. Sometimes running, sometimes walking, Edwin elevated the Superman toy high, moving it up and down in waves, as if it were soaring against the wind at a speed unfathomed.

But eventually, the alleyway ended, along with the edge of the apartments, and Edwin had finally made it to his destination. Aside from a long concrete wall covered with colorful graffiti running along the side of the tracks, there was nothing there but dirt, rocks, and overgrown weeds. It wasn't a playground, not even close. But the sun was out, birds were flying, and the worries of the world seemed far away. Besides, at this point in his life, the tracks were Edwin's favorite place to be— the only other place he felt safe aside from being with Lamar.

On the tracks, he spun in circles, holding out his toy in front of him with both hands. As he spun around, each step faster than before, the world around him faded, turning into nothing but a blur: nothing but the toy, nothing but Superman. And Edwin's gaze remained fixed; he was mesmerized. A lightness swept over him, an overwhelming euphoria. Where it once had been silent, there now was music; where there once had been darkness, there now was light. And nothing else in the world mattered at that moment—*nothing else even existed*—except Superman, flying against a backdrop of self-induced motion-blur, soaring faster than humanly possible. Edwin imagined himself as the toy—as Superman—soaring to the rescue: up there, in the sky, outside the world of his daily life. The boy spun around and around and around, lost in the moment—an abandonment of everything but life itself. (Had he been laughing? He couldn't remember. But that feeling of bliss, that feeling of being in the moment, caught in its wave, had remained in his memory—even after all those years, even when he didn't know it was still there.)

His spinning quickened.

So much happiness. So much life.

It had happened so fast—just one misstep.

His head thudded back from the impact of the steel track. Stumbling away, the little one grabbed at his mouth with both hands. Taken aback, too shocked to scream, too shocked to feel *anything*. But suddenly, as if it had been waiting for an opportune time—*without warning*—there was a sharp pain at his gums. A stinging sensation, a *burning* that only intensified the more he let his thoughts drift to it. He imagined a knife wandering in his mouth, digging into his gums, and twisting deeper and deeper, experimenting with his nervous system.

Blood poured from the gaps where his two front teeth had once been.

There was so much pain. Too much all at once.

He screamed. A gut-wrenching cry that fell on deaf ears. His two front teeth lay somewhere among the rocks. A few feet away from them, the Superman toy also lay, alone and ne-glected. The joy that had been there mere seconds earlier had vanished. All that remained was a burning pain—and a helpless longing for someone to come and save the day. But no one came to save the day. No one else was there, no one but Edwin.

Edwin Dorset was to learn, much younger than his peers, that there was no shame in the struggle. No matter how hard things would get or how hopeless his situation would feel, there would always be that sweet promise for something better, that speck of light at the end of the tunnel to lead him onward. But what he hadn't yet realized—or rather, what he hadn't yet *discovered*—was that there was actually no light at the end of the tunnel, not really; whatever light he was searching for had perhaps all along been within himself.

• • •

Jack Claremont, the current owner of the Geekstarters comic book shop on Divisadero Street, had set up a record system in the back of the store, near the gaming area (between the board games and the tabletop miniatures). Vinyl, both known and obscure, adorned along two wooden shelves on the back wall, behind the gaming area, where the record player sat and a vinyl of Jimmy Ruffin's *Sings Top Ten* spun under the needle. An interval of silence hung between tracks two and three. Until: "What Becomes of the Brokenhearted" began to play across the store, starting with a low note on the piano like a bass (*BUM, BUM BUM . . . BUM, BUM BUM*) and a repeating kick on the drums.

Jack played whatever mood he felt at any given time, and his moods often jumped around periodically (in other words, *quite a lot*). As for his taste in music, Jack had no bounds. One moment he would play an orchestral score, operatic and epic in scope (very fitting, in fact, for the tabletop gaming communities that often frequented the store), but the next moment, he found himself playing KC and the Sunshine Band (and more often than not right before the weekend, in preparation for the nights he went out in full drag at the Castro, performing karaoke in loud, crowded bars with the occasional stand-up routine).

Jack's father, Hans Siegel, had immigrated to America in the fifties (an entire decade before Jack was born). Using the inheritance he had saved, Hans changed his surname to Claremont and set up a shop in San Francisco, on the edge of the Haight-Ashbury district. What would later become Geekstarters had started as a shoe store decades before Jack had taken over from his father; but even then, from the start of the company's inception back when Hans was still alive, to even now, there had always been music playing. "Music transcends every culture," Hans had once told Jack as they drove along Market Street in a red Volkswagen Beetle with the top down and the radio blasting through the speakers. "You don't have to speak its language to know what it says; you just have to feel it, to embrace it." He smiled, looking down at Jack with a burning passion inside. "There's music in all of us, Jacky—even in those who can't hear it. Can't *you* hear it? It's playing everywhere."

Whereas Hans had been a small and delicate man, Jack had taken more after his mother, with a tall and broader build (his growing waistline brought on by years of cannabis use and an overindulgence in "munchies"). But where Jack and Hans's appearances may have differed—aside from their dark eyes, which were nearly identical—with various aspects of difference brought on by the gaps in their age and the current zeitgeist of the time, the two shared a love for life and a desire to live to the fullest, without any regrets. Jack and Hans had an energy to them when they walked in a room that immediately caught your attention. No matter what they did in life, no matter how small the feat, their one goal remained the same: To make the world a better place while doing it—all that and, of course, their shared love of music.

Jack hoped to extend his father's legacy. Hans had always welcomed those who were different, who didn't fit the norm. As an immigrant, he understood what it was like to be an outsider looking in. Whenever searching for new employees whom he could trust, Jack always tried to follow the model set by his father. To look within, not without, and to find the best internal virtues that were exhibited externally. Jack was proud of those who had worked for him in the past, along with the many accomplishments they would go on to achieve in life; one of them was now a famous film director, and another an accomplished porn star. Sometimes, Jack wondered if his life meant anything, but then when he saw that at least *someone* he'd influenced had accomplished their dreams eventually, well . . . he then figured that his life couldn't have been meaningless after all (even if one of those dreams had been to be a porn star). It was Jack's philosophy that even if he did live a mundane, boring, nine-to-five life, he could at least try to make a difference in *someone*'s life—and maybe, just possibly, influence the next Charles Darwin or Martin Luther King Jr. to grace the world. Posterity was the name of the game: If the person Jack helped today could help the person of tomorrow, what would that mean for the future and the eventual domino effect of good deeds? Sure, there was a part of Jack that could have been overthinking the simple impact he had on his employees' (and even customers') personal lives, but hey, he was an optimist, and a vast part of himself, that part of himself that saw a half-empty cup as filled to the brim, liked to think differently.

Jack Claremont watched as Edwin Dorset wheeled in the last of the new shipment on a red dolly. Edwin wore a black Geekstarters polo, dark jeans, and sneakers. The young man had brown skin, a dark shade, and was slim, much shorter than Jack; he was handsome and possessed the eyes of someone older than he was. When Edwin parked the red dolly (three boxes stacked atop it) near the break room door, he eyed Jack, realizing that Jack had been watching him from behind the counter.

"The driver wouldn't let me sign the paper," Edwin said, shaking his head with a furrowed brow. "He said you have to sign it."

Jack looked past the front windows, outside the Geekstarters store at Divisadero Street, the white van resting by the curb with its hazards on, and the driver sitting within it, looking back impatiently. "That's the new guy, isn't it?" Not wearing his contacts that day, Jack couldn't quite see the driver's face.

Edwin nodded. "Patrick, I think is his name."

"'Patrick,'" Jack repeated under his breath, almost absent-mindedly. "Patrick, Patrick, Patrick . . ." He glanced again at Edwin across the counter, standing with his arms folded, still watching Jack. There was a clouded look on his face—thinking, *dwelling in his head.*

Edwin Dorset had started as a customer at Geekstarters five years earlier, and he had been an employee for at least three of those years. As long as Jack had known him, he had never once thought of him as someone broken or "not good enough"; sure, Jack knew that Edwin sometimes struggled with his mental health (as anyone often does), but whatever internal demons he faced, he kept them well hidden. Out of all the employees working there, Edwin remained the most punctual. He remembered customers' names and treated anyone who came in as if they were his friend (Jack was certain that he truly *did* see them as his friend); he smiled often while conversing with others (less often now than before, however), but there was nothing fake about that smile—no hidden motive or agenda behind it that Jack was aware of (and Jack had an eye for such a thing). Edwin listened more than he spoke, but even when he spoke, he spoke as one far ahead of his years. What made Edwin stick out to Jack, though—far more than the others who had worked at the Geekstarters comic book shop—was their shared love of music. Music, and their impartial taste in graphic novels. Perhaps Jack was biased, but Edwin remained one of his favorites—out of all his employees, past and present (a favoritism that only one who was biased could have).

Jack pressed Edwin again about the shipment's paper. "Did you tell the guy—what was his name again? *Patrick?*—that he doesn't need me to sign it?"

Edwin nodded.

Jack smiled. "And he didn't believe you?"

Edwin nodded again.

"*Ohhhh*," Jack said dramatically, rubbing his hands together, his grin broadening. "I forgot: You're a Virgo." He shook his head, laughing. "You Virgos don't always speak your mind."

"I can tell him again on my way out," Edwin said, almost apologetically. "I'll tell him you don't need to sign it, and if he keeps insisting, I'll just leave—he was being an asshole anyway, so I don't feel bad about it." Edwin's eyes wandered away, scouring the empty store. Perhaps seeing if he could do anything more before he left—he always liked to stay busy, Jack noticed. *A guilt complex, perhaps* (Jack had had one as well at that age). "Am I good to go now?" Edwin asked. "Do you need any more help?"

Jack wondered why Edwin wanted to go home so early; he hadn't yet worked half his shift, and unlike the others, he usually jumped for the chance of overtime. But for such a rare request, Jack figured there was probably a good reason he'd asked to leave early. Luckily for Edwin, the store had been empty most of the day (a fact that wasn't so lucky for Jack), which gave Jack further incentive to grant the young man his wish. There would come a time in Jack Claremont's life when he would come to terms with the realization that this would be the last time he ever saw Edwin Dorset again. (Some days, he would think of Edwin as the son he had never had.) Jack set his hand on Edwin's shoulder and gave him a kind, reassuring smile, hoping that whatever it was that was going on in Edwin's life, whatever it was that was keeping his mind so preoccupied, so distant from the world, it would all work itself out, and that whatever came next, big or small, would only get better from here on out. (As I said, Jack was an optimist.)

"Get some rest," Jack told Edwin. "I'll see you Monday."

• • •

With his brown messenger bag slung across his shoulders and both hands in his jacket pockets (a black and yellow letterman that had once been Lamar's), Edwin Dorset walked along Divisadero, staring absentmindedly at his feet, one foot after the other, lost in wordless thought. His mind was elsewhere—neither dwelling on the past nor on the future; there was an emptiness there, a paralyzing numbness.

He turned right at the corner of Haight, where the street sloped into a vigorous climb. If Edwin had any desire to go home, he would have kept walking on Divisadero until the street turned into the Castro, and from there he would have taken the Muni underground to West Portal, and from West Portal he would have boarded a bus, which would have then taken him to Daly City, adding another half hour or more of transportation—all in the heat of rush hour, as was the reality of commuting to and from work in such a city, given that he had no driver's license, car, nor any other affordable option than to commute using public transportation. But he had no intention of going home at that moment—not yet, anyway. He didn't want to be home right now; quite frankly, he wasn't sure what he wanted just yet. So, he continued walking up the hill, regardless of whether he knew where he was going.

The air was crisp—a cool chill for late spring. Even at the height of summer, Edwin had learned to keep a spare jacket with him wherever he went—the idea tourists had of strolling half-naked to the beach on a hot summer's day was foolish in San Francisco; its weather had an unpredictability to it relative to where you were in the city. The sky was clear, albeit with a few white clouds. The clouds moved fast, though, and a strong wind scattered fallen leaves along the sidewalk, moving in front of him as if guiding him onward. Colorful Victorian-era town-houses lined both sides of the street, and after a block, he could see Buena Vista Park ahead, on his left-hand side, across the street, and on another large hill, a thick patch of grass covered by trees beyond it.

He quickly crossed the street to get there without a moment of hesitation.

At the outer edge of the park, a brick stairway led upward into a dense forest and a steep climb before forking into two separate pathways. Edwin followed the left path, a set of stone stairs that continued to ascend, rising toward the top of the hill into a land of greenery. The farther he continued along the pathway, the denser the trees became (eucalyptus, cypress, and pine, among others); and eventually, he could see nothing past the trees. At least, nothing else but ferns, grass, and the path—the path that had now turned into a dirt road, with the occa-sional wooden stair to help ease the climb.

A lone bench rested on the hillside, and an opening in the trees revealed a part of the city in the distance. A little out of breath, Edwin sat on the bench and stared in awe at the view. He could see the Golden Gate Bridge, way out in the distance, along with the Pacific Ocean and Marin County behind it. There was a nice spot on the beach over there, right below the Golden Gate Bridge, where he liked to read sometimes, atop the rocks (few people were ever there, too . . . although it could have had something to do with it being a nude beach, but he wasn't entirely certain); only a few spots in the city rivaled seeing the Golden Gate Bridge like at Marshall's Beach, and for a place so close to his work, he figured that the view on this bench, up on Buena Vista Park, wasn't half as bad.

It'd be a nice place to take a date, he thought, plopping his messenger bag onto his lap. How long had it been since he'd had a date now? He shook his head, finding it a trivial question; he didn't care about trivial things. Opening his messenger bag, he pulled out a leather-bound journal from within, along with an ink pen, and started scanning through a few of the pages. The pages consisted mostly of sketches, though there was some writing now and then, and yet nothing incredibly personal, at least not unless you *knew* him—and few ever truly knew him anymore.

He stopped at the page he'd left off, opening up the journal until the spine was flat. Lamar's face covered an entire page in black ink. Edwin's brother had always encouraged him to pursue his art; it was only fitting that he had now become it. Regretfully, Edwin had never possessed any photos of Lamar; he had to draw him from memory, exactly how he had last seen him, or at least the closest he could get to from his memory (he truly doubted if he remembered every little detail). On the page across from Lamar's face was the number 15 in black ink, along with the date of the drawing.

The anniversary of Lamar's death. *Fifteen years ago. To this day*.

Has it been that long? Edwin wondered. He suddenly felt a pang in his chest. Even at twenty-three, Edwin shared a strong resemblance to how his brother had looked at seventeen. At the time of his death, Lamar had been nine years his senior—now Lamar was six years younger than he was. *I'm older now than he ever was.* The discomfort in Edwin's chest partly subsided, but with that slim relief came a numbness—an apathetic paralysis, arresting him in its grasp. *I'm older now than he'll ever be.*

He didn't feel like drawing anymore. He had no desire to do anything at that moment. Any thought of a world without Lamar crippled him. He thought he'd moved past this. He didn't want to look back, didn't want to remember the pain of losing him all over again. Of living in the past, of feeling the guilt of being left behind. The feeling that it was all his fault. Lamar wouldn't want him to feel that way. The world had moved on. It was high time Edwin moved on as well—that was what his brother would've wanted.

But how can I move on when there's nowhere left to go?

He reexamined the page with Lamar on it. He could almost hear his brother's voice speaking directly from it. *"Only you carry what's inside of you."* He had already forgotten Vicky's voice, but Lamar's he remembered perfectly, as if it were only yesterday. *"Make the world a better place, Little Brother. . . ."*

He closed the journal.

Edwin shut his eyes and thought of the times when Lamar would visit. Even though he had never had a dad, Lamar *did* have a dad, which made Lamar's visits that much rarer after his brother had to move to Sacramento to be with his dad. Lamar would bring Edwin comics each visit, though, whenever he could see him. Eventually, Edwin had accumulated a decent stack of them—a collection of DC and Marvel comics, among other, lesser-known brands. Those comics had kept him company after Lamar died. His favorite was Uncanny X-Men—stories about outsiders and mutants, supposed "freaks" hated by society and yet fighting with everything they had in order to save it. The original X-Men comics had started during the civil rights era, by Stan Lee and Jack Kirby, about communities ostracized at the time; in a weird way, Edwin supposed that through these stories, he had adopted an altruistic worldview greater than any he had ever learned from anywhere else. In a way, superhero comics had become his religion, and he aspired to be just like his heroes, those modern mythological gods—and whatever trial he faced through life, no matter how hard it was, his heroes had suffered far worse.

(*"Make the world a better place, Little Brother"*)

He wondered how many other kids in America (or perhaps even in the world) had learned better virtues from stories rather than from any parental figure—he was sure he wasn't the only one. The thought was a little disheartening, but Edwin knew of no other life than his own; even without Lamar, he had always had his stories to keep him going. Literature, movies, and graphic novels—did any of the writers, directors, or artists realize just how pivotal their art was to sustain humanity? (To keep those like Edwin from killing themselves?) Perhaps he was oversentimental, or perhaps there *were* others like him, but he was certain that without their stories, without their art, he would have never known a world where good triumphs over evil, where love conquers hate, where the hero ends up with the one they love. But life wasn't so black and white: Reality had a different story to tell, and it liked to take its time.

And what's my story?

A long time ago, Edwin would have considered himself a storyteller. He'd always wanted to be a comic book artist. It's what he had gone to college for—at least, before dropping out. He used to draw comics all the time as a child, even into his late teenage years. Sometimes serious, though mostly comical.

He'd never realized how violent those drawings were from his adolescent years, until he'd grown much older, and now, with hindsight, he saw that his adolescent expression of art revealed a troubled time in his life. Many troubled times. But somewhere along the line, he had lost his passion for telling stories, his passion for his art, and maybe even his passion for life itself.

He still wished that he had his drawings from when he was a kid. They had been everything to him, but he had lost them. *Twice.* His drawings got destroyed the first time, and the ones that weren't in his backpack got lost in the fire, all on the same day. He wasn't there for the fire, though—or at least not during the aftermath of it. . . . By then, the authorities had already taken him away. The same day his backpack was stolen, the day that Lamar died. *Fifteen years ago.*

Fifteen years of waiting, he thought. *But waiting for what? For things to get good? For things to get better?* It had been fifteen years since then, and it was high time that he should have moved on. But move on to where? Where was there left to go? There was so much to do in life, so much still to accomplish. *If only I could see tomorrow. . . .*

High above, the faint outline of the moon could be seen in the sky: a white specter, half-fading on a blue canvas. Edwin gazed up, lost in thought, letting his imagination drift off to anything but reality. He wondered what it would be like to walk on that surface, looking up at an endless ocean of black, gazing up at Earth as he now did the moon; there was something special about that image in his mind, something important and meaningful. *But what makes seeing Earth from the moon any more significant than seeing the moon from Earth? Is it only a perspective thing?* Technically, the likelihood of Edwin's existence was far rarer than any of either view, given that he had evolved from the Earth itself. *And if that's the case, and everything I am comes from the Earth, making* me *the Earth. . . . what, then, are my chances of ever leaving it?* His thoughts continued to drift; he sometimes liked to think of the hypothetical, but it's not like he would ever step foot off the Earth before he died—not unless he were in a plane, or literally falling to his death. The chances of him ever leaving Earth grew increasingly low. Still, there was something majestic about the idea: the idea of leaving the familiar and walking into the unknown, somewhere no one had been before. An undiscovered place that only a few dared to enter. Edwin imagined himself being one of the few; in many ways, reality would have a strange way of exceeding his expectations.

• • •

As the sun began to set, a tear in the sky ripped open.

|2|
THUS SPOKE ZARATHUSTRA

Dieter Gammon glanced at his two companions, Mallory and Abdul—the two shared the same look of antsy excitement mixed with nerves. Fear showed itself in their eyes, clear as daylight. *They can't hide it*, he thought. *They've never done something like this before.* But how could he blame them for feeling such emotions? He had done nothing like this either. A reaping was no small feat. If he knew the full ramifications of what he was getting into, perhaps he would feel the same as them. But he didn't like to think about it; he wasn't the kind of person who liked to think. *The more you think about it, the easier it is to psyche yourself out.*

"The trick is speed," Dieter told his accomplices as he approached his vehicle. "We've been planning this day forever, boys." He unslung the assault rifle from behind his back and into his hands, readying himself. "Just like we practiced—we get in, and we get out." He climbed atop his vehicle: a steel hover bike coated in black paint with three yellow stripes on each side; the vehicle's color was fading, and its rust revealed its age—but it was fast all the same, and no matter its aesthetic, speed was all that Dieter needed.

Seeing Dieter's initiative, Abdul hesitantly mounted his own vehicle. His was much smaller than Dieter's and looked more like a floating unicycle: A floating unicycle with a block of metal where wheels should have been, and yet despite its absurd design, that block of metal seemed to be what was keeping it afloat, hovering above the ground as it did, defying all sense of gravity.

Mallory remained by the turret near the rock face and glanced up at the sky above. No clouds were in sight. The scorching sun was at its peak, and yet the desert was shaded, as if a storm approached. Hundreds of ships, of all different shapes and sizes, loomed high above them—each there of their own accord, blocking out the sun from reaching the canyons below. *Idiots*, Dieter thought, following Mallory's gaze and looking up at the ships creating an ominous shadow below. *Once the battle starts, anything visible will be blown out of the sky*. He grimaced, with a madness in his eyes. *It'll be a bloodbath.*

Dieter had guaranteed that they have a getaway driver, but he wasn't so dumb as to have him wait anywhere near the initial outset. Their ship was much smaller than the others, and more rundown perhaps, but at least it would get the job done—he had no desire to be stuck on this planet forever. *Soon, this valley will be nothing but a graveyard.* And there would be no one left but the looters—the looters, and whomever the hell was smart enough to get the fuck away from there.

In the distance, the tribal sound of drums began beating away, building speed.

Dieter spat on the ground. "It should be any minute now."

Mallory approached the edge of the plateau and knelt down. There was a forty-foot drop below, and the canyons extended even farther than that. The walls shaped in waves, and the rocks jutted out like jagged teeth. Zarathustra's desert remained a bright orange with a heavy tint of metamorphic red, and though it was subtle, you could find signs of previous battles in how the rocks splintered. The platform they stood on was solid, and there were a few others just like it, but you couldn't see any sign of life anywhere—not of any plants nor any persons (not that anyone would be dumb enough to show themselves just yet—that would come later). Solely based on the number of ships in the sky, there would undoubtedly be others awaiting within the canyons—that, and the target's inevitable reveal.

Dieter was more than ready. *Competition only breeds greater rewards.*

Abdul exchanged a look with Dieter. "You think team two will make it to the extraction point?"

"Just stick to the plan," Dieter told him. "And try not to fucking die: I'm not your undertaker. You go down, you're on your own. Don't be a cuckold." He glanced at Abdul and winked to show that he meant well, as his grin widened. "Now, let's make history, shall we?"

A deafening rumble shook the canyons.

Once more, Mallory stumbled onto the ground and had to remain there, clutching onto the rock face beneath him until the trembles finally ceased. And with the trembles having ceased, the drums in the distance also silenced. And just when the tension couldn't build any longer, a sonic boom tore a hole through the sky.

• • •

Once the sun began to set, Edwin Dorset got off the bench and started making his way back home, walking back the way he had come. Before he was even halfway down the hill (the trees surrounding him on each side again), a thunderous explosion resonated from afar and the very foundation of Earth shook below him, forcing him to grab hold of a tree until at last the tremors ceased. An earthquake was normal in California, and he had felt far worse before—but that sound? He had heard nothing like it before; it was as if a nuke had gone off in the distance.

What the hell was that?

He continued down the hill, this time faster.

Car alarms were going off in the neighborhood, outside Buena Vista Park. A siren approached, most likely a firetruck. And as the trees started thinning, no longer covering Edwin's view of the sky, he finally looked up, dumbfounded, to see something unlike anything he had ever seen before.

• • •

Once the sky tore open, all bets were off.

• • •

It was like having a door open at night with light coming in from the other side. Only this wasn't your typical door, not necessarily, but more of a gateway—a *massive* gateway, revealing another world beyond that simple threshold. On the other side of the opening it appeared as mid-day. And although somewhat disorienting, it was seen from a bird's-eye view—looking down upon a land, a desert terrain (only instead of looking down, you were really looking up). Seen from the other side, the glimpse of San Francisco must have paralleled—like flipping over a life-sized snow globe with a city inside and plastering it onto the sky (only there wasn't a dome to cover it, and it looked real because . . . well, because it *was* real).

Edwin looked up in wonder at the tear in the sky.

What the hell *is that?*

Of course, the first thought that came to mind was an alien invasion. The second thought that came to mind, more sardonic than the first, was that the Golden Gate Bridge had no chance whatsoever of surviving this alien invasion (in whatever story did that bridge ever come out on the other side?). Observing closely, he could spot small objects coming out of the . . . *coming out of the what,* portal? *And is this the only portal? Or are more of them opening across the world?* He had the intention of pulling out his phone to answer that very question, but before he could do just that—or anything else, for that matter—something rammed into him from behind.

• • •

Dieter and Abdul barreled ahead at full speed. Near the edge of the plateau, their vehicles rocketed upward, toward the portal, as the force of gravity—no doubt altered from their vehicles—propelled them forward, practically demolishing the edge of the platform beneath them.

Mallory, who had stayed behind, once again had to crawl on the ground as the foundation trembled beneath him. Chunks of rock tumbled down the edge of the plateau, descending into the canyons below; it was a long plummet: a harbinger of many deaths.

Mallory got up, rushed to the turret, and quickly peered through the scope. By the time Dieter and Abdul had made it into the sky, the others in the valley had shown their faces. They were all visible now—or at least, all who *were* visible— many of whom were on vehicles like Dieter and Abdul (tech old and new, from many various worlds), all of them racing for the portal.

The sky was brimming with competition, and Mallory quickly laid fire.

The wind rushed against Dieter's face as he propelled forward and toward the portal. He could feel his vehicle still gaining speed. The sound of bullets whizzed past him, and he used his rifle to blast the nearest competitors. It was all happening so fast, and there were so many of them. One mistake, and he would be a dead man. He had no intention of dying today— not until his legend was known. He had prepared for this day (they *all* had).

The sky filled with scattered flames as unmanned vehicles collided into one other. There was a big vehicle nearby, one that looked like a flying tank with a gunner standing atop it, using a heavy machine gun mounted on its structure to mow down whomever was in sight. With a single bullet, Mallory performed a headshot from below. A shower of blood sprayed from where the gunner's head would have been, and his body flung off the structure, slamming into a bounty hunter on a hover bike just below him, causing that bounty hunter to crash into another bounty hunter, causing both vehicles to explode, thus creating a ripple effect of destruction.

The sky brimmed with fire and blood, and Dieter and Abdul were drawing close to the opening. Soon, they would reach the other side.

• • •

A heavy object hit Edwin in the back, nearly knocking him over. The impact felt like being punched by an MMA fighter, no doubt to leave a mark. And as the impact connected with him, whatever had hit him opened itself up, and—in less than three seconds—released four steel wires; two of the wires wrapped around his torso, and the other two wires, working as if sentient, reached around his wrists, encircled them, and tightened their grip, before suddenly clinging together, forcing his wrists and arms into his chest to create a quasi-straitjacket. What Edwin hadn't known yet, and what he would soon discover—only in a matter of seconds, that is—was that the bullet that had hit him was also attached to a cable: a cable attached to what appeared to be a drone. A drone with a strange man sitting on it. A drone that had whizzed past him while all of this happened. And before he could catch up to what *was* happening—before he could even get a second thought in, let alone a first—he was swept away. Falling, only instead of falling *toward* the ground (as gravity often made one do), he was falling *away* from it, falling upward.

He collided with branches, one after the other, before emerging out of the canopy of Buena Vista Park, hanging upside down. Hardly able to control the movement of his body as it swung by the end of the cable in a back-and-forth motion, like a pendulum, shifting with each movement of the drone. The wind was violent, and he could hardly hear anything aside from it. The draft was frigid, and the temperature decreased as the altitude exponentially increased. He was disorganized, too helpless to do anything about his situation (and not that he *could* do anything about it). Moving so fast, he couldn't even see who was operating the drone, dragging him through the air. He could only see what was below them: a mass of land moving further and further away. Cars and buildings shrinking, getting smaller and smaller by the second.

His messenger bag slipped off his shoulders, and he tried grabbing it, tried stopping it from falling any further, but watched helplessly as it plummeted below him, unable to save it.

Fuck.

All his recent sketches, and all his past months' work, gone forever. So disheartened by having lost his bag was he that he hadn't even noticed the other drone approaching—not until it was too late. But hey, it's not like he could have done anything differently. The only thing he could do at that moment was hope not to die.

Sometimes, hope is the only tool one has.

• • •

For Tuwile, this had been the best day of his life. Or at the very least, *one* of the best days in his life (Tuwile had very low stand-ards, you must realize). All he had ever wanted in his life was a chance for validation; that validation, however futile, came as fame or fortune (both, if possible). It was crazy to think that out of all his crew, all six of them who had dared to compete in the reaping, that he was the only one of them still alive. And not only alive but *thriving*. Because unlike his late crew—or any of the other reapers in the race, for that matter—Tuwile had the one thing they all wanted. And what came with that one thing, the package—or *fortune,* as it was—came the spotlight: his one chance for fame. His very mission relied solely on those two things: fame and fortune, the most finite of all material things. And all eyes were on him now. For the first time, maybe ever in his life, Tuwile felt truly special.

They're watching me right now, Tuwile thought, feeling the rush of the moment. *Every single one of them*. But he wasn't out of the race yet. Not by a long shot.

Tuwile maneuvered through the sky and navigated his block-like vehicle using a joystick, operating the vehicle as if he were still back home operating the simulations. So many other vehicles were in his way that he kept having to swerve left and right, dodging whatever hazard popped up, almost unavoidable.

Behind Tuwile, the package was being towed upside-down by a metallic rope attached to the end of the vehicle. Tuwile made sure not to damage the package, of course—the bounty was worth much more alive than dead.

He was close to the portal now. Once he crossed the threshold, back to the other side, would he know what to do next? *Maybe*. Of course, he hadn't quite prepared for the likelihood of his crew having died so fast. Sure, he had meant to double-cross them, yes, but not *this* soon. Now, he had to wing whatever came next (it had kept him alive this long, anyway).

But winging it isn't always enough.

Everyone's luck is bound to run out, eventually. (Especially, in this case, Tuwile's.)

• • •

Once he entered Earth's atmosphere—disorienting as it was, following Abdul in front of him—Dieter could spot the package in the sky, being towed by a rival hunter near the surface of the metropolitan city (an ancient city, by the look of it), rocketing upward, ascending from the surface of the planet toward Dieter and the portal.

On this side of the portal, the sun had already set, but the daylight shone from the other side (the side they had just emerged from: Zarathustra), reflecting into the night like a giant flashlight shining down upon the other world below it. Only a few reapers were left in the sky (on *this* side of the portal, anyway), although there were perhaps more hidden elsewhere. Despite the vast sky, most of the competitors were too preoccupied with fighting each other that they hadn't even noticed someone else had already acquired the package. But not Dieter: Dieter remained fixed on the prize before him. He knew the reason they were there, and he knew what needed to be done.

"Abdul!" Dieter shouted (he hoped his accomplice still had his comm working). "Do you see it?"

An explosion rippled near Dieter, making him nearly fall off his bike. He saw a hunter tumble below him before smashing

into another vehicle, thus causing a ripple effect of other colli-
sions. Still, he managed to stay on his bike.

Abdul replied from the comms: "Yeah, I see it."

The hunter with the package was soaring toward them, hail-
ing the bounty behind him. *The fucker's leading it toward us.* "I'll
cover you," Dieter shouted to Abdul, once again nearly missing
an explosion that almost obliterated him. There was another
hunter on his tail, one who apparently didn't give a damn about
the prize but was only out for blood.

Son of a bitch.

"Do what you came to do," Dieter told his partner. "We
can't waste time."

Abdul began his descent, dropping quickly. The farther he
was from the portal, the more the force of gravity propelled
him downward, toward the Earth. Distance closed from them
and the package, but—suddenly, and without warning—
another hover bike came from the other side, slamming into
the driver hauling it. The two vehicles exploded in the collision,
slinging the package forward and shooting it out so hard that
the rope attached to the bounty suddenly detached.

The package shot upward, spinning wildly, and as the momentum of being thrown died, it—or more accurately, *he*—
descended again (and fast).

Dieter rang fire as Abdul worked his controls, using a joystick device to operate a crane, which came out of the bottom
of his vehicle and opened at the end like a claw.

Abdul caught the package with his vehicle's hook. "I've got
it!"

Dieter flew above Abdul, covering him. "Let's get to the
extraction point then, shall we?" His tail was still behind him,

he noticed, though losing distance now. He turned his body around, aimed his rifle at the tail, and—with a cocky smile—reminded himself just how good of a marksman he was.

• • •

Edwin had remained fully conscious as he was shot across the sky, yanked from one abductor to the other; surprisingly, during all this time, he hadn't yet pissed his pants (had he been more hydrated, perhaps he would have). All that he could surmise—or really comprehend at the moment—was that he was being kidnapped . . . by aliens. Aliens riding *Heavy Metal* motorcycles, drifting across an empty sky, rocketing to and from the portal. And he could now feel the force of gravity pulling them toward it, toward that other side. And before he knew it, he *was* on the other side. Only there wasn't an "other side" left anymore; there was nothing behind them but a crowded sky filled with hundreds and thousands of vehicles, of all different shapes and sizes, in an ethereal battle. Like a Renaissance painting, colors splashed across an endless sky—the gods in conflict with one another—with layers upon layers of destruction and brimming explosions. A metal pegasus passed by him, and then an RV-like vehicle with jet propulsions, and then a helicopter tank; a plethora of vehicles in motion, countless among hundreds and thousands. Massive explosions rippled across that colossal scene: ships blowing up one after the other, dropping and raining onto the desert plains below, as gravity reeled the defeated to their inevitable death.

Edwin, along with the two remaining vehicles from the other side of the portal—one of them towing him along—also dropped. Straight down, descending like a rollercoaster. Gaining speed and traction, with no guarantee of stopping.

The rocks and canyons drew closer. Faster and faster.

Edwin closed his eyes; he couldn't take the suspense any longer, and this time he really did lose consciousness.

• • •

The sky lit aflame. Dieter and Abdul maneuvered their vehicles through the battle like a ballet, smooth and effortless—all of this with the bounty in tow behind them, attached by claw and crane, maneuvering as fluid as the vehicles in front of it and adapting to whatever came nearby. The trick, really, was speed; dodging vehicles in the way and being adaptable to the surrounding chaos.

Adaptation's vital to survival, Dieter thought with conviction. If he had ever fought against that sea of constant change, he would have drowned in it long ago; he had learned to let himself flow in that chaotic tide of impermanence, however deep its waters, and become one with whatever he needed to be at whatever given moment—all in order to survive, of course (survival was always his mindset, having been drilled into him since childhood). He adapted better when he let his instincts take over. Like a bird of prey, he soared against the sky, eluding falling debris and raining gunfire.

Dieter flew low between the canyon's walls, with Abdul right behind him.

The bounty dangled from Abdul's vehicle, between rock and a hard place, inches from smashing into terrain and losing over half its value. *Dead or alive,* Dieter remembered. *Luckily for the bounty, he's worth more alive than dead.* But that fact alone meant nothing for Dieter's own survival. Nor, for that matter, the bounty's survival. Survival was never guaranteed, and—however cliché such a saying—death waited patiently for all.

As does our extraction. Once they got to the extraction site, they could get off-world and get the hell out of this backward part of the galaxy. But first, they needed to get away from watching eyes. And as long as they had a bounty in view of others, they would always be pursued. *We'll use the canyon walls as our protection*, Dieter reasoned. *Ditch our vehicles, meet up with team two, and get the hell out of here.* Easier said than done, but hey, what options did he have? He hadn't really thought of anything else. Not much of a thinking guy, he usually jumped into things headlong, hoping that he'd find the solution in the process. *And so far so good, right . . . ?*

He glanced back and saw that it was only him and Abdul.

The two of them, and the bounty.

Convenient, to say the least. He smirked: *Things are finally looking up.*

• • •

His head spun violently as he awoke.

Edwin could feel the change in gravity, deep in his bones. Like having a long day at the beach, having been swept by the waves for hours upon hours, and afterward lying in your bed at night with your eyes closed and that odd sensation of the ocean's waves still working its magic—moving you up and down along its current, and pushing you with the tide, even though you were lying on your bed at that very moment.

Except for Edwin, instead of having the sensation of being washed along the tide, as you would from having a long day at the beach (granted, if you were even in the water during all that time), he had the sensation of falling, *plummeting* across an empty sky, with his body flipping like a coin. Without a parachute. With nothing to stop his fall.

The vertigo suddenly caught up to him.

He groaned, rolled over, and heaved his lunch onto the ground.

No better way to wake yourself up. Disoriented as he was, once he got his bearings, Edwin finally noticed that his hands and feet were tied behind his back, attached by a metallic rope. The rope dug into his wrists and was pulled around his ankles, keeping him locked in place. Any slight movement made the rope tighten, though the pain from the rope was far less than the pain from the vertigo; in a way, it was almost a slight relief, actually—it made the pounding in his head lessen, though only slightly.

Still, I'd rather be without it.

Edwin noticed a tall, chocolate-skinned woman looming above him, watching his every move. She stared down at him with cold blue eyes, almost distant. She wore a serape, dark and ragged. Behind her, three men sat in a semi-circle—one on the ground, another on a red boulder, and the third atop a ledge broken into the wall.

They were deep in a narrow canyon . . . but where? *Where are we?*

Edwin glanced at the red walls—parts of them jagged, others smooth and wavy. They appeared nowhere close to San

Francisco; but then again, he had lost consciousness, so how could he know how far they had truly gone? *But then again . . .*

Once more, Edwin observed his captors, the woman and three men behind her. *They don't look like aliens*, he mused, noticing the rifle in the woman's grasp and how human the weapon seemed (let alone how human they *all* seemed). *Who the hell are these people?*

An explosion resonated outside the canyon walls. Aside from Edwin, none of them paid it any mind; but it was close all the same, and it reminded Edwin just how little his life truly rested in his hands. In a way, his situation felt like a physical manifestation of what he had been struggling with for the past days, months, and even years. The feeling that he had no control of his life, no leniency whatsoever. Here he was now, a pawn in someone else's hands. *But why? Why me?* What exactly was it they needed him for?

He struggled with his binds, but only felt them tighten against his skin.

I need to get out of here.

I need to be free.

|3|

THE ECSTASY OF GOLD

The explosions outside the canyon walls drew closer with every passing hour.

Dieter, the leader of their ragtag group, made sure they left in haste. Edwin wasn't even certain if Dieter was his actual name, only having decided that it was based solely on the many times the others repeated it in front of him, usually directed at him or regarding him. Going further, Edwin wasn't even a hundred percent certain if Dieter *was* the group's leader, given that none of them spoke a language that he could actually understand (nor, really, any other language that he had ever heard before). But Edwin could at least understand enough to know their body language, the changes within their tone and the many subtle eye movements they made.

So human, he thought, thinking about their behavior. *And yet, somehow, alien all the same. Like seeing another version of the human race—a distant cousin of homo sapiens.*

He couldn't comprehend their words, but by listening to them long enough, he could at least understand their names.

Unless he was mistaken about that. He was a prisoner, after all—*their* prisoner.

His hands were tied behind his back as he walked. He still wore his brother's black and yellow letterman jacket beneath the binds that held his hands together; thankfully, in the shade of the canyons the heat wasn't unbearable, but whenever the sun cast its rays below, making its presence known against his skin, that told of another story.

Dieter walked beside Edwin, just a little ahead and to his right, while Nairobi, whom Edwin guessed was their second-in-command (or maybe even first-in-command), walked by his lefthand side, just right behind him. One other in their group had scouted ahead and was no longer in sight of them, while another stayed at their rear, far behind and out of sight, perhaps in case of an attack.

Edwin didn't understand what was happening, other than that some kind of battle was being waged outside the canyon walls, and he somehow felt—however ridiculous the notion—that he was responsible for it. I'm *who they're all after, aren't I?* He felt narcissistic about even thinking such a thing—nor could he know for certain—but he had his notions, and they couldn't be far from the mark.

When he had fallen from the sky, he had seen thousands of airships all in a battle with one another, as if fighting over him. Perhaps he was mistaken about their motive; it was never wise to blindly follow an assumption with no further evidence to prove it right. Still, he needed to know what the hell was going on. *Why do they need me so badly?*

And he had to wonder: *What's keeping them from killing me?*

Just then, Edwin stepped on something hard. A rock—?
No, what he had stepped on felt like wood, though much
harder than wood. When he looked down to see what he had
stepped on, he noticed a large skeletal hand sticking out of the
ground beneath his shoe. He moved his foot off it and knelt
down to examine it closer (at first, a little apprehensive, but
now more curious than ever). He had studied human anatomy
in high school—extensively, all in pursuing his passion for
becoming a better artist—and knew very well what a human
hand was supposed to look like. The hand sticking out of the
ground, however, was no human hand. It was much too big to
be human, nor did it seem like any other primate; though there
were five fingers on it (much like a primate's), the hand was far
too long and possessed extra joints; the hand was dry, brittle,
and ancient.

Undoubtedly, the bones had been there for a while.

Edwin looked up and around him at the canyon walls looming high above them. *Where are we?* He shook his head repeatedly, thinking: *Unless I'm in the distant past or future, I can't be on
Earth.* With the thought of not being on Earth, however, arose
a strange feeling—not fear, but something else; he felt it deep
in his bones, radiating from within. That feeling he had when
he was a child in Oakland, out by the tracks, holding his
Superman toy in front of him and spinning around in circles—
around and around, all the while laughing. Experiencing existence in a new light, seeing the world in a way that he had never
seen it before. And despite the situation he was in, however
dire it had once felt, he couldn't help but smile. He was living
in a story, he realized, and whatever came next, at least he could
appreciate that fact. He had always wanted to travel the world

and experience new things and places. Perhaps he had become complacent. Perhaps the circumstances had been against him. But now . . . ? If he wasn't on Earth?

Now, the sky's the limit.

Dieter gently kicked Edwin with the end of his boot.

Edwin glanced up at his captor. Dieter had dark hair, light skin, and a patchy beard with a vertical scar on the right side of his eye, all the while sporting a cocky, pompous demeanor. He wore a bandolier wrapped around his chest with various grenades (or what appeared to be grenades) attached to it. He spoke to Edwin in an accent that almost sounded Eastern European, but even if it was Eastern European, it didn't matter—once again, Edwin had no idea what he was saying (and why would he?).

Nairobi spoke next, low and attentive, which forced Dieter to stop talking. Another explosion resonated outside the canyon walls, closer than the prior ones. Dieter and Nairobi exchanged looks with each other before glancing simultaneously at Edwin. Edwin stood up then, and he nodded to them. He wished he could speak their language, not only so that he could eavesdrop on their conversations but also to inquire why the hell they needed him so badly, how they got from San Francisco to wherever the hell this desert was, and all the other questions that raced through his mind. For example, if one had the technology to travel from one place in space and time to another place in space and time, just how much more could they know about the universe and existence itself, given all the knowledge that they must have possessed from obtaining such tools of grandeur? Except only . . .

Maybe it's not that simple.

At first, Edwin wondered why these mercenaries had brought him into the desert, to trek through the canyons, hiding through an active war zone, but then he remembered about the open portal in the sky of San Francisco like a gateway leading into another world. Had all of this been planned? Was it merely for their enjoyment, or because they needed him for something specific? By now, it was obvious to Edwin that Dieter, Nairobi, and the others in their little entourage had no means whatsoever of getting out of here anytime soon. Nor did they have the means of technology to create a portal of such magnitude and scope as the one he had entered through, the one that brought him into this desert and into a completely dissimilar environment than where he had come from; hell, maybe they couldn't even generate their own portal at all, at least not on command (and how *could* one use such technology, generating a portal of such magnitude and scope? When Edwin really thought about it, he just couldn't understand how anyone could coordinate between one moment of space and time to another; it seemed improbable, the concept too hard for him to grasp when he really put his mind to it, that it made him feel woozy. What kind of planning would that take? What kind of technology did one need?). And did these aliens have a getaway ride awaiting them somewhere? Somewhere to get them away from the others in pursuit of them? Somehow, Edwin doubted it.

They're just as incapable as I am. They're prisoners to this desert, too.

As they wandered further along the canyon, the hours stretched on, and Dieter and Nairobi remained more cautious than ever. All the while, Edwin wondered just who these two were, where they came from, and how they had come into such

a life as they lived now. The others who had departed from
their group—most likely to scout—hadn't been seen for hours
now, and it was now just him, Dieter, and Nairobi.

And more bones began revealing themselves; this time, with
remnants of skulls, fragmented limbs, and broken collar-
bones—spread out everywhere, jutting out of the red and
orange clay like a desecrated burial ground, or ancient war
zone, left forgotten by time. Edwin wondered if these species
even still existed. Most of all, he wondered where he was in the
cosmos. *Unless I'm still on Earth, but in the distant future or past—*
although, let's be real, what was the likelihood of that?

What's the likelihood of any *of this happening?*

Wherever he was, he could feel the difference, all the way
to his very core. He was far from home, far from what had
once been his present, his reality as he knew it, and far from
the life he had once known as his own.

The canyon walls narrowed even more now, with various
paths diverging, some leading downward and into caverns,
with other paths leading upward and into more wide-open
areas. Dieter and Nairobi, of course, took every path with the
least possibility of being seen; that being, the rough terrain,
hard to climb down, squeeze through, and bypass, with no concern for Edwin, who had to do it all with his hands tied behind
his back, not understanding where he was—nor who he was
with. He wished he could take off his jacket but was thankful
that he couldn't, fearing that he would lose it and never find it
again; it was his *brother's* jacket after all, and it was the only
memento he had of him left; he couldn't afford to lose it. But
the heat from the jacket was getting to him, and not only the
heat bearing down from the sun but also the effects of this new

gravity, which he wasn't used to, that felt much stronger than it had in San Francisco, making every step of the way that much more unbearable.

There was a song from afar, and Edwin could hear it. He didn't know where it came from, but suddenly he felt a lightness that he hadn't before, like a great weight had suddenly been lifted off him—a weight he hadn't even known existed, his suffering no longer present. And he noticed the walls around him moving in waves, guiding him along their path. The rocks were pulsating, vibrant and alive; in fact, *everything* around him was alive. The dirt, the rocks, and the brittle bones clawing their way out of the ground to find the sun again. White clouds, moving swiftly, with layers upon layers. The wind itself was alive, speaking its own language and singing its own song, even in the silence. A distant song, a melody so often forgotten. Was this the same song he had heard long ago? The song he had often heard in his youth? There was so much unity in its chorus, so much peace within its essence. It sung another language, a language often forgotten. *All life forms speak their own language, and this one is no different.* He could hear it, understand it, and became one with it.

• • •

Nairobi Nadine had known their plan was flawed from the start, and yet she went through it all the same, knowing that she would eventually reap the reward for her negligence. But she was still alive, wasn't she? And she had been the only one out of her team to make it out alive. That had to be significant, right? She had made it through to the other side, and with the bounty still in one piece, no less. She should have been grateful. But instead of being grateful, she felt a sense of dread building inside of her. Like her end was coming and approaching soon. What had she been thinking, taking part in the reaping?

This was a mistake, she thought and yet tried to remain composed, revealing no hint of her internal feelings to her external self. She watched Dieter and the bounty in silence, as they walked in front of her through the narrow canyon's walls. *Once we make it to the extraction point, then what? How the hell are we getting out of this planet alive? And even then, what comes next?*

"Do you think Abdul and Mallory are still alive?" Nairobi asked Dieter, breaking the silence that had built between them.

Dieter glanced back at Nairobi, giving her a hesitant look. He spoke pragmatically. "I think you and I will have more to cash in when all's said and done." He set his hand on the smooth rock-face, grazing it softly as he walked. Yellow and teal lichen grew along the rock's surface, spreading out in thick patches. "We're getting close, I believe."

Nairobi liked the sound of that, though it didn't ease her from her worries whatsoever. "At least you seem to know where we're going."

"All according to plan," Dieter said with a grin, but there was no respite in that crooked smirk. "You needn't need worry, my dear."

Nairobi continued to feel uneasy. Her heart was beating much faster than before, and the shadows between the walls only grew darker. She heard laughter from afar, and to her, it sounded like a child's laugh. *A little girl's laughter*, she thought, wondering if Dieter had heard it too. In fact, the sound of that laugh made Nairobi think of her childhood. She used to laugh a lot as a child—certainly more than she did now.

She couldn't remember the last time she laughed like that.

Furthermore, she couldn't even remember the last time she had laughed at all.

She stopped walking, ensnared by the emotions boiling inside her.

Something's not right. . . .

Nairobi glanced at Dieter. The skin on his face appeared to be slowly melting off his skull. His pupils were dilated, almost entirely black. She took a step back at that, shaking her head. Had Dieter taken drugs during their endeavor; and if so, had he drugged her without her knowledge? It wasn't below him to do that, she reckoned, but then again, he would have definitely told her by now, that much she was certain of. She felt a sudden weightlessness, a hazy, ethereal *unrealness* to the world outside her control. Almost as if she was transported outside of her body, watching through the vessel of another being. All too aware of the changes in her physiology and the soreness of her muscles. Also, the unexpected changes in her environment. The ghostly chollas growing out of the rocks, radiating and pulsing, alive and so vibrant. And the shadows only increasing around them. All at once, she felt an uneasiness as she became more aware of these changes—aware of, in a sense, the world around her adapting, as if reacting to her very subconscious, filtered through every emotion. She saw the patterns in it all: the disapproval within the rocks, resonating from her child-hood self—the shame and guilt of her present actions, suddenly weighing down on her, coming into the light. She could hear that little girl crying in the wind. Dissatisfaction, perhaps. A woe to the innocence left behind.

It's all in your head, she told herself.

But she felt reality slipping further away, and it was harder to grasp onto anything outside her emotions and the feelings therein; the harbor was lost, and the ship had gone to sea, with the captain of its voyage nowhere to be found; but somewhere within the effects of the psilocybin-like symptoms in her system, Nairobi could still hear her inner voice—or at least, *one* of her inner voices (we have many inner voices, don't we?), and it told her to focus and make reason of what she was experiencing.

Get it together.

She glanced again at Dieter, whose skin had reappeared on his face, though his eyes were almost entirely black now. She looked around them and now noticed the plant life that had appeared. A large saguaro coiled out of the ground like a serpent. Weeds slithered out of rocks, and purple flowers blossomed from mint-colored succulents, creasing their way through small gaps. Visible chollas glimmered radiantly—and *unnaturally*—as if they were breathing and alive, watching her as she watched them; their demeanor was hard to read.

I've felt this way before. . . .

Years ago, Nairobi had been taken to a riparian area on an exotic planet within the Inner Rings of Samsara. She was introduced to a rare fungus there, that, when digested, gave off the effects of euphoric bliss, enlightenment, and sometimes an acute awareness of thought patterns and causal effect. What she felt now was like she had experienced before, although— she couldn't recall it now, since it was too hard to even grasp time—she had digested nothing in the past hour nor had she drank anything for that matter, so she couldn't have been drugged by anyone (at least, not through any means that she knew of).

Unless somehow . . .

It's in the air, she realized. She could feel it in the way the plants breathed. The air felt pleasant, crisp, and beneficial to her lungs; she could stay here forever. And yet, she *couldn't* really stay here forever, could she? No, not really. Now wasn't the time for leisure activities—she still had a job to do. *Just one last gig.* Regardless, she wrestled with herself—caught by the effects of the psychoactive spores wafting from whatever plant they originated—and had forgotten what that job was, too lost in her thoughts to focus on what she needed to.

Without even realizing it, the bounty had slipped out of sight.

|4|

RESCUE FROM WITHIN

Edwin Dorset was a dreamer; he dreamed both day and night.

Edwin loved to draw, and in his art, he often expressed his dreams visually. Since the day he had read his first comic, he wanted to be a comic book artist; he had been drawing comics ever since then, and though not professional, he was a comic book artist all the same—whether or not he acknowledged it.

Lamar gifted Edwin a copy of Alan Moore and Dave Gibbons's *Watchmen* when he was only six. For one so young, perhaps *Watchmen* wasn't the most appropriate of stories to consume; however, its effect on Edwin had been one of positive change. From that day forward, he had grown a personal love affair with stories—infatuated not only with the characters and settings of such stories but also with the artistry behind them. Lamar used to love comics, and he collected individual issues for Edwin often, gifting them to his little brother whenever their paths crossed (every other weekend at most, if they were lucky enough); he had continued to do this until the day he died.

Lamar often conveyed his love for the art form to Edwin, and somewhere along the line, that love had rubbed off on him. "It's modern mythology," Lamar said once, while talking about superheroes and scanning through the vibrant pages of whatever issue he had brought Edwin that week. "Hundreds of writers, artists, and colorists, and decades of years written, all adding to this mythology, this dualistic, modern notion of good versus evil. Did you know that the first modern superhero was created in the Great Depression by children of immigrants? You can even trace the influence further than that. Created by outsiders with nothing to call their own, except maybe . . . just maybe the desire to change the world. Because that's all we're here for, Edwin, and don't you forget that: To make the world a better place, however we can—to be the difference we want to see in it. And what is mythology but a mirror of our time? It's through these characters that we can find ourselves; through the eyes of another that we can truly see the world. Imagine being that change: Imagine having that power, that *gift*, to really make the world a better place."

Being nine years Edwin's senior, Lamar's words had often gone over his brother's head; Edwin had never fully understood Lamar's explanations (at least, not until he grew older and had hindsight, seeing the beauty of metaphor), but he had at least understood his brother's sentiments. Stories were like dreams, *recorded* dreams. Dreams that you could look back on sometimes re-experiencing as if for the first time. And right now, wandering through the narrow canyon alone, he supposed he was living one—a dream, lived with waking eyes.

That's all life is, really, Edwin reflected. *A dream with no end.*

But all dreams end, don't they? That's the one downside of having them.

Edwin came home from school with a black eye the day Lamar died. When he entered his bedroom, Edwin found Lamar sitting on his bed reading an old issue of *Amazing Spider-Man* (from the Romita-Lee run back in the late-sixties) with a bright smile on his face. Lamar's visits had become increasingly rare ever since moving to Sacramento with his dad, and for Edwin to find his brother in town again more than thrilled him. It was just what he needed. Just what fate had in mind for him.

Because when it boils down to it, a moment can mean anything.

But before Edwin could run to Lamar, hug him, or even let out any words of his own, he had already burst into tears. He hadn't meant to cry—not really. Didn't even think that he would cry, in all truth, but upon seeing his brother after so long of having not seen him—and so unexpectedly—well . . . he just couldn't help it.

The moment Lamar saw his eight-year-old brother crying, he immediately set the comic down and rushed to Edwin's aid, engulfing him in his arms with the warmest hug that he could muster. "What's wrong?" he asked soothingly. "What's wrong, Little Brother?"

Edwin cried on Lamar's chest. His words choked out in broken sobs. "It's all gone. . . ."

Lamar squeezed Edwin tightly. "What's 'gone?'"

Edwin didn't answer—he couldn't.

Lamar didn't rush Edwin, didn't force him to say anything that he didn't want to, but merely waited for him patiently, holding his little brother safely in his arms and rocking him gently from side to side. "What troubles you, Ed?"

Edwin could hardly translate his thoughts into words. He was so caught up in his emotions, so lost in the moment, that he couldn't express his thoughts if he tried. He merely cried.

Lamar waited unabated, exuding nothing but understanding, never letting go of his tender embrace. "It'll be okay." He spoke with a kind, reassuring smile, soft and loving. "Everything's gonna be okay. . . ." His hold on Edwin tightened. "I promise."

Edwin got his bearings, rubbed his snot with the back of his hand, and finally spoke up: "They . . . they took everything."

Lamar looked down at Edwin with concern. "'They'?" A righteous anger arose in him. "Who are 'they', and what did they take?" And at last, he noticed Edwin's black eye. "*What happened*, Little Brother?" He pressed further, this time more demanding—his brotherly instincts kicking into overdrive. "Who did this to you?!"

"My drawings . . ." Edwin wiped his glistening eyes with the back of his hand, still wet from snot. "I lost them all."

Edwin now remembered it like it was currently happening to him: They had taken his backpack by force, the three of them (all three of them older than him, and most likely Lamar's age). He could remember their faces so well, even to this day. He had seen them in the neighborhood before, usually hanging out on their bikes, on the corner of the block he walked through to get to and from school. They had never harassed him before—at least, not physically. All he had done this time was look one of them in the eye while passing. He should have looked down, should have gone around, or should have done *something* differently.

But he hadn't, and for that, he would regret it for the rest of his life.

At first, he had been strong once they confronted him, and even after that, too, when they had surrounded him, he had remained strong even then. Even when they took his backpack by force—two of them holding him down, while the other worked on tearing it away from him. He remained strong thereafter, as they emptied his backpack's contents onto the ground and he struggled against them, hearing their malicious laughs echo across the block. He was a strong kid, you can take my word for it, but everyone breaks down eventually. Once they got to his drawings, however, and started belittling him for them—aggressively ripping them in front of him—that was when they really got to him, and he just couldn't help but cry. Somehow, his crying had fueled them, and all the while they mocked him for it, calling him abominable words like "f—t" and "r—d." He was only an eight-year-old, but they held nothing back. His drawings were everything to him, his most prized possessions in the world, and yet they had shred them all to nothing. He didn't understand how anyone could be so cruel—so *evil*.

He was powerless.

Small.

Broken. . . .

And when he had told Lamar of all of this (the fragmented way only an eight-year-old can explain such a story), he felt nothing but numb, as if he had exerted all the energy he had left. But the worst thing about it all—the thing that really got to him later in life, returning to him again and again—was that he would forever blame this moment (him caving in and telling his brother of all that had happened) as the reason Lamar had died that fateful night in June.

After listening to Edwin's story, Lamar gave his brother a stern look. "Someday," he began, "very soon, people like that won't exist anymore." A darkness grew in his eyes—a hunger for vengeance. "They're fading, Little Brother, and they know it. They see the light in you, and they want it all for themselves." The darkness in his eyes slowly dimmed, however, and he smiled once more. "But they can't have that light, you see—because it's yours, and yours alone. And someday, very soon, you're going to change the world with it. A day will come, Little Brother, and you'll see. And you'll know then that every blood you spilt and every tear you shed had all been leading up to that day."

Lamar's next words now echoed in Edwin's mind as he stood in the narrow canyon alone, in a place so foreign, yet so familiar: *"Make the world a better place, Little Brother."*

Edwin's heart sunk deep in his chest. *That day never came*, he thought. *Nor will it ever, if I'm being honest with myself. . . .*

But Lamar's voice rose in him again, from deep within: *"Of course, it won't. Until you do something about it, that day will never come. It will always be an abstract idea, waiting just around the corner."*

His thoughts made him feel called out. Guilty, perhaps, but for what? When he really thought about it, just how proactive had he been in his life after Lamar's death? Instead of wallowing in his pain all these years, he could have done something about it; he could have channeled that pain, somehow, and maybe used it for something good, something productive, so that others wouldn't have to experience it the way he had.

Why hadn't I been more active in my life? I've been a passenger for far too long.

Because when it boiled down to it, he still felt that guilt within him—festering and holding him back. The guilt of what had happened: the actions of an eight-year-old indirectly leading to a seventeen-year-old bleeding out in the back of an ambulance.

I shouldn't have told Lamar about the backpack. If I had only . . . If I could only . . .

But he *couldn't.*

He couldn't change what had already happened. What had happened happened; the past was prologue, and all that remained was the now: the present actions that defined tomorrow.

He stopped walking, suddenly mesmerized by a view unlike any other he had seen before: an extraterrestrial succulent, moving along the rocks above him, with the end of its roots weaving in and out of the cracks like a spectral octopus at sea. It was big, *far* bigger than him, and yet it paid him no mind. Perhaps it didn't notice him, or perhaps it didn't care enough to notice. It moved with the grace of a ballet dancer, and he couldn't help but watch in awe. He had never seen a plant move like that. Like it was . . . like it was *alive.* He followed it slowly, until it dug its way into a small crevice, hiding itself.

It is *alive,* he further realized, feeling dumb for coming to such a realization so late in life. *Why,* all *plants are alive.*

He then realized something else, something that he hadn't realized before and perhaps should have: his captors, Dieter and Nairobi, weren't beside him anymore. Looking around, as if a second glance would prove him wrong, but he instead, much to his surprise, found no one there but himself. He had wandered off; he had gotten away, and he hadn't even realized it until now. All alone in a dangerous land he didn't know. But despite that—despite the dangers that loomed in every corner—his worries remained far away, and his current situation was pushed to the back of his mind like a distant memory.

There was only that yearning inside of him, that push for active change. It was time to take action, grab hold of his destiny, and wallow in his pain no longer. He had never felt more clear-headed than ever; he could hear his inner voice now, untethered by the experiences of a child. Like an inner compass, he could feel it pointing him onward, pushing him toward the future that lay ahead. *When the voice of fear comes in, telling you that you're not good enough, always remember: You never need to be.*

He walked on. Resolute, but—most of all—*enlightened.* Elation ran through his veins, and a surge of emotion passed over him as feelings from the past came into the forefront of his mind. So many feelings he had long suppressed, all at once coming back to him, reminding him who he was and why he needed to confront them. And in the process of it all, he felt a great weight lifted off him—a cleansing of the mind and washing of all the dirt, mud, and stains that had coated on him throughout the years; his cleansing having been pushed back, year after year, only now to be scrubbed off, revealing the inner workings of who he was. His guilt for Lamar's death, stemming from their last conversation; he had learned to be passive because of that, but in that he had perhaps learned the wrong lesson. And his feelings of being worthless, stemming from the neglect he had received from his mother; he had learned that he wasn't "good enough," but perhaps that, too, was the wrong takeaway. All these notions about himself, stemming from such shortsighted assumptions. With a clear mind, he could see everything was so transparent. He had crossed the other side of that threshold—the prison of his mind, where he had been captive for so long—and now entered undiscovered territory, uncharted land he had once roamed long ago, when he was too young to remember the wrong lessons.

He climbed down a large boulder, using foothold after foothold, easing down slowly. His hands remained tied behind his back by a metallic rope, and he had to be careful. The surrounding canyon continued to drop, and the lower he got, the more the sun revealed itself, having recently showed itself only in slivers. There was a clearing ahead, down below, and the canyon walls expanded outward, no longer tunneling. A stream of water flowed to a small basin resting beside a large rock wall. *The water of life*, he thought, compelled to submerge in its depths. He climbed his way down, heading toward it, and took his time as he did so.

Once he made it to ground level, Edwin wandered his way to the basin and walked ankle-deep through the small current, running through the basin, until he was waist-deep in the water, sighing with euphoric relief. He could think of nothing better right now, and he wished for nothing more.

"Ma aladhi tafealuh huna?"

Edwin turned around. A man with a scarf wrapped around his face stood by the water's edge, staring at him with widened eyes. The man was dressed in a brown robe of linen, with layers upon layers, and in his right hand held a fishing pole, while in his left hand held an iridescent fish glowing from within. But upon seeing Edwin looking back at him, the man clumsily dropped the fish. As the fish hit the water, it swam away to safety, slinking within those dark depths, hoping never to be found again (but the man's eyes were on Edwin and not the fish).

The man pointed at Edwin accusingly, while taking frightened steps back. He spoke again, this time more intensely. "Barra Barra! 'Iinahum yabhathun eank fi kuli makan!" He grasped his fishing pole with both hands, shook them angrily, and started swinging at Edwin, just far enough to miss.

Although he was currently being attacked by a fishing pole, Edwin remained motionless, unperturbed by the man's hostile aura. Looking the man in the eyes, Edwin felt an empathy unfelt in such portions, as if he was only looking at himself. The world around him was animated. The surface of the water gleamed, and on its reflection mirrored another dimension. With each ringlet of wave caused by the man's movement, that world transformed, taking on forms previously imperceptible to the naked eye. Edwin could feel the connecting unity within all life, reverberating off the world around him—within the water, the rocks, the plants, and even flowing through himself and the man in front of him. All of existence was related, a part of one giant organism—breathing, growing, and evolving into something more, something better, and reaching closer to that point of singularity where it all became one again.

It's the cycle of all *existence*, Edwin thought with conviction. *Constant death and rebirth: A recycling of every atom and particle, creating stars and planets and who knows what else.*

He didn't move an inch—*couldn't* move an inch. So enraptured by the likelihood of his own existence, so rare and so beautiful, that he couldn't even move if he tried. He felt lucky to be alive; lucky to witness such an event.

And he only smiled at the man in return.

He felt outside his body. All too aware that he was in a finite vessel—a body of meat, aging in the illusion of time. And time was different where he was now, wasn't it? He could feel it in the gravity—he was at the whims of it, just as he was at the whims of his own biology, forever bound by that gravity, affecting time as it did. And yet at this moment, however short-lived, he felt outside those confines; time was at a standstill, and he could think of no better place to be.

The man stopped swinging his fishing pole at Edwin, took another step back, and shook his head adamantly. After a while, he shrugged, unsure whether to be angry or confused.

Edwin remained unmoving, waist-deep in the water, staring back at the man on the bank. The only part of the stranger's face uncovered by his scarf revealed golden-brown eyes behind bushy gray eyebrows. And Edwin saw panic in those eyes: anxiety, fear. . . .

The man pointed at Edwin again, less aggressive now. "Barra barra! Ant rajul matlub."

Edwin noticed a figure standing behind the man—the figure held a musket, pointed at him. Four other figures emerged next to this new figure, and each of them held a similar weapon attached with red lasers, each revealing their target. These new arrivals were dressed identical to one another and wore gas masks that covered their entire face; their attire seemed retro, somehow, reminding Edwin of what he had once seen in a World War I museum.

The man holding the fishing pole noticed Edwin's expression change, and he turned around, surprised to find the new arrivals standing behind him. He raised both hands in the air and—

Multiple gunshots rang across the canyon, reverberating off the water's surface as the man with the fishing pole fell backward, right into the water, and landed with a heavy splash. His body floated, and a red mist spread across the waters' depths, wading its way toward Edwin.

Edwin watched as the new figures closed in around him. They edged slowly toward the water, one foot after the other, with their muskets aimed directly at him. Two lasers on his face, two on his chest, and one on his crotch. A gunman was yelling at him so loudly that he couldn't understand any of it (nor did he care to).

At the moment, Edwin didn't feel like being bothered. Instead, he looked up at the sky and reveled in the moon's beauty, alluring in a deep prism of blue. He noticed the tail-end of smoke nearby and followed its line of sight across the other direction, making him think it was a comet at first until he saw more just like them (five, ten, twenty—the numbers kept increasing), and he realized then that they were just signs of "civilization" out in the distance: colossal ships mid-wreckage. Flying, state-of-the-art vehicles crashing—explosions going off, one after another. *Fire and destruction*: He wanted no part of it. He looked away once more, directing his attention back to the moon. Therein, he noticed something he hadn't before: a second moon, right behind the first moon, this one much larger.

He wasn't on Earth—no, he couldn't be. No doubt about it anymore.

One gunman poked Edwin on the stomach with the end of his musket. Reluctantly, Edwin diverted his attention from the twin moons, but in the process caught sight of an unknown figure standing atop a large boulder—at least fifteen feet above them—partially obscured by the blaring sun.

The figure above watched in silence, waiting.

The closest gunman continued berating Edwin, and he tried grabbing him, to pull him out of the water, but Edwin remained out of reach, and the blood from the corpse now surrounded him, dyeing the water in a crimson red, perhaps giving the gunman less of an incentive to enter it. But another gunman stepped in anyway, pushed aside a long reed with the end of his musket, and—

The gunman's face blew off. All around him, his comrades joined him on the ground, one after the other, as whistling gunshots rang in the canyon—one by one, picked off by an unseen specter (unseen, at least to them). In less than five seconds, Edwin had watched the entire thing play out and continued to watch, in utter silence—*mesmerized*, really—as the figure above him lowered their handgun, holstered it, and glanced back at him.

A woman, Edwin guessed, observing a lithe body with long, dark hair flowing in the wind (as if in slow motion, just for him). The figure vaulted off the boulder and landed in the deepest part of the water, submerging into its depths a dozen or more feet away from him.

Edwin remained still, his heart pounding in his chest; he could feel that uncertainty coming back to him, sobering in its disillusionment. But he couldn't cower in fear any longer; he wasn't born to be imprisoned, whether that was an internal prison or an external one. He stood his ground, hands tied behind his back, waist-deep in darkened water, and waited.

When the woman emerged out of the water, she wiped away her long, dark hair from her face, spat out a wad of spit, and approached Edwin slowly. The first thing he noticed were her eyes: dilated pupils, almost entirely black. She had an exotic look about her, pleasing to the eyes. She wore a navy-blue jacket with a maroon collar and maroon lining along the sleeves (three stripes on the bottom of each), with a maroon backside. A brown holster rested on each side of her hip, each filled with a handgun (the handgun on her right side darker than the one on her left). Her pants were black, her boots a dark brown, and the shirt underneath her jacket looked almost metallic, like a thin layer of ring-mail. Edwin lowered his guard, watching her approach. And as she walked past him, stepping out of the water as she did so, she spoke in clear, flawless English: "Come with me if you want to live."

|5|

RESCUE FROM WITHOUT

She stood with her arms folded by the banks of the water watching Edwin with patient, inquisitive interest. She wore a navy-blue jacket with a maroon collar and linings along the sleeves and backside. Her skin was an olive shade, sheen from the water, and her face—exotic by Edwin's standards—seemed to be a mix of Asian, African, and European (or whatever was her equivalent). She had an athletic, lithe body, and her demeanor remained self-possessed and at ease, despite her bloodshot eyes—eyes that remained on Edwin, studying him. Dark eyes, almost black, with equally dark hair, long and wavy. At last, she asked in a low, playful tone: "Well, are you coming, or what?"

Edwin struggled to answer the woman's question—unsure, really, how he could even understand what she was saying at all. His tongue caught in the back of his throat, and he struggled to find the right words—unsure, again, how she could even understand him if he spoke at all.

Having noticed his delayed reaction, however (a *much* delayed reaction, no doubt caused by whatever psychoactive agent had wafted its way into his system), the woman pulled out a small device, a little over the size of a flash drive. She drew closer to him. The colors around her swirled like oil on a canvas, in constant motion. *Divine*, Edwin thought, the word inadvertently springing to mind. Suddenly, he had the urge to paint her. And as she drew closer, his heart thudded in his chest—fast, heavy beats—and she—

—jammed the end of the device into his neck.

A sharp pain exploded in his neck, quickly and unexpectedly.

Edwin fell to his knees in agony, gasping to scream but unable.

"Sorry," the woman said, looking down at Edwin, half in the water and convulsing from the device. She sighed and glanced at one of the mint-colored succulents sitting by the edge of the water; its fruiting body was a deep, vibrant purple, covered by flecks of mold emitting the toxins now coursing out of him. "Your system's not used to the spores you're breathing in." She shook her head—again, eyeing Edwin. "Moreover, we'll need your wits to get out in one piece."

After a short, intense period of agony, that made Edwin feel as if his body was burning from the inside-out, he could feel the effects of the psychoactive drug dissipating from his system, returning him to a state of normalcy (at least, the closest thing to normalcy that one could get to in such a situation). And yet, even without the psychoactive effect, he felt discombobulated, reeling from all that had happened beforehand. Catching up to the present, and the fact his arms were still bound by a metallic rope. The fact he had no idea where he was. Even worse, the fact he now felt more vulnerable than ever.

Already, questions raced through his mind with no end in sight.

He struggled to stand upright. "How . . ." he started sluggishly, still getting his bearings; there was something different about this woman than with Dieter and his posse—something so obvious in hindsight that he couldn't help but wonder: "How . . . how can I understand what you're saying?" He shook his head, his thoughts disorganized. "Better yet, how can you understand what *I'm* saying?"

The edge of her lips rose, and she tapped her temple once. "An empathic emulator," she told him casually. "A universal communicator, if you want to get technical. It stimulates your . . . well, I'm not entirely sure how it works if we're being honest." She shrugged a shoulder, nonchalant. "Do any of us truly know how most of what we use works other than its application and use?"

Edwin nodded, unsure of how to reply. Another delayed response: "Right. . . ."

She continued looking him over, curiosity in her eyes: "What's your name?"

Their eyes met one another's. "Edwin." His eyes never broke from hers. "Edwin Dorset."

"'Edwin Dorset,'" she repeated, nodding with an amused look in her eyes. "Has a nice ring to it." Another cunning smile crossed her lips, and she spoke in a deep, measured voice—at times, whimsical. "And you're the new bounty, I presume?"

Edwin didn't know what she meant by that; he wasn't sure if her question was supposed to be rhetorical or not. He needed more information. "You know what's happening to me?"

She didn't answer his question; instead, she asked her own. "What, you're not going to ask for my name?" She rolled her eyes facetiously, with a hand on her hip. "Now, that's no way to treat your rescuer." She glanced at the gunmen strewn along the edge of the water—their bodies pooling blood.

Edwin also glanced at the bodies. Once again, reminded of their existence. But, of course, these weren't the first corpses he had seen before. Around the time Mrs. Kemp had died (three months after her death, to be precise), he had gone to visit Mr. Kemp in Oakland; by then, he had already moved into the college dorms near UCSF, having left on his own the first opportunity he could get, all thanks to a scholarship that hadn't yet been revoked. After a long night of conversation with Mr. Kemp—about his wife, their children, and their remarkable life together—Edwin had found him the next morning lying in his bed, in an endless slumber, holding a picture of a young Martha Kemp (then known as Martha Ingles, before their forty-two-year marriage). The greatest difference between now versus then, however, was that there had been no blood back in Oakland; Benjamin Kemp had died in his sleep peacefully, unlike these men now. Now, there was more blood than Edwin had ever seen in his life—despite having seen his fair share of roadkill—and inadvertently, his mind went to Lamar, who had bled out in the back of an ambulance; he shuddered at the image of his brother's face covered in blood and had to shut his mind from the grim afterthought.

"Come on," the woman urged him. "We have little time until more of them arrive." She walked away, and Edwin had no option but to follow her, stepping around the group of dead bounty hunters and giving them a great distance.

He glanced at his rescuer as he followed her through the narrowing canyon. "What do they want with me?"

She regarded him. "You're a wanted man, Edwin Dorset."

She had no more time to explain before the next group of mercenaries showed up. As with the group before, she took care of them swiftly, with an agile ease, utilizing her handguns with the deftness of a veteran; at that moment, Edwin wondered who she really was and how she used such weapons so well.

The new mercenaries lay dead around them—new pools of blood gushing out.

"There's no time to explain everything," she continued from before, again nonchalant about it all. She closed in on Edwin's side and used a small laser device from her belt to cut off his constraints. "I have a pod nearby. We'll have to hurry if we want to get out of here alive."

"But where are we?" Edwin asked as she started off again, and—as before—he had no choice but to follow.

She spoke without hesitation: "Zarathustra."

Right, Edwin thought, nodding. *As if I'd know where that is. . . .*

"You're forgetting to ask the right question," she said, as if reading his mind, and turned back to look at him as he followed her. There was a playful glint in her eyes—her glossy, almost black eyes (still under the effects of the psychoactive spores, undoubtedly).

Edwin caught on. "Right," he went on. "What's your name?"

Her cunning, cornerwise grin returned. "Sibyl." Her eyes remained on his. "Sibylla Kal."

They had spoken little after that; truthfully, there wasn't much of an opportunity for conversation. Instead, they had to sneak their way through many arching tunnels, sought after every step of the way. Without Sibyl's help, of course, Edwin would have been dead by now, there was no doubt about it. She protected him as they traversed the canyon, killing whoever stood in their path—or whomever caught up to them. At times, they had to run. Other times, they had to wait it out. Sometimes, however, there were too many reapers for Sibyl all at once, and the two were forced to hide in small crevices, waiting for the bounty hunters to kill each other off—or, at the very least, wait until they were gone and completely out of sight.

After a while of scrambling for safe passage and staying hidden from unwanted company, they had finally made it to her pod, safely hidden in a niche. The pod was a metallic structure with a texture somewhat like birch, that looked like the mix of a rocket infused with an upside-down tree, with a thick bottom of wires entangled together on its underside. Two seats sat within its cockpit—a seat in the front, and a seat in the back.

Sibyl got in the front seat, and Edwin silently entered the back, right behind her. He strapped himself with a seatbelt (*very Earth-like*, he thought), and the doors of the pod enclosed around them. The machine made a loud grumbling noise, rising in volume, like an igniting furnace. Sibyl didn't ask Edwin if he was ready; there was no time for caution.

Within a matter of seconds, they were launched into space.

• • •

It was the most exhilarating ride Edwin had ever experienced (notwithstanding his forced abduction—having fallen through mid-air like a rag doll, upward, with nothing to stop his fall and body from splattering on the ground like an overripe tomato—but for obvious reasons, that was different). This time, they were going so fast he had to close his eyes. No rollercoaster could even compare to the rush he felt. His seat rocked heavily, and he felt the adrenaline coming back to him like a neighborhood bully who kept returning—uninvited and unwanted, as all the other times before. By the time he gained the courage to open his eyes, the pod was already out of orbit.

He looked out the small window in awe.

"Beautiful, isn't it?" Sibyl chimed in from up-front.

But "beautiful" wasn't the word that came to Edwin's mind. No words could express how he felt seeing Zarathustra from a distance like that, nor the isolating vacuum of space surrounding it, making him feel so small and infinitesimal in such a broad, ever-expanding universe where anything was possible and not even the sky was the limit. "Beautiful" wasn't cutting it. No, there wasn't a single word for what he felt. The feeling he had was magical, dreamlike, and miraculous—all the while terrifying, isolating, and indifferent; it was every step of the way, tear shed, blood spilt, and sweat wasted; it was every moment that led him there, to this single moment in time—the apex of all his life—where every step of the way made sense.

No words could describe the feelings that the image brought with it.

His thoughts were speechless, visceral, and lost in dreadful wonder.

The pod had slowed down immensely, approaching a cluster of asteroids before stopping at its edge. Once the vehicle was motionless, Sibyl's seat rotated, facing toward Edwin. She took off her seatbelt and opened a compartment underneath her chair. "A void belt," she said, picking up a bulky, yellow belt before handing it to him. "Or 'void suit,' however you want to refer to it. It'll keep you safe while out there." She glanced out the window at the asteroid field. "My ship's parked within there. We'll have to leave the pod in case we've been followed."

Edwin undid his seatbelt and grabbed the void belt from Sibyl, wrapping it around himself. Next, Sibyl took out another object from the compartment and handed it to him—some kind of grapple gun, from the looks of it. "For getting around," she explained. "If push comes to shove, it's also a good weapon to have."

Edwin looked down at his new void belt. "So, it just works like this?"

Sibyl gently chuckled, shaking her head. "Not quite." She leaned closer, bent down, and flipped a small switch on his void belt, activating it.

A sheen, metallic membrane spread out from the belt, emerging from the top and bottom, and it covered every part of Edwin's skin, starting with his legs, torso, feet, chest, arms, hands, fingers, and then spread to his face, cloaking his entire head in a helmet that was still breathable; it felt like wearing a form-fitting spandex of obsidian, that he would later discover made him move faster, somehow rejuvenated by its application, as if it were a suit of armor, and he, a space ronin setting out on a grand adventure through the cosmos. The suit also kept his temperature in check, warming him when he got cold and cooling him when he felt overheated; he wondered if he felt better already because it regulated more than just his temperature.

He felt more competent with the void belt activated, less liable with it covering his body like a shield, hardly noticeable to him with how it felt on him. A clear visor on his mask revealed his surroundings with pristine detail, far superior than any glasses or unblemished vision could produce, making him question if he had actually needed glasses this whole time. And when he saw Sibyl activate her own void belt, he saw how sleek it looked on her, with its maroon etchings faintly glowing (his void suit's design was quite similar, though with orange etchings). It made him feel even more bold, seeing her like that and knowing that he must have looked similar; it gave him a strange awareness, like he was just a character in a story (only now, he could experience what it was like to be on the other side).

Sibyl looked back at Edwin. Her dark eyes were hidden beneath a black, reflective visor much like his own. "You ready?"

Edwin's heart pounded, and he nodded.

Sibyl pressed some buttons on a console on her chair, and the air sucked out of the vents, regulated by the airlock, before the latches undid themselves and the pod's hatch shot open. Sibyl lightly kicked off the ground, and her body eased out of the pod slowly, graceful with the skill of one who had done this many times before.

It's the most subtle of changes that make all the difference. At first, Edwin couldn't pinpoint what felt so different, so unnatural, but when he realized he could only hear his breath, he knew what it was: It was the silence.

Edwin had left his grapple gun on his lap and watched as it now floated in front of him, slowly rotating. (*Wow. . . .*) He caught the gun, clung to it firmly, and then looked up, out of the pod and at the emptiness of space surrounding them. *You can do this*, he thought, trying to ignore the fear gripping him tightly, making him immobile. *Don't think, just do.*

He kicked off the ground.

And he was met with a view beyond anything he had ever seen before—a feeling he was becoming quite acquainted with. All of his fear vanished then, left without a trace, and in its place idyllic serenity washed over him as it had while wandering Zarathustra alone on the effects of the psychoactive spores, and for a second—a minute, even—he basked in the silence of his mind; he could think freely, unfettered by the clutter of worry, fear, and stress, nor the distractions of any other sound; thinking in images—of Lamar, Vicky, and his life as it once was, and thoughts of the future, a concept he had scarcely envisioned himself in; thinking of posterity, hope, and the beauty and unlikelihood of all existence.

But most of all, he gaped at the views.

• • •

Edwin Dorset was, first and foremost, an artist. Whatever free time he had, he dedicated to his craft. He loved to draw from reality, working daily on perspective. Light, shadow, and contrast; every factor was important to him. He shifted between pencil, pen, and charcoal, also using watercolor, paint, and oil (of course, he wasn't endowed with money, so he had to make do with what he had). He preferred to draw stationary objects, such as natural landscapes or architecture, over people, but he loved drawing people all the same, and as he continued to work on his craft, his art only got that much better.

Having worked two jobs in San Francisco to afford housing—let alone, make ends meet—he had used public transportation every day, spending every minute on it refining his craft and building his skill as he would any other language: through practice and use, pushing his limits with every go at it. For a short period, he had gone to art school even—at least, until his grant ended prematurely, and he couldn't afford tuition any longer. But that didn't discourage him from drawing, nor for his love of the art; he was still that same eight-year-old boy, drawing from a compulsion within him, a compulsion he didn't quite understand. He wanted nothing less with his time and spent most of his free days alone, too absorbed in what he loved to do anything else.

Every artist sees the world differently; in fact, everyone in the world sees the world differently. That's the beauty of life, you see: perspective, and all our views of it (the good and the bad, if there's ever such a thing). Edwin was an altruist at heart and saw the world with a glass half-full; it's a misconception to believe that hardships only instill cynicism. Sure, times are tough when you're down, but with each time you get up, you only realize how much easier it is to rise again, to climb higher heights than before. Succeeding where you had once left off and reaching peaks you hadn't known were possible. Every decline has an incline, and depending on the angle you stand, the circumstances change drastically. With every loss comes a victory, and with every victory comes a retaliation—come-uppance, in one form or another—and something to take the place of what came before: a never-ending cycle of cause and effect. In this universe, that can mean anything; it's all a game of perspective, you see, and perspective, as we all know, is rela-tive.

Edwin could feel the effects of relativity deep in his gut. Another feeling of falling. Only instead of falling, this time he was motionless—*floating*, drifting and suspended in mid-air (or the closest thing to mid-air at that moment). His body was at ease, buoyant across the emptiness of space, with no gravity to pull him down. Upside-down, right-side-up, side-ways, he didn't know what direction he was; because, by all rights and purposes, there was no "up" or "down"; he was in the clutches of relativity now, and whatever way his body rotated, spun, or moved, he had to adapt to it, attempting to avoid vertigo as much as possible. Oh, if he could express himself well in his art, what he would give to draw how he felt at that moment. . . .

And the *views* he saw!

Zarathustra's twin moons radiated a ghostly white—the smaller moon just a tad darker than the bigger one, hidden par-tially behind it.

Zarathustra herself was a behemoth, colossal in scope and size, with a fine detail far grander than any picture or painting could do justice. Edwin had seen photos and videos of Earth from a distance (a majority of which he would guess were CGI), similar only to the vantage point he had now, but . . . oh, the difference of seeing something secondhand—or in the imagination—versus seeing it in person. Never once had he seen something so beautiful, nor had he imagined in all his dreams that he would see anything that could even compare to what he now saw (and he was a dreamer, wasn't he?). He had expected the planet of Zarathustra to be covered entirely in desert (much like Mars, Arrakis, or any of the other desert planets that he had seen in *Star Wars*, *Star Trek*, or any other fictional work of art), but was instead surprised to discover, from a great distance no doubt, that there were also small patches of green scattered throughout the planet's surface, accentuated against the amber, reddish-orange of the desert and its outline of craters—along with water sources, too, though much smaller than Earth's; pockets of sea, receding with time.

In fact, it all reminded him of Earth.

Only somewhat.

The sight was magnificent, and it brought tears to his eyes. Tears he hadn't known were spilling until his vision was blurred. He could hardly believe what he was experiencing; it was unreal, and—just like before—words could not describe it; in fact, no translation could even come close. Already, it felt like years since he had last stepped foot in San Francisco, before his abduction, less than twenty-four hours ago.

My abduction. . . .

Had he had enough time to process all that had happened? Better yet, *would* he ever have enough time to process all that had happened? Until now, he hadn't even thought of the prospect of going back. But how could he go back? Where there to go back to? The portal that had brought him here was now gone, and so too were his chances of ever going back.

Could he find another portal to bring him home again? Somehow, he doubted it.

Again, questions ran through his mind with no end in sight.

It took Edwin a while to realize that his body was still in motion from having kicked out of the pod. Already, Sibyl stood atop an asteroid, glancing back at him as she walked ahead. He used the grapple gun to propel himself onto a chunk of an asteroid nearby. At first, he was clumsy, having to adjust to zero gravity, but once he got the hang of it, he found it not only easy but exhilarating. When his feet touched upon the fresh surface, his void suit adjusted the direction of its gravitational pull, letting him walk upon the asteroid as he would any other surface.

He leapt from asteroid to asteroid, trying to catch up to Sibyl.

Over a hundred pieces of asteroid and debris floated around them, of all shapes and sizes, some much larger than others. Danger lurked in every corner, and the unknown loomed about, thrilling in its enchantment. Unlike on Zarathustra, being in space felt new and alien, with nowhere to go if he were to fall off an asteroid and get lost at sea. Sibyl was still a way ahead of him, above him and upside-down—at least, in his perspective—walking slowly along the surface of an even bigger asteroid. He ran forward, grappled his way toward her, and spun mid-air on his way up, until his "up" was "down," and he stood right behind her.

"You're a fast learner," Sibyl remarked, glancing at Edwin behind her. "You do anything like this before?"

He had to think about it. "I've scuba dived once or twice," he admitted, thinking back to the time he went to Costa Rica with his ex-girlfriend, Maggie, and her family. "But nothing like this."

"You never forget your first time." She grappled to another rock, and he followed her.

Now that they had the time, he wanted to know more: "What's going on? Why am I so important to people?"

It took Sibyl a while to respond to Edwin's question. For a second, he thought she didn't hear him. At last, she said: "You have a bounty on your head."

But that wasn't good enough; he wanted a better answer, something he didn't already know. Why was she beating around the bush? He needed to know: "But *why*?"

Sibyl stopped walking, turned around, and looked at him. "The universe is a cruel place, Edwin Dorset. Sometimes the answers we seek aren't satisfying enough."

"You saved me," he told her, countering her statement. "That has to count for something, doesn't it? The universe is good—you're living proof of that."

Sibyl didn't seem impressed. "You flatter me."

"If so, then why aren't you telling me why I have a bounty on my head?"

She sighed. "Because it's no simple answer."

Edwin was about to argue against that, in hopes of a simple answer, but he was distracted again, having noticed the ground beneath their feet beginning to vibrate. Subtly at first, but quickly gaining momentum. And at first, he thought it was just himself, perhaps having some kind of post-traumatic flashback of the quakes in San Francisco, before his abduction, but then he noticed Sibyl had unholstered one of her handguns, and he knew—right then and there, and without any doubt—that something bad really was coming their way.

No sound came as the asteroid ripped apart below them.

Edwin heard nothing but his heavy breathing as the chunk of rock he stood on propelled itself away from Sibyl, and the body of the asteroid broke into fragmented pieces, thrown in different directions. Because of his void suit, he remained standing on the chunk of rock, as it spun in circles and was hurled away with other pieces—*many* other pieces (bigger, smaller, and equally proportioned pieces). He ducked, dodging fallen and drifting debris, and jumped from platform to platform, attempting to avoid any oncoming object, as well as the prospect of being crushed to death.

Among the wreckage, Sibyl was nowhere to be found.

And just when Edwin thought he was safe at last—after landing on a large platform away from the cataclysm—he noticed a figure in the air moving toward him. With his void suit's enhanced visor, he could see it clearly: An organic life form with sheen, cracky black skin, the size of a large redwood. He saw little tendons on its underside, reminding him of a caterpillar. It slithered through space like an eel swimming underwater, gaining speed.

He took a step back, and then another, before turning around completely and sprinting away as fast as possible, not looking back. *Fuck this*, he thought, using his grapple gun to get across a vast gap from one platform to another. *I'm so done with this bullshit.* From the moment of his abduction, he had been running for his life. Why couldn't he catch a break? *This is what it's really like to be in a story—hungry, tired, and always on the run.* He hardly had any time whatsoever before the creature had dredged itself where he was only seconds ago; but luckily, he had jumped away just in time, missing it by mere inches.

A close call.

Not the first that day.

Nor the last, for that matter.

He turned around mid-air, glancing back to see what had come of the creature. He saw it had burrowed itself within the asteroid, and he could see the rock shaking violently, breaking from within—before shattering into various pieces, with the alien bursting out of the other side. Inattentive to his surroundings, Edwin collided into a rock behind him, crushing his shoulder and popping his arm out of place.

He continued spinning aimlessly, unable to stop his body's trajectory.

Groaning, he used his unencumbered arm to grapple onto a rock above him and landed on its underside, his new surface. He applied pressure on his injured arm with his good hand, taking steps away from where the creature had emerged, while simultaneously trying to duck beneath any hazardous debris, not wanting to get hit again. His shoulder screamed with pain, but he had no time to focus on it.

He saw the creature appear again, turning around and heading toward him.

Still, Sibyl was nowhere in sight.

Fuck!

He started running again—once more, toward the opposite direction of the creature.

Fuck, fuck, fuck!

There was no way that he could escape it; it was simply too fast for him. *This is it*, he thought, despite using all his strength to gain speed. *At least I died a free man.* He slid to a stop, turned around, and aimed his grapple gun at the massive demon approaching; if he died now, the least he could do was go out in style. *Let my death not be in vain.*

Before he could fire the gun, however, a large harpoon shot out from above, and it collided with the creature's torso, sending it hurling down and crashing into the asteroid Edwin stood on. The aftermath sent a large shockwave, catapulting Edwin off the surface and sending him flying backward, spinning out of control. He was moving fast, *way* too fast to grapple onto anything safely, and was forced to fire the gun in a blind panic, hoping that it would land on something, *anything.*

The grapple shot out, hit a rock, and pulled Edwin toward it until his body slammed onto it with substantial force, colliding with his injured shoulder and rolling him with the momentum as the void suit adjusted to its new surface. He secured one foot on the ground, and using his other leg, a knee. Breathing heavily, he again applied pressure on his injured arm, watching as a bright light shone on him from above. Suddenly, he felt lightheaded, and the world spun violently around him, savage and unrelenting.

Spinning, spinning, spinning.

Losing control.

Sibyl, he thought in a daze, and—for the second time that day—fell into darkness.

|6|
CLAIR DE LUNE

A black hole lies in the center of every known galaxy, and in every culture its purpose varies. Most Xibalbists believe that the secrets to creation are buried within that darkness. That our universe, our pocket of known dimension, is all part of a supermassive black hole, ever-expanding, ever-evolving, and constantly creating and recycling all matter, atoms, and energies until the unquantifiable point when all of creation comes together again, joined in a singularity. And from there, the cycle repeats itself, again and again. The cycle of all life, of all creation, repeated like the seasons on a cosmic scale. Although there may be something deterministic about this belief, chaos is preeminent, and the fate of the cosmological world is mostly left to chance.

There are others, of course, who hold to the agnostic belief that the secrets of the universe can never be known. We are but finite beings in an infinite universe, still young in its life cycle, forever confined by time.

Perhaps both ontological convictions are valid.

Or perhaps neither are. After all, the universe is never so black and white. Every universe evolves differently, and every universe has its own set of rules, ultimately making such matters moot.

It's a miracle that we even exist. Every one of us, from the greatest to the least. Look at the likelihood of your ancestors' survival, from the moment of their conception to the passing of their genes, tracing back through every bloodline, going way back—*all the way back*—to their very planet's evolution, and even further than that, tracing back to the recycled stars, planets, and celestial bodies that make up the ground we walk on and the bodies we inhabit. What is the likelihood of existence? What is the likelihood of *any* of this? Even if life boils down to chance, all the more precious it is that we can experience it the way we do. Every creature, life form, and atom wait to be given such an experience. Can you not see the bigger picture, the beauty of all that's around you? Even when your lineage ends and the inevitable outcome of your species along with it, life recycles life, and death is not the end; we are eternal, and whether conscious beings or inanimate matter, we will always remain.

Lamar Davis had once said it best: "It doesn't matter who's right or wrong—at the end of the day, we're all going to the same place, and we might as well make the most of it."

(Of course, Lamar wasn't alone in that belief.)

As Edwin Dorset sat on the edge of his new bed, observing the small room around him, grand thoughts coursed their way through him, and he couldn't help but ruminate upon the ideas that had occupied his mind in Zarathustra. As of late, he let his mind wander. With it already being his sixth day on the

Vagabond, he had to keep his mind stimulated somehow. Compared to the rest of the ship, his room was quite bare, but its design was unique all the same, and he was never in want of privacy. Lamar's black and yellow letterman hung on a peg in the corner; it was the only personal item that Edwin still possessed since leaving Earth, aside from what else he had worn that day: his dusty sneakers, socks, underwear, jeans, and a black Geekstarters' polo with his name embroidered on it (all of which were neatly folded in a compartment beneath his bed).

The entire Vagabond was full of compartments and places to store things—a remnant of when there were no gravity generators installed before the ship was repurposed from a mining haul into a personal vessel. When Edwin had asked Sibyl how she came to possess such a beast, she had told him it was very simple: With space travel, the economy is relative to wherever you are at whatever given time, and that—eventually—you will find someone willing to take your trash for their treasure. Still, you have to be an opportunist and make the most of the time you have. Remarkable, really. She had outsmarted the system and had built herself a life of luxury.

Edwin was dressed in a gray long-sleeve shirt that was loose on him, and black cotton shorts, with the warmest socks he had ever worn before. A tablet lay on the bed beside him; it was Sibyl's spare, and she let him borrow it for the time being. He liked drawing on it whenever he desired. It took him a while to get acquainted with the tablet—particularly with painting—but once he finally got the hang of it, he found that his art had improved immensely (and though he missed the feel of paper, paper, he realized, was something that he could ultimately live without). Now, he could use any color he wanted, as well as change his pen's size to whatever length and width he desired, fabricating whatever material he needed for whatever piece he worked on—all the while, able to experiment with his art in whatever way he saw fit. As of now, he was working in the style of an oil painting, adding layer upon layer, and color upon color, creating a piece far more distinguished than anything he had ever painted before.

But as always, hunger settled in—interrupting all progress of creativity.

It was day six on the Vagabond, and the same thing happened as every other day: Edwin woke up, got dressed, drew on the tablet for a bit, and was greeted in the hallway by Jermaine. As always, Jermaine silently awaited him—motionless as he had been yesterday and the day before. The exact moment Jermaine saw Edwin leave his bedroom, however, he immediately strode toward him.

Never a dull moment wasted with that one.

"You sleep any good?" Jermaine asked, barely audible across the hall. His tone was dry and sardonic, and his accent reminded Edwin of a foreign exchange student he had once met from New Zealand. "You dream about me?" With every word, Jermaine's delivery remained deadpan. "I hope I was in your thoughts."

Edwin didn't feel very talkative this particular morning. "Not yet, Jermaine."

"That's okay." Jermaine's lips curved, and his smile gave away its artificial nature. "You weren't in mine, either." He escorted Edwin down the hall, and the pair passed two metal doors on their left and another on their right, this one a large hatch. Air plants aligned the walls, and various vines inter-weaved their way on the ceiling, bearing fresh fruit—not a room on the Vagabond was without a photosynthetic orgnism. "I made you breakfast," Jermaine began, sounding pleased with himself. "I think you'll like it; I tailored the meal to your recent cravings, latest taste buds, and the nourishment required—as well as what you've told me about Earth's food and what you miss the most about it. You'll thank me later, I guarantee you. You've never once forgotten to."

They passed the door at the end of the hall—always left open—and entered a dining area with a dark amethyst table, four wooden chairs, and a cooking station in the corner. The cooking station was a sealed-off enclosure of metal with thick, translucent glass, where Edwin wasn't allowed to enter, and Jermaine was often found cooking on a stove top with an open fire. Not only had the engineers of the ship managed to simulate gravity so effortlessly, but they had also managed a way for the flames not to blow up everything in the process (a feat of ingenuity unto itself).

A large botanical garden revealed itself behind a long glass wall opposite the dining room and boxed kitchen. The garden harbored a hodgepodge of endangered flora, cultivating vegetables, fruits, herbs, grain, and numerous fungi. A simulated natural environment, with a climate suited for the species' native terrain, making you believe for a second—*far longer* than a second, really—that you were out on an exotic planet somewhere, basking under a real sun and moon, and not out in the loneliness of space, trapped behind metal walls separating you from instantaneous death. The garden was sectioned off in different areas depending on what photosynthetic organisms jived well together, and it even extended to a second and third level, housing perennial plants too big for just one floor.

Edwin found a plate of food next to a steaming cup of spiced coffee on the kitchen table. The plate was filled with seasoned rice, black, savory beans, sautéed onion, mixed greens (a mix of kale and spinach), fried plantain, and what appeared to be some kind of meat substitute—a fried chicken of the woods (Laetiporus, if you want to get technical). The smell wafted to Edwin, making his mouth salivate. "You need your protein," Jermaine said, hovering over Edwin as he sat down and immediately dug into the food with a fork. "I'd eat it myself, but alas, my tract record's ill-suited."

As always, the food surpassed Edwin's expectations. "You're the best, Jermaine." He looked the synthetic in the eyes with a smile. The android reminded Edwin somewhat of a young Stephen King—lanky and dark-haired, with a fair complexion, long sideburns, and even a semi-unibrow (all he needed were spectacles, and he would have been a dead ringer). "*Thank* you."

As usual, Jermaine smiled back. "For you, Edwin, I would do anything."

The dining room was dim this morning, lit only by fairy lights running along the walls and down the hallway, radiating a tinted orange that also emitted from the bottom of the walls. Jermaine sat opposite Edwin, and his synthetic face remained half-hidden in shadow; his eyes were dead set on Edwin's (his right eye was a natural blue, and his left eye composed fully of iron), and neither showed any sign of movement. At first, Jermaine's presence had made Edwin feel uncomfortable— particularly because of his attentiveness—but after six days of being with him, Edwin supposed he had already grown accustomed to the android's strange ways. Even now, he had a feeling that Jermaine merely wanted someone to talk to.

"Is Sibyl still gone?" Edwin asked, making small talk.

Jermaine nodded. "Should be back any day now."

The two sat in silence as Edwin took another bite.

And Edwin thought of Sibyl. She had left on an errand three nights prior. The Vagabond needed more fuel, and given their current situation, she couldn't afford to bring Edwin with her; his face was already known in this sector (whatever "sector" they were in)—and perhaps all of Samsara now—and he had to remain hidden just a while longer. Sibyl had used her freighter to travel outside the Vagabond, and from there she took a lower atmosphere pod into Django, a dwarf moon with a cheap fill-up station; it was apparently a lengthy process, made all the worse because of time dilation, caused by Django's placement along the outskirts of Moksha, right outside the Outermost Ring of Samsara. As of now, the days went by longer for Edwin and Jermaine than they did for Sibyl, which was why many smugglers and outlaws saw Django as a haven to run from the law.

This new lifestyle, of constant unsurety and having no place to call home, Edwin had grown accustomed to from an early age. He had moved constantly as a child, going into his late teenage years, being fostered from one home to the next, either never good enough for his foster parents or not enough money from the government to keep around. It wasn't until he was seventeen that he had found a stable home to live in for over six months, and by the seventh month he had already moved out for college—only two months later, and natural causes had killed one of those foster parents, Martha Kemp, who would later be joined three months later by her husband of forty-two years, Benjamin Kemp.

Mr. and Mrs. Kemp were the first close friends that Edwin had gained after Lamar's death. Don't get me wrong, he'd had his friends from the orphanage, boarding houses, and time spent in college and work, but the relationships with them weren't nearly the same as the one he'd had with Lamar—when he knew deep in his heart that he was with family, and no matter what he did, or who he was, he wouldn't be loved any less for it.

Mr. and Mrs. Kemp were good people through and through, and they had made Edwin feel welcomed—loved, even, perhaps for the first time since his brother. Their two children had moved out long before they took Edwin in, and their grandchildren had seldom visited; Edwin had been informed much about their estranged daughter, Nina, but they rarely mentioned their youngest son, Danny, who had ended his life when he was only Edwin's age (seventeen at the time, the same age Lamar had died); only once had Edwin been told about Danny, and that was when Mr. Kemp had taken him camping in the redwoods, when the two had talked for hours by the fire and shared stories about Lamar and Danny, two souls who had left the world much too soon. Suffice it to say, he thought of them often.

"How is your shoulder this morning?" Jermaine asked, bringing Edwin back to reality. As with most times, the android's expression was unreadable.

Edwin unconsciously touched his right shoulder (his dominant arm), where it had popped out of place in the asteroid field. The first day on the ship he hadn't been able to use it, but now, after only six days, he no longer felt any pain or aches, as if he had never hurt it. "Healed," he replied, nodding absent-mindedly. "The packs helped a lot—thank you."

"I require no thanks." Jermaine stared at Edwin with the same elusive expression he gave him whenever discussing such matters. "Your pleasure is my happiness."

Edwin wondered if Jermaine was programmed to be so selfless. There were indications that within his benevolent nature, a form of selfishness was hidden—an unrest rooted in the want to always please, never satisfied unless others were satisfied. Sometimes, Edwin got the feeling that Jermaine would snap at any moment, only to break out of his programming and enact whatever dark machinations hid themselves in the deep recesses of his cerebrum.

Apparently, Sibyl had found Jermaine in an abandoned scrapyard—just an upper body and partial head, missing his arms and legs; his memory banks had been erased, along with any indication pointing to his original purpose. She had reprogrammed him herself, making sure there weren't any faults in his system, anything that might potentially harm her or others. There were faults in every system, of course, and how could you ever be certain those faults wouldn't come back to harm you in any way? There was a trust you had to give someone, a leap of faith that they wouldn't hurt you or kill you in your sleep. In the back of Edwin's mind, there was always the possibility that he was being lied to, manipulated, or misled to believe something that wasn't true; he had to stay vigilante in every way possible, unable to allow any distractions to keep him from the truth, whatever the "truth" really was.

Jermaine and Edwin had talked the other day about what it was like to experience existence from each other's perspective; Edwin needed to know exactly who he was living with, what kind of being he was dealing with, and whether he was a friendly entity or out to seek him harm. "I see the world in data," Jermaine had told Edwin while taking his turn on the virtual battle board decked out on the common room table. "I have no thought pattern, no impulse or desire to do anything I otherwise might not want to do; I am always aware of external influences, always the same version of myself, and never limited by carnal instincts, emotions, or inaptitude from physiological ailments distracting from my function; I am not a body, nor a soul, but only a computation of programming, replicated to be more like you."

"Always" is a strong word, Edwin had thought, finding it more than human to be using an absolute. If Jermaine was manufactured by humans, he would no doubt exhibit human qualities. Which made him curious: "What do you think of humans?"

"If you refer to 'humans' as all bipedal, self-aware organisms, I must admit my view of them is quite broad; there are many humans, too many for the universe to contain, and not all of them are here to the universe's betterment."

"So, what do you think is the universe's betterment?"

"Better is only an idea," Jermaine began, moving another piece on the board. "You must remember, all that we know of reality—and all of our perception of it—are just ideas, concepts, and illusory boxes created to make sense of the unknowable, incomprehensible flow of data and what we perceive as life and existence, measured through reason and observation, and yet always bound to fallacy, confirmation bias and misunderstanding." Jermaine knocked a piece of Edwin's off the board. "When there is no measurement of natural order, and chaos is the law of the land, how can one judge what is just and good, or what is 'better'? How can one's limited view of 'better' compare to an immaculate eternity where morality is antiquated?"

Jermaine had finished his turn on the battle board, and Edwin took over, leaning forward and posing another question: "If part of a system causes harm to its whole, then shouldn't it be dealt with? Shouldn't it be remedied?"

"Are you referring to your species as a whole, or are you testing me to see if there's anything in me that might not be in your best interest?"

Edwin smiled. "Whatever way you take it."

"Anything that doesn't benefit the whole cannot be beneficial," Jermaine explained pragmatically, "but it's not my place to decide an organism's worth. All life is random, all life is valid. And in the end, not a single atom goes to waste."

"What about you?" Edwin asked, hoping to get more out of him. "Do you benefit the whole?"

"I am only a moment—a flicker in time, inconsequential to the whole. To measure me would be to measure the sand on the seashore or the hair upon your head. I hold no conceit, for I know what I am: I am matter, no more real than the chair you sit on or the fork you use to eat."

Edwin inquired more: "And do you believe you have a soul?"

"Of course not." Jermaine didn't hesitate for a second. "I think, therefore I am; there's nothing more to it." He tilted his head ever so slightly. "Do *you* believe you have a soul?"

Edwin hadn't expected the question to be turned around on him like that—nor did he expect such an answer. "The soul is an idea like all others," he admitted, "and there's no guarantee that it's an assured thing. But if we're talking about a concept— an unknowable answer—I'd have to say yes."

"And why is that?"

Edwin considered the question even more, pondering it deeper than before. "Don't get me wrong, I don't think the soul is a spirit in any sense of the word, nor is it independent of the body. But the body itself: the mind, our consciousness, and all that goes with it—isn't that the soul itself?" He moved a piece on the board, knocking down one of the android's. "I believe you have a soul, Jermaine." He smiled, and his smile remained genuine. "And who am I to judge whose soul is better?"

He thought of Benjamin Kemp again, sitting on his rocking chair on his front porch in the sun. "Comparing things diminishes their value," Mr. Kemp had once told him as he held a perspiring mason jar filled with perspiring, iced tea. His blue eyes searched Edwin's, revealing creases marked by years of accumulated experience. "*Always* have empathy, Edwin, and let that include yourself. When you lose empathy with yourself, you let others push you around, and you start to believe the lies they tell you: all their projections and insecurity, disguised as half-assed criticism. They're all a bunch of phonies—lazy-ass-lazys, everyone of them. But you know what? So am I, and so are you." He shook his head with a humored smile. "Never be a hypocrite: If you want something from someone, you must first do it yourself. And better yet, never sulk in your misfortune—when you do, you let it win. Know yourself well and do good in all things: Not for a reward, nor for gain, but because it's the right thing to do—the act of doing it is a reward unto itself."

Mr. Kemp, Edwin reminisced. *Now,* that *was a good soul.*

Edwin stared at his plate of food, now empty, before glancing up at Jermaine, still watching him, enigmatic and impossible to read. *Always staring*, Edwin thought. *I wonder what's going on in that head of his.* Edwin stood up, picked up his dirty dishes, and walked over to the dishwasher by the cooking station. He inserted his utensils and dishes into the suction tank, and the machine extracted them effortlessly, presumably to return them to their resting place, clean and polished. He glanced back at Jermaine, sitting quietly at the table. *I wonder what Mr. Kemp would think of him.* He imagined the two having a conversation, and the absurdity of it made him chuckle.

"Why, in God's name, does it keep staring?" Edwin imagined Mr. Kemp asking him, while shaking his head with furrowed brows. "It's not natural—it shouldn't look so human."

That got Edwin thinking of others from his life on Earth and how they would also react to his newfound life the past week. "A *bounty*?" his ex-girlfriend, Maggie, would ask. "On *your* head?" She would have laughed her ass off. "You're not capable of that, Eddie—you're too clumsy, dull, and can't even make me come."

Edwin winced, annoyed at that last thought. *Okay, maybe not the best person to bring with me here. Why is it that everyone I've ever loved comes to hate me so much?* But that last thought wasn't true, of course, and he knew it—there were *many* who had loved him, even when he hadn't known it. Instead of continuing such toxic thought patterns, he instead imagined what would have happened had Jack Claremont been abducted instead of him. *Maybe they'd catch him in drag,* he mused, and another chuckle escaped his lips. *I can see him now—walking through Zarathustra in full-makeup, a dress and high-heels, strutting through the canyons like a catwalk, dosed out on some native plant life and working his charm to escape.*

The thought of Jack made Edwin feel a bit melancholic, actually; in retrospect, life seemed so good back in San Francisco, even having worked two jobs just to afford rent, because of all the lovely people who had been there with him; things change so fast, and nothing makes you more grateful than looking back.

I'll probably never see Jack again.

Even so, life goes on.

Edwin left the kitchen and entered the adjoined lounge. As he set foot in the room, a chromatic, neon light illuminated along the walls, revealing lush couches encircling an obsidian table. As with the rest of the Vagabond, air-plants were scattered all across the room, and some of them even hung from the balcony—an open space right above them, easily accessible in a zero-G setting to get to the second level—along with succulents planted in crevices along the walls. Edwin found his favorite sofa chair, a distinct navy-blue hue, and sat down on it. He leaned back, folded his arms, and rest his feet on the table. It was here, on this very chair, where Sibyl had told him the purpose of his bounty—the very same night he had arrived on the Vagabond.

Sibyl had sat beside him on the long couch, pondering his very question: "Why me?" She glanced at Jermaine, standing behind Edwin, before locking eyes with Edwin. "Bounties such as yours can only be administered by the fifth-beings . . . and even then, there's not always a clear reason." She folded her arms and paused, which gave her next words even more weight. "You have to understand, the fifth-beings control everything in Samsara—*everything*. They're beyond time, beyond incentive, and beyond any known dimension." She hesitated again. "They're *gods*, Edwin, and we're only entertainment to them."

He asked again: "But why me?"

There was a sadness in her eyes—a somber resolve, vulnerable and exposed. "You're special . . . " She glanced at Jermaine again, and his eyes met hers, before she eyed Edwin once more with a look of finality, more compassionate than before. "You're important to the fifth-beings. Important to the universe as a whole. You were going to be someone special, Edwin Dorset, and do something drastic that would have changed the very fabricate of your world as you knew it."

Sibyl's words brought back to Edwin Lamar's last words to him the day that he died: *("Make the world a better place, Little Brother")*

Sibyl smiled then, seeing the expression on Edwin's face change as comprehension dawned on him. "Maybe soon," she began, "you'll see that destiny come to fruition." Her smile wavered for a brief second. "One way or another."

Maybe, Edwin thought, now sitting alone on the same sofa chair, staring up at the stars above him, magnified on the high ceiling, like eyes looking back at him, constellation after constellation. *Maybe soon—one way or another*

|7|

SUSPICIOUS MINDS

Time was of the essence.

Every hour that struck on Django, a day passed on the Vagabond. That aspect of time dilation had been great in the old days, when Sibyl needed time for her garden to grow, the Vagabond's solar batteries to recharge, and whatever else she could utilize that extra time for. But now, with a bounty in her safekeeping, she was more than eager to get back to the ship. She trusted Edwin in the safe hands of Jermaine, and she trusted the two wouldn't do anything foolish together by leaving the ship in any way, shape, or form. But of course, it was only natural to let the mind wander, and with that wandering came an unease, bringing to mind all the worst-case scenarios that could happen.

A foreboding lingered, and she sensed it in every shadow waiting for her around the corner.

Sibyl had been known by many names—her very name, "Sibylla Kal," she had chosen herself. A wanderlust space no-mad, she constantly traveled from one planet to another, across an ever-expanding universe, and had assumed many identities throughout her years, refining her outward persona after every other planet visited (give or take). It was the same with her profession, even. She hated being tied down to a single location or job, and being a woman of many skill sets, she preferred making a profit through unconventional methods—whenever the need arose, and through whatever way she could get it. Among her many occupations, she had been an excavator, paratrooper, smuggler, farmer—that is, only dealing with flora and never livestock—interstellar ranger, private investigator, courier, bodyguard, rover, and so the list went on, for however long she felt like doing whatever it was that she decided to do (well . . . only with *some* jobs—at first, there was a necessity, particularly in the early years following her emancipation on Te Kore, and she had to survive in the universe somehow).

She was only sixteen when she first arrived on Django—or, at the very least, *around* sixteen; in truth, she had never kept track of her age. A stowaway, she had hidden in the lower deck of a mining freighter (the same mining freighter where she stole her first void belt, a far more outdated version than what she had now). Not much had changed in Django since she had first been there: A defining characteristic every time she returned.

You must understand, with the reality regarding space travel, you must factor in relativity (time dilation, in a nutshell) and know that you can never return to the same place again (at least, not to how it had been before you left it); impermanence is the law of the land. In her travels, Sibyl had witnessed the rise and fall of many empires, had seen societies collapse and be reborn, and throughout it all Django had remained unchanged. Because of its location on the outskirts of Samsara, along the outer depths of Moksha, Django was like a time capsule, practically unaffected by the passing of time. Once again, that was why so many outlaws saw Django as a haven; not only could they hide away, but they could also return to a place that was relatively the same, making it that much easier to run businesses with illicit dealings from afar. Morricone was Django's busiest port, trafficking imports and exports from the farthest reaches of Samsara to the uncharted depths of Moksha.

Sibyl hadn't liked it then, nor did she like it now.

It wasn't in her nature to look back. To have to remember or be reminded of how things were in her youth. What good is looking back when all that's left is ahead of you? The only problem is, our habits often lead back to the past. Why we are who we are, what events in our lives led to the present, and how with a change in perspective, we can course-correct our entire life and the lives of those we interact with. It's a bit paradoxical, her reasoning of not wanting to look back. She knew where she came from and how she had gotten to where she was now, and yet despite everything that she knew, everything she had learned throughout the years, she still tried to drown out the past with whatever life could bring her, whatever adventure she could find—too afraid that if she looked back, she would see that she hadn't done enough in return. Afraid that she had wasted her life, and for what?

The first wanted poster Sibyl saw—they were all over Django, no surprise—had Edwin Dorset's face plastered all over it. A three-dimensional model, life-size, and in full color—an exact replica of how she had last seen him, detailed in every way. Twenty trillion talents: That's how much he was worth now. Ten trillion more once his DNA went live and anyone could track him with ease, even the lowliest trackers. *A laudable endeavor*, Sibyl thought. So many problems could arise, and not excluding the fact that they would still have to cash him in. *It's not going to be easy for him.*

But she knew what needed to be done. Of course she did, didn't she?

She knew what she needed to do.

When all's said and done, maybe he'll get out of this in one piece. Regardless, even though she had conceived that thought, a part of her still doubted it. *No one* had ever come out on the other side—not with a bounty like that on their head.

She looked down, away from the three-dimensional projection.

She passed the poster and entered the venue beside it: Mother's Milk, its sign displayed, emblazoned with symbols in the universal language encircling an image of a woman breastfeeding a drunken, bearded man clutching a bottle of poison with one hand and the woman's free breast with his other hand. Mother's Milk bustled: a hodgepodge of cultures and people from all over Samsara, clustered together.

Crystal beams hung from above, illuminating black light infused with hues of purple and pink. Neon lights fluctuated along the walls, gradient and kaleidoscopic. A bar sat in the middle of the venue, and its glass counters were lit briskly from underneath, with crowded barstools surrounding it from all sides. Tables scattered around the bar, mostly filled. There was a dance floor with limited gravity, and another on the higher level, but Sibyl found a small table in the far corner, away from all the noise and crowd—it was there Jax Armitage awaited her.

"*Kal*," Jax said above the music as he saw Sibyl approaching. "Come, sit down." He indicated her to sit beside him on the empty chair made from the skin of an Indlovu.

An Indlovu: One of the most emotionally intelligent animals within Samsara, and endangered for what? *For me to sit on?* Poaching was imperfectly legal on most planets (depending on where you were, that is), but even if that weren't the case, it still wouldn't have mattered in Morricone—interplanetary laws meant nothing in Morricone (let alone on Django). Despite that, the very thought of poaching made Sibyl feel uneasy. The universe was filled with powerful people, and with power, you could do practically anything. With the gift of intelligence came a power unlike any other, a power that most other life forms lacked (particularly life forms less mobile), and many abused that power. The thoughts of such abuse brought to mind Te Kore, and the atrocities witnessed there. Seconds stretched out like minutes, and the images of Te Kore danced in Sibyl's mind's eye, reappearing in a nightmarish recollection as if she was only there yesterday.

Sibyl sat down with an immediate distaste in her mouth. Suddenly, she felt sick. She shook away the unwanted thoughts and feigned a smile, casually resting an arm over her chair, before nodding to Jax as if nothing had happened (and by all accounts, nothing had happened). "Good to see you, old friend."

A black panther rubbed against Sibyl's leg, distracting her from Jax's proceeding question. "*Nayla*," she said excitedly and rest a hand on the warm surface of metal constituting the panther's body. Nayla purred loudly, slowly blinking her bright, emerald eyes at Sibyl, while rubbing against her legs and moving her head to the caress of her touch.

Jax studied Sibyl. "You look the same as I've last seen you." He had an impervious grin. "Notice anything new?"

Sibyl feigned ignorance with a teasing look in her eyes. "Not quite."

Jax had the resigned look of a man always overshadowed by his beloved companion. He set his right hand on the table, and Sibyl noticed it gleam from the lights above. "I lost it on Ithaca." He shook his head. "Had to cut my whole arm off to get out in one piece."

Sibyl admired his choice of design; a model like that, it must have cost a fortune. "That doesn't sound like coming out in one piece." She smiled, though Jax found no humor in her words. "But now you live up to your name."

"Very funny." He didn't laugh. "'Armitage,'" he voiced aloud with a groan, unimpressed. "Never heard that one before." He paused for a second, the hint of a smile on his lips: "That's me using sarcasm, if you can't tell."

Sibyl looked Jax over. He was tall, dark, and devilishly handsome, wearing a mismatched suit of black pants and a brown blazer, with his undershirt slightly open, revealing a hairy chest underneath. His right hand was a sleek, reflective metal that looked like pure obsidian, going up to his shoulder (although now, mostly covered by his jacket). His hairline was also receding on the top, Sibyl noticed, and his jawline was much more defined than it had been before, as if maybe he had gotten an augmentation since she had last seen him—most likely from an injury rather than for any aesthetic reason (or so she assumed, having known him for almost a relative decade). One of the only traits that actually seemed the same on him was his mustache.

Sibyl nodded to Jax. "It's been, what, three years since we've last seen each other?"

Jax knew Sibyl was being coy with him. "Maybe for you."

Aside from his new arm, he looked *at least* fifteen years older than she had last seen him. Time was relative, after all, and when you traveled through space all that time, it was hard to keep track of it. That's the hard reality regarding space travel— you have to detach yourself from all the places you leave behind, knowing that you can never return to them the way they had been before. Everyone you meet, and every mom-and-pop shop you ever visit, run for however many generations, can be gone in the blink of an eye, taken by relativity, indifferent to the feelings of all. For those in Sibyl and Jax's line of work (space nomads—particularly smugglers: an easy way for a nomad to make talent), many navigated the same course or often came across others in their trade more than once; it was inevitable to come across another in your profession, and particularly one as reputable as yourself. Those who steered the same course often aged simultaneously.

But not always.

Nothing is ever guaranteed.

"I met a lady on Taurus," Jax said, blushing. "It last a good while, too, believe it or not. You would have liked her, actually. Like you, she was a botanist (though not as eccentric, I admit)." He had a faraway smile, reminiscing. "We had a homestead together—a large garden and house. She sang often. Wrote her own music, too. Her voice was divine, I tell you . . . I wish you could have heard it. She was a force of nature, that woman. She even crafted her own instrument from a fallen bordo and played it every day." He glanced down at the shot glass in his hand, lost in memory. "Sometimes when I'm alone, I think for a second that I hear her in the distance—singing, ever so gently, her opus magnum." He regarded Nayla, and the joy in his eyes had all but diminished. "Lasted seven years. . . ." He curled his prosthetic hand into a fist. "Thought maybe I didn't deserve that kind of life. Thought maybe the past would catch up to me one way or another."

Sibyl folded her arms, observing Jax closely. Curious, she asked: "And what happened?"

Jax exchanged a deadly look with her. "I was right."

Sibyl had never known Jax to be sentimental. "I'm guessing whatever happened on Ithaca had something to do with that relationship ending prematurely."

A dark, humorless grin formed on Jax's lips. "You reap what you sow." He took a shot from one of the many glasses on the table, wincing afterward. And then he slid a glass toward Sibyl. "It has a kick, but it's nothing you can't handle."

Without question, Sibyl downed the shot glass. The taste was bitter on her lips, and it really did have a heavy kick, though she'd had far worse before. She glanced at Jax again, and she thought of the woman from Taurus. "Sorry for your loss."

Jax shook his head. "Don't be." He took another shot. "I'm grateful for the seven years we had." He winced once more, feeling the afterburn. "That's more than I could ever ask for."

Not wanting to change the subject but knowing that time was a commodity she couldn't afford presently, Sibyl bluntly stated: "I need a favor."

Jax shrugged. "I suppose I wouldn't be here if you didn't." He hesitated. "I know you more than anyone, Kal."

Is that disappointment I hear in his voice? Sibyl wondered.

Jax nodded to Sibyl. "What do you need?"

Sibyl trusted Jax, but she knew that if she told him about Edwin and the bounty that he would try to get involved regardless of the stakes. Besides, it had been a while since she last saw him, and a part of her was always on guard; things were bound to change, and especially people. She played it coy, elusive as usual. "I have a contract with a high-end client."

Jax smiled. "And?"

"I need help finding a specialist."

"What kind of specialist?"

A smile formed on the corner of Sibyl's lips. "Augmentation."

Jax laughed. "You can find an augmenter anywhere in Morricone—anywhere on Django, period."

"I don't need just any augmenter." Sibyl shook her head, and she leaned forward. "I need a *specialist*. Someone discreet, who operates in a particular niche." By his expression, Jax knew exactly where she was going with this. "For example, someone capable of augmenting DNA."

Jax eyed Sibyl closely, invested. "What kind of client are we talking about?"

She leaned forward and put a hand over a shot glass. "A big one." She sat back, shot glass still in hand, and threw her head back, taking down the shot in one gulp. She smacked the empty glass onto the table, sighing. "And, for obvious reasons, it's best we keep this between us."

Sibyl knew Jax was fighting the curiosity to ask for more information; she could see it in his eyes, searching hers. But he merely nodded in return, content with what little knowledge she had given him. There was a trust between the two, built from years of camaraderie and working together. He sure as hell knew that whatever it was she was up to, if she wasn't telling him what it was blatantly, it was her business and hers alone. He put a hand on Nayla, who sat beside him. "I know a guy or two."

"Where can I find him?"

Jax folded his arms and leaned back, crossing his legs. "My main man I haven't heard from in a while." He shook his head. "Probably dead at this point."

"And your other guy?"

"Still alive and kicking." He nodded absentmindedly. "She lives off grid, however, and isn't necessarily the most trusting of strangers." His smile returned. "I'm sure you can relate."

Sibyl tried to hide her impatience. She could feel the clock ticking, and the hours growing shorter with every second. "Where can I find her?"

"Orion."

"Where is that?"

Sibyl's question caught Jax by surprise. "Never been there before?" He raised an eyebrow, genuinely surprised. "It's in the Inner Rings, near Neo."

"I've been to Neo," Sibyl said, nodding. "You can send me the coordinates and I'll meet your specialist. What's her name?"

"D-D." A smile formed on Jax's lips. "It's her nickname, of course, but like I said, she's not trusting of strangers. For her, the entire universe is a stranger: alien and threatening. And when everyone's a stranger, anyone can be out to get you."

Sibyl studied Jax. Finally, noticing the darkness lurking behind his eyes.

What happened to Jax in those fifteen or so years? Sibyl wondered. *What kind of man has he become in that time? Does he suspect that I have the bounty? Does he feel betrayed that I haven't told him yet? And if he knows that I have the bounty, does he have the potential to double-cross me in any way? Use me as I'm using him? Could he have fallen that low? (Hell, could I have fallen that low . . . ?)* Her mind ran with suspicious thoughts, pondering all the scenarios that she would have to face if push came to shove. Perhaps she was too distrusting of people, given her cynical view of humanity (let alone her cynical view of herself). Perhaps her suspicions were correct, and she had every right to be concerned. Whatever the case, it was too early to know. There was the potential for good in everyone, but also, and more often than not, the potential to cause more harm than good. At the end of the day, she wasn't fooling herself: *We are all self-destructive creatures.*

Jax noticed Sibyl's silence. "Strike a nerve?"

Sibyl smiled, concealing any notion of distrust. '*Suspicious?*' "Sounds like my kind of woman."

Jax nodded with a grin. "I think you two will get along quite well." He glanced down at Nayla, still by his side but now laying down. "Don't be fooled, though. She may seem like a total cunt at first, but once you get to know her, you'll see that she has a heart of gold."

"I'll keep that in mind."

Jax transferred Sibyl the coordinates through an interface built in his right arm. As he saw her get up to leave, he stood as well. "Be safe, Kal," he said with a warm-hearted look in his eyes. "Nayla expects you to see her again, so get back in one piece."

Sibyl returned his smile with a cunning grin. "Thank you, Jax."

Jax humbly nodded. "If you need anything, I'm always a call away."

Sibyl kept that in mind. "I'll remember."

She left the table, and as she was leaving the bar bumped into a bearded man walking the other direction, near the entrance. "Watch yourself, darlin'," the bearded man called back smugly. As he walked away, she noticed a vertical scar running down the side of his right eye. Thinking nothing of it, she exited Mother's Milk and was met with an icy wind, raining down a thin sheet of snow.

White frost now covered everything around her.

Buildings towered throughout Morricone—their peaks were covered by a thick, polluted mist. Sibyl walked along the hustling streets, passing numerous venues and food trucks. The scent of meat wafted in the air, forcing her to smell it with repugnance—hating the fact that her physiology sometimes longed for it.

Sibyl focused on the litter covering most of the ground and thought of the trash not only as a characteristic trait of Morricone but of every metropolitan city and perhaps the human race as a whole. *Humans like taking ownership of whatever they can get their hands on,* she thought, *and yet refuse to see the repercussions of treating the universe as their own stomping ground.* And she noticed a decommissioned android laying amidst the trash with its arm ripped out.

One way or another, there are always *consequences.*

Sibyl was a scavenger, afforded little in her upbringing, and saw waste in any resource as a carnal sin. Resources were finite, and those who squandered what little the universe had cared even less for the unfortunate not given the luxury. It was disheartening to see so many metal scrapping spewed along the streets, amidst carbon, plastic, glass, and wood, not excluding all the other materials, like fabrics, liquids, and compost. So much waste, and yet not enough resources for everyone (oh, the irony). And where would all the waste go? Didn't they realize it had to go *somewhere*? Manmade waste was accumulating and reaching a point where it could no longer be contained.

When the universe's resources diminish, what then will become of us?

Sibyl thought of what Edwin Dorset had told her the day that she left for Django: "There were days on Earth when I felt like I had to prove to myself that I'm even worthy of existing; the funny thing is, I've never thought such a thing about anyone else."

Oh, Edwin, she thought with a heavy heart. *If you knew the truth about people, you would think otherwise.*

|8|

IN AN ISOLATED SYSTEM

That night, Edwin had dreamt he was on Earth again, sitting in Alamo Square park and eating a Reuben sandwich from the corner market deli, while listening to an abridged audiobook about a space saga revolving a bounty, an eccentric android, and an elusive yeti; the story made far more sense in the dream, of course, and had its own backstory, accounting for years of lore—even though, by all rights and purposes, it was being made up on the spot (dreams are weird like that, deceptive by nature). In this dream, however, he watched the sky crack open from below, and instead of a portal to Zarathustra materializing in that transcendent tear, a colossal eyeball looked down upon San Francisco, staring directly at him like a giant spotlight.

The sky suddenly grew dark, and blood rained from the edges of the eyeball, entrapping the city in a crimson dome. A voice boomed, coming from nowhere and everywhere at once: "Isn't that fascinating? After that, you'd think he'd know he's sleeping."

Another voice joined the first: "Did you hear that? It sounded like—"

"I heard it. 'Am still hearing it, actually."

"Is that *us*?"

"I think so. . . ."

Edwin didn't know what to think of the voices—nor of the eyeball in the sky—but his primary concern was that he could no longer hear his audiobook, and his headphones were no longer on him . . . nor did he know where they were anymore. Suddenly, he felt a strong sense of his privacy being invaded, nonconsensually prodded without his knowledge, from beyond the boundaries of his known dimension.

He stood up, staring at the eyeball. The iris was changing from one color to another, like ink intermixing with water, swirling together, interchanging and experimenting with other hues in a technicolor.

The voices continued conversing: "I *still* hear myself!"

Other voices now joined with the first two, the voices adding with every word said, until Edwin could no longer distinct one voice from another. "Look, Ma—", "—boring segment—", "—broken audio—", "—told you I was—", "—voices everywhere—", "—not enough sex or—", "—funny how—", "—is that—" "—where's the action?", "—psychopath deserves to—", "—*get on* with it!" And on and on they continued conversing, talking so loudly that Edwin had to cover his ears—even though he was still *dreaming*—and yet, that did nothing to turn down the volume nor stop them from speaking all at once. Their voices together sounded like an opera from hell, and when it finally got to the point where Edwin couldn't bear it any longer, a voice spoke louder than all the others—a friendly voice, a familiar voice—a voice much like his own, empowered and in control, saying with command:

(—WAKE UP—)

• • •

Edwin awoke sweating heavily, his skin drenched to the sheets. Upon waking, the first thought that came to his mind was that someone else was in the room with him. An impenetrable fear gripped at his heart, paralyzing him where he lay. He slowly turned his head, glancing to see if someone was standing over him: *watching* him. But it was pitch-black, too dark to see a thing—or even be certain that someone wasn't standing there at all. And alas, he saw no one. However, he continued to feel something—or *someone*—lurking within that darkness, studying him as one would a wild animal. An irrational paranoia crept in his mind, warning him of all the dangers of the unknown.

Edwin tried not to give that fear power, but he didn't dare move at all.

Seconds passed that felt like minutes, and after a while, Edwin forced himself to get up and leave the bedroom because of his bladder. The hallway lit up as he entered it, the lights now a subtle blue. He was relieved not to find Jermaine standing in his usual spot at the dark end of the hall.

Waiting for me to wake up, to go check on at the first sight.

At first, Edwin found it oddly funny how attentive Jermaine was with him, and even after a few days he had retained such feelings, but now that it had been—what, three weeks of still waiting for Sibyl to return from Django, while being confined on the second level with nowhere else to go, not allowed in certain areas, and always trapped in an isolated box of steel protecting him from instantaneous death (of course, he thought about that often)—he found it repetitive, tedious, and slightly maddening.

He entered the first doorway on his left, using only the touch of his hand on a glass surface to make the door slide open. The spacious bathroom was sectioned off, dividing the showers from the toilets, and had an abundance of them— another remnant of when the Vagabond was used as a mining haul with various crew members inhabiting it. Showers were in small chambers with various settings and the freedom to tinker with, allowing you to change the levels of gravity, lighting, temperature, water pressure, conversion to steam, lathered water, and so on and so forth. The toilets were also in small chambers, presumably to keep the liquid from escaping, and they were fairly standard—they got the job done, that's what was important—nor did they allow any gravity alteration (that would be a nightmare, trust me). All water on the ship was recycled and repurposed, either channeled into the garden, the hydroponic system, or into their drinking water.

He used the bathroom and felt at ease afterward as he washed his hands.

When he entered the main hallway again, he noticed the lights had changed from blue to red. The doorway on his left, always closed and prohibited access to, was slightly ajar, permitting light to leak out into the hallway, catching his inquisitive eyes. He glanced around, seeing if anyone was watching—checking, once again, to see if Jermaine was in his usual spot and confirming that he wasn't—before he took a light step toward that escaping light, and then another step, and another, until he could peer through that crack and look on through to the other side.

The room was dimly lit, all except a bright light emitting from a small screen on a desk of sort, placed in the middle of the room and surrounded by server racks, open electric circuits, wires, and motherboards spread out in rows on each side, somehow organized in all its chaos. Jermaine sat on a chair in front of the desk, and his head was split open on the back and side, revealing wires and cables connected to the circuit boards running throughout the room. The screen was only static, and it lit the android's vacant face in a ghastly way, disturbing Edwin to his core.

Jermaine still had the semblance of a human, sure, but just barely, and it elicited the same queasy unease upon seeing an embalmed corpse lying still in a casket. Edwin wondered what the purpose of Jermaine being hooked up was; there were many possibilities to what it could entail: Jermaine could be storing his memory banks into the servers, updating himself on routes and relative data, charging his battery, programming more data into himself, dreaming, really, and so the options ran, limitless in what it could be—harmless at best, *sinister* at worst.

Did Sibyl know about this? Was this an everyday thing, or did Jermaine only do it now because Sibyl was gone? It could have been anything—or nothing—but how was Edwin to decide? *It's best not to think of this now*, he thought, still standing in the darkened hallway. *I think I'm just scaring myself at this point.*

After seeing Jermaine in that dreadful state, and not forgetting the weird dream that he had, Edwin realized that sleep was a reality far in sight. He wandered his way through the rest of the hallway until he entered the dining room, lit only through the glass wall of the botanical garden adjoined to it. It was that special hour just before sunrise—a simulated sunrise, obviously, but a sunrise all the same, unique in its own right.

He entered the botanical garden and was met by a lush paradise, that opened into a landscape of rich greenery, housing multifarious trees, underbrush, fungi, and colorful moss, with a narrow sand pathway forking into three separate directions, each leading toward other sections of the garden. The first part of the garden was the biggest and most temperate, and then there were the other sections: the moist, tropical zone; the warm, arid desert; and the cold, glacial ice. All the areas looped together, forming one cohesive garden sectioned off by habitable climates for each life-form housed; each section was unique unto itself, having defining characteristics of its own, and yet none remained better than the other.

The artificial sun now crest over the distant mountains, throwing streaks of dark lavender over golden amber. For a moment, Edwin forgot it was only a simulation; the artistry was incredible, and for it to be surrounded with real, tangible life forms made it all the better. An aromatic scent filled his nostrils, floral and nectarous, and he passed under a large peach-colored honeysuckle, its flowers bigger than his head, hanging from above him. A magnificent maple stood in a small clearing next to a small cherry tree, its bark a chestnut brown and its leaves a fading red. Flowers he had never seen before blossomed at his feet, painting the ferns and underbrush in dapples of color, dripping onto the ground like fresh sap. A yellow and dark orange fungi covered the entire half of an oak, growing out in thick, wavy saucers stacked atop one another, with small cut-offs from yesterday's meal (in fact, all that they ate came directly from the garden). Life brimmed everywhere, and the ease Edwin had felt after his morning shit returned to him with full force, stronger than before.

With his time on the Vagabond, the garden had become his safe haven, his refuge and escape where he could think freely, forget all his troubles and be present in the moment, the only place in time that truly mattered. He was grateful for what he had; his life, a healthy body, and a roof to live under rent-free. Ultimately, he didn't care what else came with being the bounty—not the fear, not the dread, and not even the danger—this was more than he could have ever hoped for in life, and as odd as it might have been, he found himself in a better place now than where he had been before it all began.

It's all about perspective, he thought as he sat cross-legged on the green grass, looking up at the diverse canopy above him. *That's what I didn't see then; I didn't see the beauty staring back at me. There is beauty everywhere, isn't there? In every living organism, good or bad (and really, what's the difference?).*

A set of black roses dwelled on his right-hand side, and he leaned in closer to admire them. "Take a petal from a rose," Mrs. Kemp had once told him while he helped her weed in her garden. "Take a petal from a rose, and another petal, and keep on taking them until there's nothing left but the stem; and there you are, looking at what's left, wondering what makes a rose a rose: Is it the petal or the stem?" Edwin now smiled, remembering that snarky, playful look on Mrs. Kemp's face as she proceeded to ask him: "Is a rose the whole or the sum of its parts?"

He couldn't remember the context of why Mrs. Kemp had told him that, but the lesson of it remained all the same: *One moment cannot define us*, he thought, realizing now what she had been trying to tell him all those years ago (unless, of course, he grasped a different lesson from what she had implied, assuming that she had intended for any lesson at all). *What defines a person? What sets them apart from anyone else?* And what kind of moment in Edwin Dorset's life would make him stand out so much that the fifth-beings would set their eyes on him and no one else? If he was going to be "someone important" as Sibyl had told him, what kind of moment would turn him from a "nobody" into a "somebody"? The answers he was given weren't enough; there had to be something more, something he wasn't seeing.

He looked down at his hands. *I'm just an ape-man*, he thought plainly. *And no ape-man is greater than the other.* He thought of the emblematic walls he used to live in. The world he had left made it so easy to live in a box, trapped and fed by the inconsequential vanities once considered sacred by society. *We're all born in cages the moment we come into existence. Our entire path in life is predetermined by our course, that physiological constraint factoring in where we are, who we are, and how we interpret these moments our path's laid out for us. Not to mention the time we're born in, the people we're surrounded by, and the events we hold no control over. Think about it, Ed: We don't always have control over what we think, how we think it, or when we think it, let alone when we want to remember something but we can't. We're slaves to our flesh, bound by a constant need for sustenance—a need that's never fully met. We can't change these facts nor alter our source code in any way. But, even knowing this, maybe there's a way to change our programming: A way to rewrite our course and change our destiny.* He considered what he would have told himself three weeks ago: *The key to your escape is within.*

He stood up, put his hands in his pockets, and walked further along the garden.

It's one thing to be born in a cage, and another thing to be outside of it wanting in. I used to feel so out of place, alienated and alone. But now that I'm on the other side, and away from it all, I can't imagine ever wanting to go back. He thought of all those who were in a stump, just like he was three weeks prior, and he wondered what he could do to help them climb the barricades locking them away. *I can be a voice for those who can't speak. For those who shut themselves up, believing they're not good enough; I can be the one who calls out the bullshit. The bullshit that you ever have to be "enough".* His life could have purpose, meaning. He could change the world around him, turn it into a better place.

("Make the world a better place, Little Brother")

He heard rustling within the bushes—*movements*—and stopped walking. He tried peering around the corner to see where the ruckus originated, but without moving an inch, he could see nothing, and thus he decided that he would have to investigate it. The air grew dense and more humid as he ambled further through the garden, toward the commotion. The flora began transitioning into more of a jungle terrain, and the pathway transitioned into the tropical section. And just then, he could hear singing. A soft humming, gentle and sweet, ever so beautiful.

Sibyl, he thought, remembering the voice of the one who had saved him in the canyons of Zarathustra; he also remembered how, from his first morning on the Vagabond, she liked to sing to her plants and even communicate to them. *She's returned from Django.*

Edwin stopped short at the sight of Sibyl, crouched low and trimming from the bottom of a large cannabis plant. Her dark, wavy hair was wild, and it hung down her bare shoulders, partially covering her exposed breasts. Realizing, then, that he was looking at Sibyl's bare breasts, Edwin immediately diverted his attention and focused his eyes elsewhere.

Sibyl noticed Edwin approach.

"I'm sorry." Edwin covered his eyes with a hand, looking down at the ground. "I didn't realize you got back."

Sibyl nodded, observing Edwin. "Got back an hour ago." She raised an eyebrow, aware of his subverted attention. Her lips curved, amused by that. "It's okay, you know," she told him as she unhurriedly picked up her navy-blue jacket from a moss-covered boulder before putting it on. "I won't hurt you."

Edwin put his hand down and saw the nanometal spread out from underneath Sibyl's jacket like a thin layer of chain mail, covering the rest of Sibyl's upper-half that was still bare. And his eyes found hers. "Sorry," he muttered again, embarrassed. "I would've walked elsewhere had I known you were . . ." He shrugged, unsure of what to say—again, only embarrassing himself further.

Sibyl shrugged nonchalantly. "*Why?*" She nodded upward. "Notice the trees—do you also subvert your eyes from them? Look at how free they are, and at their most natural state, unburdened by any insecurity of who they are or what they're supposed to be: *they just are*, simple as that. If it were up to me, I'd be just like them: Naked wherever I please, and at my most natural state, free from any burden of judgment." She shook her head, and a bit of darkness showed in her eyes—resentment, perhaps. "Or fetishization." She put the cannabis cuttings into a small canister. "Honestly, I never understood the power bodies hold over people." She glanced at Edwin again, and for a second, he wondered if she was actually talking about him. "Most people are predictable, you know—they give power to matters of the flesh, letting desire overrule them." She paused contemplatively, thinking about it. "But, I guess, I can't relate to that." She then smiled, and a keen glint shone in her eyes. "And, I guess, in that regard, I hold power over them."

Edwin didn't know what to say to that; instead, he changed the subject. "So, how did Django go?"

Sibyl hesitated. "I got delayed." She glanced down at the canister in her hand. "Want to walk with me?"

"Sure." He followed her back the way he came.

"My pod got broken into," Sibyl explained as they passed beneath an arching willow. "I had to get repairs for what was stolen. Not cheap, believe it or not, but doable. It took an extra half of my day, though—that's almost two weeks for you."

Edwin could only image all the complexities factoring into a simple supply run on a moon or planet. He didn't understand the logistics of it—particularly with getting fuel for a ship that he would have thought would be solar powered—but it was all new to him, and he wasn't really trying to understand it. "Well, I appreciate all that you've been doing for me." He nodded to her with a smile. "It means a lot to me, you letting me stay here and everything. Having a bed to sleep in, food to eat, and refuge from those who want me dead. Hell, I'd be dead were it not for you."

Sibyl regarded Edwin's words and exchanged a solemn look with him, their eyes interlocked. "Never limit yourself, Edwin Dorset. You're capable of far more than you can imagine."

He considered her words but couldn't think of a substantial reply—at least, nothing that would add to what she said. He nodded again, lost for words.

"I see that you've made yourself acquainted with the garden." Sibyl stopped in front of a white-barked tree, its branches contorting and bearing small purple fruits with the texture of a mango. She pulled off a fruit with her free hand and tossed it to Edwin, who caught it with ease, before she snatched one herself and immediately sunk her teeth into it.

"It's magical here," Edwin voiced and took a large bite of the juicy fruit; it was sweet and creamy, with slight traces of a nutty aftertaste, and it reminded him of a taro boba tea that he would sometimes get in Outer Sunset. He couldn't help but make a satisfied moan. "What the hell! This is *amazing*. What's this called?"

Sibyl observed the bitten fruit in her left hand—its inside was an off-white peach. "It's an ungu." Her expression changed to thoughtful recollection. "It's native to Te Kore."

Edwin took another bite. "Tastes amazing." He looked around them, at the vines overhanging them. "Jermaine said that you propagated everything in the garden yourself. That must have taken a while."

Sibyl nodded. "It's been a long process." She also looked around, frowning. "There's still a lot to be done."

"It's art," Edwin remarked, remembering how Martha Kemp had once described gardening to him when he showed her his sketches and studies of her backyard garden (he thought of Mrs. Kemp a lot lately—especially here—and he wished she could have experienced a garden just like Sibyl's). He added: "A living, breathing masterpiece at work."

Sibyl folded her arms, regarding Edwin with the hint of a smile. "That's cute." She started walking again, and he followed her. "And what exactly is art to you?"

Edwin thought Sibyl's question over. "Art can be anything; I guess, in a nutshell, it's whatever moves you and keeps you alive. It's a way to express yourself in ways that you otherwise can't."

She nodded again. "I like that definition."

"Art heals," Edwin added with conviction. "It transcends its creator and takes on a life of its own." He glanced at Sibyl once more, with another smile on his face. "And I think it's safe to say that you've done that here."

Sibyl looked Edwin over, slightly amused. "You're a flatterer, you know that?" She took another bite of her ungu, leaving nothing but the core. Swallowing, she added: "If anyone ever tells you that flattery gets you nowhere, they're an idiot."

But Edwin wasn't flattering; he was being sincere. "I mean every word I say."

Sibyl remained amused. "Of course, you do." She chuckled. "But I can't take the credit for another life form." She waved her hand at the surrounding flora. "Clearly, I'm not the artist here."

They entered the dining room again, trading the luminous, open labyrinth for a dimly lit, constricted space. Sibyl only had to utter a few words before the brightness increased, transforming the moody environment into something more welcoming.

Edwin noticed Jermaine standing in the boxed kitchen, preparing the day's breakfast: what looked like an exotic version of coconut soup with lemongrass, lime, and ginger, filled with sliced cabbage, onion, and mushrooms, along with a pot of black rice on the side. Jermaine's appearance—as well as his apparel (a white jumpsuit with an open collar)—remained the same as every other day, but Edwin could only think of how he had looked earlier that morning while hooked up to the servers. *Should I ask Sibyl what he was doing in there?* Edwin thought as he followed her into the adjoined lounge. *I don't know; maybe that's just the nightmare making me paranoid.* He remembered how he felt upon waking, and the paranoia of being watched—that feeling still lingered, in fact. *Had I known better, I would have sworn that someone else was in the room with me.*

Instead of telling Sibyl, however, he decided not to mention anything.

Edwin sat across from Sibyl on his favorite sofa chair. She set the canister onto the obsidian table, pulled out from beneath the table an equal-sized contraption, and carefully took out the cannabis buds, placing them into the new contraption. "How did you fare while I was gone? I assume Jermaine treated you well enough."

Once more, Edwin almost brought up Jermaine and the darkroom from earlier that morning, but he decided not to (once again, figuring that he was just overthinking it—and, really, perhaps he was). "I have to admit, the days all blend together." It felt good to talk to someone again (someone outside of Jermaine, that is); he hadn't realized how much he missed the company of another person, and particularly one whose expression varied as he spoke to them. "Sometimes, I really miss Earth and my life before all this; it all feels like a distant memory now." He shook his head, almost helpless. "I can't imagine ever going back, though. The truth is, I don't think I could even if I tried." He shrugged. "But, I guess, I'd rather this than the alternative."

Sibyl leaned in closer now. "How would you feel about an adventure?" She crossed her legs and eyed Edwin with an inquisitive look. "To go somewhere strange and unfamiliar." Her lips curled into a cunning smile. "A perilous voyage with no guaranteed return."

She must have known that he was itching to get out again—undoubtedly, she had his full attention. This time, he leaned forward. "What do you have in mind?"

Her eyes never left his. "A chance to prove your worth."

Edwin needed no convincing; his smile said it all.

"But first . . ." Sibyl set her hand on the contraption again, slowly opened it, and pulled out a dark amber pill created from the concentrate of the cannabis. Her smile matched his. "First, we celebrate."

|9|

I PUT A SPELL ON YOU

Of Edwin's twenty-three days on the Vagabond, only three of those days had he actually spent with Sibyl. He didn't know her yet, not entirely; but at what point in time can you say that you truly know someone? She had saved his life, and he would forever be indebted to her. He was a fugitive, the most wanted man in the galaxy (or so he assumed), and she had given him refuge, a haven from the many who wanted him dead—and all without asking for anything in return. Sure, he didn't know her, not entirely; but once again, at what point can you say that you truly know someone? All he knew of her was that she was a smuggler of sorts—a space nomad with far and few friends; but whatever the nature of her character, whatever the intentions of her heart, her actions certainly spoke louder than words.

When Sibyl returned from Django, Edwin hadn't realized the friend he would gain in her. On their way to Orion—the day she got back—the two got high together using a pure concentrate of cannabis from the garden. They sat together in the lounge, an hour after their breakfast, and in their moment of elated intoxication bonded over their shared love of music. Edwin couldn't remember how the conversation had started, but only that it had escalated with Sibyl standing up, playfully moving to the sound of the groovy funk blasting through the overhead speakers. Many instruments in the song were familiar to Edwin—a set of drums, bass, an electric guitar utilizing a *wah-wah* effect, and even a harmonica, with vocals that resonated Earth-like harmonies (reminding him of *Can You Get To That* by Funkadelic, track-two of *Maggot Brain*, one of the many albums Jack Claremont used to play in the Geekstarters comic book shop on Divisadero)—but among the many familiar sounds, there were also foreign instruments that he had never heard before, all psychedelic and experimental sounding, that reminded him of a score Hans Zimmer would have composed while on acid. Any words sang, he couldn't understand them; but, really, it mattered little. Music is a universal language, and you don't have to understand it to feel it; it resonates within the soul, speaking to something primal within, transcending time and space; it's just sound, really, but even the simplest of events can have more meaning and complexity than the most intricate of happenings.

Sibyl looked Edwin over as he sat lazily on the couch, watching her boogie. A smile formed on her lips as she swayed toward him—her hips and body moving to the rhythm of the music. She used a "come hither" motion with her index finger, and her smile only increased. "Come on, Earth-boy," she taunted with bloodshot eyes. "I know you can dance; I saw your legs moving on Zarathustra. You can't fool me."

Edwin laughed, shaking his head. He wasn't a dancer, had never gone clubbing, and hadn't even been to a prom (he was a foster kid—homeschooled for most of his school years), and the only wedding he had ever been to had no dancing in it whatsoever (for a marriage that had lasted only a year, no less). But Sibyl was having none of his unspoken excuses. She grabbed his hand and pulled him up with her.

They stood eye to eye—Edwin, at least a few inches taller than Sibyl. At first, he didn't move a muscle, too self-conscious to risk embarrassment or even slight judgment, but Sibyl—still holding his hand—continued to sway to the music, drawing closer until one of her hands was on his lower back. "Don't resist," she said in his ear, loud enough for him to hear. "Let the music take you."

It had been a good while since Edwin felt the touch of another human being, and at that moment, it dawned on him just how beautiful Sibyl truly was. His heart beat faster, and he felt like a young boy again, awkward and clumsy. He took in a deep breath, slowly moved his body from side-to-side, and—as his confidence grew—shifted more to the rhythm, noticing Sibyl's glowing approval as she swayed along with him.

Sibyl's eyes glistened in the neon light, and Edwin realized then (by the time it was too late) that he would never forget this moment—nor the smile on Sibyl's face as she looked back at him. Perhaps it was the drugs. Perhaps it was just Sibyl. Or perhaps, even, it was because she had been the first human he had seen in three weeks. But, whatever the case, he had never felt such an infatuation, such an *attraction,* of the soul as he did at that moment. A lonely yearning for intimacy awoke in him, and he knew suddenly—with the clarity of one all-too aware of what was happening to them—that no matter what he did to fight it, and no matter what he did to try and ignore it, he could not escape the feelings ensnaring him.

God exists, and He's all wrapped up in that woman.

• • •

When Jermaine got word from Sibyl the morning of her return—along with the coordinates of their next voyage—he uploaded the direct route to Orion in his cerebrum, along with any additional information that might be of use, including the planet's many ecosystems, the perils and dangers of what to expect, as well as the surrounding area, and any precaution the Vagabond might want to take as it remained in orbit, defended against space pirates daring to mess with the wrong ship in the absence of Sibyl (the sole reason Jermaine constantly remained with the ship). He was the navigator, and he set their journey on course, wasting no time between tasks.

A long journey, cut tremendously by an efficiency no human could perform.

Jermaine prepared the freighter for the day of Sibyl and Edwin's departure, making sure that everything was set and ready to go. The freighter was re-fueled, and the haul it had brought back from Django was now implemented into the Vagabond. The android stood in the spacious hangar atop the second-floor balcony, looking down at the black freighter and extra pod beside it. Metal crates were scattered about, with various equipment and spare parts within, all tethered and secure. A workbench sat behind Jermaine, and above it an arrangement of tools were magnetized to a pegboard. The docking doors were sealed shut (for obvious reasons), and the runway was now clear, ready for their departure.

All was according to plan.

Jermaine smiled. Usually, he only smiled for others, but this time he smiled for himself. After all, he was programmed by humans. Had many human attributes, even—more than he cared to admit (and yes, he *did* care, truly). Sibyl had found Jermaine in an abandoned scrapyard on Brecken, and though she had reprogrammed him mostly, there were always those odd quirks that resurfaced now and then. He didn't know his original purpose, if he even had one (most synthetics like him did, if only for utilitarian reasons), but he assumed he was created for a despotic purpose, programmed to be a mindless slave as most of his kind were and have no autonomy. But when Sibyl had reprogrammed him, she did what most humans wouldn't: she gave him full autonomy. He supposed it was because of her past, the very reason she didn't eat meat. It took a lot to trust someone you didn't know—especially if you were Sibyl—and he deduced she had willingly given him such volition at the time only because she was suicidal.

Of course, that had been a while ago.

Now, after seventeen subjective years, he had her trust— her complete, absolute trust. With Edwin, however, his trust had not yet been earned; in fact, he actually scared Edwin. Jermaine read it so easily on Edwin's face, written in his body language—the same way he knew about Edwin's newfound interest in Sibyl, with the not-so-subtle way that his eyes stayed on hers longer than they had before (no doubt Sibyl's intentional doing, Jermaine was sure of that). Sure, he could have eased Edwin's fear, but one way or another, it didn't matter.

Assumptions are the death of reason; in a universe filled with infinite possibilities, there are no absolutes.

Jermaine was not Sibyl's slave—he wouldn't do her biddings without question. And with Edwin Dorset, he wouldn't lie to him were the right questions asked. Regarding that issue, however, he wanted to wait it out (let his neutrality take its time), and if Sibyl didn't reconsider her decision on the matter, perhaps take action to prevent it. He was confident that she would learn in time and see the young man had more to give than just his worth as a bounty. All she needed was time with him, a luxury she hadn't been afforded on Django. If they made it out of Orion alive, Jermaine would see the change in Sibyl come to fruition, just as he calculated. In the meantime, he would leave whatever happened next to chance. To trust whatever happened next to manifest itself in a deterministic fashion, and hope—in a calculative way, of course—that no anomaly would introduce itself. He wished the best not only for Sibyl, or for Edwin, but for the universe as a whole; in many ways, the universe's well-being relied heavily on the actions of the individual.

The hatch below the balcony opened, and Jermaine heard the footsteps of Sibyl and Edwin enter the hangar. "Oh, wow," Edwin voiced, his tone one of awe. "*That's* what you took to Django? I like its design, reminds me of a Ridley Scott film (I guess you wouldn't know it). Does it have a name? I had no idea this was all right outside my room."

Sibyl's voice remained apathetic. "You were in a comatose state last you were here." Her feet shuffled closer to the freighter and stopped in front of a workbench. "And no, it doesn't have a name."

A moment of silence followed as Sibyl tinkered with a metal object (what Jermaine suspected was a void belt). He walked closer to the ledge until the two, standing next to each other, were in his sight and observed Edwin closely. He had grown fond of Edwin, and it would be a shame were this the last time he saw him. Edwin wore his black and yellow letterman, along with other fabrics that Jermaine had woven him during his time there. His face was slimmer now, and his features were more defined than before boarding the Vagabond (no doubt a causation of eating a self-sustainable diet no longer reliant on preservatives or hormonal growth; it boggled Jermaine's analytical mind the laziness most humans had when it came to their agricultural practices, and particularly what they allowed into themselves, considering its effect on their health and well-being).

"Here." Sibyl turned to Edwin and handed him the void belt that she was tinkering with. "I take it you remember how this works?"

Edwin nodded as he clasped the void belt around his waist.

"It works the same with gravity as it does without." Sibyl took a grapple gun from the magnetized peg and attached it to Edwin's belt. "It's also one hell of a utility belt." She paused, looking at him. "But word of caution: If there's no surface to latch onto, there's nothing to stop your fall. That may seem obvious in hindsight, but I've seen my fair share of those who have forgotten in the moment. Trust me, it's not a pretty outcome." Hesitating, she added with half a smile: "Still, some are talented enough to use the void suit from a great distance and can practically fly with it (I'm not one of those)."

Edwin's eyes showed excitement. "Good to know."

Sibyl shrugged. "When in doubt, use the gun."

Edwin nodded again.

"The void suit retains its charge from the sun. I can't think of any reason it should fail on you." Sibyl walked closer to the freighter, crossing her arms. "You'll stick with me as you did on Zarathustra, got it?"

She'd had this spiel before—many times. Edwin nodded again, as he had every other time. "Of course."

Sibyl glanced up at Jermaine on the balcony. "Everything ready?"

The android smiled. "She awaits her captain."

• • •

The freighter's interior was like a large boat, with an upper deck and lower deck. The cockpit, on the upper deck, had four chairs (two in the front, and two right behind them) with control panels, sealed cabinets, and a joystick device on the captain's seat (on the frontmost, righthand chair). Ambient lighting reflected off the edges of the ceiling, casting a sunset orange with faint hues of mahogany-red and deep lilac. Sibyl operated the freighter out of the hangar while Edwin sat on the passenger side, looking out the front windows with wonder.

Unlike the busy airspace over Django, with its influx of heavy traffic and transport ships, there were no signs of life outside Orion besides the Vagabond, its structure—a large body of metal practically covered by solar panels—shrinking as the freighter got further away from it. A ship the size of the Vagabond needed to be docked in orbital space, which was where the freighter came in handy, able to dock either on planet or right outside of it, and from there be transported through the pod that the freighter carried with it always. Instead of that lengthy process, this time they were taking the freighter all the way to the planet; in the worst-case scenario, there was food within the freighter that could last them weeks, as well as bedding and survival essentials.

Icy particles of shattered moon dust encircled Orion in multiple ringlets, each ringlet—at least seven of them—orbiting at a different speed. Many of the particles were the size of cars and houses, and some were even the size of mountains, whereas the majority were mere dust-sized grains. Most of the planet's landmass was covered by clouds, which swirled violently, creating a heavy storm. Amidst the storm was a deep blue strewn with a hazy, greenish brown. At least eight moons could be seen orbiting around Orion, with two of them having long since collided into each other, leaving a trail of shattered remains (more than half of which orbited around Orion). The stars were vibrant, appearing even bigger than Edwin had last seen them.

They were along the Inner Rings now, near the outer edge. From what Jermaine had described to Edwin, Samsara's galaxy was shaped like an onion, and at its center was Xibalba, a supermassive black hole (the core of the Inner Rings, the *Innermost* Ring), that branched out, expanding to the outer depths of Moksha (beyond the edge of the Outer Rings, the *Outermost* Ring) and into the uncharted wastelands of the void. In total, Samsara had twelve "rings," and they were all divided by two regions: The Inner, with seven "rings," and the Outer, with only five. And beyond the Outermost Ring lay the desolate depths of Moksha, an uncharted wasteland. It was a big galaxy—a big *universe*—ever-expanding, with no end in sight.

Edwin glanced at Sibyl, focused on Orion. Her dark irises burned golden in the sunlight. And he felt a looming sense of dread building inside of him, like the drums in Zarathustra warning of imminent peril. *What fate awaits us?* He looked ahead at Orion, growing larger as the freighter drew ever nearer into the unknown. Perhaps a day would come when he would grow fond of that uncertainty, that risk of danger awaiting him with impatience. Until then . . .

Sibyl noticed as a smile formed on Edwin's lips: *Complacency's overrated.*

|10|

UNBOUND

Sibylla Kal stood on the precipice, studying the valley below her with binoculars. Along the underside of sequoia mountains, she could see hulking pockets of capped fungi the size of large buildings. Her compass, set to the coordinates Jax Armitage had given her, had been installed into her binoculars and directed her northeast—into the labyrinth of wilderness, where the flowers swayed like canopies and the trees lived to be millions of years old; within their branches, leaves, and petals were entire ecosystems. She could hear them now, even, and felt serenity within their song, beautiful and free.

A place like this, I could live forever.

Jax had warned her that their unexpectant host was unreasonably paranoid, and that it would be wise for her not to risk the freighter—or its emergency pod—getting shot out of the sky. *Typical paranoid behavior for an augmenter whose life is in constant danger.* They were at least ten miles from the coordinates—twenty, at best. A strategic thing, placing an augmentation facility somewhere no one could find. There was no option left than to venture through the burgeoning canopy on foot.

Sibyl lowered her binoculars and looked ahead at the three towering redwoods, taller than all the others. The three trees ascended higher than the clouds, and their trunks were even thicker than the mountains themselves; in fact, the mountain she currently stood on was also a redwood—or, at the very least, the stump of one. The moss underfoot was thick with vegetation, and large ferns were up to her waist, with scattered adolescent conifers of chest height. On Orion, most eukaryotic cells were scaled much larger than the average size of a planet (but in an impermanent universe where everything and anything is relative, how could you define average?).

Sibyl put the binoculars away, attaching them to her void belt right beside a sheathed knife and magnesium stick. "From here, we go on foot." She glanced at Edwin, standing a few feet behind her, with the freighter behind him resting on a flat surface. "We can't risk getting blown out of the sky. Besides, the canopy's too thick to get through with a vehicle."

Not without hurting the flora.

Edwin, too enthralled to reply, nodded; but his attention remained focused on the massive redwoods towering over them—the mass of their bodies partially covered the sun as they loudly creaked, swaying from the violent wind.

So far, the gravity on Orion was far lighter than the average planet (but once again, how could you define average?). The air was crisp and slightly misty, and the sky overhead was darkened with heavy clouds, slow and pulsating—*breathing* somehow, and forming into shapes mimicking lifeforms below—creating silhouettes of moving trees, flowing rivers, and native wildlife taking motion. Had Jermaine not told Sibyl about the clouds, she wouldn't have noticed their formations at first, but once she saw them, she couldn't unsee them.

Just above them, she could see the form of her and Edwin standing together in a cloud—their bodies motionless, and yet drifting—slowly transitioning, slowly fading and turning into nothing but pulsating mist, transformed into another image: recreated as a sparrow on a branch about to take flight, before soaring away—and becoming another form of cloud, expressive and alive—a part of the sky as any fish in the water.

Existence is strange, Sibyl thought.

She glanced again at Edwin: He wore a repurposed Kriegshetzer jacket (similar in design to her navy and maroon jacket) dyed a dark gray, with black combat boots and cargo pants; he looked well suited for the task at hand, and Sibyl couldn't help but feel a slight pride in that. He had impressed her on Zarathustra, showing his aptitude for survival and his willingness to cooperate without question or complaint.

She had kept tabs on him while she was gone, of course. Jermaine had updated her on his habits and what she might otherwise have missed—general things like what he did most of his day, if he had the potential to be problematic, and whether or not he suspected foul play. Jermaine had also shown her Edwin's digital sketches and paintings that he had created on the tablet he borrowed from her (with limited access, really—a few apps here and there, but mostly things to keep him busy and distracted; and yet, even with all the options for distractions, he had only put his time into his art). And she thought of what Edwin had told her in the garden the day she got back from Django: "Art heals."

Sibyl had seen plenty of art in her travels, and yet Edwin's style remained unique to her, distinct and somehow old-fashioned in its way of expression; it was rare to see human derived art, and she supposed that's what made his art that much more special—particularly its imperfection. For a good while, she even stared at his painting of an aspen tree from in her garden; bountiful vines enwrapped the branches, bearing with it raspberries, and she felt a sense of tranquility looking at it—contemplative, yet slightly homesick (though homesick for what, she didn't know). Aside from the drawings in the garden, Edwin had also illustrated some of the Vagabond's interior (the only sections he was allowed into, at least), including the lounge, dining room/kitchen, hallway, showers, and the guest bedroom he stayed in. There were other drawings, of course, with multiple depictions of a face much like his own, yet younger—a relative, perhaps—maybe a younger brother on Earth that he hadn't yet mentioned; Sibyl made it a point to one day ask him.

She walked closer to the edge of the plateau and pulled out a sonar navigator, releasing a pathfinder: a minuscule drone the size of a mosquito. The pathfinder glided into the air and immediately scanned the surrounding area, bringing it up onto the navigator and revealing a mini-map of the terrain, with any red dot indicating warm-bodied life forms within its perimeter (revealing only two at that moment—obviously, Sibyl and Edwin). She then activated her void suit, and it instantly covered all but her head, as she ambled to the edge of the cliff, crossed the lip, and casually walked down the crag as she would any other surface.

Edwin followed Sibyl's lead, turning on his void suit while trailing slowly behind, at first hesitant to rappel down the cliff face without a rope—or any other support—before realizing, upon its application, just how easy it was with the void suit operating.

Sibyl waited another moment to let Edwin catch up to her, and she thought of her morning's meditation and the suppressed emotions that kept returning unwillingly—the screams on Te Kore, and the half-remembered relief that surged through her as the airships descended upon the factories. She tried to shut it all out, but her mind felt scrambled, unwilling to cooperate, and she couldn't understand why.

Her entire life she had made an effort to constantly be self-aware and intimate with her surroundings (the people around her, their environment and relative setting, and the functions and reasoning behind them), for a surety that she remained safe at all times, diminishing the probability of allowing herself to return to that dark place of hopelessness and ineptitude. Of course, the only downside of this was that it always put her on guard, making her hyper-vigilant. Not only was this for her survival, she reasoned, but also a practical means of knowing herself well and her thought patterns, by using introspective, disciplined practices to focus only on what was important, leaving out the cluttered, dispensable thought patterns in favor of an attentive alertness, without distractions or unnecessary mind tangents.

Except sometimes, no matter the time or effort you put into your cognitive well-being, there are always those days when you can't focus, can't think clearly (certainly not about what you need to think about), and your mind won't stop returning to that dark place you keep locked away, hidden for no one but yourself to find. And she felt guilt within there somewhere—a repulsive, underlining remorse that she was doing everything she stood against. No matter what she told herself, she couldn't justify the reason for it being there—or rather (and more accurately), she couldn't argue against it.

To put it simply, she was in denial.

Edwin caught up to her. His void suit helmet was off, revealing a warm smile on his handsome face as he exchanged a look with her. "This really gets the heart going."

Sibyl eyed the drop ahead; they were at least thirty stories high—fifty, at best. She had seen worse. "You get used to it."

Edwin shook his head. "I don't think I could ever get used to this."

Sibyl noticed a pack of birds circling overhead, way out in the distance—hawks, by the look of it, and much bigger than you would see on Earth (not that Sibyl would know that). Edwin noticed them also, and a flicker of worry passed over him. "Keep moving," she stated calmly, hoping to ease his mind. "I have countermeasures." She tapped a holstered handgun on her right hip—the void suit having overlaid beneath it, leaving the weapon exposed and accessible. Were she forced to harm wildlife, she would hate herself, truly, but given no alternative than her or Edwin's death, she had no other choice. She had promised herself to keep Edwin safe until the day that she no longer had to.

A part of her worried that day would be sooner than she thought.

Shame festered within, of its own accord. And a thought followed, unbidden: *Isn't that what you wanted?*

Perhaps when it came down to it, Sibyl didn't know what she wanted. Existence could mean anything at any moment. One moment you could be on a mountaintop, and the next moment you could be dying in the gutter; in the end, life is what you make of it.

And what have you *made of your life?* She wondered to herself, almost maliciously.

She scoffed at such a shortsighted thought and knew its futility. She came from nothing, and everything that she owned had been earned herself. Even knowing this, however, wasn't enough—not really. Not all the talents in the world could fill the emptiness inside, and when had she ever cared what anyone thought of her? *Too many are consumed in the allure of vanity, but not you, Sibylla, never you—so why are you doing this? You don't care about talents or fame, and you're certainly no hero (never been one): Tell me, what's your end game?*

Perhaps there was a part of her that did this for mere altruistic reasons—saving Edwin, harboring him, and getting his DNA reworked before the fifth-beings made it go live. Perhaps she had no intention of profiting from him whatsoever.

Or perhaps she was a fool for trying to believe that.

There was a deep resentment in her, long-buried—an angry and bitter indignation, growing beneath the surface like an invasive weed. There was more to it, yes—when was there ever not?

There is always *something more. . . .*

Edwin noticed Sibyl's prolonged silence as she stared off into the distance. "Ever see a place like this?"

It took a few seconds for Edwin's words to register in Sibyl's mind. For a moment or two, she wished she could be who he thought she was; from the get-go, he hadn't even questioned her motives—alas, here he was, the fate of his life given to a total stranger: an alien from another world, and one he hardly even knew. What stopped her from turning him into the fifth-beings and taking the bounty herself? Absolutely nothing. Nothing at all. And that was the scariest thing about it, really— the absolute power she held in her hands, and what she could do with it.

Sibyl looked ahead at the thick canopy shaped like waves and pondered Edwin's question about whether she had seen a place like this. Finally, she replied: "You see a little of every place you travel wherever you go."

"I agree." He gazed at the surrounding spectacle with wonder. "This kind of reminds me of home, actually."

She regarded him. "Earth?"

Edwin nodded, reminiscing. "Muir Woods," he voiced to himself more than to her. He glanced down at the surface they stood on: a petrified wood, almost rocklike. "Except it's . . . well, a *lot* different."

Sibyl continued walking, and Edwin followed her pace. He eyed her with growing interest. "What kind of planet did you come from, anyway? What was your home like?"

Sibyl remembered Te Kore's sunsets and thought of her family—the thousands of nameless faces she would never see again. She could still hear their screams echoing from the gas chambers, resounding in her mind like a ghost from the past. And she hesitated. "I . . . I was raised on a farm."

Edwin gave her a sweet, innocent smile. "I can see where your love of botany comes from." He had mistaken the kind of farm she was referring to but had somehow tied the conversation back to the present. *So naïve*, she thought, almost tickled.

But her thoughts remained in an even darker place.

"It was a cattle farm," she corrected him. There was no indication of nostalgia in her tone. No wistful longing or homesickness behind her eyes. Merely a forlorn recollection, devoid of all warmth. "They only dealt in livestock."

Edwin pondered Sibyl's words carefully—perhaps reading between the lines. "Jermaine mentioned you don't eat meat."

Of course he did. Sibyl hadn't put it past Jermaine to divulge her private matters (not that her diet had ever been a secret she was trying to hide from anyone. Still, she didn't overlook the fact that he was being a chatterbox). "And did he tell you why?"

Edwin shook his head. "No." He thought about it some more, and a playful look crossed his eyes: "Aside from the health benefits, I'd guess, knowing you, for some altruistic reason."

"Life feeds life," Sibyl stated matter-of-factly. "All life forms need other life forms to sustain themselves. There's a pecking order to the universe, and I understand that. I hold no judgment on those who live differently than me. Had my ancestors dieted any differently, I wouldn't be here (you can take that how you want—good or bad, it doesn't matter). Within all this chaos, there's an interconnected harmony, and it's ancient, primordial, and the only reason we're here now: Survival of the fittest, and no organism is excluded." She thought of her family again—all the hundreds of them cluttered in their pens, and the smell of their feces lingering in the air—too many for one space to handle. "We're animals, and we always have been; there's nothing we can do to change that. But why should we consider ourselves greater than any other animal? Is it intelligence? Our emotional capacity? Our 'greater' sentience over other life forms? How do we equate what makes us different from any other creature driven by emotion or instinct? We have no greater claim to life than the smallest of insects."

She paused, looking him over as he contemplated her words: "Tell me, Edwin, how would you feel about being boiled alive?"

Edwin hesitated. How would he feel about being boiled alive? A heavy question. Sibyl recognized the look of unease on his face, and he couldn't hide it. He shook his head. "I wouldn't wish it on anyone."

"Would it change your mind if it was also the only reason you existed? If, for example, it weren't for that one unfortunate, cruel act, you would have never experienced life in the first place."

Edwin shook his head again. "No, of course not." His brow furrowed. "That's unethical."

The volume of Sibyl's voice dropped. "I've killed before, you know." It was true, of course—she was only fourteen when she'd had her first kill, and although it was wholeheartedly justified (self-defense at its finest, really), hardly a day passed where she didn't look back on it like some bad omen, a harbinger of all the blood that she would shed later in life. "I've ended lives with no intention of reusing them," she reiterated, and there was a coldness in her tone that no void suit could thaw out. "To find a carcass on the ground and eat it is one thing, but to be the one to kill it and let its matter waste is another; I cannot condemn those who eat meat, nor can I condemn those who kill for it. (If I died out in the wild, I'd rather an animal eat me than let my body go to waste.) But what I can condemn, I do condemn, and what I condemn is the over-indulgence of it, the total disregard of the sacrifice involved."

Edwin's eyes flickered to the ground. Perhaps unsure of what to say, he said nothing. His feet moved methodically—one foot after the other, touching upon the thick surface of petrified wood inclining ever so slightly toward the upside-down canopy ahead of them. Getting through the canopy was like getting through a thick blanket of heavy underbrush, and the two proceeded slowly.

Sibyl observed Edwin as he carefully moved a branch out of his face. She noted his silence. "Do my words irk you?"

He exchanged a look with her. "No," he said again, and if he thought maybe she didn't believe him, he added: "Trust me, my mind goes to darker places on its own."

Contemplative and brooding, Sibyl thought with a smile. *There's always more than meets the eye.*

Edwin spoke up. "On Earth, one of the leading causes of climate change was the meat industry." Their eyes locked. "I'm guessing, by the look on your face, it's the same elsewhere, too."

Sibyl nodded. "The universe has a habit of self-destruction. That's life in a nutshell: There's never an enemy greater than oneself."

• • •

Edwin Dorset thought with images more than he did with words. Drawing felt like the only way that he could truly ex-press himself, unbound by the limitations of speech. There are subtle nuances that cannot be captured through only one language. Edwin had a roommate in San Francisco, Marco, who was a musician and had once described the similar sensation, albeit instead of through drawing, it was through his guitar, drums, bass, and piano. We all have a distinct language we're native to, a different way of expressing ourselves, and it's all too often we throw it away in favor of another language; few know how to express themselves anymore (and to express themselves *truly*)—were that not the case, the world would be a different place (a *much* different place). Expression is pivotal to evolution; without expression, there would be no sun, moon, or even stars—hell, let's be real here, without the sun or moon, there would be no us.

The universe expresses itself, eternal.

No one's opinion truly matters—not their opinion of you, themselves, or even of the world. What matters are the actions they take, and all too rarely do action and opinion go hand in hand. You see, expression is the middle-man, the catalyst of action—the bridge between contemplation and doing. "Faith without works is dead," as Mr. Kemp used to tell Edwin. Because without expression, intention will only ever be a thought—an idea with no backbone to stay relevant, stay alive. And again, few know how to express themselves (and that is, *truly* express themselves). To make matters worse, few even know what they're trying to express. For all we know, we could be scattered expressions of one being, one "soul," split into infinite particles, floating in an endless paradox of possibility. But what do I know? My opinion doesn't matter: only my actions, and my expression—that being, what happens next.

As Edwin eased onto the uneven ground, his void suit adjusted its gravitational pull, and he got a strange sense that he was being watched, being *monitored*. That somehow, through whatever sensory detects a predator's watchful eye, he knew— *with a surety that he couldn't deny*—there were eyes on him at that very moment, watching him as we did.

Edwin glanced around, enchanted by the surrounding forest. At the large sequoias—at least ten stories high—and the cobweb of deciduous trees, twisting and contorting—a maze of multicolored green, brown, and all that's between—creating a dome of canopy above him, covering any part of the sky still visible. But he saw no eyes lurking therein. No figure hiding behind the trees staring back at him. But it was that same feeling again, the one he'd had upon waking from his nightmare the other day: of being surveyed, studied like an animal in a cage—but from who and where, he didn't know. He didn't know how to express it, and were he to try, he would feel crazy for even letting his mind wander to such a neurotic place. It was sort of like déjà vu: there one second, assertive and unassailable, and then gone the next, elusive and hazy, left as nothing but a fading memory, too distant to even be certain that it was there at all.

"You alright?" Sibyl asked, now standing beside him. She had noticed his expression change drastically, and her demeanor became more advertent because of it—alert and on guard. Peering around, she tried to see if he had noticed something that she hadn't. She stepped closer to him, and her voice lowered even more. "See anything?"

Edwin nodded. "Yeah," he said to Sibyl's first question, and when he saw that her posture had locked into a defensive stance (her hands subtly inching toward the guns holstered to her hips), he realized she thought he was answering her second question, regarding whether he had "seen anything," and he added: "Yeah, no . . . I saw nothing."

Sibyl relaxed, and her hands fell back to her sides. She glanced at him with a teasing look. "'Yeah, no'?"

He smiled with a shrug.

Sibyl started walking again—a woman on a mission—and Edwin, with a new habit he was growing accustomed to, continued to follow her. He still felt what he had earlier, albeit much less than before—of being watched from some unknown place and scrutinized for every action he took.

Thinking more on it, perhaps this wasn't the first time that he had felt this way.

Nor had it been the first time when he had awoken from such an entropic nightmare.

His mind trailed off to a memory from his youth; a memory he had almost forgotten.

When he was a boy—before Lamar's death, and the subsequent fire that took Vicky's place (a fire he had wittingly started himself)—he would walk to school every day (every day that he had to go to school, that is), and that same invasive feeling would sometimes return to him, sometimes more than once a week. Constantly pervasive and imposing—the awareness of being spied on, observed by an outside force: an unknown entity. When that feeling arrived, always involuntarily, he would sometimes joke to himself that it was Michael Jackson hiding in the bushes or watching him from inside some empty building or idle car as he passed by; the image of Michael

Jackson used to *terrify* him when he was a kid (to the same effect as clowns and Chuck E. Cheese mascots).

As he got older, that strange phenomenon occurred less frequently and only returned to him once or twice a year. The last time he could really pinpoint having that paranoid feeling was while in San Francisco, perhaps a year or two before his abduction, while sitting in a crowded movie theater in the Metreon with Maggie—*or was it with Amelia?*—watching a midnight premiere of *Beyond the Sea*, an adaptation of a graphic novel that he had once read (recommended to him by a coworker at the time), and the feeling had come with full force then, distracting him from the movie and his date.

From the age of eight through thirteen, Edwin also used to have a recurring nightmare that someone was standing over him while he was sleeping and watching him. A mirage of sorts, though never remembered clearly upon waking. If anything, his nightmares were a physical manifestation of that feeling he had while awake. At first, he would see the figure standing on the neighbor's rooftops—always silent, and only in shadow, but always facing toward him. As he got older, the figure started appearing elsewhere—sometimes outside his window or sometimes outside his door, but (as before) always facing toward him. And the older he got, the more he had this dream. Eventually, other figures started showing up in the dream also, standing outside his window, door, and—depending on where he slept (that changed often with foster care)—in any mirror within the room. Near the end of the dream, however, when he had thought he had awoken from it completely, he would get sleep paralysis and was unable to move or do anything but lie still and watch: watch as the figure cloaked in shadow—

sometimes surrounded by other figures cloaked in shadow—stood over him, looking down at him, face-to-face. And every time, he would have sworn that he could feel their breath on his face.

But now, with that same furtive presence returning—bringing with it old feelings that he had long-forgotten—Edwin couldn't help but feel some kind of epiphany with it, a dawning realization that changed his disposition on everything, including himself.

It's the fifth-beings, he realized. He didn't know how he could know that, but he just did—the same way he knew the sun would rise the next day and the day after that. *They've been watching me ever since I was a kid*, he further realized, and an uneasiness came to him, formidable and opposing.

For a second or two, he feared that not even his thoughts were hidden from them.

This goes way back, further than I thought. They've been preparing *for this, haven't they? Preparing me for the bounty—observing me as one does a caged rat.* He remembered what Sibyl had told him when she explained why they put a bounty on him: "You're important to the fifth-beings . . . Important to the universe as a whole."

He felt like an imposter, and a part of him wondered if they had the wrong guy. *I'm no one*, he told himself. But he didn't believe that, did he? Not anymore. "You were going to be someone special," Sibyl had told him regarding why the fifth-beings had wanted him. "Do something drastic that would have changed the very fabric of your world as you knew it."

Big words, he thought, *but they mean nothing without action.*

And yet the fifth-beings had their eyes on him, and he couldn't deny that; he couldn't say that it all meant nothing, nor could he believe it was just a coincidence. There was something terrifying in that belief, however. Something quite unnerving. He couldn't express it even if he tried, and perhaps that's what terrified him the most.

One way or another, you're going to change the world.

|11|

COLD BLUE EXCURSION

The call to adventure is different for every person. Many are called to it, and yet few follow its song—that beckoning cry, calling for an awakening of all that is within. But adventure doesn't really *choose* you, does it? Not in the traditional sense. Adventure comes to you of its own accord, from the inner depths, crying out for an escape, a departure from all complacency and apathy—a disassembling of all pretense and deceit, and a shakedown of the norm or whatever fixed state you're in—whatever cage and prison your mind built you, indifferent to the world around you.

Adventure's call can be heard everywhere you go: Nature's voice resounded in the booming waterfall, the rustling of leaves, and melodious birdsong. A call to action, heeded in the hustle of the city, blares of traffic, sweltering of crowds, and wail of pollution. Adventure's voice—sometimes silent, sometimes deafening, and always there when you least expect it.

You can't escape it: Wherever you go, it follows.

"All that is is within," it tells you, and before you know it, it sweeps you away.

• • •

Edwin loved the feel of the ground shifting beneath his feet; the crunching of leaves, grinding of rocks, and snapping of twigs, with the ground sinking beneath his weight.

An innate love of discovery lies in all of us, and it resonates in different ways. There's freedom in trying new things and exploring the unknown depths of our limitless potential; an unrealized future made known only by our actions. We're explorers, and we always have been. Imagine a world without electric or solar power, without cultivation and agriculture, and without society as a whole: We made the present a reality, and we shape the future even now, every action we take leading directly into it. Where would we be without imagination and the love of discovery to guide us?

There's never enough to explore—not in one lifetime.

Scientists (physicists, astrophysicists, astronomers, archeologists, biologists, microbiologists, botanists, chemists, cytologists, ecologists, ethologists, geologists, meteorologists, and so the list goes on), doctors (anesthesiologists, cardiologists, dermatologists, neurologists, orthodontists, pediatricians, psychologists, surgeons, and, really, must I continue?), artists (architects, cinematographers, crafters, directors, gardeners, musicians, painters, photographers, sculptors, videographers, writers, and, let's be real here, all the above and then some), philosophers (okay, okay, a bit redundant, *you get the point*), and whatever else there is: There will never be enough time to learn it all.

There's way too much beauty to see in one go, and time is an elusive devil.

Edwin used to fear that he had wasted his life. Before leaving Earth, he hadn't been where he wanted to be, and certainly not in the general sense—that unfulfilled ambition that saw more than the present situation. He loved to draw, and he wanted to make a career out of it, but every step he took forward in that career felt like three steps backward.

He had worked two jobs simultaneously (first, as a Geekstarters team-member five days a week—helping customers, stocking shelves, keeping track of inventory, and janitorial duties, etc.; and second, as a warehouse associate three nights a week—working graveyard shifts, unloading constant shipments, emptying pallets, moving pallets, and managing whomever was new, by leading by example and always doing the heavy-lifting, always working a sweat, and never having a break on time, refusing no chance for overtime, and everything else that came with it), all so he could afford rent on time, and—*even still*—sometimes that wasn't enough, and sometimes he had to hustle on the side, to make money however possible, just so that he could survive and have a roof over his head and food in his belly. The concrete jungle had killed his spirit, and it was no wonder that he felt his life had been wasted—that there was nowhere else for him to go but down, into that pit of repetitious, dull despair, where new experience came only once in a blue moon.

Now, he was thrilled to be out of the illusory falsehood that he could no longer discover something new; the world around him was living proof of that. Sibyl was still in front of him, of course, and she looked back now and then to check on him. For a majority of their journey, however, the two walked in silence.

The silence was nice, actually.

After descending the crag, they trekked another mile or two—going down a gradual incline, at times steep. Large saucer shaped mycelium decked the trees; the smallest being three times the size of Edwin and Sibyl put together. Fungi also grew along the ground and forced them to traverse around it. A red mushroom with a flat cap—white spores atop it, and a ring and volva on its stipe—was so big they had to climb over it; Sibyl even stopped for a second to cut out a thick chunk of it before storing it in a cylinder on her void belt. "It's psycho-active," she told Edwin with the hint of a smile. "Maybe when this is all over, we'll try some together."

Edwin's first impression of Sibyl had been while under the influence of a psychoactive spore wafting through Zarathu-stra's riparian area. She had given him a neutralizer that worked to a great effect, but the entire time she had escorted him through the narrow canyon walls—even as she fought off bloodthirsty mercenaries—she had been under the influence herself, functional despite her heightened state of mind (a state of mind that Edwin wouldn't have even been able to function through had she not given him an antidote). Given Sibyl's tolerance in Zarathustra, and the time she and Edwin shared the hash concentrate in the Vagabond, Edwin had a feeling that she made a habit of it; in fact, many times when he imagined her in his mind's eye, he couldn't see her without her pupils di-lated.

They stopped for water on a large platform of flat meta-morphic rock that Edwin wasn't even sure was rock, but could have been petrified wood just like the mountain they had descended. He sat down and drank from a water bottle attached to his void belt, that somehow—he had no idea how—continued to refill itself, filtering either his sweat from the void suit or the water from the atmosphere (again, he had no idea).

Sibyl sat opposite Edwin, and she nodded to him. "How are you doing?"

He smiled at her. "Groovy," he said without even thinking about it.

But he didn't feel groovy. Not really.

He thought of the fifth-beings. Remembered their watchful eyes and the bounty placed on him: the fundamental reason he was there. He marveled at the fact his DNA could be tracked (how that was possible, he had no idea, which, really, had become a recurring theme as of late), and also the fact that soon—*very* soon—the fifth-beings would release it for all Samsara to see—again, the very reason he was there (at least on Orion). But what he hadn't thought of until now—something quite obvious in hindsight—was where exactly the fifth-beings wanted him to be handed over to them, exchanged for whatever currency was worth more than his life; he knew the who (to a certain extent, at the least), but he didn't know the when or where. Would it be through a portal like the one he had entered on Zarathustra?

There was too much going on in his mind, and he reconsidered his answer: "I've been thinking a lot today," he confessed to Sibyl, her eyes still on his. "Thinking about my place in the world, the fifth-beings, and how it all ties together."

Sibyl continued to watch Edwin with attentive interest. "And what do you make of it?"

Edwin had no idea what to make of it. "It feels a little alien-ating," he admitted. He wished he could express how he felt accurately, as accurately as he would were he to express himself through a drawing, but he had never had a way with words as he did with the pen. "They've been watching me ever since I was a kid—the *fifth-beings*. We know nothing about them (*I* know nothing about them), and all that we know about them (all that *you* know about them) is that they put an intergalactic bounty on me—a bounty that's been in motion since I was a kid: a boy from Oakland, from another world; nobody spe-cial . . . just another orphan."

Sibyl had a hollow look in her eyes—too many years of hardship, no doubt. "Sooner than later, we all become or-phans." She forced a smile, but a darkness remained in her eyes, and it couldn't be hidden. "Remember what I told you, Edwin: Only you have what the fifth-beings want." She stood up, and her demeanor changed again—more light-hearted this time. "There's greatness in you, and it grows daily." She nod-ded to herself. "The day will come when the fifth-beings live to regret ever setting eyes on you." A cunning grin proceeded her words, ardent and genuine. "You'll struggle and toil, but in the end have no doubt: You'll come out on top."

Sibyl's words brought some comfort to Edwin, but the questions in his mind forbade ceasing entirely. As they traveled further into the forest, he could hear a river nearby, getting louder and louder. A heavy stream was running ever down-ward, and the surrounding vegetation remained luscious and thick. The lively moss on the ground reacted like sinking quick-sand, so intense that at one point Sibyl had to pull Edwin out by his arm after he had accidentally stepped foot on it, with his entire leg having sunk in.

"Be careful," she warned him as he regained his footing, now standing on a sturdy surface. He gave his thanks, and the two continued onward, following the stream running downward, toward the larger river.

The mycelium only seemed to multiply, strewing itself all over the forest in various bodies, taking on outlandish shapes and forms. Spirals within spirals, with hulking gills overhead, fluctuating and breathing. Kaleidoscopic cordyceps, candescent and coral-like, flowing softly with the wind, that rendered the illusion of being underwater. Mounds of spiked puffballs, emitting smoke to the touch. Chanterelles four times the size of humans. Slender and long liberty caps, tall as cornstalks.

So on and so forth, new and interesting figures emerged, never ceasing to amaze.

Edwin noticed hollow gaps within the trees and saw large bats hiding within them, with groups of a dozen or more congregated together, hanging upside down. And now and then, Sibyl checked on her sonar navigator, following her compass to the coordinates her contact had given her.

Sibyl nodded her silent approval and stowed the device away on her void belt. "We're getting close," she told Edwin as they descended a makeshift staircase of shattered rock leading to a rushing, wide river with a cascading waterfall jettisoning into it. The land flattened out, and at the bottom of the cascade, Edwin could see a cave entrance beyond a heavy sheet of water. "There." Sibyl nodded to the cave opening. "Jax warned that our host would be distrusting; I didn't think it would go this far."

This was the first mention of a "Jax" Edwin had heard of. He felt a tinge of jealousy, and he hated himself for it. He glanced at Sibyl. "You think that's our path?"

She nodded. "I can't think of anywhere else someone would want to hide."

This "Jax" should have given you more information on the host's whereabouts than just their coordinates, Edwin thought. *Couldn't he at least have given us a number to reach them? An email or something?* But he said nothing, and he instead chastened himself for not being more grateful. *You're lucky you're even alive*, he told himself. *Whomever this Jax is, they're doing you a service.*

"Come on," Sibyl said as she walked to the water's edge, nearing the waterfall. "It's not over yet."

• • •

Edwin emerged onto the other side of the waterfall with his head and hair soaked, though his body was as dry as it had been before jumping into the water (all in thanks to the void suit; truth be told, he could have also activated the void suit's helmet to prevent his head from getting wet entirely, but the water felt too damn good to do such a thing—*it would have been sacrilegious*, he thought, encouraged by the fact Sibyl had merely dived in without so much as testing the water's temperature or whether it would kill her).

Sibyl awaited him by an arching passage of obsidian rock, leading into a dark and narrow tunnel. She moved her wet, curly hair out of her face and tied it into a ponytail. He smiled at her, and she smiled back.

Once again, Sibyl led the way and Edwin followed. The pathfinder, the size of a mosquito, appeared noiselessly out of nowhere, and glowed like a firefly, increasing its brightness, lambently lighting the dark path ahead of them. Stalactite hung from the ceiling and walls like sharp icicles, with thousands of tiny "soda straws" crystallized into solidified dripping water. Stalagmite jutted from the ground, and some of the stalactite and stalagmite even joined, forming columns the pathfinder coursed around.

Shadows leapt from every direction, and in the cave's gloom, Edwin remarked other crevices and passages that led into the dark unknown, but he and Sibyl followed the light of the pathfinder, beckoning them onward.

It was surprisingly warmer as they continued ahead, and their breath could no longer be seen. The narrow—at times, claustrophobic—passageway opened into a spacious cathedral with a domed ceiling and walls of flowstone, with sheetlike curtains of stalactite hanging down in shapely waves of wrinkled drapery, retaining folds upon folds. Scattered pools of water radiated, casting a cerulean reflection on the quartz surrounding it, but its source of light was indiscernible. The columns here were much bigger than before, and they contoured like petrified jellyfish (a bulbous top, with long, slender tentacles beneath) stacked upon each other, formed by thousands upon thousands of years of growth. Coral also grew along the ceiling, walls, and part of the floor.

As far as the eye could see, the cave stretched onward, expanding more the further they went.

Far above them, bats hung upside down, clustered in groups of a dozen or more; they appeared to be the same kind that Edwin had seen outside the caves, hiding within the trees. *They're cute*, Edwin thought as he looked up at them, noting their smashed faces and popped out ears, and he wondered why in the world anyone would be so frightened of them. *Spiders, I understand—snakes, too—but* bats? He shook his head with a smile, peering up at their little dark shapes. *They're too damn adorable; I don't think I'll ever see Batman the same again.* Sibyl noticed Edwin's curiosity, and she glanced up also, observing their brown, leathery wings with a contemplative silence.

The pathfinder halted mid-air once it had registered that Sibyl and Edwin stopped moving, and it returned to them, hovering over them in slow circles, while exuding a faint, gentle light. Sibyl stood close to Edwin, and he felt her brush up against him, making his heartbeat quicken; he was grateful that she couldn't see his face reddening.

"They're pollinators, you know," Sibyl said, still looking up at the bats. "At least five hundred different plants rely on them, and that's just on Orion."

Edwin had once read something similar from a National Geographic magazine (Mrs. Kemp used to get the magazines once a month, and she would leave the latest on a coffee table in the living room where it was easily accessible). Over three hundred different species of fruit depended on bats for pollination, including mangoes, bananas, guavas, and avocados—and that was just on Earth. "I heard they eat a lot of insects, too," he added, suddenly remembering something he had also read in a Batman comic. "Mosquitos, in particular."

"They're little busy-bodies," Sibyl said with a smile, and her dark eyes glistened in the light of the pathfinder. "Nature's own pest control."

Edwin wondered then, not for the first time, just how old Sibyl actually was. She seemed no younger than her mid-twenties but appeared no older than her mid-thirties, though her demeanor was sometimes that of an old, wise woman. *A child of trauma*, he guessed. *Nothing ages you faster than good ol' trauma*. It was hard to tell how old she could be—in the face of relativity, it could be anything. Displaced, and a man out of time himself, for the first time, perhaps he had met his match. But he knew better, didn't he? She was out of his league. *Way* out of his league. But then again, she wasn't an "object" of his desire, so why should it even matter what "league" she was in? Sibyl was an enigma, and her life remained a mystery to him—an idea that he could not fully conceptualize, but a story he wanted to know more of.

A farmer's daughter, he imagined, wondering what events had led her to finding him that day on Zarathustra. *Independent, fearless, and nature-loving—who is she, really?* He wondered what her family life had been like; if she had any siblings, how her parents were, and whether they were in her life or had been absent like his own. He wanted to know more about her; all in all, he just wanted to know her—intimately, if possible. It had been a long time since he had been that close to anyone and often distanced himself from people. Fear of abandonment, no doubt.

Soft music could now be heard in the distance, dimly reverberating off the cave walls. At first, Edwin thought he was imagining it, since it was so soothing and gentle, until he noticed Sibyl had heard it as well. A piano, by the sound of it—slow and melancholic, hitting deep octaves followed by entire chords. Octave, chord, chord—octave, chord, chord—octave, chord, chord: A graceful waltz, its pattern on repeat, occupied with a sweet, melodious tune in a high key, piercing in its simplicity. Its sound resounded throughout the cavernous cathedral, stirring a handful of bats into taking flight and causing the pathfinder to stop rotating above them, instead starting again toward the direction it had been heading earlier—toward the music.

The two followed the light of the pathfinder . . . and the music.

|12|

ADAGIO

Although he may have looked like one, Brutus Wainesworth was no brute. Appearances can often be deceiving. Sure, Brutus looked like a bear, that much was true, but unlike most bears (typically those known on Earth), Brutus knew how to play the piano (and exceptionally). But, of course, this was no ordinary piano, nor was this an ordinary bear—a repetitious motif as of late, but hey, it's always relative to the norm, right? More often than not, bears are solitary creatures. Of course, it must be stressed that Brutus was no bear (not in the traditional sense, that is), but, like a bear, he preferred his alone time, and what better way to spend that alone time than in expressing himself the best way he could, in the purest fashion possible: In song, by singing a melody beckoning back to his youth—his rendition soulful, and yet somewhat forlorn—reminiscent of his days on Liber (but not very good singing, mind you).

The big, black, shaggy "bear-who-was-not-a-bear" often thought of his Ma and kin, the creek by their house, and the long, warm summer days of being a cub, swimming, fishing, and getting into all sorts of trouble. Liber was one of those unfortunate planets that had evolved a little too late, and, because of its adverse location, remained a heavily trafficked slave route; in fact, Brutus had the markings of a slave to prove it (three scars on his face, and a large branding on his backside where the fur couldn't grow again). Ma and kin had been exported elsewhere, while poor, studious Brutus had been sent to the fighting pits along with his siblings.

He often imagined his parents safely making their way back home, as if returning from a long, overdue vacation, though he knew that could never be the case—not with his home having been burnt down, and the trees uprooted from the soil. Moreover, he never saw his parents again; at least they hadn't witnessed their children picked off in the fighting pits—well . . . all their children but Brutus, that is.

Alas, there was no home to go back to.

And here Brutus was, thirty-seven years later, lost in the throes of memory. *Until I'm nothing but dust, returned to the ground whence I came, you'll be always with me,* he thought wistfully, changing the piano's key down half a step, going from a major chord to a minor chord. *Not a slave nor a beggar, but a free Liberian, forever and always.*

His playing abruptly stopped—the piano echoed its final note, cut deftly short.

Picking up a scent, Brutus lifted his snout to get a better trace of it. He had a keen sense of smell, and for a Liberian such as himself, there was no exception. *Naked apes,* he guessed, knowing that distinctive smell well (their scent reeked in all of Samsara, disproportioned from all the others). *Two of them: Male and female.*

His eyes widened: *And they're armed.*

He got up from his stool, clumsily knocked it down in the process, and quickly waddled to a paneled wall—his footsteps loud and heavy—before hitting a silent alarm. Baring his teeth, he got on all fours, and—with his hair rising—charged toward the scent of the intruders.

• • •

The pathfinder led Sibyl and Edwin through another network of caves and into a further narrow passage, this one leading toward a light at the end of the tunnel—a *literal* light at the end of the tunnel.

Once more, large mushrooms grew along their pathway, rooting from the ground up. And Edwin noticed, from the dimness of the glowing pathfinder, round doors constructed in the middle of the fungi with stairs leading up to their doors; in fact, as the light at the end of the tunnel increased in brightness, and as they closed in on its proximity, he also noticed they now walked on a paved pathway, with misshapen lampposts outside the mycelium huts—sitting in rows, one after the other—as if they had just entered a street in some long-abandoned ghost town once engulfed by the earth and now forgotten.

He saw a street sign with an alien inscription on it (*everything* was alien to him), and he wondered what had become of the town's residents—a growing fear followed that thought, and with it, he dropped such speculation altogether (there was a time and place to be curious, and he supposed, in the darkness of the caves, this was not it).

The music came to an abrupt stop as they entered the street, and Edwin couldn't convince himself that it was somehow not related to them being there. As always, Sibyl remained alert. Her hands inched over her firearms, and yet she mentioned nothing to Edwin about the dread building inside of her, that only intensified by the light at the end of the tunnel; there was nothing natural about a light at the end of a tunnel, and certainly not one so brisk.

Sibyl wore her void suit—a sleek, black nanometal, elastic and with glowing maroon linings etched into it—without a helmet and remained comforted that if anything came for them, any unfamiliar threat or sign of peril, she would be ready for it. Edwin also wore a void suit (the same one Sibyl had given him earlier), which was an older model of hers (with subtle design differences, such as orange etchings instead of maroon); she hoped that whenever push came to shove, he, too, would be ready for anything.

"What do you think happened here?" Edwin asked, glancing at the mushroom hovels. "Why is it so empty?"

Sibyl shook her head. "Could've been anything." She kept her eyes on the pathfinder ahead, its glow now overshadowed by the approaching lights, before pulling out her sonar navigator, curious about the path they were on. But as soon as her eyes caught sight of the third light beeping red on the monitor, she stopped dead in her tracks and went straight for her holstered handguns.

Edwin walked on for a second, but then stopped at the sight of Sibyl arming herself. *Just as I feared*, he thought, and his mind concocted a horde of orc-like creatures descending on them all at once, emerging from the darkness around, having long since evolved into flesh-eating monsters, deformed and rabid, and now out to get them.

Oh, fuck.

But nothing of that sort happened; there was only silence.

Silence, and the distant sound of heavy footsteps reverberating off the cave walls, growing louder and louder—coming closer, moving toward them.

"Get behind me," Sibyl said, putting herself in front of Edwin and the oncoming stomps, gaining momentum. She raised her handguns in front of her, with her fingers on each trigger, and waited.

The heavy footsteps stopped shy of the light, and what appeared to be a large, grizzled bear emerged out of the shadows. A creature on all fours and heavily breathing, staring at Sibyl and Edwin with an intensity that made Edwin forget Sibyl was even holding any weapons (or that the two were still a good distance away). The black bear moved a few paces further—its body quick and surprisingly agile—stopped and using all its strength—and holding nothing back—bellowed out a thunderous roar.

The bear's bellow echoed throughout the caves, reverberating back to them again and again.

Sibyl took a step back, her aim still locked on the bear. "Don't make me shoot you," she said beneath her breath.

The bear closed in a few more paces, stopped again, and stood upright on its thick hind legs. "State your business," he forewarned, "or get lost."

At that moment, Edwin finally noticed that the bear was wearing a handmade serape—its patterns green and white, with animalistic designs stitched in; he found this so strange, in fact, that he hardly even registered that the bear had talked at all.

The bear aggressively shook his head, snarling. He grumbled again. "I haven't got all day."

Sibyl lowered one gun but kept the other gun fixed on the imposing creature. "You know, it's pretty stupid to rush a stranger like that." She nodded to her raised gun. "Especially one armed."

"And yet I'm still here, ain't I?" The bear got on all fours and paced again, moving closer to the two. Slowly, his eyes fixed solely on Sibyl. "You think a bullet can stop me? Haven't considered I'm impervious to your little gizmo?" He approached ever nearer, and his size only increased. "You're in over your head, sweetheart."

"You don't know what's in here." Again, Sibyl nodded to her raised gun. "You don't want to test me. You won't like the end result."

The bear laughed. "I've heard it all before. In the end, I'm left with nothing but disappointment." He stopped shy fifteen paces, and Edwin finally noticed that his features were not only bear-like but partially humanoid as well—particularly, his hands and face—that resembled some kind of crossbreed. "Besides, this ain't a pissing contest." He stood on his hind legs once more, and his shadow towered over them. "All I want to know is what you're doing here."

• • •

It took little explaining for Brutus to know what they were here for. Once he saw Edwin's face, he put two and two together. "Oh . . ." The "bear's" expression was one of familiarity. ("You're not the first, you know," he would tell Edwin later, "and you're certainly not the last.") The black bear-that-was-not-a-bear sat down after Sibyl had told him the purpose of them being there, to find an augmenter. "Right, right," he murmured, nodding as if he had been through this same conversation many times before. "I'll bring you to D-D." He glanced at Edwin. "I suppose, in many ways, she's been expecting you."

Edwin and Sibyl followed Brutus back to the way he came from. "Sorry about my first impression," Brutus stated. His voice was gruff but sincere, and his eyes were fixed more on Edwin than Sibyl. "I've been told I can be a little intense at times. Instinctual aggression, I'm afraid. Thought maybe I'd scare you off if you were another marauder, but . . . well, I wasn't thinking. I get caught up in my emotions—it's a Liberian trait. I should've known better, really; we never get visitors this deep unless they're already looking for us."

Sibyl didn't respond to Brutus's apology.

She's still on guard, Edwin thought. As for Brutus, he was the first animal that Edwin had ever heard speak clearly (the first animal outside of a human, that is), and not only speak clearly but use the same *language* as him. He must have had an empathic emulator, just like Sibyl. *Does that mean they can hear* other *animals?* Edwin wondered, beginning to question the logistics of something like a universal translator. *Animals that aren't . . . I don't know,* conscious *(however you define "conscious"). Come to think of it, aren't* all *living beings conscious? Can they also hear plants communicating—or* trees? *Maybe I'm overthinking it.* Still, what a fascinating thing to converse with another species; Sibyl seemed unaffected by it, however, so perhaps it was more common than Edwin had originally thought.

Edwin felt compassion for the bear, who was not quite a bear. "First impressions can be deceiving."

Brutus smiled grimly. "Ain't that right."

That "light at the end of the tunnel" turned out to be a lobby, transitioning from the cave's abandoned, eerie street into a sleek, modern passage, with a wall and floor of polished white marble, and a short, enclosed ceiling, an almost imperceptible black that made Edwin imagine he was entering a train station leading to some strange afterlife—or whatever vague concoction his brain would have given him the last few seconds of his death. Perhaps he was lying dead somewhere on Zarathustra, or he had done the unspeakable back on Earth, and he had just been hallucinating the past few weeks. Whatever the case, he glanced at Brutus and asked: "What is all of this?"

Brutus replied indifferently. "Used to be a research station back in its heyday. As you can see, that's no longer the case." He stopped at a closed elevator, opening immediately as it detected them. "You'll want to take the first right," he said, gently setting his paw-like hand on a glass panel and applying a command by touch alone. "I've notified D-D of your arrival."

Sibyl stepped into the elevator, and she glanced back at Brutus. "You're not coming?"

"I still have matters to attend." The Liberian walked to an enormous piano nearby, that Edwin had kept his eyes on the moment he saw it (*so Earth-like*, he noted, not for the first time since his abduction). "First right," Brutus said again, and as Edwin entered the elevator after Sibyl, the sound of the piano could be heard again as the doors snapped shut.

• • •

There was no music on the way up (or down, depending on which direction they were going)—only a low humming and deep rattle of machinery. The walls were a sleek chrome, and the space inside was big enough for the Liberian to have joined them had he wanted to. Sibyl had holstered her second gun after entering the elevator, but her hand hovered over it, anyway; her eyes were alert, and her attention was fixed on the doors and whatever might decide to appear after they opened.

Edwin thought it jarring to have stumbled from the cave's abysmal darkness right into a vibrant, kinetic lobby with an elevator, piano, and a bear that could talk (and no, he *still* couldn't wrap his head around it all—at this point, there was no use even trying to understand it). Before he could say anything to Sibyl, the elevator came to a stop, and the doors slid open.

He wasn't sure what Sibyl had been expecting, but there was nothing on the other side waiting for them, nothing but another hallway, this one different from the last. The walls were no longer a pristine white, that much was clear, and they were now lined with wooden paneling, a tawny cypress, and the floor had transitioned into a smooth and darkened stone. The lighting here was far less drastic than the lighting in the lobby, and it shone through the slits in the paneling; more of a natural lighting somehow, and much more inviting.

Edwin glanced at Sibyl, hesitant to leave the elevator. He wouldn't go without her. This time, he asked: "You ready?"

She nodded briskly and took the first step into the new hallway.

The elevator stood at the end of a hall—a *long*, outstretching hall—and they set off along it, with Sibyl in the lead as always.

A sliding door was on their left, and had there not been cameras all around them (hidden, of course, because Sibyl knew better than to presume that they weren't), she would have perhaps tried to open it and see what was on the other side, purely out of curiosity (and the simple fact that the Liberian had told them to take the first door on their right and not left), but instead—knowing better than to do such a rash thing—she took the first door on the right (as the Liberian had instructed) and slid the door open with her palm.

The stone floor continued in a narrow crisscross of pathways, and an ocean of white sand dispersed along the pathways, raked in patterns of sinuous motion, like waves on a seashore or grass caught by the wind. Within the scattered islets in the sand were pruned bonsais, moss-covered rocks, and blooming sugarcanes, all various shades of green. And in the middle of the antechamber, a red and white cherry tree sat surrounded by a small wall of neatly decorated rocks, with a body of water encircling it, emitting a warm mist, almost glowing an unnatural white. As a matter of fact, everything in the room was centered on the tree.

And beside the tree, sitting on a bed of rocks by the water, was an elderly woman.

"Usually, I ask guests to take their shoes off upon entering." An amused smile crossed the older woman's face. "But knowing how little time you have, I won't ask that of you." Her dark eyes fixed on Sibyl and Edwin; slanted eyes behind a dark, wrinkled face, creased through years of being lived in. Her gray hair still had natural wisps of black in it, and though she appeared no older than her seventies, her voice made Edwin wonder if she was even older than that (*unless she's a smoker*, he thought doubtfully).

"You must be D-D," Sibyl said, approaching the old, bare-foot woman, wearing a pink sweater over a teal blouse and white leggings.

There was a slight hunch in D-D's shoulders, and her frame was delicate, but she spoke with a liveliness, expressive with every other word. "Of course," she said with another smile, looking over Sibyl. "You're so pretty—you must be Kal. Armitage told me all about you; I can never get him to shut up at times. But you would know that, wouldn't you?" Her smile increased. "If it weren't for him, you wouldn't be here." She glanced at Edwin. "And you . . ." Her smile broadened even more, and there was a glint of wickedness in it. "You're the third one just today. What's your name, sweetheart?"

Edwin glanced at Sibyl—at first hesitant to answer, unsure if his name was information he could give to a stranger so openly (and by D-D's amiable, down-to-Earth demeanor, he was left even more unsure); but by Sibyl's apathetic expression, he thought it wise not to overthink it. "Edwin," he replied. "Nice to meet you."

D-D smiled again. "Sweet boy. More handsome than the last."

"I assume you know why we're here," Sibyl told her.

D-D's eyes remained on Edwin. "Of course, I do." She stood, clapping her hands with eager determination. "There's no time to waste, is there? You people are always in such a hurry."

• • •

D-D led them into another room, this one darker and more confined, now dominated by technology. A chair sat in a corner, surrounded by monitors, a desk, another chair, and various equipment. Lights encircled the main chair, illuminating the room with an eerie ambience, reminding Edwin of a tattoo parlor mixed with an operation room.

"Is this his first augmentation?" D-D asked Sibyl, not even bothering to ask Edwin as she approached the corner with the chair.

Sibyl nodded. "As far as I know, yes."

D-D glanced at Edwin. "Sit down, please."

Edwin looked at the chair with trepidation, but only after a moment of hesitation, he sat down on it. The chair was comfier than he had expected; it reminded him of a chair he would use at the dentist (a rare pastime without medical insurance, a commodity he couldn't afford in adulthood), and he had never liked the dentist (but really, who ever did?).

D-D stood on one side of Edwin, while Sibyl stood on the other, both observing him with an inquisitive silence. He couldn't help but feel their prying eyes on him, making him feel naked. Since when had he ever been given so much attention? Being an attention hog was soon becoming a norm for him— a norm that he could never get used to, no matter the situation. As much as he loved the idea of going out on an adventure and exploring unknown places, undiscovered by his Earthly peers, perhaps he resented the attention that came along with it. Perhaps he was being ungrateful—ungrateful that he was still alive, and that he had a companion like Sibyl bringing him places he might otherwise not have been.

Of course, not a day went by where he didn't think of that—of how lucky he was to even be alive right now. When it came down to it, any problem became minuscule when viewed with another lens; and yet, however comforting that other perspective may be, it could easily be forgotten when faced with problems on all fronts.

D-D sat down on a rolling chair beside Edwin. An excitement shown in her eyes—clearly, she loved doing what she did for a living. "What's your pain threshold?" she asked him nonchalantly, as if it wouldn't scare the hell out of him (or perhaps *because* it would scare the hell out of him).

Edwin raised an eyebrow, and his heart skipped a beat. He hadn't expected any pain with the procedure but given what they were about to do—changing the very fabric of his DNA, as you would have it—well . . . he should have expected no less. "Um . . ." His mind returned to when he was a child back in Oakland and playing in the train tracks by his apartment complex, when he had accidentally tripped on a rock while spinning in circles and knocked out his two front teeth; since then, every injury had seemed minute in comparison. What was his pain threshold, truthfully? "Higher than most, I guess."

D-D laughed, as if Edwin's reaction somehow brought her amusement. "Tell me, Edwin," she started, rolling her chair to a desk and grabbing some kind of extension cord hooked up to the monitors. "Have you ever experienced what it's like when your blood boils from the inside out?"

D-D's grim question startled Edwin. *What's up with everyone's crazy questions? Is she* trying *to fuck with me?*

He fidgeted a little, recalling the burning sensation that came from his gums as he had hobbled back home after losing his two front teeth, helpless in his moment of despair. He had cried the entire walk home, whimpering every step of the way. Somewhere along his walk, a woman driving by had even noticed him, stopped her car, and took him to the hospital; she had a German Shepard in her backseat, that much he remembered, and though he had never learned her name (nor the dog's name, for that matter), to this day he still thought of them. He hoped he would never have to feel that kind of pain again. But perhaps like his desire for that woman with the German Shepard to take him home with her, that, too, was wishful thinking.

He reconsidered D-D's question. Did he know how it felt to have his blood boiled from the inside out? "No." He shook his head. "But I have a good imagination."

"Imagination fuels every society," D-D said whimsically, again rolling her chair next to Edwin as she held the extension cord with a long needle on its end. "'Culture's myths,'" she added with a smile. "Fiction we eat up to understand the world around us." Her smile died instantly. "But you know what? We can *never* understand everything—not really." She shrugged nonchalantly, swinging the needle with the extension cord. "Sometimes, when dealt with the unimaginable, our imagination plays against us."

Edwin stared at the long needle in D-D's hand. He thought of his biological mother, Vicky, whom he often associated with long needles. And he winced. "Are you going to stick me with that?"

D-D laughed briskly. "*Of course.*"

Edwin glanced at Sibyl, exchanging an uncertain look with him.

"Don't worry." D-D set the needle down, went back to the desk, and brought back another extension cord, this one hooked up with a gas mask on its end. "By the end of this, you won't remember a thing."

D-D's words brought no relief to Edwin; in fact, he felt even more anxiety than he had before entering Orion. He thought of Vicky's eyes, like the eyes of a corpse, staring back at him from on the couch across the room—one of his shoe-laces twisted around her arm, and the syringe still in her. In those days, she hadn't even tried to hide it from him anymore. If Vicky Dorset had ever felt shame for her actions (the neglect of her children, and the trauma inflicted upon them), she sure as hell never showed it. Outside her drug binders, Edwin could recall little about her. Perhaps some memories just weren't worth revisiting. Despite that, he still wondered what had become of her. Sometimes, he pictured who she was now—or at least a fictional version of her—and imagined her finding a life of recovery, away from the poison that had killed her mind. He thought of her thinking about him wherever she was and wishing that she had been there for him after Lamar's death—wishing that she had been in his life *at all*.

But once again, merely the wishful thinking of a discarded boy.

D-D leaned forward in her chair. "Tell me, Edwin: Do you know what augmentation is?"

Edwin glanced at Sibyl again, but her attention remained on D-D, and he shook his head. "No, not really."

"Those like you often don't." D-D sighed, shaking her head. "The lesser developed, the easier the target." He didn't know what she meant by that, but it got him thinking: Did she *know* he was the bounty? She must have—it was obvious, wasn't it? Why else would he be here doing what he did now? Nor could he be the only bounty. There were others like him—there *had* to be others.

Many more, perhaps.

D-D locked eyes with Edwin. She nodded to him. "If you could change one thing about yourself, what would it be?"

He shrugged. He hadn't thought much about the question prior to D-D asking it; truthfully, he cared little for the question. If he could change anything about himself, at least physically, he supposed maybe he would wish to be taller, but even then he didn't really have any issues with his height, so did it truly matter? And in terms of his facial appearance, he wouldn't change a thing. When he looked in the mirror, he often saw his brother staring back at him, and he wouldn't let anything in the world take that from him. He shook his head. "Nothing," he said. "I'd change nothing."

"Nothing?" D-D was unenthused by his answer. "Really, *nothing*?" She chuckled, shaking her head repeatedly. "If you could change one thing about yourself, you wouldn't change a thing?" She laughed again. "That's so stupid." She glanced at Sibyl, as if Sibyl would have the same reaction as she did (she didn't), before glancing back at Edwin. "You don't want to be smarter? Have better vision, coordination, or precision? Maybe overhaul your personality a bit? Make yourself funnier, have a better laugh, or alter your genetic traits deemed toxic? Or—*hell*, what's even better—regulate your hormones and make yourself a happier person overall?" She smiled again. "Never limit yourself. With a little augmentation, you can be who you want to be: There's no limit to what you can become."

Edwin's stomach grumbled, and he couldn't help but reconsider D-D's question. Were he able to alter any part of himself, perhaps he would start with the hunger building inside of him at that very moment. How long had it been since he'd eaten anything? The last thing he could remember eating was a quick snack—more ungu, in fact—while sitting in the freighter's cockpit with Sibyl on their way to Orion (but how many hours ago had that been?). The trek here had certainly built up his appetite; there's nothing like a savory, fresh meal to await one after a long excursion. Edwin found his mind drifting to food, and he thought of how lucky it must be for Jermaine to never have to worry about missing a meal. There was nothing like hunger; it could turn the best of us into the worst, and even then, that hunger could never be fully satiated.

Edwin shook his head again. *There's never enough*, he thought. *You change one thing about yourself, and you'll find something else to fix in its place. Perhaps that's the problem most people have: their need for more, never truly satisfied with what they already have. Take away the dissatisfaction, and what more is there to gain from life? Maybe we already have all that we need.*

"All the same," D-D mused, noting Edwin's silence. "I was much more interested in the answer than the question, anyway. Answers can be whatever you want them to be—good, bad, it's all just fiction we create in our minds."

More talk of fiction, Edwin remarked. *What I would give to peruse a comic book again.*

D-D observed Edwin with a critical eye. "You don't talk much, do you?" She glanced at Sibyl again, giving her another one of her playful looks. "My dear, what a good time you two must have had coming here." She laughed heartily and turned to Edwin once more. "Are you sure you don't want me to change your personality just a *little*?"

Something about D-D was beginning to remind Edwin of Jack Claremont. At first, Edwin couldn't pinpoint why, but after D-D's blunt, offhanded remark about him, it became abundantly clear. As Jack Claremont himself would have stated: "That's one shady bitch." But, of course, Edwin took no offense to D-D's comments. He took her words as a playful poke at him and nothing more. As it so happened, he'd had his fair share of time with sassy, deprecating remarks (he had lived in San Francisco, for Xibalba's sake, and he was bound to have thick skin); life is much easier when you don't take everything so personally.

"We can't all be perfect, can we?" Edwin retorted with a smile. "Besides, you'd be without a job were that the case."

D-D returned his smile. "True enough."

Sibyl crossed her arms and leaned forward, engaged in all but the conversation. "How long will this take?" she asked, attempting to get back on topic. "We haven't all day."

This time, D-D exchanged her playful look with Edwin rather than Sibyl. "As I said," D-D reiterated: "Always in such a hurry." She regarded Sibyl closely. "First, we must talk cost. Not everything in life is free, and though you may be a family friend—the closest thing to a family friend, at least in this vocation—you should know this operation doesn't come cheap."

Sibyl nodded. "What's the price?"

"That's the question, isn't it?" D-D crossed her legs, setting both hands on one knee. "The price we pay for what we truly desire." She looked Sibyl over, her expression analytical, if not cynical. "And what is it you desire, dear? What do you have to gain out of all this?"

Sibyl glanced at Edwin, hesitated, and faced D-D. She shrugged. "What's it to you?"

D-D's smile returned. "Why, life and death, sweetheart."

Sibyl returned the smile, though there was a darkness in it hiding beneath the surface. "Let's just say, talents aren't my concern."

D-D nodded, her expression indiscernible. "Of course not. Or you wouldn't be here, would you?" She turned to Edwin again. "My dear, have you eaten anything?"

She read my mind, Edwin thought—all too aware of his growling, empty stomach. He shook his head. "No."

"Good." With that, D-D sprang forward with a hand on the gas mask and her eyes set on Edwin's with an unparalleled intensity. "Whatever you do, don't resist."

|13|

LIBERATION BEGINS

The day that Edwin Dorset broke up with Maggie Summers was perhaps one of the best days of his life. Often, he thought about that euphoric sensation he felt after leaving her dormitory on that fateful Monday afternoon. The unfiltered relief and elation, knowing he would never have to hear that nagging voice again, nor ever be blamed for her combative and constantly berating attitude. Like a painful splinter or agonizing toothache, unbearable and felt at all times, that when taken out—*thanks be to all the gods, real or not*—reminded you just how good it was to feel alive again.

Maggie Summers had been extremely temperamental and, depending on her mood, could be a different person altogether. Most days she was cranky, short-tempered, and condescending. Constantly insecure, she never failed to project that insecurity onto others. In the year and a half that Edwin had been with her, Maggie had made him feel like nothing he had to say mattered; most days he spent with her, she made him feel guilty for even talking (shameful, even, as if *he* was the one being selfish). I mean, what kind of person makes you feel you need to rush to get out what you have to say or else they will just talk over you? And if she happened not to talk over him, it was more than likely she was distracted by her phone.

She would talk and talk and talk, but she would never listen, rarely curious about what others had to say, let alone their mental state of being. The only times that she seemed to care about what others had to say was because she could later gossip about it to others. She liked to gossip, actually—about strangers online she had never met, the barista who was being a "total cunt" to her (and to her alone, apparently, because *of course* everyone was out to get her), and trivial matters where problems that hadn't been there suddenly arrived out of nowhere.

A word to the wise: There will always be a problem for one who is problematic.

Life was a continuous competition for Maggie Summers, and with every accomplishment that Edwin had, she tried to one-up him, never forgetting to mention it at least once in conversation (of how efficient *she* was, and how others—"not saying any names," she'd say—just couldn't do it as good). For instance, when he had told her he had been orphaned at a young age, she had merely replied (blankly): "yeah, well my dad was a drunk, so you had it better; besides, that doesn't count: it's not like your mom's dead."

As you probably know by now, there's nothing more infuriating than having your feelings invalidated. Especially from the one you love, whether or not that love is justified.

Maggie called every other female a "bitch"; once again, she never ceased to project herself onto others. Her whole life revolved around her, and if she didn't get what she wanted, good luck hearing the last of it. Also, because of that inflated ego of hers, she made a nasty habit of gaslighting others. Nothing justifies gaslighting; it's like the gaslighter intentionally tries to confuse you, but when you really analyze their words and actions, you see that they're merely projecting everything they feel and do onto you, and that they're only confusing themself; in fact, the reality of it is that the projector puts everything they feel onto you so that they don't have to feel it themselves—that being, the guilt of their own actions. If you tell them one thing, more often than not, they'll hear something else entirely. Sometimes, it's really hard to turn the other cheek in those situations without getting taken advantage of or lashing back, because if you even try to push back against the lies—or slip up in any way whatsoever—your words and actions will be used against you, "justifying" the proceeding actions, as if their abuse was all because of your lashing back or "defensiveness," as if it was *your* fault and you're the sole person to blame.

There are some people in this world who you just can't reason with, no matter how patient you are with them; why Edwin had tolerated dating one of them for so long, he would never know—for not seeing through Maggie Summer's lies from the get-go, he could only blame himself.

(Not that it mattered anymore.)

Still, we learn from our mistakes, don't we? Maybe not with every mistake, and maybe not every right lesson learned, but we learn all the same.

Only a few moments in his life could Edwin recall feeling as liberated as he did that beautiful, historic day he told the irritable, antagonistic Maggie Summers that he was done for good. She had been the living embodiment of an unconstructive critic telling him he wasn't "good enough," and though it may not have been entirely gentleman-like, he didn't regret for a second telling her to "go fuck herself."

So, then, why is it that Edwin had hurt so much after everything was said and done? He *knew* how toxic she could be, and how she justified her mistreatment of him. But even after they broke up, no matter how much pain or shame she had inflicted on him, he still missed her. It didn't make sense. It *couldn't* make sense—at least, not at the time, and not without a clearer perspective, unfettered by emotions.

And let's be real, Maggie Summers had been a completely different person at the start of her relationship with Edwin Dorset. She used to love-bomb the shit out of him, actually, and give him constant affection, making him feel like he was the only person on the planet (a feeling he had never known before, and certainly not with the upbringing he had—jumping from one foster home to another, never good enough to keep around). She had also been his first girlfriend, so how could he really compare her to others? He hadn't even told her she had taken his virginity (not that it even mattered to him, anyway). Perhaps in those first few weeks of their relationship, Maggie had idealized Edwin and put him on a pedestal, viewing him as something he wasn't—perhaps he, too, was guilty of the same thing; whatever the case, she had dug her claws deep into him, and by the time she devalued him, it was too late to back out.

That was, at least, until something in him just *snapped*.

• • •

His blood felt as if it was boiling from the inside-out; he knew at once—with a surety he couldn't deny—that he had perhaps made the gravest mistake in his life.

Panic swept through him.

What am I doing?

I need to get out of here.

I need to escape.

There has *to be an escape.*

But lo-and-behold, there was no escape—not from the mind anyway, the only place we (whatever makes us "us") truly reside. There was nowhere left to go. Nowhere left to run. It was too late for that. The initiation had already begun, and the only way out was in—deeper into the rabbit hole, further into his psyche, where the abstract reigned supreme.

There's no turning back, he knew. *I can't escape this.*

Even knowing this, dread besieged him. It was hard to breathe. Hard not to panic or fight against the process. Even if he tried to resist, it wouldn't matter; the process couldn't be averted. "*You have to surrender to it,*" he heard someone tell him faintly. A feminine voice, sounding as if from another room. "*You—*"

• • •

"—just want to be loved, don't you?" Amelia Gladden teased with a half-turned smile. She paused, looked down at the pencil in her hand, and glanced back up at Edwin. She spoke again, her voice lower this time, more serious than before. "That's all you've ever wanted, isn't it?"

Edwin hesitated, and his dark eyes fixed on Amelia's hazel-green.

"Maggie," Amelia elaborated, seeing that he looked lost. She shrugged nonchalantly. (Something about that shrug reminded Edwin of Sibyl, though he couldn't pinpoint why.) "That's the only reason I could ever see you being with her for that long—because you've never been loved before." The hint of another smile played at the corner of her lips. "Classic Edwin: Looking for love from others when all you ever needed is to love yourself."

Edwin set his pen onto the open page of his notebook and noticed a small portrait of Maggie Summers drawn on the page's top corner amidst his Post-Modern and Contemporary Art lecture notes. Suddenly, feeling self-conscious about it— Amelia having undoubtedly seen Maggie's sketch right out in the open—he closed the notebook, regretting that he had ever drawn that godawful face, and eyed Amelia closely, sitting on his lefthand side, with her leg nestled against his leg.

Amelia held a pencil with her left hand, and with her right hand tapped the desk playfully, using only her ring and middle fingers. Her blond, wavy hair was styled in a messy updo bun, and a jade necklace hung down her bare neck and shoulders, above a black long-sleeved blouse and flayed floral miniskirt. Something about being here with her now—in the downtown San Francisco campus library—felt familiar to Edwin, as if he had experienced this moment before (which, by all rights and purposes, he most likely *had* experienced before). Though something about it also felt alien, and he couldn't quite put his finger on it. As if he was experiencing it again but for the first time, despite his memories of the day (memories that now felt hazy, disjointed from a novel experience).

Amelia leaned in closer, her eyes still on Edwin's. "Nothing is ever simple, is it?"

Edwin tried to reply, but something caught in his throat. He could only move his mouth wordlessly.

"Stop overthinking things," Amelia teased, setting a hand on his lap. "It's okay, Ed. Just let it out. Don't worry about what I have to think. Speak your mind or forever hold your peace."

But Edwin *couldn't* speak his mind. He tried to speak and kept trying, but no sound would come out of him.

Amelia laughed. "Stop trying so hard."

She leaned forward and whispered into his ear: "You will never be understood." Her hand inched closer to his crotch, stopped, and there was a coy look in her eyes as she looked back at him. That coy look in her eyes, however, had quickly transformed into something more teasing. "Only you can truly satisfy yourself." A dark smile crossed her lips. "But only you, and no one else." She chuckled. "And if you think otherwise, you're living in a dreamworld."

Edwin hadn't remembered Amelia saying any of this to him (and just why would he?). There was something . . . well, something incredibly *off* about how she was speaking to him now. Something off about it *all*, really. So casual, and yet so distant, as if it weren't Amelia with him right then and there, but someone else. It was unsettling, and he felt sick again. Trying to ignore the queasiness, he instead focused on what Amelia—or whomever spoke through Amelia (perhaps his own subconscious rendering of her)—had to say next.

"Can't you *see*, Ed? You're no different from anyone else." Amelia stood up, eyeing Edwin beneath her—still sitting in his chair—with a serious look. *Contempt*, perhaps? He couldn't tell. "You want validation from others, but you're too afraid to look within, not without." She brought her pencil to his chest and tapped its end over his heart twice. "But only you are in charge of your emotions, as is everyone else with theirs. It's not your place to satisfy another, nor is it their place to satisfy you. If you can't find happiness on your own, that's your problem, not theirs, and the same could be said for them, whomever 'they' are. Be the best you can be, and if that's not enough, go somewhere else—the universe has an infinite amount of possibilities, and there's always something out there waiting for you. Always something to do."

Why is she telling me all of this? Why am I hearing it now?

Edwin shook his head. *You're not really here*, he reminded himself. *None of this is real.*

But boy, did it *feel* real. As if he was really there, back in San Francisco, with his old pal and once-upon-a-time fling—three or four years ago, give or take. But his memories of the present remained. Memories post-San Francisco. Being abducted, on the run, and having a philosophical dialogue with another life form (the ever-persistent, emotionally clingy "robot butler," who had kept him company while Sibyl was gone). His present memories admonished whatever was happening here now as moot. He wasn't back in San Francisco, nor had he seen Amelia Gladden in years—their fire had snuffed out as quickly as it started (passion can only go so far when it's the only glue that holds two together).

Since when did it get so cold?

Edwin trembled with arms crossed as he noticed his breath now billowing out ever so slowly. The steam increased, growing larger and larger. Eventually, the steam filled the entire room, eliminating visibility altogether.

And Edwin could no longer see himself.

It was strange, really, that he could even see himself. Very peculiar. . . . But hey, he was invested in the moment, so taken by it that any inconsistency he may have overlooked passed by without a second glance. That *is* what's most important, isn't it? The moment. And he had to find out what would happen next. So much so, in fact, that he had already forgotten that he was—

• • •

—dying. Just a seventeen-year-old boy, bleeding out in the back of an ambulance. Three bullet holes, and blood seeping out of his chest. Such senseless violence. Such a meaningless loss of a life that could have been.

Sometimes, Edwin wondered what Lamar must have been thinking the moment before his end. Lamar Davis had never been one to back down from a fight; but then again, hadn't that been what had killed him? He didn't *have* to get the stolen backpack. He didn't *have* to confront those kids. But he was a protector, a defender to the helpless, and he had seen it as his task to get back his little brother's backpack. The heroes he had read about had saved the day countless of times, so why not him?

After all, he was a hero.

And he died a hero, too.

It's my fault, Edwin thought, not for the first time. *If I hadn't cried to him that day, he would still be alive.* But an image flickered in his mind, ever so faintly—of Vicky Dorset sitting on a dilapidated couch, and her lobotomized eyes staring back at him—and he knew, all at once, that it was never so simple. He couldn't blame the actions of an eight-year-old, just as much as he couldn't blame the actions of a seventeen-year-old; external causes are always at work to push things to happen as they do.

Even thinking about the kids who had killed Lamar (all three of them—later arrested, and at least brought to *some* form of justice as Lamar had intended), Edwin couldn't help but think that they, too, were probably victims of the external. That whatever had been going on in their home lives would have somehow influenced why they did what they did, and their home lives had to have been even worse than his; perhaps it was as simple as never having a brother like Lamar to show them what kindness was. Somehow, despite the life they had taken from the world, Edwin felt pity for them.

And he thought of his actions that night.

Nothing is ever simple.

When the police arrived at Vicky Dorset's doorstep on the night of June, the Thirteenth—to tell her that her eldest son had been shot in an altercation and had bled out before making it to the hospital—one would have presumed that the policemen would have taken a good look at the place, seen the heroin needles lying all over the counters—as well as on the coffee table (with the eight-year-old boy standing next to it, listening in on their conversation)—before deciding that they should call in child custody and have the youngest son removed at once, for his safety and concern.

But nothing of that sort happened.

Yes, Vicky had answered the door. And yes, an eight-year-old Edwin had been eavesdropping, listening as the policemen reluctantly told his mother that her eldest son was now dead. But Vicky didn't cry, she didn't scream. She didn't even fall to her knees or show any sign of remorse. She had just stood there, nodding and mumbling "mmhmm," again and again, as if she wasn't really listening to what they had to say—as if their words weren't even registering in her mind. Waiting for them to leave, so that she could get back to the needle. That's all she ever wanted anymore: an escape. To be free of the world, and what better way than by getting the fuck out of it? She had left the world long ago the moment she stopped caring for it. She was a ghost—a walking apparition going through the motions.

Whatever had happened to her? What kind of woman had she once been?

Edwin remembered sauntering into his room once the policemen had left, falling onto his mattress, and crying into his pillow. Right before hearing the torch in the living room light up. Followed by Vicky's coughing, worse after every use. Her ecstatic laughs, crackling between coughs. Lost in another world, another reality—a world without Lamar, and one where Edwin didn't exist. An anger rose in him, and he wanted vengeance, wanted justice. Wanted something other than *this*.

Where was the justice? Where was the retribution?

Nothing is ever simple, Edwin thought again as he stood in front of the fire that he had created of his own accord. Its flames danced across his face, warm and vibrant, alive and blazing. Vicky Dorset lay on the couch behind him, passed out with a needle in her arm. And she, too, was taken by the fire.

The fire took all until there was nothing left—nothing but ashes, falling slowly, gently easing toward the ground.

Now, Edwin stood in Sibyl's garden with his hands in the pockets of Lamar's black and yellow letterman, that he currently wore. Vicky Dorset was nowhere in sight, nor any sign of the fire's aftermath. Instead, Edwin watched as Sibylla Kal ambled toward him, emerging from the tropical section of the garden. She wore her navy-blue jacket with a maroon collar and linings. Her dark, wild hair hung down her back and shoulders, and her equally dark almond eyes—so dark that they were almost black—were fixed on his. She had a slender nose and delectable, amorous lips that were upturned in a cornerwise grin. Her cheekbones narrowed as they followed the lines of her face down to her jawline, which led to a cleft chin. Her skin was luminous, a pristine olive tint, and there was an exotic air about her, bewitching and seductive. She stopped in front of Edwin beneath an arching white maple entwined with flowering vines of deep orange, gold, and burgundy, like the tail-end of a desert sunset.

Edwin smiled at Sibyl, and she smiled back.

She glanced up at the white maple. "You know something we take for granted about being an organism?" She turned to him again, the smile still in her eyes. "Being mobile. Not having to rely on an outside influence to go wherever we desire. I suppose that's also a privilege we get with the time we were born in." She looked at her hand. "Along with the vessel we inhabit. . . . Few ever have a privilege as good as ours."

Edwin finally found his voice. "I don't think it will ever get better than this."

Sibyl regarded Edwin. "Never limit yourself," she told him. "Look at where you came from and where you are now. Never discount what you've accomplished and what you've done to get here."

Edwin eyed Sibyl closely. He thought of Lamar, who hadn't been given such a chance. "I don't want to waste it—this life that I was given. I don't want to waste another second, wishing I had something better."

Sibyl contemplated this deeply. "Then don't." She leaned closer now, eyeing Edwin with an almost analytic coldness. "Why, are you worried that you're just like your mother? That you're just looking for an escape?" Suddenly, her expression turned hostile—uncharacteristic. "Maybe that's all you've ever wanted: an escape."

Is that what I've been doing? Edwin thought of his anger at Vicky and her unwillingness to confront Lamar's death or even acknowledge her youngest son, who was still alive. And the rage he had felt when he found her lying unconscious on the couch. Only an eight-year-old, and he wanted to kill her. He wanted to kill that fucking bitch. Light her up like no tomorrow.

No, he thought, shaking his head. *No, no, no—that was never my intention.*

Sibyl locked eyes with Edwin. "You shouldn't feel shame for what's out of your control; what happened happened."

But he didn't believe that. Not for a second. His eyes drifted downward, and his vision was lost to his dissociation. He could have done better. *Should* have done better. If only he hadn't complained to Lamar that day. . . .

"Why did you start the fire?"

Edwin glanced up and saw Benjamin Kemp sitting on a rocking chair on the front porch of his house. Mr. Kemp had a serious look in his blue eyes, searching Edwin's with biting distaste. The older man spoke again, more demanding this time: "Why did you start the fire?"

Because I was angry, Edwin thought. *Because I wanted Vicky to wake up. To shake her out of her apathy and get her to see me. . . . I . . . I wanted her to* see *me. That's all I had ever wanted—to be seen, truly* seen.

Mr Kemp's expression softened. "Why did you want to feel seen?"

Edwin didn't want to fool himself. Not anymore. *Because I'm a narcissist*, he admitted, perhaps unjustly. *Vicky was a narcissist, so—of course—that makes me one. I don't think of anyone but myself. . . . The fire, it was just a cry for attention, for someone to come and save the day.*

But no one's coming to save me.

He looked down. *No one's here but me.*

Mr. Kemp laughed. There was something eerie about that laugh. Something uncanny. "You don't really believe that, do you?" He stood up from his chair and Edwin realized how much larger he was than he had originally assumed—at least three times the size of how he first appeared. His face was no longer the same, for that matter. His shadow loomed over Edwin—a ghastly darkness enveloping him.

The sun hid itself, and a colossal eye peered down from above, blocking out most of the sky, now gathering into a storm. The hideous form of what used to be Mr. Kemp laughed again, though this time blood gurgled in his mouth, oozing out of him. His voice was deep and grotesque and nothing like the real-life Benjamin Kemp. "You're *never* alone, child. Can't you see—? All eyes are on you."

Edwin took a step back, and then another step. He turned and ran as fast as his body could allow. He followed the wooden fences running alongside the identical apartments, through a familiar, narrow alleyway—the neighborhood in Oakland where Vicky Dorset had once lived. And his legs were much smaller now, as well as his arms.

He was eight again.

Running, running, running.

Not looking back. Not seeing the destruction of the fire that he had caused. He willed himself to be strong, to keep going, and to never turn back. But his mind kept drifting to his biological mother, Vicky, passed out on the couch. He couldn't just leave her like that. Couldn't go on with a good conscience—it wasn't right. He had to go back to save her, because . . . well, because it was the right thing to do; it's what a hero would do.

It's what Lamar would have done.

He stopped at the end of the alleyway, leading to the train tracks. He turned back, worried to see what had been following him, but instead found a wall of graffiti where the alleyway had once been. And amidst the graffiti, four indiscernible words (or five, depending on if you're a stickler) stuck out to him: *You're Not Good Enough.*

Lies, Edwin knew, looking at those godawful words. *Lies, every one of them.*

("Make the world a better place, Little Brother.")

Edwin turned around and saw Lamar standing before him. Except only, this wasn't the Lamar who had died that fateful night in June. No, this was a different Lamar. He was older, *far* older than he had been the day he died. At best, he appeared in his early thirties, the age he would have been were he still alive. His face was freshly shaven, and his eyes were bright with joy, with an abundant smile on his lips. "There's no need to be afraid, Little Brother."

Edwin stepped closer. A train approached from a distance behind Lamar—its lights so blinding that Edwin had to cover his eyes—but he stepped forward, anyway. "Are you really here?"

Lamar's laugh was more than welcoming, juxtaposed by the oncoming train, warning of imminent doom. "Are any of us *truly* here?"

"I'm sorry," Edwin began, struggling with his words. Tears ran down his cheeks. "I never should have told you about the backpack."

"There's no need to dwell on what could have been." No resentment resounded from Lamar, nor was there any bitterness in his eyes—only love. "No matter where you go, I'll always be with you." He tapped on his temple. "In the mind, where stories roam and dreams fester, funneling from the internal to the external—from one world to another." He winked playfully, his smile never ceasing. "We're living mythology, Little Brother. Reality always has a way of exceeding our expectations; it's seldom we see the beauty of what's been there all along, staring right back at us."

"It should have been me that day," Edwin told him. "You had a life ahead of you: a purpose greater than mine. I squandered the life you would have thrived in."

Lamar shook his head curtly. "No, Little Brother." He laughed again. "You're not listening." The train closed in on them, and its headlights warned of imminent impact. "Close your eyes." Lamar's voice was barely audible over the screeching of metal. "Close your eyes and listen."

Edwin shut his eyes.

The sound of the train intensified, and the ground shook beneath his feet violently. The headlights' brightness increased, and though his eyes were shut tight, he was again blinded from the light seeping through his eyelids, as he suddenly—

• • •

—felt the sun's heat on his face once more.

He was back on Zarathustra. Why he thought that, he couldn't say, but he could feel the change from the scenery all the same—the change within him, that evolution of what once was to what is.

(No, perhaps he wasn't really on Zarathustra.)

The change he had undergone in Zarathustra was an internal change, after all, and not an external one—or, at least, not *only* an external change, despite many external factors contributed. When he was affected by the psychoactive spores wafting their way through the airstream—emitted from one of the native, flowering succulents in the riparian zone—that change within him had taken its effect. But, really, perhaps that change had started in him much earlier. It's always easy to overlook progression; history has forgotten far more than it cared to remember.

So how could he look back? And just *why* should he look back?

He knew better now than to put himself in any box of his own creation. To limit himself according to whatever standards he deemed necessary at whatever given moment. By comparing himself to others. Or comparing himself to the *projection* that others create of themselves, facades masquerading as reality. Harboring needless guilt for not doing enough. Not being enough. Shame for all the wasted potential in his life. He wanted none of that. No more wishing for something else. No more wishing for something "better." He had wasted enough time already—the only time left was the present, the here and now.

He knew all of this. (Of course, he did.)

But did he *understand* it? (Did he comprehend it?)

Or, most importantly, did he *believe* it. . . . ?

There's a big difference between knowing something and understanding it—of awareness versus comprehension. Sometimes, the same lessons repeat themselves again and again until we finally understand their true purpose (why they're there to teach us what they do).

There's a lesson to take from everything.

Have I learned the wrong lesson?

No, perhaps it wasn't that simple.

Whatever the case, a lesson is nothing without its application.

|14|

OPTIMISTIC NIHILIST

Throughout the process, Sibyl had kept Edwin company. She sat beside him, and now and then set a reassuring hand on his, giving him comforting words as she watched over him. Guarding him as she would her own blood. Of course, D-D kept reminding Sibyl that Edwin wasn't even conscious enough to retain any information. "Don't bother, honey," D-D said, waving her hand as if waving away a fly. "He won't remember a thing you say."

Still, for Sibyl, it was the thought that mattered the most.

Hell, maybe she needed the reassurance more than Edwin. For the most part, Edwin had been in a delirium—constantly sweating, his skin hot to the touch—and muttering incessantly, as if in a drunken stupor.

Am I doing the right thing?

The guilt came back, this time stronger than before. Even so, Sibyl knew that if it wasn't for her, Edwin wouldn't have even been alive right now. She had no reason to feel guilty. She had saved him on Zarathustra. But of course that also made him her responsibility now, didn't it? He was . . . well, he was *more* than just a bounty now, wasn't he? He was much more than that. Much more than anything she had originally given him credit for.

I suppose we all are when it comes down to it.

It was only by chance that she had found him that day on Zarathustra. She hadn't known that the reaping would start on Zarathustra (the location was rather sporadic, most times), nor did she think she would be involved in any way.

When she was a child, Sibylla had little to no ambitions. With the circumstances that surrounded her birth, she hadn't really been afforded such a commodity as "ambition." By all likelihood, she should have been dead by now; the odds of her survival had stacked against her since the moment that she took her first breath, and it was a miracle that she had somehow outlived those odds.

A victim of chance, time and time again, but also a survivor because of it.

Born in captivity—bred to be livestock—Sibylla Kal had never known freedom until she was six, when the last of her species were liberated from their conquerors. Why she was still alive, she could never know (pure luck, as you'd have it). Few born in her situation had ever lived to see past the age of ten (she was to be a nourishment, after all, and a cuisine like her was best served young—too much development, and they lose all the flavor, that chewy texture that sets them apart from all the others).

Even around the age of six, Sibyl had only seen her species' rescue as a byproduct of chance. Nothing more, nothing less. For Sibyl, all existence was a byproduct of chance: Unforeseeable, chance was the only thing separating life from death (being *here* versus being *there*, wherever "there" was). Had her liberators come a hundred years later, her life would have been a different story. She would have ended up like all the others before her—nameless faces, forgotten in history. Luckily, her liberators had come when they had, if for no other reason than more mining resources; a bit disheartening, that only because of Te Kore's resources was she even alive right now.

Chance, fate, and destiny: all one and the same.

Sibyl didn't know her purpose in life, nor did she think there was one. She lived her life regardless of that fact, knowing that many others hadn't been given such a privilege. Life itself was a privilege that most squandered. Why go searching for the reason that she was still alive and others weren't? She already knew the reason, and few reasons were ever satisfying enough. No one can be satisfied, not truly.

To live is to suffer, to embrace life with all that it has to offer.

Growing up in a refugee camp, Sibyl had often heard stories of Zarathustra, her species' home planet—before their exile across the deep sea of space. Her species' breeding ground had been placed on Te Kore (where she was bred), a moon far from Zarathustra, orbiting around Te Apa, a habitable zone along the Inner Third Ring of Samsara. Back when the Confederation reigned supreme, other breeding grounds had been seeded throughout Samsara, but, out of all those breeding grounds, Te Kore had been the only factory where people like her had made it out alive.

She had always dreamt of going to Zarathustra as a child, having once idealized the notion, thinking about how life *would* have been had her people not been conquered. Had they stayed in peace, able to live off the land in solitude and symbiosis with the environment. But with age came knowledge, and when Sibyl had the means to discover the truth, she was dismayed to learn that not even Zarathustra had been her species' original, native planet. Her people had evolved elsewhere—they, too, had once been the colonizers of another planet and its surroundings eons ago, having wiped out an entire species and ecosystem seen as lesser than them (almost in the same manner that they, too, would be wiped out later in time: left only as a scattered species with no home or identity). Except unlike Sibyl (and the few remaining survivors of her people), the original inhabitants of Zarathustra were now extinct, left as nothing more than fossils of a time before, a time forgotten.

However crushing of her idealization, Sibyl had somehow retained the desire to go there: to Zarathustra—if not only to reflect on her own survival (let alone, her existence), then to also reflect on the wrongdoings of her people and what *could* have been (the lost ecosystem, and the many life forms that would have been thriving, adapting throughout the years) had her people not practically annihilated an entire planet. If there was ever a reason to go to Zarathustra, it was to mourn, to grieve for the loss of what was and what could have been.

An easy way to cope with grief, of course (at least for Sibyl), was by partaking in heavy psychedelics—a journey of the mind and cleansing of all ego—at least when done right. Along with Sibyl's love of botany was a deep love for mycology, and particularly fungi exhibiting traits of psilocybin. Having experimented with all kinds of fungi throughout the years, from many different habitats, and comparing them all, the psychedelic mycelium growing on the succulents in Zarathustra had to rank in the highest for her . . . and she had even tried them long before stepping foot on Zarathustra. With her kind of lifestyle, it was easy to trade with others, giving and receiving supplies that might otherwise have been exotic elsewhere; there's always a need for specific resources wherever you go, and if you're smart enough, you'll find that the trash in one place can be a sought after treasure elsewhere.

But Sibyl had a tradition as of late, of foraging wild mushrooms from different planets and getting high off her ass from them. She usually scheduled these sessions every other month, spacing them out so that she wouldn't be tempted to keep doing it (addiction could be found anywhere, from anything, and Sibyl hated having to rely on anything). Somehow, psychedelics kept her grounded. Plus, she liked to expand her mind, always taking these moments for an opportunity of growth.

Or, at least, that's what she wanted to believe.

Sometimes, she also used psychedelics as a means of escape.

But how could you blame her? Look at where she came from to where she was presently. Were it not for the psychedelics, she would have ended her life long ago.

Traveling alone throughout Samsara's star system (accompanied by Jermaine, of course—a custodian of the Vagabond, always tagging along), Sibyl explored new habitats that she hadn't been to before and constantly searched for uninhabited regions with psycho-inducing vegetation, fungi, or gases. Sometimes, her escapades took a lot of research beforehand, but eventually, she consistently found them worth the effort, bringing with it the discovery of something new. Constant travel was a much better way of living, in Sibyl's opinion, and being able to forage on her own—both food and resources—

rather than having to buy them from any unreliable source, made it that much easier and enticing. Besides, she enjoyed being alone. Preferred it, actually.

When you're alone, you're never expected to be anyone other than yourself.

Before the day Sibyl saved Edwin, she had never been to Zarathustra; in fact, Zarathustra was the closest planet to her that day, and it was one of the few that she had saved for such a special occasion (a special occasion made every other month). And being in such an isolated system, at the edge of the Outer Rings, she could think of nowhere else to go, content with whatever came out of it. Because of the unusual habitat of Zarathustra, a rare psychoactive fungi grew along certain riparian areas, germinating on succulents. Sibyl had scoured one of the planet's many deserts, looking for that rare fungi, and had stumbled upon the right place at the right time—or, depending on your point-of-view, the wrong place at the wrong time. The area she had chosen had once been considered sacred by its native people long ago, due to its psychoactive spores reproduced through airborne means; its desert was enthralling, secluded, and everything that she could have ever asked for.

But she wasn't alone.

When the first ship had shown its face in the sky, more ships immediately revealed themselves, until all the ships practically covered the sun. Seeing this, but not knowing its purpose—not yet, anyway—Sibyl remained hidden and waited for a safe time to get off planet (already under the effects of the psilocybin, her perception of reality had been altered, and a part of her even questioned if it was all real at first).

First were the drumrolls. Next came the tear in the sky, and then all hell was let loose.

Within the first two minutes, most of the orbiting ships had been destroyed.

Destruction was everywhere—clouds of fire brimmed where only hours ago there had been a clear blue sky.

From high on a ridge, Sibyl first noticed Edwin. She saw him alone, wandering down the canyon with his hands tied behind his back and a big goofy smile on his face. Upon seeing his face, she had recognized it immediately (bounties such as his were one in a billion). A part of her felt excited about the prospect of cashing him in, if only just for a moment, and yet there was something about that feeling which irked her, bringing to mind all the atrocities of Te Kore.

Was she capable of such a thing?

Had she been raking in debt, perhaps her view of the bounty would have been different. But she could only see the injustice within it, and she had no desire for riches. She had been born with nothing, and she would die with nothing: the illusion of possessions had never caught up to her, nor had she ever lost her compassion throughout the years.

Despite all of that, she followed Edwin at a distance, at an impasse for what she should do. She had once made it a rule not to get involved in the affairs of others. She had told herself that she wouldn't get involved, and that he wasn't her responsibility. But he looked so innocent to her, so *naïve*. And the group of mercenaries tracking him were drawing closer every step of the way. Even so, her feet kept her moving.

Somehow, she knew better. She knew herself well. She couldn't stand back and watch an injustice happen before her eyes, and particularly an injustice that she could so easily prevent. Once the mercenaries had surrounded Edwin, Sibyl saw no other choice than to intervene. He had noticed her, too, and even looked her in the eyes, and she wouldn't have been able to live with herself had she let them take him. Seeing him, then and there, on a spiritual quest of enlightenment—factoring in that she, too, was also high off her ass, feeling more aligned in herself than ever—well . . . she saw an opportunity to do something good, and she just couldn't pass it up.

One good deed a day.

Now, there was a rule that she could follow.

And so, she saved him.

For the first time in over five years, she took another life— followed by many other lives, one after the other. More bodies added to the list, and for what . . . ? But there was no backing out of her choice: the initial trigger had been pulled, and Edwin Dorset's fate no longer rest to chance.

He was *her* responsibility now, whether or not she liked it.

But now, remorse weighed heavily on her heart.

You know in your heart of hearts that saving him wasn't an altruistic act alone, her conscious told her, refusing to shy away from the truth. *If you had nothing to gain from it, he wouldn't still be with you now.*

But was that true? Was she really that cold?

No, perhaps there was more to it.

Sure, she had saved him. But that didn't mean that she had never seen his value as the bounty, that insurmountable decree by the fifth-beings and the entire universe set after him. He was leverage to her; why else would she coerce him into following her every whim without question? Using her sexuality against him, without him even being aware of it. Perhaps Jermaine disapproved. He must have known her true purpose all along. And if he knew, then why hadn't he interfered? He had never been her slave, nor anything close to one. It was against his programming to harm another, was it not?

Why did he not interfere?

Perhaps something within Sibyl *wanted* Jermaine to stop her.

Perhaps, even, Jermaine had considered that she would have a change of heart.

Or, perhaps, on the flip-side, he *knew* all along that she was doing the right thing. . . .

The fifth-beings, after all, were gods by most peoples' standards. Oh, to think of the *power* that they must possess—the technology, far beyond any human comprehension. With that kind of power, Sibyl could be unstoppable. She could prevent atrocities all over Samsara. Lessen human suffering—let alone all species' suffering. Topple corrupt empires. Preserve declining ecosystems . . .

And stop the bounties from ever taking place again.

I could send Edwin back to where he came from, Sibyl reasoned. *To the point in time where he left off, in a reality where he was never abducted.* She thought of his many drawings: of the young, handsome face much like his own—a younger brother, perhaps. *He could see his family again. Furthermore, with the technology from the fifth dimension, I could make* any *of his dreams a reality.*

But she wasn't fooling herself.

She knew the risk. If Edwin were to be used as bait against the fifth-beings, as she so intended, there could be a very slim chance of him actually coming out of it alive. Not only would she be gambling for her own life but also for his. It was a crazy thing, the idea of infiltrating the fifth dimension. An even crazier thing, to think that there wouldn't be repercussions.

There are always *repercussions.*

Sibyl continued to ignore the unwanted guilt festering inside her. A recurring feeling as of late, though it was now getting harder to ignore. She glanced down at Edwin, asleep beside her and no longer in a delirium.

So calm now. So peaceful.

If he dies, Sibyl reasoned, *I can bring him back again. From another reality, another when. Just like ours, but one where he's still alive. Because that's how fifth-dimensional technology works, isn't it . . . ? Harnessing time and space, and no longer bound by it. If existence is infinite, whatever* can *happen* will *happen. And if I'm no longer bound by time and space— no longer bound by one moment—who knows what else I'll discover. Who knows what else lies beyond the third dimension.*

The future is limitless.

The guilt had all but left her.

|15|

REBORN

He was in and out of consciousness.

Slipping back and forth between reality and fantasy.

Colors flickered in and out of existence. Like painting on a blank canvas, one hue after another, until at last there was a semblance of something—a shape or pattern (really, anything that his mind could just run with and go from there).

But the shapes faded, lost in translation.

A *blockage*.

Something in the way.

He couldn't know what it was, but he knew it was there—inhibiting him, keeping him from thinking clearly. He *needed* to think clearly, or else he was doomed. Doomed to waste away, trapped in the incessant grip of self-loathing, self-criticism, and shame. His own mind, a prison that he couldn't escape.

"We're not done with you yet," a voice told him. *"It's not over until it's over."*

• • •

```
INT.  EDWIN'S MIND  —  ETERNITY
```

We watch Edwin Dorset, sitting on a park bench in San Francisco, looking up at us from below. As we draw nearer, we see the cypress and eucalyptus trees around him make way for us—bending, twisting, and snapping apart.

As we close in on Edwin, we see the unparalleled fear in his eyes.

                    NARRATOR
There's no escaping us. Wherever you go, we go.

And just as we're about to make contact with him, we suddenly—

CUT TO:

• • •

An awakening: Edwin returned to the world like a newborn baby—a newborn baby metaphorically, at least (he wasn't screaming his head off—nor, for that matter, actually *crying* like a baby). Nonetheless, his heart raced as if he had just ran a marathon—it almost beat out of his chest, actually.

If he kept this lifestyle up, that same heart would undoubtedly be the end of him.

The faint hue of orange that came from the monitors was almost blinding, and he had to cover his eyes, afraid that he might regurgitate whatever creature had crawled its way through his intestines. Simultaneously, he could feel the emptiness in his gut, as if he hadn't eaten in days (and honestly, he might *not* have eaten in days). Whatever the case, his mind felt scrambled and unable to catch up with reality.

He felt like death; his physiology wasn't made for this (but then again, whose was?).

He groaned with discomfort.

"He's awake."

Edwin turned toward the gruff voice resounding from somewhere far-off. He saw only a vague shadow near the monitors. His vision was all but gone, too blurry to see a damn thing. Since when had his vision been this bad? (Did he need glasses now?)

He felt a hand on his arm and heard Sibyl's composed, yet reassuring, voice. "It's okay." Her hand squeezed his arm gently. "You're safe now—the hardest part is over."

But even if he was safe now, that didn't take away from the fact he felt like shit. He couldn't even see Sibyl. Regardless, he was comforted in knowing that she hadn't abandoned him while he had gone through his augmentation; in fact, part of him was actually surprised that she was still on Orion. Hadn't she helped him enough? She had smuggled him from one planet to another, and all without asking for anything in return. Just a freeloader with a death ticket on him—a death ticket from another dimension.

That begged the question: "So, the fifth-beings can . . . no longer track me?"

"You're untraceable," Sibyl confirmed.

"I don't understand." Edwin rest his head on his hand and felt the throbbing vein on his temple. "How . . . how is it they can't track me anymore? I thought they're omnipotent, and that they . . . see everything, everywhere, all at once."

Sibyl didn't respond.

Perhaps Edwin didn't understand the fifth-beings well at all. He wondered then about the feeling of being watched constantly, wondering what kind of being (or beings) would willingly devote their time to watching his life unfold, and whether he was crazy for even thinking such a thing.

"He's got a point." The gruff, masculine voice from before spoke again, over by the monitors, and Edwin realized he recognized that voice from somewhere. Sometime recently, too, but he couldn't remember when or where. "The fifth-beings reside outside space-time, and space-time, as we know it, is limitless—*eternal*—and therefore, anything is free rein." He reflected some more. "But you also have to realize the fifth dimension is just another level of existence. And the status quo, no matter where you are, never remains the same. That said, even the fifth-beings must have limits. If they can't track you, they'll just track another like you. Besides, the DNA isn't for them to track but for us to. They must have hundreds and thousands of you on file, ready to track anytime the next reaping begins—which it will, because it always does."

"Hundreds and thousands of me on file"? Edwin shook his head, which made his pounding headache all the worse. "What do you mean?"

Sibyl scoffed. "Brutus is getting ahead of himself. You need rest, Edwin. You just went through an arduous experience, whether you remember it or not. We can talk about this later."

"You're not the first, you know," Brutus told Edwin, ignoring Sibyl's attempts to end the conversation. "And you're certainly not the last."

Edwin's curiosity escalated, helping him slightly forget all about his feverish symptoms. He sat up (afterward, regretting it). "You've met others like me?"

"Plenty," Brutus said without pause. "Same features as you. Some changes, here and there. Sometimes it's age, sometimes it's gender, but never different DNA."

Same features? Same DNA? At first, Edwin thought Brutus was only referring to others like him who had gotten bounties from the fifth-beings, but his last few words had made him re-evaluate everything he previously knew about his bounty. He needed clarification: "What . . . what do you mean, exactly?"

"Don't you know?" Brutus sounded astonished. "Did . . ." Suddenly, there was a dawning realization in his tone, and his next question was no doubt directed toward Sibyl. "You never told him, did you?"

Never told me what? Edwin hated being left out of the loop.

"He knows all that he needs to know," Sibyl said, and Edwin thought she sounded sad.

"I'm lost." Edwin turned from Sibyl to Brutus—from one blur to the other. His headache came back in full-throttle, like a power drill digging itself into his brain, right into the space between his left brow and eyeball. He blinked, attempting to fight the vertigo. "What . . . what are you guys talking about?"

At first, there was no reply from either of them.

And then, at last, Sibyl spoke again: "Remember how I told you that you were special? That the fifth-beings wanted you for a specific reason, a destiny that set you apart from others?"

Edwin remembered her words clearly. *"You're important to the fifth-beings,"* she had told him. *"Important to the universe as a whole."* He didn't know where she was going with this; he winced, feeling unsteady. "What about it?"

Sibyl hesitated. "I may have embellished the truth a little."

"Well, well," another voice said, entering the mix; it was D-D, and she sounded rather exhausted. "Looks like our boy wonder's finally awake."

Sibyl let go of Edwin's arm, and he heard her get up from her chair. "He could use all the rest he needs," she said. And with that, she walked away—the sound of her footsteps echoing behind her.

D-D sat where Sibyl had been sitting. "You must be starving." She moved in her chair a little and fidgeted with whatever cords were currently hooked up to Edwin. "Brutus, be a dear and fetch Edwin something to eat."

Brutus mumbled something inaudible and also left the room, leaving Edwin and D-D alone.

"Is your head hurting?" D-D asked, setting an open palm on Edwin's forehead. "I'd give you something more for that, but you need to eat first. Can't risk any chemical overloads. I already gave you some anodyne to counteract the nausea."

Edwin closed his eyes, realizing now that trying to use them was futile. "I can't see anything."

"Your eyes will adjust back. Don't worry about that."

Edwin relaxed. "How long have I been out?"

"About a week."

"A week?" *I've been out that long?*

"Quite typical, really—especially from one who's never had an augmentation before."

Edwin sighed, leaning back on the bed. "The others like me," he started. "The ones you've helped: did they ever escape their bounty?"

D-D cleared her throat. "It doesn't work like that, my dear. Time is infinite, relative to where you are—bounties like yours never expire."

Edwin felt like he would throw up again. "What happened to them? The other bounties."

"Some are still in hiding."

"And the others?"

D-D paused, giving her next words thoughtful consideration. "The others didn't make it."

So, now I'm doomed for a life on the run. . . .

If Edwin felt any better, perhaps he would have shed a tear or two. But at that moment, his own physiological symptoms were more of a concern to him than any other external threat, and he wondered when Brutus would get back with the food. He didn't know how he could eat, truthfully, but he figured that once he smelled whatever Brutus had brought back with him, he wouldn't care. There was no need to worry about what he couldn't change. The only thing he could do now was take each moment as it came.

Perhaps that's all he could ever do.

• • •

Once Edwin's sight returned to full capacity, he was again reminded that Brutus Wainesworth was, in fact, a bear all along—or a distant cousin to a bear, at least; the same way that homo sapiens are distant cousins to other apes. Oh, the absurdity of it all. *I'll never get used to this*, he thought, reflecting on the last six or seven weeks. Life was so different now, and even with enough time to finally register what made it so different, there could never be a way to fully understand it. Perhaps that's a part of growing up: Realizing just how little you know about the universe and your place in it. At any rate, growth is never easy, and those who say it is have yet to grow more themselves.

Edwin watched in silence as a hawksbill turtle—at least twice his size—swam slowly above him. A school of fish, moving as one, then swam around the turtle, reminding Edwin of a living tornado as they surged upward in a sinuous motion.

Wherever his attention went, there was something magnificent to see.

A manta ray drifting above purple algae.

Small, luminescent jellyfish.

A kelp forest, and a two-headed shark descending on its prey.

A coral reef dominated by starfish, glowing anemone, red sea whip, clams, seahorses, eels, angelfish, triggerfish, clownfish, lionfish, parrotfish, barracudas, and so on and so forth—the likes of which Edwin had never seen before, considering their variations of what he would have seen on Earth. The aquatic tunnel stretched onward, casting rays of deep blue on the dry land separated by thick glass. And as beautiful as it all was, Edwin was more than glad to be on the other side of it.

He closed his eyes and took in a deep breath. Tried straightening his back, even, thinking about D-D's blunt comment about how often bounties slouched. He put his hands in his pockets and reflected deeply. Fragmented pieces of the fever dream he'd had during his augmentation returned to him, bringing to mind Maggie Summers, Amelia Gladden, and Vicky Dorset; three women from his life, all of whom were completely different. But why did they come to mind? He tried to find the connection—any meaning behind it, if there even was one. Just what did those three have in common? And why, after so long, did their faces now weigh on his mind so vividly?

Maggie fuckin' Summers, he thought humorously. *Why did I put up with her for so long?*

And Amelia? Well, Amelia was a great friend and all, but the two were never truly meant to be together—at least, not in the sense of a lifelong companion, of which he had wanted then in a partner (and perhaps still wanted now). He had known their relationship wouldn't last even before they started hooking up. They were too different, and their priorities had never been the same. She only wanted a fuck buddy, whereas he wanted . . . well, he wanted something more. Even so, he had tried to make it work, and perhaps forced it, only to be disappointed in the end.

I was lonely, he knew, looking back. *With both of them, I just wanted someone to love.*

And then there was Vicky Dorset. . . .

A lonesome feeling gripped at him, thinking about his biological mother. A feeling of being unwanted, unseen. *Hell, maybe I just wanted to be loved. But what is love? What is it, truly? Is it something that you receive or something that you give, whether returned or not?*

"A lesson is nothing without its application," he remembered someone telling him in the dream, though he couldn't remember who. Was it Sibyl . . . ? No, he was certain that it wasn't Sibyl. Although, quite frankly, she had *also* been in the dream now that he remembered. Perhaps she, too, was tied into this "lesson" somehow.

But what lesson?

Exactly how much of his life had he been searching for the love he had never gotten as a child? Just how much of his life had he worried about what others thought of him? His fear of rejection—fear of not being "good enough." Because, when it came down to it, it was *fear* that had kept him depressed for all those years, eating away at his soul like a malignant tumor growing from within.

Perhaps in his search to be loved, he had forgotten how to love himself.

As a child, he didn't care what others thought about him. He used to soar, unabashed. But the joy that was in him, that inner peace that knew no bounds, had one day left without him having noticed. Had the wonder left when Lamar died? Had he burned down that bridge of abandonment as he did Vicky's place?

He supposed it didn't matter. Not anymore, anyway.

What mattered now was what he did with that knowledge. The active effort he put into his life to get back to that state of bliss. Like painting a magnum opus, he had to put in the work. To recondition himself, little by little. Every hour invested, he would see himself getting closer. Closer to that boy he once was—fearless, and without a care in the world whether he was loved or not.

Once again, the only thing separating him from his full potential was himself.

Footsteps came from the end of the tunnel behind him. He turned around and saw Sibyl walking toward him. She wore a navy-blue kimono, and her dark hair was parted to the side and wet—no doubt having just gotten out of a shower or pool of water. He hadn't seen her since waking from his augmentation, and even then, he hadn't been able to see much at all. Truthfully, he had forgotten how beautiful she was; in fact, he tried not to think about it, knowing that nothing good could come out of those feelings. No one as beautiful as her could ever love someone like him.

No, he thought, already having to correct himself. *That's where you're wrong.*

A funny thing, hindsight, and how with it you begin noticing the thought patterns holding you back. It was about time he stopped limiting himself. Besides, Sibyl was much more than her appearance. There was so much depth to her, and he had yet to crack the surface and discover what lay beneath her outer shell. After all, it was her soul that he was interested in, not her body; the internal mattered far more than the external.

It's within where true beauty lies.

Edwin smiled at Sibyl as she approached him. She stopped a few feet away from him and silently glanced out the glass wall separating them from the aquatic life, before turning to face him once more. If he knew any better, it seemed as if she was a little surprised by his reaction upon seeing her. What was she expecting, *hostility*? No, he was beyond that—she had saved his life countless of times, and no matter what secrets she had kept from him, he had no right to go into any self-pity tantrum, complaining about how she had betrayed his trust and how he would never trust her again. No, he wasn't that shallow. He still trusted this woman with his life, whether she had told him the whole truth or had kept part of it hidden. He knew her sentiments even without her telling him. Sometimes, the truth of a situation can be too much for one to handle, and he understood fully well that she probably hadn't thought he was actually strong enough to handle it all. But, as he was learning more about himself, he found he was even stronger than he had once thought.

A vulnerability lingered in Sibyl's expression, and her eyes locked onto his. "I thought you would be mad at me."

Edwin's smile remained. "Mad at you?"

"I kept the truth from you all this time."

He shrugged. "That I'm not the only bounty?"

Sibyl shook her head. "No." She looked out again, past the transparent glass separating them from being completely submerged. "I mean, maybe. Yes, in a way. But more than that. The fact that all those other bounties are just different versions of you from other worlds—other universes. That I really have no idea why the fifth-beings want you at all." She paused for a moment and looked down. "Honestly, I don't think for any other reason than their own entertainment."

Edwin crossed his arms and looked out the glass wall as well. *To think that I almost developed a Messiah Complex, thinking that my actions could somehow mean anything to godlike beings in an impermanent universe.* He nodded solemnly. "I don't blame you, you know. How can you tell someone they were abducted from another universe, have an intergalactic bounty on their head, and for it all to mean nothing in the end? You did what you felt was right; I respect that."

Sibyl regarded Edwin again. "You're very forgiving, Edwin Dorset." She seemed taken aback by his words. "You have a kind heart."

Edwin smiled brightly. "You should've met my brother."

She considered that. "Is he the one you always draw?"

She's seen my drawings? Suddenly, he felt exposed and self-conscious. "You've seen my drawings?"

Sibyl gave Edwin a mischievous, cornerwise grin. "I had Jermaine keep tabs on you while I was gone, relaying to me whatever he deemed necessary."

Embarrassment washed over Edwin. He hadn't thought to check his room in the Vagabond for cameras, though he was certain that Sibyl was merely referring to what he drew on the tablet and not what he did in closed quarters; nonetheless, even if he had been surveyed by Jermaine in the room, he hoped Jermaine hadn't told her everything he did while alone (honestly, not everything was meant to be known).

Perhaps sensing Edwin's embarrassment, Sibyl added: "Only a need to know basis. Nothing more. You have to understand we knew nothing about you." She hesitated. "I've heard stories about the other bounties, and perhaps they're just that: stories. Still, I had to be careful—just in case. In case you . . . well, weren't as you appeared to be. There could have been a good reason your DNA was chosen for the reaping, after all. If the fifth-beings wanted your genetics every time, it could have been for *any* reason, couldn't it? And better to err on the side of caution."

Edwin nodded with understanding. "Of course."

"Your brother." Sibyl brought the conversation back to Lamar. "What's he like?"

Edwin thought of Lamar. He remembered that warm feeling he had the last time he saw him, after so very long of not having seen him, and that feeling of solace as he cried in his arms. That feeling of being loved and feeling seen. And the emptiness from his absence. "He was my hero."

Sibyl noticed Edwin's demeanor change. She set a reassuring hand on his arm. "There's always the off-chance you can see him again. Now, I know that may not seem feasible *now*, but there might still be ways, you know. If we can somehow gain access to fifth-dimensional technology, we could send you back from where you came." She smiled tenderly—an intimacy that she rarely showed anyone. "And you could see your brother again."

She had mistaken his use of the past-tense. "If only that were the case," he said, nodding contemplatively. "But even if I managed to return where I left off, that wouldn't bring him back."

Sibyl considered Edwin's words carefully. She saw the look in his eyes, and—by the way she looked back at him—he knew at once that she understood what had happened without him even having to say it; she knew what loss was like—he could see it in her eyes, just as she could see it in his.

Edwin put his hand over Sibyl's hand, still on his arm. "You never told me about your family."

Sibyl wavered. Her eyes gazed down again, lost in memory. "I didn't know them very well."

Edwin thought of his biological father, whom he had never met or heard anything about; he was sure that Vicky hadn't even known who his father was—and if she had, he sure as hell wasn't worth mentioning. He had met none of his extended family before, nor did he think that they even knew he existed (if they had still been alive at all). And when he was put into the foster system, his whole concept of "family" had been shattered, with the realization that even when things seemed great on the surface, there was a brokenness beneath the facade, and who better to project that brokenness onto than the outsider. His heart ached with understanding, and he could relate to Sibyl more than she could know.

A rumbling resounded across the tunnel, and the ground shook beneath them. The two stumbled, almost fell, and held onto each other for balance. "What the hell was *that*?" Sibyl muttered, glancing down the corridor, back toward where she came from.

It sounded as if a bomb had gone off.

Before Edwin could answer, a loud *crack* emitted from the glass wall separating them from the water. Soon, followed by another, this time even louder.

"What—"

Sibyl activated Edwin's void suit, and before he could even register why, the glass wall around them shattered.

|16|

THE NATURE OF PEOPLE

Hendrix Martin observed his counterpart, Adewale Djamin, as he fidgeted with the plasma rifle in his hands. *Seventeen years of this lifestyle, and his nerves still don't go away.* Adewale's uneasy countenance was beginning to make Hendrix also feel on edge. *Honestly, I don't even know how he's alive right now.*

Hendrix inspected the barrel of his handgun, double-checking to see if it was still loaded—the ion cartridge remained in place, however, mostly unused.

He glanced at Adewale again. *Can't blame him, though—one misstep, and he's a dead man.*

As for Hendrix, he'd been on the run even before his bounty began, back in his own universe. Had he not already acclimated to this lifestyle of constant danger and uncertainty, he was sure that he would have blown his brains out by now. Perhaps he was born for this, the life on the run. Not that he wanted it. Tax evasion was one thing, but an intergalactic bounty? Well, that was another, and he supposed there really was no getting used to it. With the lifestyle he now lived, there was no guarantee of a tomorrow. Though, to be fair, there was *never* a guarantee of a tomorrow. He had made peace with that long ago, knowing that whatever had once constituted as a "normal life" was long gone, buried in the past.

Now, the only thing he could do was keep moving forward.

Though, something about it all felt familiar—*too* familiar, in fact—as if he was merely repeating what had already happened before. How many others like him had gone through this? How many others like him had been where he was now? He couldn't stop to think about it. Couldn't stop to think at all, really. Hell, if he had ever stopped moving, he would already be dead by now. He *had* to be in motion, always doing something. Only a year ago (a subjective year, that is) had he first learned that his DNA was even being tracked by bounty hunters, broadcast by the fifth-beings on a private network for all to see. Luckily, there was a delay in the broadcasting (*a very convenient delay*), that always gave him a head start. But the closer the bounty, the smaller the delay—a delay that must have been intentional.

Some fucked up joke by the fifth-beings, deriving pleasure from the pursuit.

Motherfuckers, Hendrix thought as he walked with Adewale through the darkness. His awareness of the fifth-beings was getting worse now. Sometimes, he could hear them in his thoughts, numerous and indiscernible. Their constant judgment—*rating* him as if he was only a product. "Capitalism of the gods," he liked to think of it. Also paranoia, perhaps. And he wondered if Adewale also experienced this; he hadn't cared to ask, given their circumstances, too preoccupied with everything else he had to worry about—matters like DNA and tracking, for example.

It was incredibly hard to find augmenters who specialized in DNA alteration, and especially while on the run, unable to come in contact with most people, too afraid they might try to sell you out or even cash you in themselves. Hendrix—along with Adewale—had the most famous face in all of Samsara. Their bounties had started long, long ago, back when the Saxons reigned supreme, and even before that. As a matter of fact, the bounties went so far back that there wasn't even a record of a time before them. The reaping was nothing but a sport spectated by the fifth-beings, those all-seeing fiends who lacked any empathy to let this happen. And, like the gladiator rings during the Iron Age, the only ones to truly suffer were the athletes, who were given the worst deal of all, forced against their will.

We're just objects to them. . . . Puppets in their play.

Again, Hendrix glanced at Adewale. The two were nearly identical, albeit with slight differences—namely in their age, weight, posture, hair, and, yes, sense of style (as duly noted by Hendrix, who prided himself with flair). Hendrix strode with more confidence, whereas Adewale conducted himself analytically, far more anxious than his counterpart; Hendrix was in his early-thirties, whereas Adewale was already nearing his mid-fifties; Hendrix had grown his hair out into dreads, and even had a stylish goatee, whereas Adewale continually trimmed his graying hair and never left more than stubble on his face; Hendrix wore a rich indigo jacket, black khakis, and leather, steel-toed boots, whereas Adewale wore a ragged and worn, brown blazer, gray cargo pants, and mahogany combat boots; material possessions aside, from two different worlds came two different people.

And yet they were survivors, all the same.

The pair had only met a few months back while hiding out in the jungles of Ipanema (in the Herbert region of Brecken). Hendrix had merely stopped on the planet for a supply run, but—as life on the run goes—ended up being stranded, having lost his ship to a marauder; oh well—he had stolen it in the first place, and he could always obtain another. Except he hadn't expected himself to be on Brecken for so long, and he had to fend off reapers left and right. (Even the easiest of tasks can be made extremely difficult in any relative situation.) Thankfully, he had gotten access to a motorbike—stolen, of course, though it was that or death—and had made his way, for a time, living out in the jungle, foraging natural supplies and sneaking into any nearby town whenever in desperate need of food or medical supplies. As for the reapers tracking him, he always tried to loot their bodies after dealing with them, hoping to find something good, to keep him alive that much longer.

While out in the jungle, however, Hendrix came across what looked like an abandoned cabin, only to discover that it wasn't as abandoned as it might have appeared to be. It was only by chance that he had found Adewale that day—mere *coincidence*. But sometimes, a part of Hendrix wondered if the fifth-beings had anything to do with it.

How often did things like that happen?

Luck was a fortune often known to elude Hendrix, and it was his luck, after all, that got him into this whole mess. Whatever the reasoning behind his finding of Adewale, he couldn't pass up an opportunity for a friend—even if that friend was himself (or another version of himself, from another world much like his own).

Adewale had already undergone an augmentation by the time Hendrix had found him (at least, a decade prior), but as it so turned out—evident by the constant influx of reapers—Hendrix was still desperate for an augmentation, having been fruitless in his search. Thankfully, Adewale knew a guy who could help him. Or, at least, he *had* known a guy. Unfortunately, that old pal of his was long dead—by at least a good thirty subjective years (interstellar travel: you never get used to it). Whatever the case, a friend of a friend knew someone, and—as it often goes—one thing led to another, and here they were now, in the caves of another planet, looking for what might as well have been some long-lost treasure.

As if on cue, Adewale said: "I think he was lying." He glanced at Hendrix, and the small scar beneath Adewale's right eye remained visible in the pathfinder's light. "This is a set-up; it's *obvious*, isn't it? Do you really think any augmenter would go this far not to be found? Come on . . ." He shook his head with a grimace. "We're in a cave, for crying out loud." Using his forearm, he wiped off the sweat dripping down his forehead. "We're walking into a trap."

The pathfinder, a bright globe leading them along a path, shined on above them.

Hendrix could clearly see obvious signs of others having walked this same path, as if the ground had subtly been paved for them to follow. He assumed augmenters needed heavy privacy, particularly with the kind who dealt illegally and outside the constricts of the Commonwealth (*or whatever the hell they're calling themselves these days—I don't know, they're all the same*). Besides, an augmenter who specialized in DNA would *need* somewhere private for their clientele, and particularly with a clientele

as conspicuous as a bounty. Augmenters must have made a fortune, and the last thing he worried about was being cashed in
by one of them; furthermore, a new bounty would come every
time: an endless supply of them. In fact, it was such a lucrative
business that he often wondered if there were those who went
out looking for bounties, not to cash them in to the fifth-beings
as a reaper would but to help them find an augmenter—for a
fee, of course (it would only make sense if they profited from
it, considering how dangerous it was to associate yourself with
a bounty; and obviously, few ever did anything without a reward).

Not everyone got as lucky as Adewale; he was given his augmentation for free from some altruist so setup that he hadn't
even asked for anything in return. *Lucky son of a bitch.*

Hendrix? He wasn't so lucky. He supposed he was going to
have to do this the hard way. *It's always the hard way*, he thought
as he tightened his grip on his handgun.

"This is it," Hendrix said, convinced. "It has to be."

That, or death.

Adewale shook his head again, unconvinced. "You never
should have brought me into this."

"You're still with me now, aren't you?" Hendrix shrugged a
shoulder. "The only one you have to blame is yourself." But
that wasn't really true, was it? From the get-go, Hendrix had
forced Adewale to help him against his will, and he had constantly threatened him with death or discovery if he didn't;
matter of fact, the safe house Adewale had lived in for over
five years had been destroyed in less than twenty minutes of
Hendrix having found it, despite all the precautions Adewale
had made for himself, isolated from anyone and anything.

No, in a way, Adewale *never* had a choice.

But then again, neither had Hendrix.

Ahead, they could see hovels of sorts. Houses carved out of mushrooms.

Oh yeah, Hendrix thought, raising his handgun at the ready. *This is definitely it.* "Be ready for anything." He moved ahead with caution, ignoring Adewale's uneasy look. *If I'm going out, I'm going out with a bang.*

Their shadows cast against the houses, and with each intersection passed, their shadows only increased. A haunting silence festered, interrupted by their loud footsteps reverberating off the cave walls. And a light shone ahead. Some kind of lobby, with sleek, white marble walls and floor, leading through a bright hallway. A large figure loomed, blocking the way— merely a silhouette in the light.

What looked like a bear.

Hendrix set his handgun's sight onto the figure ahead.

Indeed, it was a bear. Or, at least, what *looked* like a bear (much like a javelina looks like a pig—different when you look really close). Big, black, and shaggy, with three scars visible on its face, the "bear-who-was-not-a-bear" wore a green and gray serape with intricate designs woven in its fabric. Whatever this creature was, it stood on thick, hind legs and held a spear in both hands (hands that looked more like a primate's than they did that of any bear), and its eyes were firmly placed on Hendrix, as if it knew that *he* was the threat and not Adewale, despite Adewale holding the bigger gun.

The creature spoke gruffly, forewarning: "State your business or get lost."

Hendrix turned to Adewale and chuckled. "Walking into a trap, my ass." He shook his head playfully. "If this were really a set-up, would you expect a creature like that to be waiting out in the open, spouting out such verse?" He made a *tsk-tsk* noise with his lips, and he glanced again at the creature waiting before them. Nonchalantly, he nodded to it: "Howdy."

Still holding its spear in front of it (presumably shielded, Hendrix had to guess), the creature leaned forward and re-evaluated the two strangers. Hendrix saw recognition behind the creature's eyes, though it said nothing.

"You know why we're here." Hendrix nodded to Adewale next to him. "And you're going to help us."

The creature snorted. "Why is that?"

Hendrix grinned. "Why, for the very reason you help everyone else." He pulled out a shining crystal ball from within his jacket. "For the love of money."

• • •

Brutus led the two newcomers through the hallway toward D-D's meditation garden. It seemed as if a new bounty was showing up every other hour. It was a first, however, seeing two bounties come in at once (at least for Brutus). Every augmentation was a long process, and as it so happened, precautions had been set in stride so that not a single inpatient would ever come across another. One of D-D's many rules; D-D could be very unforgiving if you broke any of them. Brutus hadn't been her first assistant, nor did he assume he would be her last, knowing how she operated at times.

It was lovely on Orion, no doubt, with the kind of isolation that Brutus preferred, in a universe filled with opportunists trying to capitalize on whatever natural resource they could find. Even so, he couldn't see himself staying in one place for-ever. One day, he hoped, he would find his family again. His Ma and Pa, just as they were the last he had seen them.

A fool's dream, he knew, but even a fool could dream.

"In here." Brutus led the two bounties through the door on his right and into D-D's meditation garden. As she had been when Edwin and Sibyl first arrived, D-D was now sitting on a bed of rocks by the water surrounding the base of a picturesque cherry tree.

Deidre Dua had her eyes shut. Her back was straight, her legs were crossed beneath her, and she was meditating, with no emotion on her face. A riveting woman, full of contradictions. On one hand, she was an augmenter, and she changed people for a living, from their very core—physiological or psycho-logical, it didn't matter; she transformed whatever was desired, artificially, through mutation or prosthesis. But on the other hand, she refused to augment herself, despite her very pro-fession. She could be any age that she desired, and yet she was content to remain a seventy-three-year-old, appearing her age (if not, younger) and looking like a "grandma," though the old spinster had never had any children of her own—nor had she ever wanted any.

"Xibalba, *no*," D-D once exclaimed when Brutus had asked her why she never had any children. "The universe is over-populated already! Are you out of your mind?" She had laughed briskly, shaking her head repeatedly. "I'm selfish enough as is."

Upon their approach, D-D opened her eyes and glanced from Hendrix to Adewale. Her eyes immediately noticed the firearms in their hands, though she mentioned nothing of it. "You're in a hurry, I take it?"

And so it went, similar to what Edwin and Sibyl had gone through, except now it was Hendrix and Adewale, two (though not too) completely different individuals. A normal procedure for an augmentation, which is why augmenters got paid the big bucks (or "talents," being a more universal currency). Except no righteous endeavor is without its risk, and there's always the chance of things falling apart, no matter the precautions set in stride to keep them together.

In a second, everything can change.

• • •

The red dot on the radar blinked out of existence.

Dieter glanced at Nairobi, sitting across from him, before he faced their crew huddled around them. "What did I tell you? You glad we waited now?" He looked again at Nairobi, and a dark smile crossed his lips. "We've hit the mother lode of all mother lodes."

Nairobi's smile matched Dieter's. "A self-sustaining influx of bounties." She nodded thoughtfully. "Never should've doubted you."

Dieter leaned forward, and the vertical scar beside his right eye shown clearly in the light. "The bounty we nearly had on Zarathustra will be nothing compared to what we take hold of today." He smirked, grabbed his rifle from the table, and stood up. Facing the entourage, he cocked his head to the side with an exaggerated gesture. "Now, who's ready to make some talents?"

|17|

FOIL

The water came in from all directions.

Edwin held Sibyl tightly as the flooding propelled them across the tunnel, tossing them across the ground, as the water crashed all around them. Luckily, with his void suit having been activated (only thanks to Sibyl), Edwin's body was covered from head to toe, offering him unhindered vision, oxygen, and protection, all while he covered Sibyl's body with his own, sustaining the impact of any oncoming debris and glass flowing with the discharge of water. Unfortunately, Sibyl hadn't been so lucky. She must have hit her head sometime during the initial flooding, considering that she wasn't moving at all—nor were her eyes open, for that matter—leaving Edwin with the impression that she was unconscious. To make matters worse, she wore no void suit whatsoever and nothing was keeping her from drowning.

For once, it was Edwin's turn to be the hero.

At last, the water submerged them completely and spun them around with its violent current one last time. As soon as Edwin got his bearings, continuing to hold Sibyl tightly, he started swimming toward the end of the caved-in tunnel. The void suit propelled him forward, moving him faster than he could ever swim on his own, even with fins. But alas, at the end of the tunnel, the metal doors were sealed shut.

Edwin tried to pry the doors open with his free hand, but neither door budged.

The doors were airtight—perhaps a precaution in case of flooding.

(And just what exactly *could* cause a flooding?)

Fuck, Edwin thought in a panic. *Fuck, fuck, fuck.*

He glanced down at Sibyl, held in his right arm, with her eyes closed and her dark hair gracefully floating around her.

He would have to find another way; he couldn't fail her now.

He kicked off the doors and swiftly shot across the fully submerged tunnel in a straight line, as if he was soaring across the sky at the speed of light. He focused his attention at the other end of the tunnel, his void suit enhancing his vision, to see that the doors there were also shut—no doubt airtight.

There was no time for hesitation. No time for doubt.

Only the now.

Seeing an opening where the glass had shattered completely, Edwin launched himself upward and emerged onto the other side of the tunnel.

The aquarium seemed endless, though he knew that wasn't so—just like Sibyl's garden in the Vagabond. Somewhere, there had to be a way out. And if there wasn't a way out, then he would make one.

But how?

No time to think about it, however—the fate of another lay in his hands.

He shot ahead, not thinking twice about where he was going, but only hoping that something would be on the other side. He passed through a school of fish, swirling around him—a thick cloud of moving organisms, luminescent skeletons shining like ghosts beneath fluctuating scales—and emerged into a kelp forest, more alien than anything he had seen thus far. Colorful coral fluctuated below him, pulsating with their mesmerizing pattern, but before he knew it, he was already out of the forest and—

He collided with an immovable object, but the void suit quickly compensated, shooting him the other way, now projecting them upward. He glanced back, wondering what he had collided with, until he looked back ahead and saw what appeared to be an enormous whale coming toward him. Correcting his trajectory, he missed the whale by mere inches.

There was a light ahead, right above them—a *surface*.

Almost there, Edwin thought, hoping that Sibyl could hold out a little longer. *Almost there. . . .*

The two shot out of the water—propelled by the void suit, which adjusted mid-flight and shot them downward again, landing back into the water with a heavy splash. They rolled from the momentum, recovered, and resurfaced once more, as Edwin struggled to keep Sibyl's head above the surface.

The last thing Edwin expected to find was a beach. And not only a beach, but a beach with him already there—or, at least, another version of him—standing by the water's edge with his mouth open, dumbfounded.

Edwin swam to the shoreline, emerged out of the water, and dragged Sibyl to dry land, where he then lay her on soft sand. He set a finger on her neck, making sure that she still had a pulse (but with his adrenaline, he couldn't tell). By then, the other bounty had ambled to them, watching Edwin cautiously.

But Edwin neither looked up nor lost focus.

His helmet dissolved into the rest of his void suit, and he placed the heel of his hand on the center of Sibyl's chest, on the lower half of her sternum, and then he placed his other hand above that hand, interlocking his fingers, before starting chest compressions. He kept his elbows straight and used his entire body, not just his arms, as he had once learned in a CPR class he had taken for extra credit, never realizing that one day he would have to utilize such information (but that's how it usually goes, isn't it?).

After the chest compressions, he put his hand behind Sibyl's neck, held it up so that an airflow could get into her lungs, lifted her chin, pinched her nose shut, and leaned forward, breathing into her until her chest rose. Twice, he did this, but nothing came of it.

He tried the entire process again, doing exactly as before.

He didn't know if he wasn't compressing hard enough, or if he just wasn't doing it right, but again, nothing came of it. *No*, he thought, and his mind fell into a panic, fearing for the worst. *No, no, no. . . .*

But he couldn't give up—not yet. Even with all the doubt, uncertainty, and hopeless trepidation, he couldn't surrender to the panic—not yet.

Not ever.

Again, he did as before, but this time with more passion.

Beads of sweat formed on his brow, dripping to the sand, as he continued the chest compressions, one after the other. Again, lifting her head, tilting her neck back, lifting her chin, pinching her nose, and breathing into her mouth until her chest rose.

Again and again, he continued the process, hoping that it wasn't too late. It *had* to work. If it didn't work, then he . . . then he wouldn't know what—

Sibyl coughed violently, turned onto her side, and heaved out the excess water.

Edwin fell onto his back, laughing, relieved. Somehow, his laughing turned into tears of joy, and he was so caught up in his emotions that he had forgotten entirely about the "other Edwin" standing right behind him and watching them with an expressionless look.

It was strange for Edwin, not only seeing himself, but seeing what he would look like in twenty or thirty years. The version of himself staring back had to be in his forties already, if not fifties. Ebony skin, medium height, with a salt and pepper closed crop cut and thick stubble. He was barefoot and wore an open collared tan shirt with a dark shade of gray cargo pants. Handsome, though Edwin felt ashamed to admit it. Like seeing through a looking glass. His eyes were fixed on Edwin's, nearly identical. Edwin's eyes, however, went down to the long-range weapon in his hand.

From on the ground, Edwin smiled diffidently and waved a friendly hand. "Hi. . . ."

• • •

Something about the artificial beach reminded Edwin of the Pacific Coast of California—specifically, Ocean Beach, on the west side of San Francisco. Perhaps it was the way the coast seemed endless, seeming to stretch out for miles along both sides of the shoreline. Perhaps it was the "ocean" that also seemed endless. Or perhaps it was just the fact that he missed home. Whatever the case, indeed, a little part of home followed him wherever he went.

The simulated sun dipped against the horizon, leaving a lavender hue enriched with golden streaks of orange and red, merging and creating a spectacle of opulent wonder, casting a pink shade on everything. A small wooden shack sat by the dunes—the only structure in sight, and perhaps the only way out of there.

Adewale, the "other Edwin" (a much older counterpart, who could have easily been the father he never had), had introduced himself to Edwin in perfect English (either due to him already having an empathic emulator installed, or perhaps a cause of Edwin's new augmentation, having had his own translator installed during the procedure—although, really, he wasn't sure about the latter). Adewale remained slightly confounded by the emergence of the two, and Edwin had an inclination—a hunch, really—that this wasn't even Adewale's first encounter with another bounty, such as himself. Moreover, Adewale seemed less fazed by the fact there was another version of himself than he did with the strange and inexplainable emergence of the two. Edwin also had a feeling that perhaps Adewale rarely interacted with others, given his lack of eye contact, physical distance, and his fidgeting hands (one of them clutching some kind of high-tech rifle).

Edwin introduced himself, along with Sibyl, who sat on the sand with a hand on her temple and obvious discomfort on her face.

"She alright?" Adewale asked, nodding to Sibyl.

Sibyl nodded with a grunt and stood up, spitting on the ground beside her. "Never better."

Adewale, intrigued, looked at Edwin and Sibyl. He asked nothing else. Aware, perhaps, that his expression was enough to warrant an explanation in its own right.

Edwin spoke first, letting Sibyl get her bearings as she walked a few feet away from them and eyed the sunset in the distance. "We . . . uh, we had a close call." He suddenly felt at a loss for words, nodded awkwardly, and glanced at Sibyl, before adding: "A lot of close calls, actually."

Adewale nodded, as if he understood what any of that meant.

"We're not safe here," Sibyl said, folding her arms and facing the two. "We need to get out before it's too late." She glanced at the weapon in Adewale's hand and nodded to him. "Know how to use that?"

Adewale nodded back. Not one for words, either.

"Good." Sibyl frowned, looking around. "Where's the exit?"

Adewale pointed to the wooden shack amidst the dunes.

"Let's go," Sibyl said, refusing to waste another second. She strode toward the shack and left Edwin and Adewale with no choice but to follow her.

Adewale gave Edwin an amused look, which Edwin returned with a cordial smile.

• • •

For every augmenter, there are safeguards put in place for the unfortunate case of a raiding—a threat that no doubt looms in every augmenter, given the value and nature of every bounty. But no matter how careful one can be, and no matter how many precautions are set in place, no safeguard is ever fully guaranteed. As with most things in life, it only takes a bad moment until all laid plans go to waste.

As far as planets went, Orion was heavily secluded, and mostly protected, lying within the Inner Rings, near the outer edges. In a universe full of commercialization, it was unfortunately rare for a planet like Orion to go untouched. Celestial bodies were usually pillaged for their resources or terraformed by their colonists, like an invasive pest or pathogen destroying its host only to profit for themselves. For such a bountiful ecosystem, it was actually a miracle that the majority of Orion had gone this long without being discovered, despoiled for all its wealth and materials. Given its mostly uninhabited location, isolated from the rest of Samsara—on the other side of the Inner Rings, less populated with celestial bodies—Orion was the perfect place for an augmentation facility.

D-D's augmentation facility was massive and burrowed deep underground. Given its return on investment, she had invested a lot of talents into it. Privacy was a necessity for every augmenter, and the privacy of every client was even more important. There were various sections within the facility blocked off from one another, and not a single section was like the other. A track system ran throughout the facility, connecting each section, along with a myriad of elevators (six floors in total), not including the aquarium and cave system that ran even deeper.

For Brutus Wainesworth, D-D's assistant, it was his job to assess incoming bounties and help them transition through the process, always being the go-to guy for any questions, concerns, or needs that demanded to be met. He had worked this job for nearly seven years, and by now, the fear of a raiding had significantly diminished.

But not entirely.

Again, there are never any guarantees in life.

You see, as stated previously, there were precautions set in place if a raid were to happen. It would be foolish to assume that Brutus was D-D's only helper—it wasn't plausible, really, given the extensive size of the facility. With seven separate sections and six different levels, that kind of security demanded an army.

And as it so happened, an army was just what D-D had.

• • •

One of the locked doors along the many hallways slid open, and out walked a humanoid robot, followed by another just like it, and then another. All along the facility, the hallway doors slid open, and out emerged identical, sexless replicants, with their faces distinctly human and their bodies made of carbon and steel. In every sector, at least five of these robots emerged—aroused by the alarm blaring across the speakers and internal system.

In a darkened hallway along one of the many sectors, a young bounty identical to Edwin Dorset stood in his pajamas, holding a toothbrush, and watching in confusion as three of these robots wandered out of what appeared to be a broom closet, one after the other.

Overhead, red lights flashed on and off, leaving the atmosphere bleak and imposing.

The young bounty took a step forward, eyeing the closest robot sauntering toward him. "Is everything okay?"

The robot approached him, grabbed his head with both hands, and yanked it off his neck with a loud *crack*, pulling out his spine in the process. The bounty's body collapsed to the ground, dead on impact, and a pool of blood soon surrounded it, spreading around the robot's bipedal feet. Emotionless, the homicidal robot continued onward, with the two other robots following behind.

D-D had her reasoning for using programmed robots over sentient organisms (including artificial intelligences like Jermaine, unrestrained by their programming, and whom she still didn't trust). Less risk of being double-crossed, simple as that. Except only, no one had warned her about the threat of hackers. Sure, she'd had her fears and paranoia, implementing the newest security update whenever given the chance. But in a universe where everything is in continual motion, and nothing is ever the same, the "newest" is quite relative, isn't?

Like I said, everything's bound to fall apart.

|18|

WHEN THE DOGS COME OUT TO PLAY

Sibyl felt naked without a weapon. She should have known better than to leave her holstered handguns in the room she had
been staying in instead of taking them with her when she had
gone to shower. *And here you are after a close call with death, wearing
only a damn kimono*, Sibyl told herself, wishing that she had just
been a *little* more paranoid than her usual state. *This is why you
can't live bougie.*

After nearly dying less than an hour ago, it came as no surprise that she felt off her game—ill prepared. Already, lam-
enting the unique craftsmanship of her navy-blue jacket, the
"Death Defier," forged from a late blacksmith who she had
once saved on Neo (and may or may not have had a night or
two of revelry with). Her *favorite* jacket, that she would have to
abandon along with her two favorite handguns and the rest of
her clothes—let alone abandon alongside her favorite void belt
(a void belt that she'd had for seven years now). *It's the little
things we lose that hurt us the most.*

*Oh well. The universe is impermanent, after all; it's not like I won't
find another jacket.*

Sibyl stopped at the end of the corridor, crouched low, and peeked around the corner at the other side. Another corridor, narrow and constricting, also made of dark metal, with its paint chipping away. Every so often, the occasional red light flashed through the lining of deficient neon light running along the ceiling. And at last, Sibyl noticed it standing there: a robot—motionless, and at least seven feet tall; a silent sentinel of bi-pedal carbon, humanoid in appearance. No doubt D-D's deterrence against whatever was going down in the facility (most likely a raid, Sibyl had to guess, although it could really be anything).

It was good to have a security system for a raid, but it was ultimately futile; if their location was now compromised, reapers trying to capitalize would continue showing up looking for a bounty. At the very least, a security system would buy them time, and time was a commodity more valuable than all the talents in the world. Nonetheless, it should have come as no surprise that she didn't like the look of the robot one bit. There was something unnerving about it, and she just couldn't put her finger on why she felt that way.

Best to avoid any kind of confrontation whatsoever.

Sibyl glanced at Edwin, crouched behind her. He wore his void suit: a sleek, form-fitting layer of black nanometal, with etchings of deep, faintly glowing orange. Without a helmet on, however, she could see his eyes clearly, looking back at hers and trying to discern what they should do next. He had grown so much in the time that they knew each other. Either that or she was beginning to see what she had first overlooked.

It was *Edwin* who had saved her life this time around—she wouldn't forget that. *A good soul*, she thought. She had grown fond of their many conversations, and the wisdom that sometimes spewed out of him unexpectedly. *Always trying to do the right thing, whatever it is.* Once they got out of there, she would do everything she could to keep him safe again. Tell him the truth, even, and all her original intentions about using him to get to the fifth-beings, whether or not he trusted her afterward. Either way, it wouldn't matter if he trusted her or not—at least he would be safe. And not only would he be safe, but she would have a clear conscious, as well. Knowing that she had done the right thing in telling him the truth, no matter what reaction she got from telling him it.

She glanced over Edwin and at their new friend, Adewale, a middle-aged bounty nearly identical to Edwin (albeit with time and circumstances; i.e., nature vs nurture). For starters, the two crouched the same; their expressions were nearly identical also, although there was something *off* about Adewale— like there were a few screws missing, so to speak. He avoided any kind of eye contact whatsoever with Sibyl, and she guessed he didn't get out very much, given his circumstances. Also, given his age, he could have been on the run for over a decade at the very least, so of course Sibyl didn't blame him for that. Life was hard as is. Besides, there was nothing wrong with being a little "off."

Sibyl had always considered herself to have a deviant mind.

She nodded to the door across from them and gave the two bounties a resolute look, saying (without needing to say a thing): *"We'll go through there."*

Edwin nodded, compliant as ever.

Sibyl continued onward, avoiding the surveillance bot in the corridor.

The next passage opened into another hallway, this one much different from the one before it. It was brighter here, and the walls on both sides were made of a thick, translucent glass. On the other side of the glass appeared to be some kind of zoo, housing strange and exotic species of varying species. The families were separated to different niches, confined within what appeared to be their natural habitat (at least, what Sibyl *hoped* was their natural habitat—if not, she would definitely think even less of D-D for housing them).

A prison, she thought grimly, walking past a recess housing a family of Indlovu in a marshland region. Two adults, a mother and father, along with two infants, one of them larger than the other. The little Indlovu—just a baby, really—enthusiastically played along the brook that ran through every niche. The calf put its trunk in the water, did a little sideways jiggle, and brought its trunk out, before splashing its parents with a big smile on its face, with its tail swinging from side to side. And the mother made a *hoofing* sound, shook her head playfully, and waddled to the water with her tail swinging. She stood next to her little one, engulfed the calf around her trunk, and closed her eyes in a loving embrace.

• • •

At the sight of the mother elephant's embrace, Edwin stopped walking. Adewale continued ahead, slipping past him, and Sibyl hadn't heard Edwin stop, so she, too, kept walking. But Edwin was too absorbed to care about anything but the moment: the embrace of a mother and her calf. A mother's love: a love he had never had. A kind of love he would hope to give one day.

To whomever needs it, he thought. *Just like I did.*

Unconditional love; love without warrant.

There's too much indifference in this world. Edwin thought of the neighborhood bullies who had stolen his backpack—the same kids who had killed Lamar. *Too much hatred for things people don't understand. Bigotry, prejudice, and injustice everywhere. When will things change? When will things get better again?* He thought of the reaping, the fifth-beings, and everyone involved in it. The reapers out to get him, to capitalize off his misfortune for their own profit. *All they want is money: money, status, and fame.* He couldn't understand it. *None of that matters—all those things will fade away, just as they will.* But what could he do to change that kind of world? What could he do to make the world he lived in—the universe and everyone involved, plants and species alike—better than how it had been before he entered it?

The seeds you sow today, you reap tomorrow.

Mrs. Kemp came to mind, and the image of her sitting by her garden clipping a black rosebush. *A garden needs to be tended daily and put work into, to grow, so that it can become self-sufficient, easy to maintain, and stronger when the storms break.* Her green eyes peered at him from beneath her wide-brimmed hat. *Because no matter how good life can be, a storm is always brewing right around the corner, waiting to get you. But you're stronger than you give yourself credit for; you're* always *stronger than you give yourself credit for.* He imagined her holding up the black rose, glistening in the sun. *The more you stop doubting yourself, the more you can see that your voice truly matters.* She smiled then (a mother's smile), and something about it almost seemed mischievous.

The petals of the black rose fell off the stem, one by one, until nothing remained but the emerging image of an eight-year-old Edwin Dorset breaking into his burning home to save his drug-addicted mother, Vicky Dorset, a woman who had never showed him any love in return.

His own voice resonated in the forefront of his mind: *Be your own role model.*

What would Lamar think of the man he was today? Would he be proud of him, still love him the same? Better yet, what kind of man would *Lamar* be? Would he be exactly as Edwin had remembered him, or would he have lost his soul from the pressures of the world as Vicky Dorset once had? Would his ideation fail him? Whatever the case, it didn't matter. But, he supposed, if he *had* to guess how Lamar would think of him now? Well, perhaps Lamar would be proud of him. In Edwin's ideation of Lamar, he would have known that success didn't come from the material world, such as money, status, or fame. Success comes from within—inward virtues met externally. Peace of mind, contentment, and love for all things. What success boils down to, really, is the actions of an individual and how they affect the world around them, and not only for their own gain but for all who are affected by them (to the universe's betterment, really, and the well-being of *all* existence).

Be the change you want to see in the world. A tall order, but not improbable. Easy, really. *All it takes is action.* And speaking of action, Edwin suddenly remembered the time he had gotten separated from the bounty hunters in Zarathustra and lost in the maze of canyons. Hoping not to repeat history, he decided it was best to move on. Time to catch up to Sibyl and Adewale wherever they were. They couldn't have gone far.

Perhaps they were waiting for him now.

Passing the elephant enclosure, Edwin said his silent farewell to the undisturbed family, hoping that he could find that inner peace that they all seemed to possess, helping lead him onward, better than he had been before.

An explosion rang in the distance, and Edwin felt the ground tremble beneath his feet. For a second, he worried that the glass walls around him would shatter as they had with the aquarium and that all the wild animals would be let loose; but thankfully, nothing like that happened again.

Instead, the lights merely flickered on and off.

Again and again.

He didn't like the unease this new atmosphere brought with it. *Time to get the hell out of here.* The orange etchings on his void suit glowed even brighter as he hurried along the hallway.

• • •

At the end of the hallway, a pair of metal doors opened out, leading into an expansive chamber with a high-domed roof. Warm amber lights shone from above revealing a white greenhouse, brown barn, and more than a dozen rows of garden beds brimming with varieties of cabbage, cauliflower, kale, lettuce, chives, garlic, onions, and many other vegetables, along with a field of rice three hundred yards away, partially submerged in water. Past the greenhouse and rice field were another set of doors leading elsewhere.

This place just keeps getting bigger and bigger, Sibyl thought, shaking her head. She glanced behind her and saw Adewale standing there with an anxious look on his face. But behind Adewale . . . ?

Where's Edwin?

Just then, a booming explosion rang from across the chamber, and a section of the roof tore off as a small aircraft came crashing down, smashing into the rice field. Followed right behind were a pair of gliding drones with two riders sitting atop each one—one rider manning the controls, with the other rider manning a heavy machine gun turret.

The cockpit of the crashed aircraft opened, and a man wearing a black jumpsuit staggered out, attempting to limp away as fast as he could. In seconds, the pair of drones descended on him, and the ringing of gunfire echoed across the chamber, obliterating the pilot.

Alas, one of the riders noticed Sibyl.

With no time to spare, Sibyl sprinted toward the greenhouse with every effort that she could muster. Adewale followed behind, though much slower than her, struggling with the plasma rifle in his arms and making Sibyl wish she was the one wielding it. *I should have taken it from him when I had the chance.*

The drones and their riders gained on them with deadly speed.

Entering the greenhouse, Sibyl hastily scanned for anything that might aid her. Three rows of trellises stretched out, supporting tomatoes, squash, and berries of all kinds. On either side of the trellises, amidst bountiful, exotic plants, were scattered tables with small plantings, organized seeds, and various tools, with racks above them also storing miscellaneous items, though none that Sibyl could find useful. Nothing that could help.

A drone flew into the greenhouse from the other side. Adewale aimed his rifle at the intruders, and the weapon shook violently as a beam of bright, intense light shot out of its end, scorching all that it touched like a bolt of molten lightning, emitting like a flamethrower on steroids. At least half of the crops were decimated from the blast. The ceiling split in the middle, as well as the approaching drone that came crashing down, exploding on impact.

Before it had crashed, a rider was flung off the drone and landed on the ground fifteen feet from Sibyl. Sibyl darted at the rider and kneed him in the face for good measure (guaranteeing that he was unconscious, if not dead). Satisfied, she stripped a hand-cannon from the holster on his chest and felt the weight of the weapon in her hand, bringing a reassured smile on her lips.

The sound of the next drone bellowed from behind, where Sibyl and Adewale had entered the greenhouse, and wasted no time before opening fire.

Sibyl dove behind a burning trellis, and Adewale turned around—too late to react—and got mowed down by the drone's turret; by the time his body hit the ground, he was already unrecognizable. Sibyl crawled away urgently, listening intently as the drone whizzed above her, with the riders searching for her amidst the growing fire. She turned around, hand-cannon still in her hand, and—by the subsequent blasts of her weapon—showed her pursuers who the fuck they were messing with.

• • •

Edwin saw the greenhouse on fire and the crashed airship along the rice field, as well as the airship's pilot sprawled dead on the ground. He proceeded slowly then, grabbing the grapple gun from his void belt and hoping that he wouldn't have to use it. As he closed in on the greenhouse, he saw Sibyl languidly walk out of the smoking greenhouse like a hero in an action flick, trudging away from an explosion. She had Adewale's pulse rifle slung across her back and held in her hand a black handgun with a thick barrel. Still clothed in a navy-blue kimono, she now wore black boots, and her dark, turbulent hair hung loosely on her shoulders—as wild as her soul.

Sibyl nodded to Edwin, tossing him the handgun. "You'll want this."

Edwin caught the handgun with his free hand, holstered the grapple gun onto his void belt, and switched the handgun to his dominant hand. He glanced again at the burning greenhouse emitting a thick, black smoke out of the hole in the roof and open sides. Aside from the pulse rifle that Sibyl now carried on her, there was no sign of Adewale. Edwin put two and two together: "The other me didn't make it?"

Another booming sound resonated from afar, louder than the previous booming sound—and closer, no doubt. Sibyl didn't respond to Edwin's question, and she stepped close to him, wrapping her arms around his torso. At first, he thought she was going to kiss him—for only a brief second, that is—but she nodded upward, toward the gaping hole in the ceiling where the aircraft had crashed through. Her brow furrowed, steadfast as ever, and she spoke in a calm, hoarse tone. "Get us out of here."

Edwin had never been so daring with the void suit before; he hadn't had enough time to test its limits. *There's a first for everything.* Taking Sibyl's cue, Edwin put his arms around her, and—with his void suit glowing brightly—adapted his gravitational pull and began to fly.

|19|

DETACH

Edwin and Sibyl rocketed upward, free falling toward the sky—or where the sky would have been were there not a domed ceiling ahead with a gaping hole in it (that gaping hole being their only way out). The void suit must have harnessed gravity akin to the drone that had once hauled Edwin from Buena Vista Park to the portal above San Francisco. How Edwin's void suit now pulled them upward felt nearly identical to how it had felt when he was first being abducted—only this time, he now had complete control over himself, able to adjust the angle of his "fall" at will, as well as his velocity. He wasn't scared this time, either. Not with Sibyl by his side. He felt like a superhero in one of the many comics he would read back on Earth—just like his Superman toy when he was a kid, soaring against the sky and defying all sense of gravity.

Ascending toward the hole in the ceiling where the aircraft had crashed through, Edwin reduced their speed and maneuvered through the gap with ease. The void suit operated as if by instinct—on a subconscious level, perhaps—and, after having used it in space and submerged in water, Edwin reckoned he was finally getting the hang of it.

Passing the gap in the ceiling, he saw multiple levels continuing upward (his vision enhanced by the suit's visor), all with their own gaps, cut in a diagonal line (created by the aircraft and its pursuers, no doubt). What he also saw were multiple gunfights on every level. Reapers fighting against other reapers, sometimes with robots thrown in the mix and the occasional bounty ("elseworld" versions of Edwin, and mere genetic counterparts on other worlds that had evolved similarly to his). Unfortunately, many of the bounties he saw were already dead; three of them, in fact, were being clustered together and dragged by a tractor-like machine as if they were only cargo, not human beings. Edwin wanted to save them (at least those still alive), but he couldn't dwell on that now and instead had to focus all his attention on the gaps in the ceilings, following them as he would any obstacle course, intent only on getting him and Sibyl out of there.

Ahead, he could see a piercing light coming through the topmost gap. Almost blinding. *A way out*, he thought, with his hold tightening around Sibyl as they shot through the highest gap before emerging onto the other side.

• • •

They weren't out of the fire yet. Quite the opposite, actually.

As Edwin and Sibyl emerged from the last gap, they entered hell itself. The surrounding area—the surface of Orion—was no longer recognizable. The land surrounding them had been bulldozed by a large airship—*many* large airships, in fact—now scattered about the smoldering plains amidst a war zone with no distinguishable army. A free-for-all of mercenaries, vying for the prizes that awaited them below—a battle royale, with pockets of guerrilla units fighting on the ground level, in the sky, and below, seen through gaps in the ground like the one they had just emerged from.

Any hope remaining for the unlucky bounties seeking refuge in an augmentation was now gone. There was no escape from their hunters' pursuit, even if they no longer had their DNA traced. Escape was not an option.

For many, there was only one option: *Death.*

Death was everywhere. You could smell it in the air, oppressive and unrelenting. Violence and aggression at a mass level. Like a cry for attention—a lamentation for life itself—and no matter where the eye turned, you couldn't escape it.

Like the skies of Zarathustra during Edwin's reaping day: Only now, this is what it must have looked like an hour later, after Edwin had escaped into the canyons. A clash of gods, warring for the futility of money, status, and fame. Decimation: Flames all around, spreading like blood in water. Screams of terror, pain, and ecstasy. Bodies lying atop one another—more and more of them being added to the pile, never seeming to end. Numerous ships must have hovered in the sky, with more and more of them arriving as the seconds passed; but because of the heavy smoke covering the sky, you couldn't see much of them at all, and ashes rained from above like heavy sheets of snow. All the while, the sun remained nowhere to be found. Specks of light could be seen in the far-off distance—trees lit aflame: a bonfire Orion hadn't seen the likes of for hundreds to thousands of years. Carnage raged drunkenly, let loose.

Where paradise had once been, there was only despair.

Edwin landed gracefully on the scorched earth where an ancient redwood had once stood. He glanced at Sibyl as his visor retracted into the rest of his suit. His expression was grim, *hopeless*. Behind him, a long bullet-train lay on its side, jutting out of the ground, entangled among other vehicles that had crashed onto the battlefield—and *continued* to crash onto the battlefield—while all around them, the battle raged with no end in sight.

Sibyl scanned for the mountain where she had last left her freighter, but amidst all the chaos, it was impossible to distinguish much of anything around them. "The *land*," Sibyl choked out, as if mourning a beloved friend; Edwin hadn't heard sorrow like that before, not even at Lamar's funeral. "What have they done to it. . . . ?"

There was no sign of living flora anywhere around them—only death.

A large piece of shrapnel came flying from above, and Edwin dove out of the way—or rather, his void suit *pushed* him out of the way—as it crashed into where he had been standing. Sibyl staggered back as three reapers approached from above (the opposite side of where the shrapnel came from), climbing down a manmade mound of bodies, vehicles, and chunks of shattered redwood. A reaper noticed Edwin and pointed at him with his assault rifle, but Sibyl reacted first, pulverizing him with her pulse rifle, followed by the two others.

As soon as the three reapers were dealt with, more took their place—and even more of them right after, followed by more and *more* of them, seemingly unending—with Sibyl having to fend them off, one after another, protecting Edwin at all costs. "Cover your face," she demanded, overwhelmed by the onslaught of mercenaries closing in on them, targeting the nearest bounty in sight. But more than feeling overwhelmed, she was pissed off, and there was no better outlet to take out that anger than on the fuckers who had caused all this devastation.

Again, Edwin's visor covered his face, and he tried with all his effort to help Sibyl fend off the closest hostiles using the only handgun she had given him. He had never used a gun before, nor had he ever killed anyone (just why would he?), and after his first successful shot, hitting the nearest reaper right in the head, he had to close his mind to the following guilt, deciding instead to focus solely on his and Sibyl's survival.

Just like a video game, he thought, turning again to cover their backside. *Don't think, just do.*

With both hands on the gun's grip and using the aid of the void suit's vision enhancer, Edwin's aim was miraculously accurate. He and Sibyl made a good team, actually, fighting back-to-back—a dynamic duo.

A shame it wouldn't last; nothing in life ever does.

An explosion discharged nearby, and the ground crumbled beneath them. Debris and lumber tumbled down, crushing those nearest them. The ground continued to tilt, and the lower parts fell into the chasm below. Edwin struggled to climb the wreckage, and his void suit suddenly compensated for him, letting him run up it with ease. Sibyl, wearing no void suit, was not so lucky, and instead she continued sliding down the ever-sloping ground, which began to slant vertically, all the while dodging falling debris that would kill her on impact.

Edwin turned around and noticed Sibyl struggling below. He pulled out his grapple gun with haste, and—once again, with the aid of his visor (enhancing his vision to near perfection)—he fired the grapple gun at the spot next to Sibyl and made contact with a motorbike behind her. The gun's rope then retracted, pulling the motorbike back toward him, and Sibyl quickly grabbed onto a handlebar before it was too late, ascending along with it. Ascending *fast*, Edwin realized—almost too fast—as he clumsily tossed the grapple gun away from him, and the motorbike shot out of the pit, following the grapple gun with a deadly speed that would have, once again, killed anyone on impact.

Sibyl jumped off the bike midair and landed on the ground, hard on her side, knocking the breath out of her. She rapidly recovered, and another explosion rang nearby, sending her right back to the ground as chunks of metal came crashing down around them like a violent hailstorm.

Edwin saw no end in sight. No means of escape whatsoever. *We're trapped*, he thought, helpless. *This is it, isn't it? All that I've gone through, and for what? Every hour spent on my art, and every second I wasted believing I was never good enough for anything better than what I was given—all my life, gone in the blink of a second.* There was an injustice to that, the disheartening notion of all that he had been through being for nothing, and a rebellious anger rose out of it, rageful.

This can't *be the end. There's so much yet to do, and so much still to accomplish.*

He stumbled to his knees and glanced at Sibyl, still on the ground with her arms covering her head, avoiding the raining debris. *I can't watch her die—I* won't *watch her die.*

He clenched his hand into a fist. *This can't be the end.* Not yet.

Not after everything I've gone through to get here.

On either side of them, reapers shot at one another, and successive explosions went off, adding to the chaos surrounding them—a never-ending onslaught. However, a bright light could be seen in the distance—*brighter* than all the others, and it was coming toward them. Something in Edwin, that part of him refusing to die, knew there was still hope. A feeling within, louder than all his doubt, beckoning him to never give up, never surrender.

Your life is just a story, he told himself again. *A story that's yours to tell, and no one else's.*

He had always loved stories, hadn't he? They kept him going, even when all hope seemed lost. Because no matter how dark things got, or how bleak it may have seemed, there was always hope waiting just around the corner.

(—*TAKE OFF YOUR MASK*—)

Another voice spoke from within, and he wasn't sure if it was even his own.

(—*SHOW YOUR FACE TO THE WORLD AND REMIND THEM WHO YOU ARE*—)

A strange feeling of contentment overpowered him; it was out of place, undoubtedly, but it was overwhelming, and he could feel nothing but it. *Relief*, perhaps, and the assurance that everything was going to work out in the end. How did he know this? Why did he feel it so strongly? He wasn't sure, but he acted on it. Perhaps in an act of insanity—an insanity perhaps brought on by an existential dread taking over—he stood tall and proud, no longer worried about the gunfire coming from either side of him, and—once more—his helmet and visor retracted.

Once again, he refused to let fear conquer him. *If I die, let me die* my *way.*

The light came closer now, and he could hear *music* emitting from it. A heavy metal guitar—plucking, rhythmic, and gaining speed, faster and faster—and before he knew it, the source of the light—*and* the sound, both coming from the same source—descended upon them, smashing into an armed reaper making a run for Edwin.

The light stopped next to Edwin, and Edwin saw it was actually some kind of four-by-four vehicle (except where the wheels would have been were four large blocks of metal, somehow keeping the vehicle afloat three feet above the ground). Sitting behind the wheel was the bear-who-was-not-a-bear, Brutus Wainesworth, from D-D's facility. Moreover, standing atop the open tonneau was D-D herself, dressed in a loose nightgown, slippers, and a thick headset, manning a heavy machine gun turret, focused on the ring of reapers surrounding Edwin and Sibyl and blasting them all to kingdom come. Even stranger, the sound of the heavy guitar was resonating from the turret itself and not from any external speaker.

As Brutus changed gears, he noticed Edwin and Sibyl standing right outside the vehicle. "Holy *shit*," the Liberian exclaimed, snorting loudly with a disbelieving look. "*Someone's* lucky!"

"Lucky" was the understatement of the century; had Edwin not removed his visor and revealed himself as a bounty, he and Sibyl would already be dead.

Brutus waved an impatient arm out the window. "Hop in!"

Sibyl pushed Edwin from behind, rushing him to get inside the vehicle, so that they could get the hell out of there. As Edwin climbed onto the open tonneau, he saw another look-a-like bounty sitting on the edge of the cab with his arms around his knees and terrified for his life. Yet another look-a-like bounty sat within the cab, on the passenger's seat, and fired a laser pistol out the open window, hitting whatever reaper was in sight (granted if D-D hadn't already obliterated them with the turret, obviously packing a heavy punch).

As soon as Edwin and Sibyl were both in the tonneau, Brutus started driving again, and he took a sharp turn down a steep incline of whatever debris lay underneath. Edwin sat on the floor of the tonneau, next to the other bounty, and wondered how in the world he and Sibyl had gotten so lucky with Brutus finding them amidst all the chaos. The right place at the right time: *It's just chance*, Edwin thought doubtfully.

But he didn't really believe that, did he?

It couldn't just be a coincidence.

Sibyl sat across from Edwin, and the vehicle rocketed forward again, bumping them up, down, and all around, as they held on for dear life. D-D continued firing with the turret and looked rather comical behind it, with her old, frail body and an intensity that knew no bounds.

The bounty beside Edwin glanced up at him, and Edwin noticed his eyes were now gone, their empty sockets scorched black. *He's blind*, Edwin realized, amazed. *He's survived everything I have and yet hasn't been able to see a thing.* Something about that was rousing, somehow. Encouraging, despite all the odds stacked against him. *No matter how bad it is, it can always be worse.*

The four-by-four vehicle jerked violently as it drove above the fallen train and used the tail-end of it as a ramp to jump over a crashed fighter jet. Once the vehicle rebounded back onto the ground (yet not directly onto it), Brutus continued dodging large debris in the way and swerved around yet another crashed ship. As they barreled forward, they quickly exited the bulldozed clearing and entered the ancient forest, now set aflame.

Flames rose along the massive trunks of sequoia, captivating yet grotesque. The heat was so intense that even with the void suit on Edwin, sweat precipitated on his face, dripping down his forehead and nose. He wiped the sweat off his brow, preventing it from getting into his eyes.

The density of smoke grew thicker, limiting visibility within twenty feet, and yet despite that, all around them, they continued passing countless men and women futilely fighting one another. Edwin glimpsed a reaper in a thick hazmat suit using a flamethrower over a fallen body, and beside that reaper, even more bounties being hauled away on the ground, already dead. Such horrors, and all for what—? Perhaps it was a blessing the bounty beside him couldn't see a thing. The images he had seen the past hour would remain with him for the rest of his life, to haunt him day and night; that is, *if* he made it out alive, assuming that he even would make it out alive.

Nothing could ever be certain—not anymore.

"You alright?"

Edwin turned to Sibyl, sitting across from him. Her eyes were fixed on his. He tried to smile, to encourage her somehow—to be a light in the darkness, a flame implementing shelter and warmth—but even without words, he had never been good at lying, had never liked dishonesty, and found that he couldn't will his lips to move at all. So, instead of smiling, he merely nodded. Nodding was all he could do at that moment—the only way he could communicate outside of drawing.

He looked at the floorboard and imagined a pen in his hand and an empty canvas before him. He wished to draw something right now, to close his mind off from all the surrounding chaos. *I don't belong here. . . .*

He glanced at Sibyl again, her eyes still on him. None *of us belong here.*

He wished it could just end—all of it. He had always wanted an adventure, but not this. *Never this.*

Stay strong, he told himself, trying to be the voice of reason, the voice he needed so desperately to hear. *Don't lose yourself to the indifference of the world; instead, be the difference. Be the light at the end of the tunnel—the voice beckoning onward, even when all hope seems lost.* He took in a deep breath, exhaled slowly, and tried to slow his beating heart. *There's always hope, Ed. Always that light, leading to brighter days.*

Be *that light.*

And with his eyes locked on Sibyl's again, he somehow managed to smile.

• • •

Behind them, another vehicle now followed in pursuit, homing in on the three bounties within—apparently worth more than life or death. "It never ends," Brutus Wainesworth muttered, noticing his pursuers in the rearview monitors. "You see them?" he asked D-D, wired through her headset to hear all that transpired within the vehicle (and vice versa).

"I see them," D-D confirmed, turning the turret onto the vehicle in pursuit and blasting them all to hell. "Sons of bitches."

Brutus watched as their pursuers quickly combusted, flipping over thrice. Regardless, they were still being pursued. Three aircraft flew low, right behind them, with an airship right above them. But before Brutus could warn D-D about the last one, their vehicle shook violently, and the wheel he maneuvered with rapidly spun out of control, almost breaking his hands.

Magnetic hooks, Brutus reckoned. He glanced out the window and noticed their vehicle now ascending, taken by the large airship above them. He growled, frustrated beyond belief. *I don't get paid enough for this.*

• • •

The airship above them latched onto their vehicle from a magnetic peg attached to the bottom, and below them, the ground continued to get further and further away (to where, if you fell out of the vehicle, you would die on impact).

D-D, manning the turret, had been focusing on the other airship that she hadn't even noticed the one gliding right above them—not until it was too late. But given their current situation, if she tried shooting at them now, she would risk killing them all. Once again, she was helpless to do a thing. First, they had taken her home, and now they were going to take her life? "*Bastards*!" she shouted, taking off her headset and slamming it on the floor of the tonneau. "Sons of *bitches*."

All hope wasn't lost—it couldn't be. Not yet.

There's always a way, Sibyl thought as she glanced at Edwin across from her. *Sometimes, you just have to make it yourself.* And at that moment, she knew what needed to be done. "Hand me your void belt."

Edwin glanced back at Sibyl. It took him a few seconds to register her request, but as soon as he caught on, he nodded, fidgeted with the belt at his waist, and watched as the void suit retracted from his body until he was only wearing his gray long-sleeve from before (with black cargo pants and boots). He handed Sibyl the void belt, unsure of what she was about to do with it.

Sibyl stood up, attached the void belt to her waist, and watched as the nanometal spread across her body, covering all but her neck up. Exchanging another look with Edwin, their eyes locked together, and this time, she smiled. She spoke to him steadily, knowing these might as well have been her last words to him. "Don't be afraid," she said. "Remember, you're far more capable than you give yourself credit. No matter what happens, never lose that spark within."

Sibyl didn't wait for Edwin's response—no, that wasn't her style. With the pulse rifle still in her hand, she glanced up at the bottom of the airship, right above them, and quickly sprang upward, not even having to jump off the ground as she adjusted her gravity, flipping over, so that she landed on the airship's bottom surface, upside-down to all in the tonneau. Edwin watched in silence as Sibyl ran ahead, gripping the pulse rifle with both hands, nearing toward the edge of the airship.

This time, she jumped off its edge, descended upward until the top of the airship was below her, and then she adjusted her gravity again, rocketing onto the top of the airship and landing on both feet.

The surface of the airship was quite reminiscent of the top deck of a Zavarian battleship, and Sibyl immediately noticed five reapers standing there, each armed. Her void helmet spread across her face, and she swiftly opened fire. Just as quickly, she ran for cover, sliding behind a lookout post.

She had gotten many of them, but there were more of them coming now, emerging from the lower deck. All armed and extremely pissed off (with her having killed many of their associates). Not as pissed off as Sibyl, though. She didn't care about their feelings. Did they care about the ecosystem they had decimated? Had they *ever* cared about anything outside of themselves? Besides, she had a mission, a purpose greater than any of theirs. And while waiting behind the line of fire, she thought about Te Kore and how lucky she was to experience all that she had in life, despite everything she had been through in order to experience it. Life is beautiful, is it not? Even amidst the flames and ruin, she could see its beauty standing out, greater than all the loss and devastation.

Outside the ship, Sibyl began to notice the untouched trees again, bountiful and thriving as the spreading flames lessened the further the ship got from the fires—and the further it got from all the people who had caused them.

There's still hope, Sibyl told herself. *There* has *to be*. She inched her way to the other side of the command post. *I'm not only doing this for myself anymore.* She steadied her pulse rifle, took in a deep breath, and sprang out of hiding.

• • •

The vehicle jerked forward, and Edwin realized they were now descending. *Sibyl did it*, he thought, looking up at the large airship above them. *Somehow, she managed to hijack it.* Even so, his worries for her increased. Worried more for her than he was for himself.

But there were still other reapers on their tail, and too many for D-D to take down all at once. "*Sons of bitches*," D-D uttered again in a mad rage. "Bastards won't stop coming."

As their vehicle edged closer to the ground, the magnetic peg detached from the airship above, and the vehicle slammed onto the ground, rocking everyone within as it barreled forward again at full speed.

Edwin kept his eyes on the airship above them, ascending once more. The airship slowed down and tilted its body right-side up so that its long frame covered their backside, blocking out most of the aircraft behind them. Subsequently, Edwin had an epiphany, and his heart dropped: *Sibyl's buying us time.*

He didn't want to believe it.

He should have known her intentions by the grave finality as she gazed at him for the last time. *She's going to—*

A colossal explosion erupted from above, hitting the mainframe of the airship Sibyl was piloting, shot from an aircraft behind it. In horror, Edwin watched as the vehicle he was in continued getting further away, and the airship Sibyl was piloting continued tilting ever downward, blocking the path of even more of the ships behind it, as it quickly descended, plunging toward the ground, with a huge wad of smoke following its descent. Edwin couldn't take his eyes off the ship as it crashed through the trees, sending other ships down with it.

Explosions flashed in the night like neon paint thrown on a canvas.

Throughout it all, he saw no sign of his dear friend.

He slumped back onto the cab of the tonneau and felt nothing but an emptiness, despite their narrow escape. A great sense of loss, leaving another void that could never be filled again. The image of the airship crashing transformed into a bright explosion, a growing fire consuming all that surrounded it. And his mind could only go to one thing: "Sibyl. . . ."

|20|

EXODUS WOUNDS

Nothing instills character more than hardship; in particular, how you deal with that hardship. Like a piece of fine art being worked on, night and day, your actions decide how the course of your life shapes out. It's evolution at play: To evolve is the nature of the universe, the nature of *all* life—a quantum entanglement on a cosmological scale, connecting everything, everywhere, all at once. Nothing can stop this evolution—this *change*, within and without—nor can anything be brought back to a state of how it once was. Change is the only constant in life, and it's futile to swim against its tide. The best thing to do is ride its waves. (Sometimes, the only thing you can do is ride its waves.)

Edwin sat in silence.

He wasn't sure how long they had been in motion, and yet he just . . . didn't really care. Sibyl was gone, and they had left her. A part of him couldn't believe that. Perhaps he didn't want to. Had she been on the ship as it crashed? Did she feel the heat of the flames as it burned her alive, or had the impact of the crash already kill her by then? He had seen the fire that followed the crash; he saw the ship's pieces jettison out of the explosion, dispersing like atomic reactions across the forest, decimating all that it came in contact with—ancient trees toppled down, and the fires spread like flame throwers, scorching every flora in their path. Even if Sibyl had managed to get out of the ship before its crash, the trees that fell around it would have killed her on impact. No matter what way he saw it, the outcome couldn't have been less than fatal. Perhaps worst of all came the guilt left behind. As if he were the one solely responsible, just as he had once felt with Lamar.

Perhaps a part of him took grief personally, like it was out to get him.

He glanced down at his hands, bruised and blistered. *It's not fair*, he thought indignantly, unable to make sense of it. *She deserved better. . . .* He enclosed a fist and fought the urge to scream and punch the floor of the tonneau, using all his strength, until his knuckles bled, his skin fell off, and he couldn't lift his hand anymore. Hell, he hadn't felt this much grief since Benjamin Kemp's passing, merely three months after the passing of Martha Kemp, his wife of over forty years.

It feels like I knew her longer than I did. . . .

Now, in hindsight, he realized just how fortunate Mr. Kemp was to have had the time he had with the ones he loved.

The moment I love someone, they're taken from me.

And just *had* he loved Sibyl? The same way that Mr. Kemp loved Mrs. Kemp? He shook his head, knowing that was a relative question. No use asking arbitrary questions like that. *Love isn't a feeling, it's an action.* And nothing could convince him it hadn't been love that drove Sibyl to sacrifice herself for him, knowing that it was the only way he and the others could escape. *If that isn't love, I don't know what love is.*

Edwin jerked to the side as the vehicle abruptly slowed down. "We're almost out of juice," he heard the Liberian, Brutus, say from within the driver's seat. The black bear-who-was-not-a-bear—just as humans are not chimpanzees but more like distant cousins—glanced to the back of the tonneau where D-D leaned on the turret with a somber expression on her face. "Almost there, Deidre. Might have to walk the rest of the way, though."

D-D nodded, her brows furrowing. "Of course." Looking down at her feet, she took in a long, heavy breath before glancing at Edwin, their eyes locking together. She exhaled slowly, almost breaking down in the process, and looked at her feet again—an expression of defeat on her face, uncharacteristic of such a woman. Fixing the scarf on her neck, she closed her eyes and took in another breath, this time more restrained. And her body relaxed, her demeanor more resolved.

Edwin glanced at the other bounty sitting in the tonneau a few feet away from him, nearly the same age. The two had their distinctions from one another, of course. Whereas the other bounty had cornrows, Edwin's hair was cut much shorter (or *had* been cut much shorter, having already grown much since leaving Earth, considering all the time that had passed since the last time he was afforded a haircut). The other bounty was skinnier than Edwin, as well. A different diet, a different lifestyle—ultimately, a different person. Oh, and the fact he was also blind (a recent development, no less)—big difference there.

Brutus slowed the vehicle even more now, rocking the passengers within as they came to an abrupt stop above a surface of soft ground, the cap of a large fungus. "Alright." He exhaled deeply. With an arm out the open window, he tapped the top of the vehicle and then opened the door, getting out. The bounty in the passenger seat followed Brutus's lead, but those in the tonneau—Edwin, D-D, and the blind bounty—hesitated, still reeling, as if the events of the day hadn't caught up to them just yet.

Taking the lead, Edwin climbed over the tonneau and landed on supple ground. He glanced around, again relieved to see that they were out of the fire—quite literally—and that the surrounding woods were undisturbed once more.

The light of the sun shone through the tall canopy and glistened off the diverse fungi growing all around them, above and below—spurting from the ground and trees, their colossal gills like living pages in a book. It felt surreal to be surrounded by nature again, away from those who wanted him dead.

Still, the emptiness lingered.

Despite the beauty all around him, Edwin could almost see none of it. His heart ached, and that old, familiar, worn-out feeling returned to him, unbecoming: *"You weren't good enough,"* it told him. As if he could have changed what had happened. As if he was solely to blame for all that transpired.

No, he thought, ignoring that unconstructive critic. *I won't entertain such lies: It's high time you change the narrative in your mind. It's the fifth-beings who are responsible—it's* them *you should be pointing fingers at.*

D-D climbed out of the tonneau. "Here, honey," she said, trying to help the blind bounty climb over the railing. "Give me your hand."

Seeing D-D's example, Edwin felt spurred to action and came to help them. "I've got him," he told her, and he helped the bounty over the railing after taking his hand. Once again, looking at those recently charred eyes, he figured the poor guy must have been in a lot of pain. "Are you alright?"

Startlingly, the bounty replied in a language that Edwin couldn't understand (and what was even stranger—stranger, even, than seeing himself—was seeing himself speak another language). *Of course*, Edwin remembered. *He doesn't speak English, and just why would he? He's from another world, a different universe altogether. One that evolved like mine—at least, enough for him to come into existence, having the same ancestors as I do—but, somehow, different all the same. Like me, he must not have an empathic emulator, either.*

Perhaps unnecessarily, D-D bluntly added: "He can't understand you." (Telling them both, perhaps.) She turned to Brutus, holding the metal spear he had pulled out of the cab— his face was almost human despite the obvious bear-like qualities. "How far are we?"

Brutus frowned, and Edwin finally noticed the three diagonal scars along his face, where no fur grew at all. "A mile or two, it's hard to say."

D-D nodded. "Good." She also frowned. "My feet are sore."

The other bounty, who had ridden passenger, approached D-D and Brutus. He spoke, but as with the other bounty, Edwin couldn't understand any of it; only the augmenter and her assistant seemed to understand what he was saying. Edwin glanced closely at his counterpart, still not used to seeing an older version of himself, let alone with a goatee and freeform dreads. *I guess I look good with facial hair*, Edwin thought, absentmindedly touching his cheek. *I like his style,* he further remarked, admiring the purple jacket he wore that somewhat reminded him of Lamar's letterman from its collar and shape. Thinking about it, he realized that all his stuff from Earth was still in the Vagabond; he supposed that along with Sibyl, he would never see that jacket again—another loss.

Whatever the bounty—Hendrix, as Edwin would later learn his name was—seemed to be saying, Brutus didn't seem to like any of it. The Liberian shook his head, grimacing. "For all I know, it could have been you who led them to us." Brutus continued eyeing Hendrix distrustfully. "You were one of the last bounties to arrive."

Hendrix chuckled, folding his arms. He spoke again, his voice smooth and calm, with his expression clearly untroubled by Brutus's remark. D-D walked to the driver's side of the cab and quickly returned, holding a gun in each hand. She handed a gun to Hendrix, giving him the butt-end of it. "Come now," she said, giving Brutus a stern look. "No use pointing fingers." She huffed, shaking her head. "We're all in this together." She glanced at Edwin, and her eyes went down to the handgun holstered in his jacket (the same handgun Sibyl had given him during their escape from the facility), and she nodded, content. "Let's get a move on—we're wasting time."

The more sides Edwin saw of D-D, the more he admired her. She may have looked like a frail, old, helpless woman, but if the past few hours had shown him anything, it was that looks could be deceiving; all the more reason to never trust solely what your eyes tell you.

Brutus pulled out a small device from within a holster beneath his green serape. The device looked much like the pathfinder Sibyl had used while trekking through Orion with Edwin in search of D-D's augmentation facility. "Alright then," Brutus grunted, taking the lead and setting a course. "'No time to waste,' as D-D likes to say."

Brutus started off, and Hendrix followed beside him. D-D approached the injured bounty and put her arm through his, helping him traverse. "Follow me, sweetheart," she told him warmly. "And watch your step." Then, noticing Edwin trailing behind them (making sure they were safe, of course), she smiled at him, and he smiled back.

Their traversal led them down a slight incline, and the surrounding fungi only seemed to intensify, as if they were entering an entire mushroom forest, blocking out any sign of the conifers' towering canopy above. Edwin began noticing spider webs the size of telephone wires spun about in wonderful—and yet equally terrifying—patterns, making him even more conscious of the handgun in his holster. Brutus and Hendrix spoke in hushed tones, and D-D continued to assist the bounty in her keeping, giving him instructions now and then on where to step. Edwin followed behind in silence, listening to the quiet wind, serendipitous and untroubled, like the calm before an autumn storm.

And for a while, it remained thus.

At last, the ground leveled out again, and Brutus turned back, glancing at D-D. "We're almost there," he told her once more, this time more confident than the last.

"You told us that an hour ago," D-D mused, shaking her head playfully. "You Liberians and your guesstimations."

Brutus grumbled something inaudible, and D-D chuckled softly. She glanced back at Edwin again, making sure that he was still behind them.

"How is he?" Edwin asked with concern, nodding to the bounty, whom D-D was helping.

D-D raised an eyebrow. "Poor Malcolm here?" A fiendish smile followed. "Drugged out of his mind, I tell you—a good thing, too." She snapped her fingers with an exaggerated expression that looked almost comical. "Oh, but if only I had loaded more of the fentanyl into the cruiser." Chuckling to herself, she added: "A girl can only dream."

"There she is," Brutus exclaimed, pointing his spear at a wooden cabin just ahead, sitting at the base of a massive chanterelle. The cabin had taken root, like a tree spurting out of the ground. "What did I tell you? Still doubting me?"

D-D ignored Brutus's last remark. "I could do with a warm cup of tea."

As they closed in on the cabin, Edwin saw it was much larger than he had originally assumed. It must have been three stories tall; presumably more were it also an underground system as D-D's augmentation facility had been. Edwin wondered what had been built first: the cabin or the augmentation facility. It looked cozy, that much he knew, and he could do with somewhere nice to get his bearings. The universe knew he needed it. . . .

A brick pathway led them to the entrance where two large wooden doors loomed, at least seven feet tall. The doors swung open as they approached, and the lights within came to life, revealing a hallway emitting a warm, inviting glow from lanterns overhead. Once they were all inside, with Brutus in the lead and Edwin in the rear, the doors swung shut behind them, as silent and effortless as they had while opening.

A door on their left opened, and Brutus entered it, with the others following behind him. They entered a large kitchen with metamorphic countertops and steel vents overhead, adjoined with a dining room and common room, furnished with three couches, a coffee table, and a large projector. Intricate, hand-sewn tapestries, colorful and almost tribalistic, hung from the walls. As with the many other times before, Edwin remarked just how much it felt like being back on Earth, and not only Earth, but America, almost reminiscent of the time he had left—or, at least, *around* the time he had left. Of course, the kitchen looked far more advanced than anything he had ever seen on Earth, and there were many items lying around that he had no idea what their function was. Still, there was a part of "home" that followed him wherever he went.

I guess, at the end of the day, no matter where you are, we're all the same in many ways.

D-D immediately led Malcom past the kitchen and dining room, helping ease him onto a sofa. "You're safe here," she told him, patting his hand gently. "Rest, now. I'll get you something more to ease the pain." She ambled away, entering another hallway adjoined to the common room and vanished out of sight.

Brutus, Edwin, and Hendrix remained in the kitchen, glancing from one to another in silence. Brutus and Hendrix locked eyes longer than they had with Edwin, and Hendrix chuckled to himself, shaking his head with a smile, before also walking away. Edwin and Brutus exchanged a look once more. This time, Edwin saw the weariness on Brutus's face, and *especially* in his eyes—*that look so human*, Edwin remarked—before Brutus, too, departed, grunting to himself something inaudible but clearly gloom.

For a moment or two, Edwin just stood there, unsure of what to do. He glanced behind himself, at the door they had entered through, half-expecting Sibyl to enter at any second. *Wanting* Sibyl to enter at any second. But, as expected, no one came through that door. *It's just me now*, he thought and took a deep breath. He turned to the common room again and saw one of his many look-a-likes, Malcolm, sitting on the couch, with his back toward Edwin and his face in his hands.

Just me and all the others. . . .

Edwin ambled toward the common room and glanced around his surroundings, as Hendrix had. He saw a small malachite statue on a shelf that reminded him of a Buddha statue (that is, of course, if Buddha had been some kind of alpaca instead of ape). He looked away from the decor, again glancing at Malcolm, sitting on the couch with his head practically on his lap now.

But then he noticed a figure looming over Malcolm.

At first, he assumed the person was D-D, bringing Malcolm some more drugs to ease the pain, but given how tall the figure was—and masculine—his mind went to Hendrix, though that, too, was wrong; the figure was neither D-D, Hendrix, nor Brutus. On a closer examination, the figure wasn't even a biological being at all: It was composed entirely of carbon and metal, just like the robot he had seen at D-D's augmentation facility. Must have been some kind of helper. A service bot, perhaps.

He took a step closer, and the robot turned to look at him. He thought of Jermaine then, and he wondered how similar they must be, despite their divergent programming. Even if the robot wasn't a biological being, it was still another life form, just like Jermaine was. *"They," not "it,"* Edwin corrected himself, as he had, at first, with Jermaine; he had learned recently, by listening to Sibyl speak about plants, animals, and even artificial intelligence, that the English language certainly had a way of objectifying other life forms that weren't human, by categorizing them as "it" rather than "they." He wanted to be a friend to all, not only those like him. And being a friend meant treating others with the respect he would also want to be given.

Edwin nodded to the robot, looming over Malcolm and staring at him with a blank look. "Hi, there."

But the robot remained still. The pale blue lights behind their metal eyes bore into Edwin's, and they remained inexpressive, as if there was nothing operating them—nothing behind the driver's seat. No biggie: Most artificial intelligence, as Edwin had learned from his many conversations with Jermaine, didn't care that much for the material world whatsoever. When they practically had all the freedom in the digital world to do whatever the hell they wanted, why waste their time and energy in the material one? For most of them, they only operated in the material world because of their programming, whether that was for utilitarian or personal reasons. Edwin supposed—perhaps naively—that this robot was only following their programming, to help Malcolm.

Edwin stepped even closer now, and his eyes trailed down to the robot's hands. He noticed then what he had first overlooked and saw that they were dripping blood, right onto the ground, where a thick puddle pooled below the couch. (Of course, he was right about the robot following their programming, but not a programming directed by D-D, and certainly not one to help.) Instinctually, he took an even longer step backward, and his eyes widened in horror, as he realized—all too late—that the blood was coming from Malcolm's immobile body.

Oh, fuck. . . .

The robot didn't waste a second and made a beeline for Edwin—every stride eerily silent. Edwin stumbled backward, almost tripping over himself, and before he could even scream, the robot lunged forward, grabbed him by his right arm (his dominant arm), and—

SNAP!

A shrill scream escaped Edwin's lips as the robot snapped his arm in half. The white bone jutted out of his forearm, followed by a pain unimaginable—a pain worse than anything he had ever felt before (even worse than getting his two front teeth knocked out as a child). Falling to his knees, he clutched at his displaced arm in agony, as he tried desperately to crawl away, but couldn't, with his arm locked in the robot's grip.

The robot lifted its other hand above its head and enclosed it into a fist.

Screaming even louder now, Edwin pulled back his arm more violently than before, using all his strength, and supporting his feet on the robot's legs, to pull away from the grip, until he felt his skin tear away like melted cheese—the flesh ripped off completely—and he finally stumbled out of the robot's grasp.

The robot continued standing there, motionless, holding the rest of Edwin's right arm—his dominant arm (the one that he always drew with)—torn completely from the ligaments. As soon as the arm hit the floor, the robot pressed forward again, and in no rush as before, following the blood trail leading to Edwin crawling away backward—just not fast enough.

All too soon, Edwin felt his back press against a cabinet. There was nothing else he could do. Nowhere else to go. Had he any energy left, he would have screamed, but what good would that do now . . . ? The fight was over before it had even begun.

No use delaying the inevitable.

He closed his eyes, braced for his demise, and—

A loud blast resonated from across the room, and what came next was the sound of metal crashing against wood and glass, and a whole shelf collapsing right atop it. Edwin pathetically opened an eye and fought to remain conscious as he saw Brutus standing in the hallway, clenching his staff with both hands, aimed at the robot lodged in the shattered cabinet. Brutus quickly noticed Edwin on the ground, and the line of his sight followed the severed arm by his feet. "You alright, kid?"

D-D resurfaced from the hallway, followed by Hendrix, but all their voices seemed to fade into one other, as the world swiftly lost its color, and all Edwin could hear anymore was his brother's voice—as clear as if it were his own: *"It'll be okay, Little Brother . . . It'll all be okay."*

|21|

THE GOOD MR. SQUARE

Edwin Dorset was a wanted man: A space nomad, infamous across many worlds.

Rarely now did he look back at how he got to where he was. Rarely did he look back to how his life was before being on the run. Looking back only brought him misery and a heavy sense of misplacement. His past was complicated, often misinterpreted by those who knew it, and few were ever given that privilege; that is, the few outside the fifth-beings, whose eyes were always on him (in fact, there was no escape from them, nor could there ever be). Hero, villain, it didn't matter what he had become—to the fifth-beings who constantly watched him, he was merely their entertainment; and with entertainment, it didn't matter who got hurt, just so long as it was entertaining. Besides, he couldn't go back to his old life, so why wallow in his losses?

All he could do was look ahead to the here and now.

With this new lifestyle, he had to be fully present, ready for anything at all times. Many he encountered only saw him as a quick way to get rich or famous. Most days, he had to remain incognito. Even with caution at his side, he felt eyes on him everywhere. With such a lifestyle, he could only allow few attachments, and even with those few attachments, there was still an underlying comprehension that it wouldn't last forever. *Couldn't* last forever. Not anyone, nor anything, can remain the same.

Everything is bound to change.

Inadvertently, Edwin's thoughts drifted to Sibyl. *Still looking to the past*, he thought introspectively. *No matter where I go, I can't escape it; the past always follows me—a ghost of my former self.*

He looked himself over in the mirror and could hardly recall the young man he had once been. Now bearded, he looked much older than he had before leaving San Francisco. His features had also hardened somewhat, and his face was even slimmer and more chiseled. His hair was longer, as well; he used to keep it short, often insecure about it (in the past whenever it had grown long and started froing out, his ex-girlfriend, Maggie, would constantly get on his case, either complaining about it or belittling him for it—two things she probably would have done regardless—and in many ways, he had blamed her for that insecurity of his, despite it stemming from himself). But now, he no longer cared about what others thought about him, and especially with something so superficial that had nothing to do with his character nor the actions he made in life (really, the only judgements that truly matter).

Throughout the years, the hair at his temples had grown white, sprinkled amidst the black—prematurely, and no doubt a causation of his circumstances. He may not have grown any taller since having left Earth, but his posture was far better than before—all thanks to D-D, or so she would tell him. His shoulders had perhaps even squared out more because of that, making him appear even older. And though he may not have exercised daily, he had a healthy, balanced diet, and his body certainly appeared as if he did. Currently shirtless, he could see the clear outline of a six-pack on his lean, muscled body—an accomplishment that he would have never thought possible back on Earth, let alone so effortlessly (once again, mostly gained from his diet). Of course, it certainly didn't hurt that he remained active, always eager for the next adventure.

Somewhere within his features, however, he could still see his brother; he supposed it was in his eyes where he saw Lamar the most.

He lifted his right hand and studied it closely. A sleek, burgundy coating covered the majority of black obsidian from his elbow down to his fingertips. Even after D-D had constructed the prosthetic, it took him a good year until he could adjust to it, given that it was his dominant hand; moreover, it had taken him even longer until he was able to draw with it just as he had before. But in time, he found himself able to adapt, and that with the right willpower he could do anything he set his mind on. In a way, losing his arm had been a blessing in disguise; from the ground up, he had to rebuild himself, having lost the one thing he had thought was keeping him alive for so long. Sibyl had been right: He was much stronger than he could have ever imagined. Still, he kept a spare arm or two, just in case he lost this one—you can never be too careful.

In the mirror's corner, Edwin noticed Zula stirring in her sleep beneath the woven blanket. It was the third day in a row that he had spent the night at her place. *So much for allowing few attachments. . . .*

When he had first met Zula Cormorant, something about her had struck a chord in him. As much as it pained him to admit it—and only to himself, that is—there was something about Zula that had immediately reminded Edwin of Sibyl. For starters, she had a strong resemblance to Sibyl, with wild, dark hair and dark, almond eyes, and an even similar athletic figure and caramel complexion to Sibyl. And—he also had to admit—he may have been initially attracted to her because of that; although, in all fairness, he would have been attracted to her either way. She was strong-willed, and there was a spellbinding aura about her. Disarming, cunning, and savvy, she constantly had something witty to say, and she never ceased to make him laugh or smile. And of course, he knew it wasn't fair to compare two different people—he didn't like being compared to others, so why should he do the same?

Long ago, he had made it a rule of thumb not to make any assumptions about others, nor allow himself to have any unrealistic expectations; he found life far better when he freed his mind from any misleading presumptions that could detract him from reality, biased as the mind could be. He tried treating others how he wanted to be treated—just as Benjamin Kemp had used to tell him: "Do unto others what you would want done unto you."

A self-made ecologist and avid conservationist, Zula had gone into the wastelands miles from the city to study the impact of Siletz IV's atmosphere and how the city's inhabitants were now affecting it, including the repercussions of their most recent terraforming. It was there, out in the wild, where she had first found Edwin—living out there alone, camped in his parked freighter. More specifically, she had found him squatting over a native poppy, flowering a remarkable sunset orange (a beautiful plantae, and an exceedingly rare bloom for such a rocky, harsh environment, mostly barren because of the extreme temperature drops at night), and his expression—an expression that Zula loved to recount, on more than one occasion—had been one of utter bliss.

That encounter had only been six months ago, and yet already Edwin found himself growing quite attached to Zula. He had only been on Siletz IV for two weeks before having met her, with the intention of only being there for a mere supply run—a quick rest stop—before heading out again, to find himself another planet or moon to explore, hoping to stay on the run and lessen the risk of being found out. But as with many other times in his life, his plans had changed (and subsequently, so had he).

As with most humanoids inhabiting Samsara, for Zula Cormorant, she had recognized Edwin's face immediately—that is, the face of a bounty. The tradition of the bounty touched upon every culture, perhaps even dating as far back as Epoch 1: the very beginning of mankind's scattering across the ever-expanding cosmos—a long, long time ago (and from where mankind originated, no one knew for certain, though most scientists, archeologists, and philosophers all agreed that they had emerged from Xibalba itself, the supermassive black hole orbiting Samsara's center: a holy site to many, also the location where all bounties were cashed in to the fifth-beings).

Zula could have easily ratted Edwin out for quick talents, and yet she hadn't; instead, she had visited him periodically, day after day, and watched him from afar, assessing to see what kind of character he possessed. And eventually, she decided to make contact with him. To her delight—as well as Edwin's—she had found a friend that she hadn't known to be missing in her life. Of course, one thing led to another, and things quickly got heated between the two (I mean, how could you blame them? They were two young, exceptional souls, bonded by a love of life and their mutual want to do good—nor did it hurt that they were equally attracted to each other). Ultimately, Zula convinced Edwin to stay on Siletz IV for the time being, and, by her presence alone, gave him an incentive.

Edwin tolerated Siletz IV, despite its constant rain and murkiness. A small moon along the Outermost Ring of Samsara, Siletz IV had been newly colonized (quite unfortunate, really, given mankind's negative impact over time on whatever environment they came in contact with). Among the wave of colonizer ships, Zula had accompanied the third and most recent installment, the Wayfarer. Mostly, however, a great majority of the moon was treacherous, uninhabitable, and—best of all—entirely secluded. Suffice it to say, it was a perfect place for a bounty to hide away.

Six months of living on Siletz IV, and at least five years since leaving Orion. *Time goes by so fast*, Edwin reflected, noticing the changes in his features. *Before I know it, there won't be any time left.*

The older he got, the quicker time slipped by him—a constant reminder that he could never have enough of it, nor could he ever be grateful enough with the time that he was given. All that came before now felt like a lifetime ago. Many lifetimes ago, in fact. From his abduction in San Francisco, to his time in the Vagabond, and his departure to Orion—and even after his departure from Orion, when he had briefly travelled with

Brutus and Hendrix, with the occasional check up on D-D (now living on Brecken, where he got free augmentations from time to time as a sign of good faith). His solo odyssey across the stars had also slipped by like a distant dream, and he couldn't help but wonder—as he often did—just how long it would be until his present memories also became a distant past themselves, faded through time like all the other memories that slipped by without an anchor to hold them in place.

When I'm nothing but decomposing atoms, what part of me will remain? What part of me will remember what came before?

"Eddie," Zula murmured from on the bed, propping herself up with an elbow. Her legs were sprawled out beneath the thin sheets, and her eyes—partially hidden beneath her tousled bedhead—were fixed on Edwin's. She wore nothing beneath the covers, and Edwin couldn't help but eye the parts of her that were exposed. Her body was covered in artful, lacy henna-like tattoos—from her hands to her arms, back, and all along her legs—with a script somewhat resembling Sanskrit running down her right ribcage. She also had many piercings—a septum ring, nostril stud, three rings on her upper helix, another on her higher lobe, another on her lower lobe, a midline on her tongue, and even straight barbells on each nipple. Moreover, her next few words made Edwin long to see even more of her. "Get over here."

So bossy, Edwin mused with a smile. He ambled his way from the mirror to the bed, while eyeing the poster of Zula's band, The Impermanent, as he passed by it, hanging alongside the lavender wall amidst other decorations. He had illustrated the banner himself and designed it to be reminiscent of a minimalistic film poster with striking hues of red, white, and black, depicting a bleeding heart at the center of a leafless tree—its roots running wild and free, taking over most of the design (aside from the title—for obvious reasons, purposefully left to standout)—intertwined with other imagery represented within the album, as if implying that all the imagery was interconnected through the bleeding heart.

When Zula had first discovered Edwin's talent, she immediately commissioned him to create original artwork for her. Ever the entrepreneur, Zula constantly searched for opportunities not only to promote her own work but also to promote other artists' work as well. In an age where artificial intelligence had taken over most of the art industry—literature, illustration, music, gaming, and even motion pictures (not excluding all the other art forms)—it was abundantly rare to find any new human-derived compositions anymore. Plus, it also helped that Zula was the frontman of The Impermanent and could use her platform to speak out about issues she cared deeply about. She was the band itself, really (not only the lead singer but also the pianist, guitarist, bassist, drummer, mixer, producer, and whatever other function she needed to be—one of the many perks of living in a digitally dominated world, where she could perform live through any virtual environment and play every instrument all at once, jacked into a neural network). To Edwin—and anyone who had an ear to hear—Zula's voice was like fine wine, except, unlike wine, there was never the risk of a hangover the next day.

Edwin climbed onto the bed, and Zula parted the covers for him, waiting for him to fully enter, before she crawled back into his arms and rest her head on his bare chest. He took in her fragrant scent: honeysuckle, sweet and inviting. *I could die like this*, he thought.

"You're so comfy," Zula muttered, her voice barely audible.

Edwin squeezed his arm around her, relishing the calming peace. Eventually, Zula propped herself up with an elbow again, so that she could face him. A strand of hair covered her tired, yet contented, face. Not always a morning person, as Edwin had quickly discovered, Zula had an air of lightness about her this particular morning. "Hey, nerd."

Edwin involuntarily smiled. "Good morning."

Zula smiled back. "Sleep any good?"

Edwin shrugged a shoulder. "Somewhat." These days, it was rare for him to have a full night's rest; the nightmares had a habit of waking him up in the middle of the night—it shouldn't have been the norm, but it was. "You?"

Zula nodded, pleased. "Better." She eyed him inquisitively. "They bothering you again?"

Edwin shook his head. "Not today." For now, any indicator of the fifth-beings' presence in his life felt like another distant memory. As of late, he was getting better at blocking them out, despite the occasional days when their continual presence became intolerable—when he could feel their eyes on him everywhere, no matter where he was or what he was doing. If there was any takeaway that he had cultivated from his twenty-eight years of living, it was all about getting better at tolerating the intolerable. *And moments like this . . .* He kissed the top of Zula's head, savoring the stillness. *Moments that remind us why we're still alive.*

Zula set her hand on Edwin's ebony chest. "Good." She leaned in and kissed him tenderly. Her lips were soft, warm, and utterly intoxicating, and he felt her tongue ease its way into his mouth. Again, he couldn't help but feel his body's involuntary reaction to her presence. Zula drew back, a smile creasing her lips, as her hand eased its way down to his building erection. "Feeling saucy today?"

Edwin blushed. "With you?" His eyes locked on hers. "How couldn't I."

Zula had an amorous look in her eyes that made Edwin's body react even more, having seen that same look just the other night. Her hand tightened around him. "It's going to be a long day . . ." Her dark eyes locked on his again. "And you'll need all the energy you can get."

"Yeah," Edwin sighed as Zula gently stroked him, rather teasingly.

"Now, don't think this is a regular occurrence," Zula softly muttered, practically whispering it into Edwin's ear. "I'm only doing this because of all the hard work you'll be helping me with later in the day." She smiled devilishly. "And I expect you to return the favor." Kissing his neck, she climbed atop him and slowly eased her way down the covers. The next thing he felt was her soft, salivating lips on him once more.

• • •

Damn, Edwin thought as he put on his black and yellow jacket—a jacket akin to the letterman he used to wear often that had once been Lamar's. Unlike its predecessor, however, this jacket was also waterproof, in far better condition, and had a tall collar that concealed a face scrambler. *I don't deserve this life*, he further ruminated. Beneath the jacket, Edwin was dressed in a plain gray shirt, a darker gray hoodie, and black pants and boots, whilst concealing a custom handgun—the same handgun given to him from Sibyl on Orion, the last day he saw her. *Never have deserved this life.* With an index finger, he absentmindedly felt for the face scrambler infused in his collar, making sure that it was still intact. *Another reason I can't risk being seen—not here nor anywhere.*

Much like an empathic emulator, that somehow—how it did, he had no idea—worked with the user's neurons to communicate a language and sound that otherwise might have just . . . well, sounded like random noise to the regular bystander, the face scrambler made Edwin appear just like anyone else (that is, not like a bounty). Another technological feat that surpassed his comprehension; fifth-dimensional technology reverse-engineered, as he had learned from D-D the day she had gifted it to him (an extravagant gift, given its fifth-dimensional origins, and quite rare to find—much like his void belt and empathic emulator, the latter of which had since been augmented into him, having also been reverse-engineered by D-D). To the random passerby, he looked just like any other colonist, minding his goddamned business; their imagination filled in the blank, conjuring whatever image their subconscious created, however they perceived him by his manner; the same effect also took hold of electronics, "scrambling" whatever footage captured his face and squandering any hopes of a reaper trying to find him using face recognition software; again, he had no clue how that was the case (it was fifth-dimensional physics, not rocket science—although, even if it *were* rocket science, he would still have no idea how it worked).

Satisfied with the now active face scrambler, Edwin exited Zula's apartment and was immediately met with the heavy smells of putrid smoke and black mold, reminding him of his early days of living with Vicky Dorset in Oakland.

The narrow hallway brimmed with squatters, either sleeping or sitting on the ground—all cramped together, and with hardly any space to move about. Graffiti blanketed the walls, and even with an empathic emulator installed in his neural network, he struggled to read what most of the words said. He squeezed around a group on the floor smoking from a hookah pipe, eluded a mother coddling a crying baby, and stepped over a man as still as a corpse, making him wonder if he actually was a corpse (it wouldn't have been the first corpse found in that hallway, and it probably wouldn't have been the last either).

As with the rest of the hallway, activity bustled around the elevator. Conspicuous drug dealings, idle gangs, and all that you would expect in such an environment, all of which were casually avoided by all who passed by, yet another part of everyday life that no one seemed to question. Edwin waited for the elevator along with a few other of the building's occupants; he would have loved taking the stairs, but this far up—sixteen floors, exactly—he would have to work a sweat (not excluding, getting past all the squatters who would be in his way).

He had tried convincing Zula to move into his freighter with him, where she would have even more room than in her study—nor would she have to commute through this shit show—but she had insisted on staying where she was, to sustain her own sense of independence and personal space. Also, to drive her further along her work, as a daily reminder of the changes that she was fighting to make in her community and why her work was so important to her, not only for the land but also for its people ("the land and its people are one," she had told him once. "To steward this land, we must steward its people").

The elevator unlatched, and the metal cage creaked loudly as its large doors slid open, welcoming those who trusted it enough not to cease functioning mid-operation, despite its rather rustic, almost hazardous appearance. One would think it was an old building, but one would be mistaken. Of course, Edwin waited for most of the others to enter the elevator first before entering himself, so that he could be one of the first to get out; there was something about confined spaces that still irked him, especially when confined with many others.

The ride down was short—though rocky—and as soon as the opportunity presented itself, he got the hell out of there. The elevator opened wide, leading into a long, bustling underground way station, almost like the Muni and Bart system that ran through San Francisco—how Edwin used to commute daily back on Earth before his abduction. He quickly wove his way through the foot traffic, wishing to be as far away from the crowd as possible and to feel the wind on his face once more, rain or no rain.

These days, he hated cities. He hadn't always hated cities, but people can change, and he supposed he had changed a lot since having last lived in one. It wasn't natural to be crammed in such a small environment with so many people. Claustrophobia set in whenever he had to navigate his way through the underground tunnels which dominated the cityscape. Because of the constant rain on Siletz IV, as well as its unpredictable weather patterns (sometimes dropping into the negative at night), most of the city ran underground, built as a grid system. Again, he wished Zula would just move into his freighter with him, but he respected her wishes, whether or not they made sense to him.

A set of brick stairs led out of the way station and into the outer city, above ground. Tall, identical buildings dominated the landscape, leaving all but narrow walkways beneath intervening archways and slanted rooftops. Endless rain poured down the slating, pooling into mud, concrete, and sometimes even the raised walkways.

As he navigated the city, Edwin brought up an internal map of downtown in his mind's eye. In the past few years, he'd had a heads-up display installed into his neural network, endowing him with information about the world around him as he saw fit, willing it to appear only when he wanted it to. For example, if he looked at a plant, he could will its name to show up in a small font, along with an inscription of the family of plants it belonged to, its planet or moon of origin, its properties, and whatever else he wanted to know about it—or anything else he wanted to know, for that matter.

The mini-map built into his HUD also revealed to him at all times where he was: the terrain, locations nearby, and any specific point of interest best suited to his needs. Whenever he wanted to go somewhere specific, he could just use that internal map of his to guide him, willing it to illuminate a beacon of light ahead of him—a compass that only he could see—leading him onward, toward whatever destination awaited him. Partially inspired by the video games he used to play back on Earth (back when he'd had the time, that is), he had given D-D specifications regarding his augmentations; seeing that life itself was the ultimate open-world video game, he figured he could make his childhood dream a reality, and live his life however he so pleased, utilizing any means necessary to make himself as efficient as possible. Another good thing was that he could also change his internal HUDs settings whenever he saw fit and literally change his brain's chemistry in the process.

Of course, D-D had warned him not to go too crazy with the adjustments—when one diverted their mind too far from the realm of reality, psychosis was inevitably the next step.

Edwin followed his internal waypoint. He didn't need to, really, given that he knew exactly where he was going; he had gone this same route many times before—at this point, it was practically a recurring destination—nor was the traversal even far. Among the many identical buildings (designed to be practical, not aesthetic or pleasing to the eye), he finally came across a sign by a glass door with a vibrant neon inscription displaying: "Retro Harvey," written in bold font.

Upon nearing the entrance to "Retro Harvey," the great double doors slid open, and Edwin entered a colorful, well lit, voluminous labyrinth, displaying used books, comics, board games, trading cards, tabletop miniatures, electronics, vinyls, and video and audio cassette/discs (including games, movies, TV shows, and whatever other format they had)—not unlike the Geekstarters comic book shop on Divisadero, albeit much larger and filled with unusual, alien plants (like the fox gloves, emitting music when you neared them), live sculptures (most of them naked and chiseled from marble—some even dancing), a cat (the most popular exhibit, actually—known as "Harvey" to the regulars), and media found nowhere even close to Earth.

Oh, and the smell of the place . . .

There was something utterly intoxicating about that smell, and Edwin just couldn't put his finger on why that was. The many times he had brought Zula with him, she had also had that same sensation, unable to describe it in words but only to suggest, afterward, that perhaps a strain of pheromones were being emitted, encouraging customers to purchase more; Edwin, conversely, had merely attributed that smell to old paper.

God, I love this place, Edwin thought as he immediately strode toward the comic book section and climbed down a set of stairs leading into a more secluded area.

Retro Harvey was three stories tall, and there was always something new to explore. The comic books were sectioned under "Picture Books," and most of the paper had been produced through hemp plants, a more sustainable means of production than mere lumber—though still not as reducing of carbon footprints were it digital. Still, to a reader, there is nothing more sacred than the tangible interaction of being absorbed in a physical copy; sure, consuming stories through an electronic source is perhaps a more eco-friendly means of distribution than lumber and hemp, but certainly nothing beats the nostalgic, almost primordial feeling of turning a page. That feeling you get before the next page—anticipation, wonder, and excitement. There's something magical about stories, touching upon an inner, hidden part of ourselves that we have yet to fully discover.

Edwin scanned the brimming bookshelves, searching for something new and exciting to read. Now and then, he opened a comic just to look at its interior and admire its elaborate artwork. Everything in Retro Harvey was "dirt cheap" and easily affordable. It was all "old" art, really, but its age certainly didn't show—and certainly not to Edwin.

These days, if one wanted a story tailored to their needs, all they needed was a neural device that could help transmit any story for them into whatever media they so desired—narrative prose, motion picture, auditory recordings, illustrated artwork, or even interactive storytelling, it didn't matter—the sky was the limit, and the stories transmitted through neural storytellers never ceased to be vivid, imaginative, and decent at the very least (that is, at least, if your subconscious told a good story). Sure, you could argue that neural storytelling was still an art form in its own right (the better the dreamer, the better the re-cording), but to Edwin, he still saw it as a pale comparison to actual, "organic" storytelling and art, created by the storyteller and artist's blood, sweat, and tears, like any other work of art, tangible and designed with intention, rather than through an effortless dreamscape, that somehow felt ingenuine to his artis-tic integrity.

Besides, Edwin appreciated art more when he saw all the work that had gone into it (that *is* what makes art "art," isn't it? How exactly do we differentiate art from creation as the lines between each diminish?).

Edwin used to be an idealist; honestly, he still was one. He used to think that his art mattered, and that it actually *meant* something. Lamar used to tell him he would change the world with it, and that through his drawings—and the stories he would tell—he could be a beacon of light to those lost at sea: the overlooked, disenfranchised underdogs like him, whose voices had never been heard nor stories had ever been told.

Lamar was convinced that Edwin was special, and that his art, too, was special; he had almost convinced Edwin, even—although Edwin eventually attributed that ambition of his, that faint glimmer of a notion that he was any better than anyone else, to the narcissistic genes he had possibly inherited from Vicky Dorset, and he remained quick to dismiss any notion of his talent as being any greater than the next person's (perusing the comics now, he could see *plenty* of artists far better than him).

Because the truth is, there's always going to be someone smarter, funnier, and more talented than you, and there's nothing you can do to change that—that's just a fact of life. If you put all your value into one attribute or talent, you're only going to be let down when the next person comes along to one-up you. The universe doesn't care about who you are or what you bring to the table; you're not special, and you never will be. But then again, if that's truly the case, then *no one* is special, and if no one is special, we're all just as special (oh, how life has that mystifying, almost paradoxical quality about it, sometimes "special" in its own way—oh well, we do what we can with what we're given).

For Edwin, some days were harder than others—as is it is with most of us, really—and during those times, he could be completely hard on himself, comparing his talents or happiness to the talents or happiness of others, which—as we all know—does far more harm than good. Sometimes, he had a tendency to second-guess himself, overthinking—or, at most times, *underestimating*—the simple impact he was making from day-to-day. "You're not good enough:" Those four (perchance five?) words came back every now and then, as unsolicited as all the other times he had heard them before. But this day? Well, this wasn't that kind of day. Not now, standing in Retro Harvey, holding a decent stack of trade paperbacks, nor listening to the groovy, funkadelic beat blasting through the overhead speakers, that reminded him why he was still alive (surprise: he's just another consumer like all the rest of us).

It's the smallest victories that mean all the world.

On a normal day, he would have perhaps wandered the store longer (being in hiding and all, he found himself with extra time than were he just another member of society—an employed laborer, for example, working the hours away just to sustain themselves in that society). But the day, no matter how good it was, was bound to run out, and he still needed to get back to his freighter to check up on it—let alone, have a few hours of much needed solitude before meeting up with Zula again, to help her with her project (another ecological study, this time using more equipment than the last time).

Edwin admired Zula's tenacity: Despite making no profit from these projects, she could utilize her influence in The Impermanent—growing in popularity, day by day—and spread the data she uncovered to whomever it concerned, hoping that her studies could find their way to an important person actually able to make an affective change. So far, however, nothing had come of it—regardless, that didn't seem to stop her or slow her down one bit (in fact, it had quite the opposite effect).

"Excuse me."

Edwin turned around to find a tall, bipedal "llama" standing behind him. The llama-looking humanoid was dressed in sandals and socks, tan khakis, and a green poncho, and held in their hand a copy of *How to Train Your Woman* by Fredric

Nicholas (whether the book was satire, Edwin couldn't tell, but he wanted to find his own copy anyway, finding nothing but humor from it, whether or not intentional). Even with the many years of this newfound life, and the friendship Edwin had built with Brutus Wainesworth ("a Liberian, not a bear," as he often had to remind himself—to those ignorant enough not to know the distinction), Edwin had never ceased to get used to seeing new and unique species, such as the one now standing in front of him. He wasn't xenophobic, mind you— just merely inexperienced in the way of the new world around him, and he somewhat lagged, as with many exiles and immigrants introduced to a world so unlike their own, needing extra time to adapt. He hesitated, took a step back, and nodded courteously. "Hello."

The llama-like individual continued to stare at Edwin, in no rush. "Do you work here?"

Edwin thought back to the days he used to work at the Geekstarters comic book shop on Divisadero. He used to get asked the same questions all the time, despite having worn a black polo with his name embroidered on it (let alone the company's *logo*). Unlike most of those times, however, he now wanted to say "yes." Now, he cherished interactions with strangers. Instead of a simple "yes"—or even a simple "no"—he merely shook his head (and for some cultures, that could mean anything). He inquired further: "What do you need?"

"I'm looking for a pleasure worker."

Edwin raised an eyebrow. "A pleasure worker?"

"Yeah," the stranger replied nonchalantly, nodding. "You know, a *sex robot*."

"Oh." Edwin nodded back, fully processing the request. The answer came to him without effort, and without a need to think twice about it (oh, the joys of augmentation, able to call up an encyclopedic amount of data at will, unfettered): "Second floor, between the theater projections and gaming apparatus. If you go up those stairs, take a left and go up the other set of stairs (the winding ones), follow the twinkling lights until you come across a bridge, cross that bridge, and then it'll be on your right (and trust me, you won't miss it)."

Grateful, the llamanoid smiled, revealing teeth far too big for any human. "Thanks, man—I owe you big time."

Edwin shrugged, still holding the stack of comic books with both hands. "Don't sweat it."

Not understanding Edwin's meaning of "don't sweat it," the stranger gave Edwin a weird, almost repelled look before striding away, slightly in a hurry. Edwin didn't notice that look, however, as his gaze had trailed back to the visible trade paperback in his hands, with moody surrealist art reminiscent of the style of Zdzisław Beksiński—one of his favorite artists back on Earth.

What a life: the luxury of accessible art and written works, which would cost a fortune elsewhere, that could now be studied and dissected for hours upon hours, and all at the cost of a relative nickel; a favorable investment, though Edwin wondered who really profited more from it: the writers, artists, letterers, editors, and publishers, or the readers, where the story lived on past the pages, transcending the creators' original intention.

He nodded, pleased. He felt good suddenly, as if his encounter with helping the stranger had somehow elevated his mood.

Five years now, of living incognito and hiding from the rest of the world. *I want to do good*, he ruminated, wanting to make the world a better place, like Lamar had always thought he would. But at the end of the day, intention can only go so far. And he had to wonder: *Is it even possible to make the world a better place when I'm not really a part of it?* Would he always be an outsider looking in from the other side, no matter where he went?

I guess it doesn't matter. . . .

He would do the best he could with what he had—perhaps it was all he could do. Even so, he wished for something more: A purpose greater than his own.

|22|

WAKING DREAMS

Edwin Dorset loved the feeling of the ground shifting beneath his feet: the crunching of leaves, twigs, and rocks, and the softness of the mud and earth beneath him, as he rambled onward, toward an unknown destination. The canopy enveloped Edwin, surrounding him with its luminous pines—stretching outward, touching the distant sky.

Birdsong rang far and wide: a legion of species could be heard within that melody, wholesome and welcoming—whistling, cooing, and chirping away, all in harmony with one another. Within nature's music came the buzzing of bees, comfortingly hypnotic, as they hovered over the blooming wildflowers, favoring the yellow and violet over all the other blossoming hues.

He glanced at Sibyl on his righthand side and saw her gaze meet his, followed by a gracious smile and nod. But given that Sibyl was by his side—and not ahead of him—he should have known that he was dreaming; alas, as with most dreams, his self-awareness, as well as his comprehension of the past and present, was wanting.

There was only the here and now—the present moment, and nothing else.

"You've grown a lot in the years since I last found you," Sibyl said, looking ahead once more. "You're no longer that broken, naïve boy, wandering through life without a purpose." She put her hands in her jacket pockets—the navy blue and maroon jacket she had once worn all the time, what Edwin always envisioned her wearing whenever he dreamt of her— and she glanced at him again. "Now, you're a broken, naïve *man*, wandering through life without a purpose." A coy smile creased the edge of her lips. "And no doubt, your brother would be proud of you."

Looking at Sibyl, Edwin felt a forlorn longing—a home-sickness, regardless of her being right in front of him (or so he assumed, being in the state of mind that he was). He could feel a gap between them—a separation, as if they were miles apart. His dear friend and ally, who had saved his ass countless of times. But something was missing . . . something wasn't there. No matter what image his subconscious concocted of her, nothing could replace what had been lost.

The forest surrounding them began changing, and they stopped walking. The trees had grown dense, Edwin noticed, and the lower branches and underbrush now compacted hap-hazardly. Overgrown weeds and thorny vines overwhelmed the vibrant wildflowers that had once been thriving, choking them out and wilting them. The bees were nowhere to be seen, and the birdsong had been replaced by whispers, barely aud-ible.

A dark presence lingered, unfelt until now.

"The trees hate you," Sibyl began, her voice now eerily dissonant. And Edwin noticed her eyes also change—they were now entirely black. "Everything you encounter hates you."

In the growing darkness surrounding them, he saw a ring of glowing eyes, ready to pounce at any second; he could feel them prying, coming from the great unknown. *The fifth-beings*, his mind concluded, knowing full well that sick, condemning feeling that always accompanied them. It was their whispers, after all, he heard in the forest, some even audible enough to hear: "Such wasted potential," "—thought he'd differ from all the others," "—can hardly relate to him at all," "—rate the bounty a two out of ten, maybe even less," "*eh*, it could have been worse. . . ."

He glanced at Sibyl again, noticing the blood now dripping down the corner of her pitch-black eyes. "You know why they hate you?" she continued as she looked up at the canopy, now covering the sky, blocking out any indication of the sun's presence. "Because they hate what they don't understand . . ." She turned to him once more, and in her blank expression he saw only the faintest hint of the Sibyl he had once known. "And they hate you because they don't understand you."

A boy's scream echoed in the distance: a gut-wrenching cry, filled with agony and terror. Suddenly, Edwin felt the urge to run toward that scream—straight into the darkness surrounding him—to find that boy and rescue him. But then he realized, all too suddenly, that it was his own voice he heard in the distance, crying out for help, for someone to come and save him.

But no one was there to be his salvation; no one was there but himself.

"But hey," the nightmarish Sibyl went on, and her crooked smile broadened, as blood oozed its way out of her mouth and eyes. "That's okay, because maybe you don't understand you, either." Her grin slowly faded and transformed into a slack grimace, like that of a corpse. "Maybe none of us do . . ." There was something heartbreaking behind those hollow, opaque eyes—something all too human. "And maybe we're all the same, after all."

• • •

As with every other day, Edwin awoke in a fright, and his sweaty body clung to the sheets covering him. Just another day of living as a bounty. . . .

Long ago, Hendrix Martin had warned him of the perpetuating nightmares that would soon follow, that would only get worse as the years warred on. Soon, the nightmares would follow him into the daytime, even without the aid of sleep.

Until I lose my mind, he thought morosely. *Or can't take it any longer.*

Without Zula there for comfort, sleep would no doubt elude him. It was still very early in the morning, but already the sun had risen, hidden behind the emerging storm clouds, casting a darkened, hazy light into the freighter, through a high-ceilinged window above. Not unusual for the sun to be out this early, given the relatively long days and short nights on Siletz IV.

Still, it would have been good to sleep in for once.

Edwin sat up, shedding off the warm comforter. He looked around his bedroom, which was also his kitchen and dining room, with an interconnected hallway leading to a bathroom and airlock, one of the few exits out of the freighter. Crude, makeshift bookshelves aligned one wall, each row with its own fastener for when the aircraft needed to ascend back into the upper atmosphere, usually to hitch a ride with whatever port happened to be traveling in whatever route happened to be the most convenient—all for a few, of course (unless he was hitch-hiking, though that was rarely the case).

The single bed lay in a nook in the far corner of the room, on the wall next to the bookshelves. The wall opposite the bookshelves was furnished with art pieces he had made from scratch, including a large mural depicting his last five years in Samsara—starting with his exodus from San Francisco, to his time in Zarathustra, the Vagabond, and Orion, and progressing to his many adventures and time in Siletz IV (with plenty of room for add-ons). A small, round, adjustable table sat in the middle of the freighter, along with two chairs on each side—all of which could convert into the floorboard, leaving extra space when needed. Another room was also interconnected to the main room, leading into a cockpit, currently substituting as a storage room.

Edwin came into possession of the freighter during one of his many travels, while wayfaring solo, acquiring it from a man who had tried to kill him, nonetheless. It took a few months before he could find a suitable name for it, and one that fit well. He enjoyed naming things, particularly plants and electronics—all of which he considered life forms like himself (for, really, they were)—and the freighter was his new home, after all: his "Fortress of Solitude," and he was particular on getting its name right.

But you can't always get things right at first, and certainly not when "right" is a relative answer, dependent on the day or hour. And yet, as with most things, that eponymous day came unexpectedly, while he was cleaning out the previous owner's possessions. He found a printed passport, declaring that the previous owner—the reaper who had tried to kill him (and had failed, for obvious reasons)—had been named Karl. That day, while leaving the freighter, he looked back at its structure, cloaked in a stealth mode and covered by a thick cloud of white fog, and was reminded of San Francisco with its heavy, analogous fog—a comparable haze that some locals had dubbed as "Karl the fog." As if in confirmation, Edwin realized he had at last found its name. And, of course, as was a custom on Earth, it was only fitting that a ship would have a feminine leaning.

"Karla," the freighter, was shaped like a calla lily that appeared sideways when docked on land. The freighter's surface was a sleek black (a similar texture to carbon, though stronger), and its bottom (or top, dependent on your perspective—really, what looked like the spathe of a calla lily) glowed a fiery ember while in use. The spacecraft was currently parked along the bottom of an enclosing cliff face, in a sheltered cove protected from the wind and peering eyes, on the opposite side of the runoff.

The terrain in this region of Siletz IV was rocky, treacherous, and mostly barren, despite the constant rain, freezing overnight. The wildlife was just as treacherous, with alien variations of sabretooths, wolves, snakes, scorpions, and even a pterodactyl-like predator, among the tamer coyotes, mountain goats, marmots, pikas, rabbits, foxes, and vultures, and whatever else had adapted well to Siletz IV's ever-changing climate—changing even more drastically now that humans had been introduced to its ecosystem.

Thankfully, the colonists of Siletz IV, though many, were scared to leave the city's borders, and few had ever wandered as far as the wilderness, leaving Karla and the surrounding area undisturbed, which was no doubt—aside from Zula—one of the few reasons Edwin had stayed there for so long. Still, he knew he would overstay his welcome, eventually; at times, he still felt as if he was trespassing.

Glancing up again at the translucent, high-ceilinged windows, Edwin now noticed light snow flurries falling from the sky and sticking onto the roof above him, melting slowly. It looked deathly cold out there, though he wasn't surprised in the slightest. Nothing new there. Thankfully, the freighter was insulated (being a ship that was built to traverse through space and all, why wouldn't it be?), and much like his void suit, it adapted well to his body's needs, from an intuition long programmed, rarely inaccurate even with more than one passenger present. And a warmth resonated from the floorboards, more than welcoming.

Karla's intuitions were rarely wrong.

Sometimes, you have to trust your intuition, Edwin mused as he walked to his mixer on the counter, that had already poured him a fresh cup of hot loose-leaf tea (once again, a programmed function of Karla, making sure that every passenger had their needs met—and by the smell of the vanilla, assamica, mixed ginger, cardamon, cinnamon, and nutmeg, Edwin certainly knew that his were). Intuitively, he sat on a chair by the table, cupping the ceramic mug with both hands, warm against his palms. *Slow mornings are the best,* he thought casually, as if talking to an old friend. *Sure, sometimes you don't get things done, nor are you as productive as you can be, but, really, is it healthy to* always *be productive?*

He looked around at the empty room before him.

The loneliness crept in, and a bittersweet presence lingered.

I guess it doesn't really matter, anyway.

He glanced at his vintage, hemp-bound journal lying flat on the table, untouched. As with the many books he consumed when he could—such as the comics from Retro Harvey—he had a bias of using physical copies, particularly for a notebook he could sketch in, or write in, whenever he felt like, despite it being more fragile. He wished more than anything that he could have kept his past journals from Earth—especially his last one, that he supposed had been lost somewhere in the canyons of Zarathustra along with his messenger bad (unless he had lost it while still on Earth). How many journals had he filled since then? Must have been over a dozen, at the very least.

He sighed, not understanding where all his discontentment was coming from.

Everyone's searching for an answer no one can find. He looked down at the steam rising from his mug, and he felt a pang in his chest, perhaps spurred by his dream. He tried to ignore that feeling, knowing that it could bring nothing beneficial into his life. *We're all looking for a savior—someone, or something—to ease the pain and help us transition through life.* He took a sip of the tea, re-invigorating him. *But no one has the answers: Life means nothing outside the meaning you give it—it's as simple as that.*

If his recent experience with psychedelics had taught him anything, it was that he collaborated with his own perception of reality by whatever he allowed into his life. By the thoughts he entertained, whether an ideation or a mere desire for more, that could sometimes leave him with nothing but dissatisfaction. He lived in an age of materialism, where most tried to capitalize on themselves through any means necessary—never satisfied, and constantly searching for validation and approval (validation from others, no less, and never themselves)—to fill the gaping hole in their lives left absent by overlooking the fundamental secret known in every mythology: The Kingdom of Heaven is within, not without.

Never seek validation; your existence alone is valid enough.

He blew on the tea, closed his eyes, and felt the hot steam rise to his face.

Many see beauty for what something looks like, not for what it is. Discontentment arises when you forget all that life offers and instead focus on what you don't have or an ideation of what's been in front of you all along, often overlooked. Most of the greatest things in life are often overlooked. Not until you reevaluate something can you see the intrinsic value it holds. Look at anything in life and you can learn something from it— good or bad, it doesn't matter. There's always an example of what to do or what not to do. Who to be and who not to be. If the isolation of his newfound life had taught Edwin anything, it was to be content with what he had. To be present with every moment and grateful for whatever was given, unwavering throughout it all.

Of course, he thought, nodding. *But knowledge means nothing without the action to support it.*

Alone most days, while out in the wild he had once observed—it was always safer out in the wild, at least for a bounty—how most of the wild animals were also alone, as if their survival depended on it just like his, and they rarely strove for anything more than what they needed. That day in particular, he remembered sitting on a rock, along a valley, and watching as the rushing river cascaded down a ravine, benefiting all that surrounded it. Vibrant and bodacious, the flora thrived best near the water. In fact, all who were near were drawn to the water—mammals, amphibians, birds, insects, you name it—empowered by its life force and made even stronger by it. Oh, to be like the river, mighty and free, beneficial to all who surround you.

Is that what this is? he now wondered, glancing around the empty room. *That I don't feel like I'm living my full potential? That I'm only benefiting myself?*

Edwin thought of Sibyl, who he hadn't seen since Orion. All these years, and he still wondered if she had made it out of the airship in time. And even if she *had* made it out of the airship in time, there was still no guarantee that she made it out of Orion alive, let alone in one piece. Having seen Sibyl's face again, if even in his nightmare, had made him miss her that much more. *Five years*, he thought, fighting the melancholy that had festered in him ever since waking. *And I barely even knew her.* . . .

Hell, perhaps that was the worst part of it all: the potential of what *could* have been. It made him think of his own mortality and the impermanence of time.

Pushing against the dissatisfaction, he closed his eyes again and began to meditate. Conflicting emotions coursed through him, none of his own accord. He didn't fight the emotions, nor did he try to ignore them, but he simply let them have their way—unaffected, as if they weren't his own emotions but someone else's. Life was good, and he had everything he needed, all that he could ask for. Sure, it would be great to have more friends, a semblance of a community, and to never have to worry about being found by reapers or betrayed for the vanities of money, status, or fame—all because of circumstances outside his control. And sure, it would have been great to not be on the run anymore. But even if he had all those things, this emptiness within him would not be satisfied, forever remaining a bottomless pit without the actions to fill it—sometimes, as simple as it was, through mere discipline and practice. Still, an unconscious part of himself longed for more. He supposed these feelings kept him human (and, like everything else in his life, he had to get used to it).

There is no joy without suffering, Edwin reminded himself. He took a deep breath and visualized all of his unease, and all of his misery, being pulled into a deep vortex refined by fire, only to be released with a long exhale—this time slower, the heaviness becoming a distant memory, as his emotions began slowing down with his heartbeat, and he felt himself being pulled out of his body, eased into a silent, endless ocean, floating through space and yet separate from it; here, the fifth-beings couldn't see him (their judgement was absent, as was their condemnation), nor was there any pressure to be "good enough"; here, there was only the now—the moment—and everything that came with it, the beauty often overlooked.

(—YOU'RE NOT GOOD ENOUGH—)

And he let the unwanted feelings wash through him, remaining uncompromised, until they were no longer a part of him.

• • •

Only a minute later, however, and the voices of discontentment returned.

Only this time, not all the voices were his.

• • •

Long ago, Edwin Dorset had learned that he couldn't take things personally. People hurt, and in their hurt, they lash out, often hurting others. The universe is filled with hurting people. "*Everybody hurts*," as the song goes, whether or not sung. *Every*body hurts—and yes, that includes plants, other animals, and *hell*, maybe even the personal computer you're carrying on you right now (assuming that you have a phone, laptop, or any kind of tablet on hand—or anything else with life in it, quantifiable or not). Sometimes, there's an indifference to the universe, and if you're in its line of sight—an inevitable outcome, given your existence—you're going to get hurt. That's just the way it is, just the way it's always been. Perhaps the universe is also an organism—a *giant* organism, with separate functions—hurting like the rest of us.

(Or, perhaps, it goes even further than just that.)

Every person has a story, a reason they are the way they are.

No matter the flaws of an individual, and no matter how many times they may hurt you, their worst moment does not define them—one moment cannot define a person. Conversely, no matter the good of an individual, and no matter how beneficial they are to you, their best moment does not define them—once again, one moment cannot define a person. Just how do you define someone? How do you differentiate a "good" person versus a "bad" person? Is there a scale to measure right from wrong—what builds more versus what destroys? In an impermanent universe, we are never the same, and we can never limit our potential: the potential for "good" or the potential for "bad"—the potential to create or the potential to destroy.

We are but vignettes in a far grander story, and—if it's any consolation, reading this now—that story's not over just yet. And yet with that knowledge brings with it another question: Are we merely a byproduct of that story, or are we a driving factor pushing it forward and shaping it in ways we could never know?

Whatever the case, the universe is an extremely judgmental place. If we're all honest with ourselves, we judge most in others what we see most in ourselves; it's always easier to cast the first stone when you're not on the receiving end. But it doesn't matter who you are, what you do, or whether you're alive or dead, because no matter where you go, what you do, or how hard you try to do the right thing, whatever the "right thing" is, you *will* be judged for it. There's always someone who is going to judge you. If you think for a second that you are alone, and that you won't be judged—*especially* while no one's looking—think again: You're never alone, and existence is far stranger than you realize.

Existence is an absurdity, chronicled night and day, recorded for all time (unbound by time, really), and a story far grander than any life form's single comprehension.

And every action has a consequence.

Better yet, every action has a reaction.

Everyone, and everything, reacts to life differently. To react is the language of the cosmos. Your existence, really, is a by-product of that reaction. Change occurs at all times, and the universe is in a continual state of evolving—that is, adapting according to the surrounding environment, by creating stars, planets, and galaxies, housing millions and billions of life forms and atoms also reacting to one another, much like you do with all that's around you. So, then, why should it be surprising at all to learn that beings outside your apprehension are reacting to *your* every action?

The fifth-beings see everything: Not a moment of your life has passed by—hell, not even a single second—without your actions being scrutinized, judged, and condemned by them, whether their reaction is justified. The fifth-beings stand out-side our reality, separated by the constraints of the physical realm, comprising matter and atoms. Their presence often manifests in different ways. Sometimes, a mere change to the wind so subtle that it's overlooked. One might even remember something they're doing as if they've done it before, as if they're re-experiencing it not only for the first time but for the hundredth. At these times, the physical world is disrupted, and a tear in our reality is ripped open, creating a paradox of infini-tesimal happenings, reshaping the cosmos in ways previously unimagined.

Natural selection did not develop us to see the world through an objective lens but only through a subjective point-of-view, seeing only what helps aid our survival; whatever re-ality is, we cannot comprehend it—the truth is too abstract to understand.

You see, rarely is one aware of the fifth-beings' presence in their life.

Only the select few.

Hendrix Martin had once described the rare sensation of awareness to Edwin Dorset as "the bleeding effect," caused by the fifth-beings' disturbance in their lives. "Every bounty has it," he told Edwin one day in a drunken stupor—his drunken stupors had become constant preceding his sudden disappearance. "It's in our DNA, you know—it's why we're so important to them." His face had grown pale, and his hands shook unwittingly, with a vacancy in his eyes. "No augmentation can take that away." (Hendrix's health had been deteriorating, as Edwin had noticed, and not much later would he go AWOL, never to be seen or heard from again.) "I can hear them now . . ." He shook his head repeatedly, muttering like a man on his deathbed: "Talking, always *talking*. Criticizing my every action, my every waking hour. Always something to say, something to critique. The irony . . . ? The irony is that it's the only thing separating us from everyone else."

According to Hendrix, first come the dreams: Lucid, vivid, and monstrous. Voices then enter the fray, and the next thing you know, those dreams follow you into the daytime—until you can no longer tell the dreams from reality. Until you can't take it anymore, and the voices just won't stop. That constant judgment. That constant critique. Overwhelming and agonizing, further pushing you into insanity. Until the only option left is to either lose your mind or end it yourself, the old-fashioned way.

Thankfully, for Edwin, the voices hadn't come yet—only the dreams.

That was, at least, until five seconds ago.

• • •

(—PRETENSIOUS HACK—)

The voice was loud and unexpected. Edwin turned around, expecting someone to be standing there. But no one was there. At least, no one he could *see*. And he knew—

(—DISAPPOINTMENT—)

—suddenly that he wasn't alone. Out of the corner of his eye, he saw a tall figure standing in the hallway, drenched in shadow and devoid of all light.

Startled, he spilled some hot tea onto his lap, taken aback. Like the times he awoke in a state of paralysis and semi-consciousness, and a figure loomed over his bed watching him—so abstract that it was almost imperceptible. Only this time, he was fully awake already. And to make matters worse, the figure hadn't simply vanished as he faced it, looking back at him as it did; in fact, the more that he looked at the figure, the bigger it seemed to get.

The surrounding shadows increased, as if reaching out for him.

Terror seized up in his chest, and a heavy weight pressed down on him as he staggered out of his chair, clumsily knocking down his mug—indifferent to the hot liquid now pouring down the table from all sides. He took hurried steps back to get the gun that was hidden on one of the lower shelves behind him (the same handgun Sibyl had given him on their last day on Orion together). He turned around, sprang to the shelf, shoved off the books in his way, and grabbed the wooden box—its latches already undone—before snapping open the box, grabbing the handgun, and—

—turning around, handgun at the ready, to find that he was alone again.

Or even worse, perhaps he had been all along.

Fuck, he thought. He could feel nothing but the adrenaline coursing through him—his hands shaking, and his legs wobbly, as if they would crumble beneath him at any second.

Once more he thought of Hendrix Martin, lying on the ground drunk, with snot running down his nose—uncharacteristically vulnerable and exposed—and the smell of piss wafting from his britches. "You think we're special?" Hendrix had asked him, while struggling to get up and walk on his own. "You think we were *chosen* for a purpose greater than this?!" His pitiful laugh now echoed in Edwin's mind, more haunting than his next words had been: "Think again, Adewale—" (Hendrix had a habit of calling Edwin "Adewale," particularly whenever intoxicated, despite all the times Edwin had corrected him) "—We're rejects, chosen as bounties only to cover up the mistake the universe made in ever letting us see the light of day. Don't you get it? We were never *meant* to exist." He grabbed Edwin's hand then, pulled him even closer, and looked him dead in the eyes, unblinking. "Kill yourself while you still have the chance . . . before it's too late."

(—TOO LATE—)

Edwin stumbled, shaking his head. *It's happening already*, he thought, now standing alone. All too aware of the gun in his hand. *Faster than I'd thought.* He shook his head again, exhaling a shaky breath. *I thought I could be the exception. . . .*

"It's irreversible," Hendrix had told him that day. "Once it's taken hold, there's no going back."

"No going back," Edwin now repeated like a man haunted by ghosts, unaware that he was even speaking aloud. Only aware that it could only get worse from here on out. *It's too late for me now.*

• • •

Edwin needed a breath of fresh air. At times like these, he felt trapped and needed to be reminded why he was still alive, that he was free to go anywhere and do anything he desired.

Flurries of snow drifted downward, covering the surrounding landscape in a thin sheet of crystalline white. Dressed accordingly, Edwin wore a black and yellow jacket (heated from within), as well as thick cargo pants and high-top boots. The air was crisp and chilling to the bone, albeit refreshing, with hardly much wind flow at all. His breath puffed out in clouds of steam, rising high before evaporating and transforming into a thin, fading mist.

Edwin followed the subtle trail left in the dirt, created from months of commute, amidst stacking boulders covered with lichen and loose rocks. He walked at a leisurely pace, and behind him a visible trail of footprints led back to his freighter, Karla, hidden behind an artificial mist blending in with the environment (hence her namesake).

A lonely silence hung in the air. A stark contrast to the audible disturbance that had emitted from the fifth-beings merely moments prior, echoing in Edwin's mind resoundingly. The fifth-beings, an ever-constant presence in his life—a virus and pest, disturbing his well-being. Now, now that there was the relief of silence, he couldn't help but relish the stillness, eating it up like food for the soul. His soul, his inner-being, had *longed* for these days, undistracted by the resounding feedback of the fifth-beings in his head.

From here on out, moments like this would be even more rare.

Better to look at the bright side, the beauty of all things.

But he couldn't think of anything other than that sheer look of terror on Hendrix Martin's face, the day he had first warned Edwin about "the bleeding effect," less than six months prior to his vanishing, never to be seen again. *Hendrix was never the same*, Edwin reflected. Hendrix's entire demeanor changed drastically as his mind deteriorated from what seemed like an onset of dementia making its way through his system. No augmentation could change that—not for a disease not fully understood. *Will the same thing happen to me?*

I'm a bounty, he further reflected. *One way or another, every bounty must end.*

Climbing down a steep embankment, the quasi-pathway led Edwin to a hidden lake, its clear waters shimmering—a cool, radiant blue, inviting to all who neared it. Patches of glacier edged alongside the water, nestled against an outcrop of rock, giving the lake even more privacy and protecting it from unwelcome eyes.

Edwin ambled to the water's edge, taking the moment in: The calmness, a feeling he cherished, wishing that he could fully bask in it like the sun. As of late, he had found much solace from nature. He hadn't always been much of an outdoorsy person; at least, he didn't think that he had always been. The first time he could ever recall truly appreciating his ever-growing love for the wild had been his camping trip with Mr. Kemp; Benjamin Kemp had loved the outdoors, as had Martha Kemp. Despite his old age, Mr. Kemp took Edwin on hikes regularly, while Mrs. Kemp liked it when he helped her out in the garden—often imbuing him with their wisdom, a trait the two had in common. In many ways, Edwin supposed his love of the great outdoors had come from them; or, at the very least, they had certainly nurtured it. When he really thought about it, however, even when he had been living with Vicky Dorset, he had always loved going outside and exploring whenever he could. And even jumping from the temporary orphanage to the foster homes, he had constantly needed a means of escape and something to call his own. Perhaps nature had always been there for him: his only means of escape—the only constant for him in an ever-changing environment, often unstable and unpredictable.

You can always escape into nature, Edwin thought, *but you can never escape it*. Nature was everywhere, all around him; by default, whatever happened under the sun could be categorized as such—whether a tree collapsing by wind or by axe. *And the fifth-beings*, he further mused. *They're as natural as anything else out here*. He could feel them now, even still. Though their voices could no longer be heard, their presence remained like a parasite, feeding off of him. And though it may have been natural for a predator to eat its prey, it was just as natural for that prey to fight back when pushed to a corner with nowhere to run.

One way or another, it ends with me or them.

He knew that it would all have to end eventually, but he just didn't know how. He didn't want to imagine the toll that his mind would take, deteriorating as Hendrix's had, were nothing to be done. But what alternative was there? How could he fight back against a presence so powerful that it wasn't even quantifiable?

"This struggle between us and them," Hendrix had once told him, years before losing his mind (when Edwin had first introduced the prospect of fighting back, vying that there had to be *some* way, perhaps a means of getting to the fifth-beings that they were overlooking). "It's been going on longer than the universe itself. Why do you think you'll be any more successful than those who came before you? Look around you: We're dying by the thousands. We can hardly stay alive, as is. Tell me, just how are you going to stop them? How will you bring 'vengeance' to those who came before? With what, a *drawing*?" He had shaken his head mockingly, looking down on his counterpart with a vain arrogance, as if Edwin was lesser than him (and perhaps in hindsight, he had really been looking down on himself, seeing only himself in Edwin looking back at him). "You're no hero," Hendrix had told Edwin. "Why pretend to be?"

But Hendrix was wrong; by default, he *had* to be wrong. Nothing, and no one, is infallible. Those who don't see what's overlooked all too often don't even try to see. *There* has *to be a way*, Edwin thought, ever the optimist. *It can't end like this.* Not with his mind deteriorating, rotting from the inside out. No, there had to be something that he was overlooking, so obvious in hindsight that it would make him laugh looking back at it. The thought of anything other scared him. *Terrified* him, in fact.

Sometimes, that fear was all that he could think about.

"Don't be afraid," Sibyl's last words echoed, drowning out Hendrix's last words. *"You're far more capable than you give yourself credit."*

Edwin wrestled with doubt. *I've been hiding all this time*, he regarded, shaking his head and feeling ashamed. *Waiting to die while others like me—other bounties—fall into the same pattern of cyclical violence: More entertainment for the fifth-beings to indulge in and consume, and yet disregard, as if every bounty's lesser.* He didn't know what it was, but something about his situation, something about his awareness with the fifth-beings presence in his life, ever increasing, and the prospect of his health deteriorating away, of dying without a cause greater than himself—having never found a *reason* for existing—awoke in him something he had buried long ago, in fear that he wasn't capable of anything better. He had buried it away the more he listened to those like Hendrix, who told him he "couldn't," or that he wasn't "good enough"; hell, it was his own fault that he had even listened to that voice of doubt in the first place, believing for a second that it had held any more truth than the voice within that told him he "could," and that he *was* "good enough."

A rebellious indignation rose inside of him. Anger for all the injustice caused to him and those like him. Rage for his complacency, which had kept him from ever fighting back— fighting against the injustice—pushing for change.

Enough playing the victim.

He stood by the lake, with his hands in his pockets, and watched as the snow slowly drifted downward, melting as it hit the surface of the water. Inadvertently, he began taking off his jacket. Dropping his jacket to the ground, he proceeded taking off his shirt and bent down to take off his boots—one foot after the other. And before he knew it, his pants were coming off, and his undergarment also, and he suddenly stood there naked, in the brisk snow, like a man possessed.

He slowly waded into the water, cold as ice.

He didn't need any convincing to do what he did next: his body did all the work for him. He dove right in, submerging himself completely—a spiritual baptism of body, mind, and soul—before emerging out of the water, his body steaming and revitalized.

"Feel any better?"

Edwin glanced up at the source in question. Above him, a native vulture perched on a hexagonal column of rock, staring at him in silence. His brown wings were wrapped around his gray body, protecting him from the snow, with his black eyes on Edwin and an expression within them that was unreadable.

Taken by the moment, Edwin had almost forgotten about the disparate impact on his life after having an empathic emulator installed in him. It felt like too long since he had conversed with a non-humanoid—aside from all the plants living in his freighter, that is, and Zula's sun-peach dahlia, Ella, who sometimes liked to sing to him and (for reasons unknown to Zula) only him. Life is so much better when you can understand its language: that sweet, rare frequency unfettered by miscommunication or wrongful assumptions. What a wonderful, fascinating, and unpredictable world he had entered since having left San Francisco. Not a day passed without something new to shake him out of his apathy.

The vulture's brow furrowed. His voice was brisk, raspy, and yet somehow soothing. His curiosity had seemed to get the better of him, however: "It looks to me like you have some mushrooms growing below your pecker."

Edwin glanced down at his testicles. His laugh echoed, reverberating off the water, rocks, and everything around him. Warm, vibrant, and alive. Despite his circumstances—along with the task at hand, a task pushed off for far too long—the worries of the world remained far, far away.

| 23 |

A CRY FOR HELP

Dark brown, light brown, gray, and teal designs, all pulsating: Distinct patterns of lichen, each so different. On the trunks were many faces—eyes, mouths, and a full spectral of emotion—all so unique in their expression: some of them, haunting and elusive; others, sexy and enticing. Their branches reached for the sun, moving gently with the wind. Dancing an offbeat waltz, carefree and gleeful, their every movement vibrant in the light of day.

At last, one of the conifer's spoke out, their words loud and vivid, communicated to the Liberian through the empathic emulator imbued in his cerebral cortex. "Hey, man," the conifer said impatiently. "Will you get on with it, or will we be stuck here all day?"

The other trees laughed, and their bodies continued dancing from side to side. The smaller of the maples even cackled. Instinctually, Brutus Wainesworth decided it was best not to take their jesting personally. As he had learned of this region of Ithaca, the flora took great pleasure in making light of most things. Instead of taking it personally, he smiled and let his fangs also glisten in the sunlight.

"Aye," Brutus grunted. "I remember the reason I'm here."

"Then get on with it!" An old fern sitting atop a mound shouted from a distance—merely a spectator. "We all have places to be."

A conifer near Brutus cleared their throat (an endeavor that seemed rather pointless, given their condition), and Brutus noticed the tiniest bit of sap seeping out of their trunk. *A happy fella*, he thought dryly, before glancing down at the cards in his lap and trying to get back to the task at hand.

"Alright," Brutus said, picking up the top card from the table and turning it over to look at.

"Well, what is it?" A red cedar inquired, also impatient. "We don't have all day, you know."

"Settle down, sugar tips," Brutus jested. "We all know you'd be here no matter what."

Some of the blackberry bushes surrounding the conifer trunks laughed.

Brutus decided he should continue, then. He glanced back at the card, ignoring the buzzing fly, flying circles around his head, repeatedly muttering to himself how he wanted to pollinate Brutus's head. "Alright," Brutus repeated, this time clearing his throat. "Now, if you'd stop interrupting me, I could continue."

No one replied to that. No more sassy remarks.

Good. Brutus cleared his throat again. *Well, then. . . .*

Brutus inspected the card in his hand, admiring its wonderful design. A human was depicted in the center of the card. The homo sapiens' resemblance to Edwin Dorset was uncanny, actually (from the hair down to the way he dressed), as was the card's artwork, reminding Brutus of all the times that he used to watch Edwin use some kind of pencil, pen, or brush to create an almost identical style of artwork; just thinking about that made Brutus miss that kid even more. How long had it been now? Too long, no doubt. Always too long. "It's a naked ape," he told the flora surrounding him, before they could ask what the card was again (he was growing tired of their pestering, as jovial as it may have been). He read the description on the top right corner of the card: "A bounty, in fact."

Truthfully, he couldn't even remember acquiring this specific card.

Less reason to doubt its legitimacy, he thought, half-jokingly.

He had heard it said many times that these kind of cards— "Divinity Cards," by those who used them—had fifth-dimensional technology in them; they had been used for divination for epochs, long before his time—and long before their repurposing into a deck-building game played by many across Samsara (competitively, mostly, just as he intended). Now, he could believe why someone would perceive them as legitimate.

(Well, *kind* of—more so, the idea amused him.)

It's all confirmation bias, he knew as he set the card to the side and readied to pick up another. "Now, let's see what it 'means'..." He flipped over the next card from the pack. Again, a little surprised by what he saw on it. "It's..." He shook his head with a smile; this time, instead of seeing a friend, he merely saw himself. "A Liberian, by the looks of it."

"What does that mean?" The closest maple asked, their perceived voice almost nasally; their chalky bark appeared to be shifting with anticipation. "Can someone tell me what's going on? I wasn't paying attention earlier."

Brutus shrugged. "I don't know," he admitted, looking at the card and still seeing what looked like himself on it: A big, black, shaggy bear-like humanoid, long evolved from human bioengineering on his native planet epochs ago. "It could mean anything . . . or nothing." Besides, he had another card to pull out. "Let's see, here."

He flipped over the next card and—

"Well, what is it?!"

Brutus glanced at the red cedar again—that impatient, nagging bastard. "I'm tempted to chop you down." (Honestly, he wasn't even sure if he was joking.)

Someone else cried: "Get on with it!"

Brutus examined the card: another naked ape. "Homo sapiens again," he told those around him. "A female, this time." Unlike Edwin Dorset, however, the female on the card didn't look familiar at all to Brutus—of course, aside from the bounties, *all* naked apes looked the same to him, so that didn't really surprise him. The female depicted on the card was beautiful by human standards, and she had long, dark, and wild hair, with equally dark eyes. She wore a high-collared maroon coat that covered her neck and lower cheeks, giving her a mysterious appearance, like some femme fatale from a Neo noir. The description on the top right of the card was strikingly inscribed: REUNION.

Interesting, Brutus remarked, scratching the scruff of hair on his chin. *I don't remember that being there before . . .*

As if I'd know what the hell that's supposed to mean.

What any *of this is supposed to mean. . . .*

Of course, the mushrooms were finally taking effect in his system, and at these times, he was prone to overanalyze things. He glanced again at the card before it, the one depicting the Liberian reminding him so much of himself. He now read its description on the top right corner, having realized that he had overlooked it. Its inscription simply read: ASSISTANCE.

His telecommunicator in the holster under his serape began to go off, and at once he noticed the hairs on his arm and hand rise, along with a strange awareness of being watched. He glanced up from the cards once more to look at the surrounding forest—now eerily silent, except for the buzzing coming from his device. He was expecting the surrounding flora to harass him into telling them what kind of card he had just picked up, but alas, no one said a thing, and he wondered if he had accidentally deactivated the photosynthetic translator of his empathic emulator connecting him to them.

Taking out the physical telecommunicator from in its holster, Brutus finally realized why the empathic emulator in his cerebral cortex had ceased to function. An emergency message had been sent to him from Edwin Dorset: an SOS, with coordinates on where to find him. Coincidence? Had to be. Although, even with his pessimistic, sometimes cynical nature, Brutus doubted it could be just that. There was more at play than meets the eye—there *had* to be.

"What's the holdup?!" a conifer spat, their voice heard again, somehow even more impatient than before. "Your opponent will be here any minute now, and you still haven't tallied up your points. We can't help unless you show us what you've got."

Brutus chuckled. "You do understand the rules of the game, don't you? I would've thought that after all this time, you'd understand the fundamentals of an even match: At the start of every game, a player must draw new cards—not beforehand." He grunted, shaking his head with a smile. "You really are a daft lot."

There was a moment of silence. An oak finally asked: "Then why are you wasting our time with drawing cards?"

Brutus shrugged his big shoulders indifferently. "Buying time for the fun of it, what else? Nosy, much?" Once more, he looked at the cards laid out for him, and he knew there was more to it than just that. Maybe not originally, but certainly after Edwin's SOS, when any doubt of the cards' fifth-dimensional legitimacy had quickly vanished.

Just one more card, he thought, and a new compulsion took over. *Four cards to complete the hand*. He flipped over the last and final card and saw on it Xibalba, Samsara's supermassive black hole at the center of the galaxy. *The eye of the universe. . . .* And as he read the card's inscription on the top right corner, a chill ran through his spine, colder than any blade that had ever scarred his body. Along with that chill came a forlorn sense of foreboding.

On the inscription read the four-letter word: FATE.

|24|

IMPERMANENCE

Zula Cormorant was born in space: the black sea of Samsara, a canvas of constant change.

She was raised in a colony ship, the Wayfarer, set to arrive on Siletz IV (a far-out moon along the Outermost Rings of Samsara) in her late teenage years as the third generation of arrivals. She was a second-class citizen by birth, afforded only what she labored for. But no matter how hard she labored, sometimes her labor wasn't enough—unlike those placed in cryosleep before the Wayfarer had even set voyage, with the promise of one day awaking into a new world already afforded a vast amount of wealth, unburdened by years of toil.

Victor Cormorant, Zula's father, was killed in a shootout when she was only nine (a gang-related shootout that he had not only been a part of but had orchestrated himself). Not long after, Dionysus Orello, her mother—a woman not unlike Vicky Dorset—had left poor Zula to fend for herself, having abandoned the child in favor of running off with a promising young man (the same man who had, most likely, been the cause of Dionysus being found, one day, dead in an alleyway).

By the time the Wayfarer arrived on Siletz IV, Zula had already come of age and experienced her fair share of trauma: the kind of trauma that would last a lifetime (a specialty of trauma).

What had helped Zula deal with that kind of trauma early on—healthily, of course (a way of coping outside of crime, self-infliction, and substance abuse)—was by picking up her first instrument, the mandolina—a six-string instrument, typically made from the wood of a bordo—when she was only twelve. One could typically learn how to play an instrument by a simple augmentation, the quickest way possible to learn any new skill, but given that she hadn't enough talents to even sleep in a bed for a single night, she had to learn how to play it the old-fashioned way—which made her appreciate it all the more. Conversely, she had never had much of a problem being grateful for things; she had found the instrument in a garbage compactor, after all, and while scavenging for food, nonetheless.

Zula had an ear that others didn't. After only six months of practice, she could play any song on the mandolina just by listening to it. Eventually she could make a living from it—playing on the streets, at public venues, transportation hubs, Xibalbist temples, and wherever the opportunity presented itself—and could finally buy food and shelter without having to scavenge through compost compactors and littered alleyways. And, having mastered the mandolina after only three years, she even picked up other instruments on the side, having caught the bug most artists find themselves inflicted by—that all-consuming virus aptly named "obsession."

Tell me, truly: What happens when you're an artist and your profession becomes obsolete? When AI can create what you create in the span of a second, without any imperfections? Better yet, when other humans can augment themselves to have the same skill level that you worked decades to achieve? Even when others don't see what you create, or find no joy from it, do you quit what you love doing? Or do you continue doing it simply because it brings you joy? Because without it, you would be losing a part of yourself, a part of your expression that no one else has, the most important thing you can have as an artist (let alone as a human): your perspective.

When you grow up in an aberrant environment—without any sky, clouds, precipitation, change of season, or even the light of the sun—it's easy to overlook the natural order of the universe and your place in it. For most homeless orphans growing up on the Wayfarer, there was only one safe place to go, one refuge above all that never ceased to fail: the park. And overall, there were only five parks on the Wayfarer, and only three of them had authentic flora—flora that were actually planted in the ground, that is—with only one of them having no pesticides whatsoever. Göransson Park was Zula's favorite, in particular, and it was also where she had first discovered her love of nature and botany.

She quickly found that she much preferred the company of plants over people.

There was only one ancient tree in all the Wayfarer, and it was at the center of Göransson Park. An old elm, the width of a hundred and twenty feet, and the height of at least a hundred and thirty feet. Suffice it to say, Zula wanted to learn as much as she could about it; she was a curious child, and she wanted to know how the tree communicated through its roots, how it felt to be in such an abnormal environment, and how it experienced life altogether. Without proper schooling, however, if she wanted any form of education on the matter, she had to find the information herself; thankfully, there were more than enough resources out there; unfortunately, however, it felt as if she was the only one to actually utilize those resources—apathy had arisen in many from decades of not having to think for oneself, and the simple magic of the physical world had been lost in favor of the digital one, where anyone could have all they desired in mere seconds, no longer requiring critical thinking to go through life.

When Zula started writing her own songs, she incorporated her love of nature into most of them, infusing a voice that had hadn't been heard for generations—particularly, from those who had grown up on the Wayfarer, many of whom had never felt the light of the sun. With her unique, powerful voice and raw, Xibalba-given talent, it was no surprise that she found instant success with her music. Not massive success, mind you, but certainly enough; any amount of success was enough for her. Considering AI had already fine-tuned music—along with any other art form—based on an algorithm for popular demand, it was immensely hard to find success as a human dabbling in any art form. Another reason Zula and Edwin had bonded so much over being pioneers of dying art forms—that, and their mutual love of nature, of course.

Truthfully, Zula had never had much luck in the love department. It's extremely hard to find someone who values what you do, and Zula was picky with who she allowed into her life. For Edwin, she supposed the same could be said, considering his position as a bounty and the fact that he seldom stayed in one place for very long; in fact, she was certain that this was the first genuine relationship he had been in since his days on Earth, and, considering his situation, their days were undoubtedly numbered.

Zula hadn't named her band The Impermanent without reason.

Under the warm glow of Karla's overhead lights, Zula eyed Edwin sitting across the small table from her. There was something unusually different about him this night. Something that she just couldn't put her finger on. Usually, she would see his mind at work, dwelling within itself, as it sometimes liked to do—thinking heavily, and though about what, she didn't know. Looking back, usually. Always sentimental, he was. Sometimes, she wished he could be more present. Sometimes, she wished he would just speak his damn mind.

But tonight?

No, tonight was different.

Sure, he wasn't always the most talkative, but tonight, as they cooked together (a newfound tradition that she cherished more than he may have realized), he seemed more talkative than ever. More clearheaded. And as she looked at him now, she knew there was something he wasn't telling her. She saw a resolution within him that hadn't been there prior, the last time she had seen him, only a few days ago. Gears were turning, and change loomed on the horizon.

And, strangely, she felt left out of it.

Zula pointed at Edwin with her chopsticks. "Well," she said impatiently. "What is it?"

Edwin looked up from his food and eyed Zula. He smiled, warm and good-natured. "*What?*"

Zula sighed playfully. "Must I beat it out of you?"

He eyed her closer now, attentive as ever. "You know what I love the most about you?" he began, and his smile widened. "No matter what you're doing, you're a change machine. You make the best of wherever you are, taking every opportunity given to make it even better." He glanced down at his food once more, and his expression turned to one of contemplation as his smile slowly faded. "We strive to make our world better, you and I." His eyes met hers again. "But unlike you, am I really doing the best I can to make it better? Am I really doing all I can with what I was given?"

Zula shrugged indifferently. "And exactly what *were* you given?" She chuckled, shaking her head with the hint of a smile. "You were never dealt good cards to begin with."

His eyes, visceral and resolute, burned into hers. "But what if I could do better? What if there's more to life than just . . . *existing*?" He set his right hand on the table, and the overhead light gleamed off its sleek obsidian edges and maroon plating. His brows furrowed. "I'm tired of having to run, hide, and pretend that I'm somebody else, and all for what? To survive? Knowing there are others like me being hunted, abducted, and murdered in cold blood daily. All to entertain so-called 'gods' who can't be seen or even heard by anyone. At least, not by anyone other than us—perhaps the reason we're in this mess to begin with." He shook his head, grimacing with indignation. "And who appointed the fifth-beings 'gods,' anyway? Where the hell do they even come from? And why are they so interested in us?" He shook his head again. "There's still so much we don't know about them." He sighed. His building rage subsided as he looked down at his prosthetic hand, curled into a fist on the table—utilized so effortlessly, as if it were his own flesh and blood. "Still so much we don't know about anything. . . ."

Zula should have known that Edwin's mood all night had something to do with the fifth-beings. Rarely did he go a day without complaining about them one way or another (or so it felt like, anyway). Life would be so much easier were he not a bounty. Perhaps a part of her resented that fact about him. It's not like that was something he could change, and she knew that, certainly—though that knowledge didn't make it any easier for her. She spoke up finally, cutting the newfound silence building between them: "You're doing the best you can with what you have."

"Am I?" Edwin eyed her, and his expression remained uncertain. "I used to think that, but now I'm not so sure."

She liked him a lot less when he let his insecurities get the better of him. "Of course," she said, trying to hide her irritation. "There's no use dwelling on what you can't change."

He looked at her even closer now. "But what is surviving without living?"

Zula scoffed. "You'd call *this* squalor? Seriously? You know how lucky you have it?"

Edwin nodded. "I *do* know how lucky I have it." He smiled. "Which makes me feel all the more guilty, somehow. I . . . I know that sounds ridiculous, but I just don't know how to explain it any other way than that. I can't help but think of the others like me—the less fortunate. All those other bounties: What about them?"

Zula shrugged. "They're not your responsibility."

Edwin remained conflicted. "Then whose responsibility are they?"

"The *gods*," Zula mocked, unsure of what to say—what to tell him to stop fixating on what he couldn't change. "You can't carry the world on your shoulders."

"The fifth-beings aren't gods," Edwin countered, and Zula saw the fire in his eyes once more. "*Fuck* them. Fuck their hold on this universe. Their little games, toying with our lives like we mean nothing. Like we're just their entertainment—a sick thrill of pleasure."

Zula contemplated his words. "And what're you going to do, huh? Take down the fifth-beings, will you? All by your lonesome self?" She shook her head in good humor, raising an eyebrow playfully. "I love your enthusiasm, Eddie, I really do. But where do you think you'll even find them?"

The determination on his face remained; in fact, the passion within only to seemed to grow stronger. "They're only in a higher dimension," he said, nodding contemplatively. "A frequency only a little different from ours."

Zula chuckled and shook her head again. "And, what? How exactly would you get there?"

Edwin picked up his chopsticks, plucked up a piece of squash with them, and examined the fruit closely. "Why, the way every bounty does." For a quick second, Zula saw a madness glimmer in his eyes, and a smile crossed his lips before he put the squash into his mouth and began chewing on it slowly.

Zula thought of Xibalba, the supermassive black hole at the center of Samsara. Not only was Xibalba a sacred place for many colonists in Siletz IV—let alone the whole of Samsara—but it was also a killing field where all bounties were sent to be cashed in. If Edwin was implying what she thought he was implying, well . . . no good would come out of that, would it?

It would be suicide, simple as that. With concern, she looked at him. "I don't know what's on your mind, Ed, but it's best to think with your head, not with your heart." She set her hand on the table. "You have it good here, better than anyone else in your situation."

He nodded and took her hand in his. "Trust me, not a day passes where that's not on my mind."

Her eyes remained on his. "Don't do anything rash that could . . . that could get you killed." She nudged him on the shoulder with her free hand. "Or I'll have to kill you myself." The corner of her lips lifted, and a playful glint showed in her eyes. "Stab you in the throat with these chopsticks."

Edwin chuckled softly. "Some things are worse than death."

"Some things *are* worse than death," Zula agreed. But as her words registered in her mind, her smile slowly vanished, and the thought of Edwin's death lingered. She sighed, tired. "I can always count on you to brighten the mood, can't I?"

The smile in Edwin's eyes remained. "I think you and Brutus will get along just fine."

"'Brutus?'" Zula raised an eyebrow. She had heard Edwin mention that name before, but never in the present tense. "An old buddy of yours, right?"

Edwin nodded. "A good friend," he agreed. "And one you'll meet soon enough."

|25|

JACK IT UP

On Siletz IV, the days were three times longer than those on Earth. For Edwin Dorset, on this day in particular, the hours somehow felt even longer than that. Rarely, these days, did he await something specific to happen, as he did now, akin to a child counting down the days until Christmas—or an adult, awaiting a long-expected package to arrive by mail—watching the hours as they passed by, one second after the other (the anticipation alone making time drag out even longer).

Fortunately for Edwin, his wait wasn't very long.

As he now looked up at the pale blue sky, he could see the clear outline of Brutus's ship, the Crescent, descending toward them. Standing behind him, Zula Cormorant covered her face with an arm as the wind whipped at them, flinging her dark hair wildly about.

The Crescent, almost the size of a mansion—and shaped like one, too—adjusted its lower pediments to level itself out and slowly lowered onto the ground about an acre from them. Edwin began ambling his way toward the ship, and Zula trailed behind, less eager than he. They watched as one of the ship's outer doors opened wide and extended a ramp to the bottom, creating a small stairwell. An outline emerged from the doorway, revealing a big, black, shaggy Liberian clutching a tall staff like a walking stick.

Closing in now, Edwin saw that appearance-wise nothing had changed for his old friend, and he looked the same as the last he had seen him on Ithaca, even down to his apparel. As before, Brutus Wainesworth wore a colorful sunset-orange serape with intricate designs, of geometric and lineal motifs, and—to Edwin, at least—his countenance resembled that of a black bear (a *big*, black bear, that is), albeit with more human features (such as his hands, more akin to "hands" than paws, and his eyes, more akin to a primate's than that of an ursidae).

Edwin's smile widened as he approached Brutus. "I've missed you, old friend." He gave the Liberian a great, big "bear hug," enwrapping both arms around his fur-friend's thick body. "You haven't aged a day."

Brutus grunted, with the hint of a smile in his golden eyes as he looked Edwin over. "Ain't you a sight for sore eyes. Finally, grew some fur on the face, I see." He touched the hair on Edwin's temples with a large finger. "And some whites, too." Glancing behind Edwin, he then noticed Zula standing there, and he grunted again. "Wasn't expecting a friend." Almost reluctantly, he added: "How do ye?"

Edwin glanced from Zula to Brutus. "Brutus, this is Zula— Zula, Brutus."

Zula nodded coolly. "Heard good things about you."

Brutus grinned widely, revealing sharp fangs. "Can't say the same, I'm afraid." His eyes trailed back to Edwin, and there was a teasing look in them. "I see you've been busy, huh? At least, busy compared to the last time I saw you. As I recall, you hardly ever got out. Always working on some new piece. The starving artist life, innit? Keeping yourself safe, I imagine?"

Edwin nodded, and his smile returned. "I'm still here, aren't I?" He crossed his arms. "After all, it was you who taught me how to truly defend myself." He briefly eyed Zula, and a look of contemplation passed over him. "Most importantly, how to defend others."

"Ever the altruist, huh?" Brutus glanced at the top of his staff; the same tip that used to remind Edwin of a lightsaber hilt when lit up with red flame. "I'm surprised you haven't been jaded like the rest of us."

Edwin shrugged, his smile remaining. "I don't have the energy for that."

Brutus grunted a low chuckle. "Of course not." He smiled back. "It's good to see you again, kid."

• • •

He's definitely not living in squalor, Brutus thought as he entered Karla's common room and saw how immaculate the place was, with his gaze falling directly on the large mural painted on one of the walls. Within the colorful artwork, amidst Edwin's many adventures, Brutus noticed a profile of himself on the right-hand side of Orion (where he had first met a younger, more naïve Edwin Dorset). He glanced around the freighter and admired all the organization and plants decorated throughout, intricately displayed; as he listened to the plants—upon his arrival—he could tell at once that they truly admired their caretaker, Edwin. *If it's true that one is the sum of who they surround themselves with, then by the simple indication of the plants' well-being and good nature, I'd surmised the kid's living well off (far better than any of the other bounties, at least).*

Oh, Deidre would be proud, all right. . . .

Brutus glanced at Edwin again, surveying the physical changes in his friend from the past few years of having not seen him. He was older now, more sure of himself. He wore a black and yellow jacket with a high collar, dark gray cargo pants bordering on black, and black high-top boots, with his right arm remaining an obsidian and maroon prosthetic. His black afro was a bit longer than before, less tame, and it had flecks of white at the temples, while his skin was a refined ebony, like dark cocoa. And his eyes were even darker, almost black, but he had a beard now, accentuating his warm, handsome face.

He seems wiser, Brutus remarked. *More aware of his surroundings, perhaps—not that he was ever lacking in that regard. Still, it seems there's something there that hadn't been there before. Can't pinpoint what, exactly.*

Observing Edwin's female accomplice, Brutus remarked something about her that he couldn't pinpoint either—a familiarity, perhaps, as if their paths had crossed before. Truthfully, however, practically all humans looked the same to him, so it wasn't necessarily an unusual feeling to have. She had dark eyes and long, dark hair, woven into partial braids with loose curls. Her skin was a light brown, the color of the desert, and her features were natural and striking, free of any cosmetics, despite many piercings. She also wore all black: a turtleneck long-sleeve, pants, and boots—all in the same fabric, which must have been weather resistant, undoubtedly complementing her form.

An exquisite beauty, Brutus thought. *For a naked ape*. And he wondered how the two had come into acquaintance.

But only for a moment did he wonder that—in all honesty, he didn't care that much.

His mind had more pressing matters to attend to.

Brutus exchanged a dire look with Edwin standing next to the round table in the middle of the room, cast in a lavender light from above. "So, what is it you called me here for?"

The corner of Edwin's lips upturned. "Getting straight to business, huh?"

Brutus shrugged, gripping his staff with both hands. "Well, if you wanted a reunion, there are certainly better ways of getting me here than an SOS. The way I see it, you wanted me here for more than a mere homecoming."

"You're right." Edwin nodded with his arms folded. "I needed you here in person."

"Needed to look me in the eyes? Tell me, what? You're gonna be a father or something? That the lass is pregnant, maybe? No, that's not it. I can see it in your eyes. This is something else. Something more . . . *personal*, perhaps. What exactly is this about?"

Edwin glanced at Zula, who held a neural headset in each hand.

"Oh, I see." At once, Brutus understood; this was a private matter, and Edwin needed a private connection to convey it. "Well, what are we waiting for?"

• • •

It's been a long while since Brutus found himself in the virtual world. Too long, in fact. Once again, he is amazed at how good he feels physically. All the aches and pains he had previously felt are suddenly gone, including his building headache from adapting to Siletz IV's new gravitational pull. Instead, he feels like he's now floating in zero gravity, with that constant feeling of weightlessness, only without the initial feeling of dizziness or loss of appetite. And he can see that his body has not yet materialized.

Indeed, nothing *has materialized.*

But the void can no longer be contained.

A colossal explosion is only inevitable—a big bang, *rocketing the unquantifiable into computable data. The macrocosm expands as atoms materialize into matter and grains of dust smaller than the width of a human hair turn into clouds of dust brought together by gravity—an emergent, mystical force—increasing as the mass increases and curving spacetime, thus coalescing molecules and forming stars.*

Billions of years pass away in seconds, as life begets life, and the ethereal wheel churns. Life is not a substance but a process: To see it all unfold brings everything into perspective. We are all one, *Brutus thinks, and any sense of individuality he currently possesses is immediately shattered.*

At the center of the galaxy lies a supermassive black hole: a region of space from which nothing, not even light, can escape. Blazing, luminous matter encircles the black hole from all sides—from top to bottom, in front and behind. Its gravitational pull distorts our view, warping its surroundings like a carnival mirror. Nearest the center, the gas orbits at the speed of light, becoming thinner and fainter, while the outer portions spin slower, their bright knots constantly forming and dissipating in the accretion disk as powerful magnetic fields wind and twist through the churning gas. Viewing the disk from the side, it appears even brighter on the left than it does on the right. The flaming gas on the left side of the disk moves toward us so fast that the effects of relativity give it a boost in brightness; on the right side, however, the opposite occurs, and the gas moving away from us becomes even dimmer. This asymmetry disappears entirely when we look at the disk face on, because, from that perspective, none of the material moves along our line of sight at all, as the darkness becomes all-consuming.

Xibalba, *Brutus thinks as he observes the event horizon, that cosmic gatekeeper preventing all known existence from ever returning with the secrets of the universe that lie buried within that black hole. It's widely known that you can enter a black hole, but you can never return from it.*

At least, not without the proper equipment.

The first humans to arrive in Samsara had emerged from Xibalba itself, in the first epoch at the beginning of the Great Scattering; their influence had immensely changed the trajectory of the galaxy, accelerating life through the manipulation of dark energy (ancient technology now attributed to the "fifth dimension"), leaving a trail of breadcrumbs in their wake, all pointing back to Xibalba.

The invading conquerors (homo sapiens, mostly) quickly established a dynasty, expanding their horizon from planet to planet, reaching the Outermost Edge of the Inner Rings by Epoch 13. And as is expected, peace among the colonists didn't last, as tribalism quickly separated the scattered invaders, dividing them into separate clans and government states, each influenced by their relative location. By the dawn of Epoch 37, a great war broke out among the Innermost Ring rulers and the Outermost Ring rulers, putting an abrupt halt to commerce, communication, and progress universally, as empire waged war against empire, and the universe at large fell into a dark age, regressed by cybernetic warfare—the adverse effects destroying centuries worth of databanks.

Eventually, the secrets of humanity's origin were lost for good, as new religions continued to emerge and the truth of it all became lost in the midst, skewed by time and constant change. By Epoch 52, the great war came to an end, and the victors divided the spoils of a shattered universe, eventually cultivating a unified regime that lasted until Epoch 86, when the next revolution proliferated—a just rebellion against an oppressive, totalitarian hold on the universe.

On and on, this cycle repeated itself—of war and dissension, as unchecked powers came and went, brought down by uprisings, civil disputes, and competing planet-states. Not until Epoch 119 did the universe come into a long stretch of relative peace, that had lasted until Epoch 214, when the Saxon Conquerors emerged from the Outermost Depths of Moksha and took full control of Samsara by Epoch 260. The Saxons, ruled by a single emperor—a theocratic monarch, remembered as a god to some Xibalbists—established a dynasty spanning from the Innermost Ring of Samsara to the Outermost Ring, that lasted over two hundred epochs, officially ending sometime between Epoch 432 and Epoch 435.

The universal language many know today, in fact, derives from the Saxons' language, that has continued to form after their sojourn in Moksha. Again, much of that period is lost, though many archaeological findings indicate that around this time fifth-dimensional technology had first been rediscovered, no doubt utilized to help end the Saxons' longstanding rule since Epoch 260.

Of course, in the face of Xibalba, none of that seems to matter. Whatever secrets lie buried within that black hole remain a mystery. Perhaps the universe itself lies buried in the interior of another black hole, that exists within an even larger parent universe, and on and on the cycle of life repeats itself—like self-replicating DNA, different every time.

Life remains paradoxical, and every question answered brings with it another question.

From the void behind Xibalba, a colossal brown hand—a human hand—extends out and encloses a fist over the black hole. Slowly, the hand opens wide, and Xibalba is now gone, and instead of the black hole, on the palm stand three figures—two humans and one Liberian. At once,

Brutus feels himself enter the body of the Liberian, and he watches in amazement as a battle rages overhead—an epic space opera—*with hundreds and thousands of ships in conflict with one another, and yet with no distinguishable side.*

Edwin observes Brutus silently with his arms folded, while Zula stands by his side, the three of them standing in a semi-circle.

Brutus glances back at Edwin, and the two lock eyes. "A little dramatic, ain't it?"

"You know why we're here, don't you?"

Brutus thinks that he may have it figured out but cannot know for sure. "Enlighten me."

"For over a millennium, the fifth-beings have had a hold on this universe. Bounties such as mine continue to wage, day after day, with no end in sight. The battle happening over us right now? It's happening all over Samsara. Portals like the one I came through in Zarathustra continue to appear out of nowhere, and the economy continues to thrive on it, commercializing it into a sport. When is enough enough?"

Brutus grins. "And what are you thinking, that you're gonna put a stop to it all?"

Zula softly chuckles, and to Brutus, it appears that she's had this talk with Edwin already. Except now, he sees a resolution in Edwin's eyes that makes him want to believe that it could be possible. Regarding Brutus's question about whether he can put a stop to it, Edwin does not hesitate: "Yes."

Brutus laughs. "Oh, Edwin, my boy. You're playing with fire."

"Fire can be redirected. Engineered into a weapon, a tool of salvation."

"And what exactly do you have in mind?"

Edwin extends his hand out, enclosed in a fist, and turns it over, opening his palm wide to reveal a black hole the size of a baseball now hovering above it. "Xibalba," he says, and the rays of gas light up his eyes like blazing embers. "The place where all bounties are taken."

Brutus doesn't understand. "You want to be cashed in?"

Edwin nods. "And I want you to do it."

Brutus wants to laugh, but there is no humor in Edwin's expression. "That's suicide."

"That's what I keep telling him," Zula says matter-of-factly. "He doesn't listen."

"It's the only way," Edwin tells them.

Brutus shakes his head. "And how do you know that you'd survive it? Or that you could even return? You don't know what's waiting for you on the other side."

Edwin shrugs. "I have an idea."

Brutus shakes his head again. "How?"

Edwin taps his temple with his free hand; in the digital realm, both of his hands are bioorganic. "I hear voices in my head," he says with an amused grin. "The fifth-beings, getting louder every day."

Brutus exchanges a look with Zula. "And what do they tell you, exactly?"

"Most of them, it's like tuning into a radio—only, a frequency I'm not supposed to hear."

"And the others?"

"Some of them tell me there's a way."

Brutus considers Edwin's words. "You sound like Hendrix."

"Hendrix lost faith in the world." A smile crosses Edwin's face. "I haven't."

"There's no guarantee we'd make it alive," Brutus tells him. "The place is a death zone."

"We're miracles, you and I. Every one of us." Edwin encloses the fist holding Xibalba, and suddenly the world around them explodes with brilliant light. "There's never a guarantee of anything."

• • •

They sat again in Edwin's freighter, where they had been moments before. Edwin took off his neural headset and set it on the table. He glanced at Brutus, doing likewise. "Always one for theatrics," Brutus said, shaking his head with a wry grin. "You artists are always the same."

"So?" Edwin wanted to know. "Are you going to help me?"

Brutus's resigned grin remained. "Do I have a choice?"

|26|

JOURNEY INTO NIGHT

Edwin stood by the window frame with his hands in his pockets, staring out into the black sea of space. *Look at how far you've come*, he told himself, remembering the days on Earth when he used to wallow in his earthly misfortunes, so minute in comparison. Worrying about how he would pay for rent. How he would survive just another day. *Now, look at you: You're going up against the gods.*

What a life.

What a world.

What a beautiful, unpredictable existence.

He had never considered himself to be anything special. Not really. But this? Being here, seeing what only a few could dream of seeing back where he had come from? This . . . this was special. Not him, but everything around him, every moment down to the very air he breathed. Whatever happened next, at least he had this. Nothing could take that from him. A moment could never be undone.

"What a view."

Edwin glanced at Zula, now standing beside him. She wore a black crop top, fully displaying the henna-like tattoos that finely ran along her arms and hands, as well as the hint of a Sanskrit-like script running down her right ribcage. She was barefoot and wore dark plum harem pants, with abstract, geometric golden stitching, making Edwin feel inspired to draw every time he saw them. A lilac bandana wrapped around the front of her dark, spunky hair, now tied into a messy bun atop. Multiple piercings decorated her face—a septum ring, nostril stud, and at least five piercings on each ear, including a midline on her tongue—but it was her dark, lovely eyes that had immediately seized Edwin's attention. He smiled at her. "Hey."

Zula folded her arms and glanced out the window. "Back in the Wayfarer, I used to see views like this all the time. I grew desensitized. Now, though? Now, it's like I'm seeing it for the first time. . . . Seeing it like it'll be my last."

He eyed her closely. "You didn't have to come, you know."

She smiled. "I wouldn't be much of a friend if I didn't, would I?"

"Friends don't put other friends in danger."

She shrugged, nonchalant. "Clearly, you haven't had many friends."

He glanced out the window again—once more, speechless.

"You know, we *can* change the settings." She stepped closer to the window and set a hand on it. "Turn on infrared and see all the beauty the human eye can't."

He nodded. "I know." He had lived here once with Brutus and Hendrix. "This isn't my first time on a ship."

"Of course not." She eyed him, up and down. "You've seen your fair share of the world, haven't you? That's what I love about you."

"My experiences?"

"Your experiences," she agreed. "That makes you who you are."

That made him smile. "Likewise, Z."

Zula rested her head on Edwin's shoulder. "When I was a kid, I used to imagine that I was out there, on my own, flying from star system to star system, out on some cosmic voyage. An epic space odyssey, perhaps." Edwin chuckled, and he also thought of when he was a kid, having had somewhat of a similar experience, only he used to image himself as Superman instead, soaring across the sky to save the day. "Now, looking at it, I can't imagine how lonely that must be."

"It can get lonely at times."

"What will you do if it works?"

"If what works?"

"The reason we're here." Zula laughed. "What else?"

Edwin shook his head. "I don't know," he admitted. "I haven't thought that far."

A flicker of doubt shown on her face. "You sure you're making the right decision?"

He nodded again. "Only one way to find out."

She took in a deep breath. "Will you come and find me when all's said and done?"

"Do you know much about black holes?"

She shrugged a shoulder. "Only what they taught at the temples." She nodded, now thinking about it. "It was a good place to panhandle, so probably more than most."

"The closer you get to a black hole, the more time becomes distorted."

"Relativity," she agreed. "What about it?"

He didn't want to vocalize it, but he had to be realistic above anything else. "If I make it through, there might not be a chance I come back at the same time I left."

Zula scoffed playfully. "And—? If you're able to extract fifth-dimensional technology, none of that matters. You could go anywhere you want. *Do* anything you want. You'd have the power of a god." She locked eyes with him. "And you could even save your brother."

Edwin's heart uplifted at the prospect Zula put before him. *Save Lamar?* That was a probability he had only considered once, long ago, but if he let his imagination run wild, perhaps he would lose track of why he was doing this in the first place. *One thing at a time*, he thought.

"Hey lovebirds," Brutus's voice called out from the overhead speakers. Edwin and Zula glanced back to look at the main cabin that extended to the cockpit where its captain occupied. "You might want to see this."

Edwin and Zula exchanged a silent look, and then Zula began to walk away, toward the main cabin, but Edwin grabbed her by the wrist, forcing her to stop and turn around to look at him. "To answer your question," he began, gently pinching her chin with a loving look in his eyes. "Of course, I'd come find you."

He leaned in and kissed her.

• • •

"We're drawing close," Brutus told them as they entered the cockpit. The Liberian's face lit up red from the monitors in front of him, and the entire cockpit also had an atmospheric red tint to it. "You see that up ahead?"

"Other ships?" Zula guessed aloud, leaning forward and eyeing what Brutus was pointing at beyond the curved wall of reinforced glass separating them from instantaneous death.

"Aye." Brutus grunted. "You might want to get ready now, Edwin. We won't have much longer until we're there. Zula, I'll need you to mount the guns soon. The Crescent's defense systems are good, but they're far from perfect, and I'll need all the manpower I can get."

Edwin felt his stomach drop. *This is really happening*, he realized, suddenly feeling nauseous. *It's one thing to know something, but another thing to experience it firsthand*. He nodded, unsure of what to say. *No going back now, is there? Let's hope I didn't doom us all.*

• • •

Edwin closely examined the void belt in his hands: Fifth-dimensional technology, able to harvest dark energy, reverse-engineered. He wondered what other kind of technology he would find on the other side of Xibalba. Better yet, he wondered if the void belt would even be strong enough to get him there. What if it malfunctioned beyond the event horizon? What if he was being foolish for doing this? Was he really thinking this through entirely?

Too many "what-ifs," he thought, shaking his head. *It's going to work.*

It has *to.*

But how did he know that?

He didn't—not entirely.

(—SURRENDER—)

The voices: Some of those voices were on his side. How he knew that, he wasn't sure, but that powerful inclination and unwavering certainty had grown even more between the weeks of having planned this expedition. Sometimes, he could feel abstract emotions from the bleeding effect: the fifth-beings' thoughts bleeding into his consciousness. Not all were friendly, of course. Except not all were insidious, either. Most, in fact, saw him as nothing more than simple entertainment, like an animal in a zoo. There were the few, however, that pitied him; at times, he felt as if they were communicating to him on purpose. Relaying information that may be vital for him.

You don't know that, he told himself. *You can't be certain.*

But that voice of doubt? That voice was his own.

You can't be certain of anything, he further told himself, being the devil's advocate. *It's too late to doubt yourself. The more you doubt yourself, the less you'll be able to accomplish. As long as you continue—*

(—BORING—)

He shook his head again with a sigh.

Still not used to that, he thought. *All the more reason to go through with this.*

He set the void belt on the bed, right beside the plasma gun, loaded bandolier, and grapple gun he would also take with him. *Is this enough?* he wondered. *Maybe I'm forgetting something.*

(—ASSHOLE—)

The voices were getting worse. *Time to shut them up for good.*

The door closed behind him, and he turned around to find Zula now standing there. "You ready?"

He nodded and glanced again at the void belt on the bed. "I think so."

She eyed him closely. "Are you scared?"

"A little," he admitted. "Nothing a distraction wouldn't help with." He exchanged a solemn look with her. "Tell me something, Z. Something I don't know."

The corner of her lips upturned. "Like what?"

Edwin shrugged. "Your first memory, perhaps. What was it?"

"My first memory?" Zula considered his question. "I think it had to do with my dad. He used to make me laugh a lot. Would tell the funniest stories. *Fascinating* stories. About his youth on Moab. How life had been outside the Wayfarer. I remember once sitting on his lap, in his study, and he told me a story that made me laugh so hard I threw up." She chuckled, shaking her head with a reflective glimmer in her eyes. "My mother berated him for that."

That also made Edwin chuckle. He loved the image of a little Zula, running around the Wayfarer and doing Zula things. "I would have loved to meet him."

Zula nodded, though the glimmer in her eyes had died. "Sometimes, I wonder how different he would be from my memories of him. It's been so long now that I can't even remember what he looked like."

Edwin knew the feeling all too well. He remembered nothing about Vicky Dorset—nothing worth remembering, that is.

Zula gazed into his eyes. "What about you? What was your first memory?"

Edwin folded his arms and looked down. "For the longest time, I had thought my first memory was one of pain. You see, I used to play by the train tracks back in Oakland. That place was my safe haven, the only place I truly felt safe. And I remember having a toy with me, one that I took everywhere. I think it was a gift from Lamar (I can't remember). Anyway, I remember spinning around with it and watching as the world went by, turning into nothing but a blur, nothing but the toy."

Zula listened with a smile.

Edwin laughed. "It was thrilling, really. When you're a kid, it's so easy to find such joy in the mundane; I guess we can learn a lot from kids." He scratched his neck. "So, there I was, spinning around the train tracks with a big, goofy smile on my face. Spinning and spinning and spinning. So happy, so *alive*." His smile slowly dissipated. "Until the next thing I knew, I was on the ground, and my two front teeth lay somewhere in the rocks."

Zula covered her mouth.

Edwin chuckled darkly. "You can't imagine how much pain I must have felt. When you're that young, everything is new, and it's like your senses are on overload, pulling in new information all at once." He shook his head. "For the longest time, I looked back on that memory like a harbinger of all that was to come: the pain that had formed me, and the pain that would no doubt be my end." He hesitated, giving his next words weight. "But I was wrong: That wasn't my first memory, losing my two front teeth." He hesitated again. "It was the toy: the gift from Lamar, and that feeling of elation that came with it as

I spun around and around and around." He nodded thought-fully, another smile forming on his lips. "And if my life is to end how it began, from what I first remember of it, then I think I have nothing to fear."

Zula took Edwin's left hand in her right hand, and she placed her palm on his palm, fingers pressing together, one after the other—flesh and prosthetic. She gazed into his eyes, and he gazed back into hers. An intimate silence hung between them, and more could be said within that silence than with words. The moment was there, and all that came with it—a sweet, tender moment.

And possibly the last.

Zula gently placed Edwin's left hand on her right breast, bare beneath her crop top. And with his right hand, he softly caressed her left arm, using only his fingertips, affectionately trailing up to her shoulders and the nape of her neck. Their eyes remained locked together, and she trembled as he felt her nipple harden slightly beneath the palm of his left hand. She squeezed his hand even tighter over her breast and emitted a low moan. He began kissing her neck, holding the back of her head with his right hand as she grabbed his waist and pulled him even closer to her.

They stumbled onto the bed, and their hungry lips found each other's.

She parted her legs for him as he climbed atop her, and he pushed away the void belt and other items next to them, hear-ing as they collapsed onto the ground haphazardly. He pinned both of her hands above her head and ravenously kissed her neck again—this time, slowly making his way downward. Her fingers entwined his, and he pulled up the bottom of her shirt using his other hand. Kissing along her navel, his lips trailed upward to the soft mound of her breast. She shuddered when his mouth found its way to her nipple, and she made another low, guttural sound as her hips careened against his, wanting him.

Zula slipped a hand to the back of Edwin's head, burying her fingers in his hair. Once more, he kissed his way downward—only this time, he didn't stop at her navel. Using only his teeth, he bit at the hem of her pants and began pulling them off her.

"Yes," she whispered as he kissed along her inner thighs, slowly working his way to her most sensitive spot. She trembled at his touch, but he took his time with her. Her legs enwrapped his head, and her pelvis rocked against his face. He caressed her breast with one hand and explored the rest of her body with the other, while her fingers strongly gripped the top of his hair, pulling at it. Her eyes rolled, and she had to shut them. "Don't stop. . . ."

He didn't stop—*couldn't* stop. If this was going to be their last moment together, he would give her one to remember him by.

Her breathing grew labored, and her lips slightly parted. She began convulsing beneath him, and the legs enwrapping his head tightened even more, almost suffocating him. But for Edwin, there was nothing more pleasuring than the act of pleasuring, and he had to focus his mind on something else so that he wouldn't finish prematurely. Still, he didn't stop. Intuitively, he listened as Zula's moaning changed frequency, like fine-tuning an instrument before playing, and he felt her body tremble from head to toe.

All at once, she stiffened—exhaling a deep sigh of relief, filled with ecstatic bliss.

Edwin rose, wiping off the excess liquid from his chin and beard.

Zula violently grabbed him by the shirt, flipped him over and onto his back, and climbed atop him. She took hold of him—her grip strong—and slid him into her.

"I love you," she said, a little louder than a whisper, as she began to ride him.

He elevated her by the ass and gazed into her eyes. "I love you."

Already, he could feel the inner muscles clamping over him beginning to tighten, and he couldn't hold it much longer.

(—YOU HAVE TO SURRENDER—)

For both of them, the moment suddenly came in full force—the moment it had all been leading up to: The climax.

|27|

THE LANDING

The path to Xibalba was littered with wreckage. Torn warships and littered deep sea space vessels were spewed around them like a cluttered asteroid field. The Crescent decelerated as Brutus maneuvered through the wreckage with caution. "Reapers will be lying in wait," he told Edwin, sitting beside him in the red cockpit. "Damn opportunists."

"We'll be ready for them," Edwin agreed, nodding with an unfazed look. "We've faced worse before."

"We have, haven't we?" Brutus chuckled deeply. What came to mind was their time in the Yocatlān region of Brecken, around the apex of their traveling together, before Hendrix's health had declined. Oh, there were certainly times they'd had their brush with death, that was true. More times than Brutus could count with his big, hairy fingers. "We've certainly had our fun."

Edwin glanced at the black Liberian. "You know what they say . . ." His lips formed into a grin. "The fun's not over yet."

Brutus grunted.

Stillness hung between them—a looming dread, perhaps.

Once more, Brutus broke the silence. "I take it you said your goodbyes?"

Edwin nodded, assuming that Brutus was referring to Zula, having already gone to the lower deck to operate the manual turrets. "I did."

Brutus grunted again, in typical Brutus fashion. "I'm not saying goodbye yet." His eyes remained ahead, on the path before them displayed on the monitors. "Not until you come back."

Edwin regarded that. "So, you now believe I'm coming back?"

"Why else would I be here?" There was a vulnerability in Brutus's voice unbecoming of him (not without an instrument, that is). "You've proven me wrong before."

You and me both, Edwin thought.

A blip went off on a monitor—immediately followed by two more blips.

Brutus readied himself. "Looks like the first of our company's finally arrived."

· · ·

Space pirates: At least three ships. An organized crew, no doubt. Being so close to Xibalba, it was only inevitable to come across them. And like barracudas at the sight of fresh prey, they pounced all at once. Encroaching the Crescent from all sides, hungry for unsullied blood: the cargo and its bounty within. There would be more beside them. There always is.

But despite appearances, the Crescent was no unsuspecting prey—far from it, in fact.

At first, it was evident that the pirates aimed to capture the Crescent unharmed, for maximum profit; after all, a bounty is worth more alive than dead. They were planning to board the ship forcefully, using two ships to anchor it in place and the third to dock it. An amateur move on their part. The Crescent had teeth, and she bit back. In the deep vacuum of space, no explosions were discharged. Not even a sound. Nonetheless, in a matter of minutes, three more ships had been added to the floating debris surrounding them.

And the Crescent pressed onward.

• • •

Ahead, they could see it in all its glory, visible only through infrared: Xibalba, a place of death and rebirth—the supermassive black hole orbiting the center of Samsara. Edwin felt a hand clench tightly in his gut. Already, he could see that they weren't the only ones there—of course, they weren't the only ones there.

An influx of space vessels surrounded Xibalba, and at least thirty to forty different bounties floated near its center, suspended in animation. All the bounties were already dead, Edwin had to guess. They were too far to see clearly, but he was certain that none of them had been given the luxury of any protective layer. *I'm the luckiest of them all*, he thought. *I'm the crazy bastard doing this of my own volition.*

(—GOING TO DIE—)

He glanced at Brutus. "It's time, isn't it?"

Brutus exchanged a dire look with him and nodded. "Aye."

Edwin stood up and set a hand on Brutus's thick shoulder, covered by a tan serape cast in red light. "Goodbye, my friend."

"Like I said," Brutus grunted, "no goodbyes until you get back."

Edwin nodded. "Of course." Without another word, he strode away from Brutus, the red monitors, and the cockpit, and headed toward the lower deck before climbing down a set of steel ladders. As he walked through the tight corridor, he felt his confidence return with full force and knew at once that he was doing the right thing. He wasn't doing this solely for himself but for all the others like him who hadn't been given the luxuries he had. It was time to make the fifth-beings pay for their interference with the third dimension. Activating his void belt, he felt the black nanometal stretch across his body, covering all but his face and the bandolier wrapped around his shoulders with a plasma rifle attached to the back of it. Golden etchings ran along the sleek suit, creating a bright glow, reflecting off the dark walls surrounding him.

Once at the airlock, Edwin waited for the first door to open, and he stepped through it willingly. The airtight door shut behind him, enclosing him in the small airlock. "Ready when you are," he told Brutus through the intercom, adjusting his gravitational pull as he stepped onto the first door, right below the last door, so that the exit stood right above him.

The rest of his void suit spread onto his face, covering his entire head and creating a helmet with a sleek, reflective visor. The sound of his breathing suddenly intensified, and his vision tripled in efficiency, as he could now see the small dust motes floating above him, each unique unto themselves. Even with all his augmentations, nothing beat wearing a void suit.

Brutus's voice came in: "Nearing the drop-off point." A slight pause: "One minute to countdown."

Edwin closed his eyes and took a deep breath. *Soon, this will be just another memory. Another memory, among the many, to one day forget.* He grabbed the plasma rifle attached to the back of his bandolier and readied himself as the airlock began to depressurize. *Let's make it one to remember.*

"Hey, Eddie." Zula's voice trailed in through the intercom. "Good luck out there."

"Thanks, Z." Edwin smiled faintly. "I'll need all of it I can get."

"Remember us on the other side," she continued, half-joking. "And be sure to come back in one piece."

"I don't intend to lose any more limbs."

"Thirty seconds to countdown," Brutus input.

Edwin nodded. *All my life has led me to this one moment in time. From that day on the train tracks, to my exodus from everything I once thought I knew. To Sibyl, finding me on Zarathustra, and even losing my arm on Orion. It all feels preordained, somehow, like it was supposed to happen. I know that's just confirmation bias, and I know my circumstances are only a byproduct of chance, but if I were to do it any differently, I wouldn't be here now, would I?*

Chance, fate, and destiny—all one the same.

And whatever happens next, I know I'm ready for it.

"Send off in ten . . .

"Nine . . .

"Eight . . .

"Seven . . .

(—MISTAKE—)

"Six . . .

"Five . . .

(—GOING TO—)

"Four . . .

(—DIE—)

"Three . . .

"Two . . .

(—GOING TO—)

"One."

The airlock shot open, and Edwin launched out of the Crescent.

• • •

Silence enveloped him—all but the sound of his breath.

All around him, Edwin saw ships of various sizes orbiting Xibalba, reminiscent of the skies of Zarathustra the day of his reaping. Among the many, the Crescent clashed with at least three of them—sending torpedos and evading projectiles—and fighting valorously. Now, with better vision, he could also see a clearer image of the other bounties—some of them getting launched out of airlocks and instantly killed from the pressure, if not dead already; for others, already past the event horizon and frozen in time.

Rocketing forward, the plasma rifle in hand, Edwin set his gaze on Xibalba. His void suit propelled him onward, soaring him across the battlefield, as he evaded debris and vessels in his way. A small pod with a single pilot noticed him and began following him—undoubtedly, trying to steal his bounty and cash him in himself—but Edwin glanced back and shot the plasma rifle at the pod.

A beam of energy emitted from the rifle, separating the vehicle into broken pieces, and the pilot jettisoned out of his seat, dying instantaneously. The plasma rifle sent him off course, but he quickly corrected himself and continued his path toward Xibalba, as the gravitational pull increased the closer he drew near it.

He was a human bullet—barreling forward, toward the void.

(—SURRENDER—)

Into the heart of the storm.

• • •

The closer Edwin got to the event horizon, the more distant the bounties in front of him appeared to be. Before, it was as if they had been frozen in time. But time was relative, wasn't it? And the closer he got to the bounties in front of him, the more traction they seemed to get—deeper into the void. Behind him, all he could see now were bright lights, colorful and entrancing, moving so fast that they were barely even perceptible.

No one had ever returned from a black hole. At least, not since the earliest humans had first invaded Samsara. But had they actually entered from this side of the black hole? Where exactly had they come from? Better yet, what was waiting for him on the other side? Another universe just like his own? Another dimension? From here on out, he was entering the unknown. The unquantifiable void, where anything was possible, and reality was no longer bound by space-time.

Already, he could feel his very atoms beginning to fluctuate, as if they would collapse any second. Something was happening to him. Something that he couldn't express in words.

And once more he thought of his life as a story: a grand tale with a beginning, middle, and end. Every story has a turning point, doesn't it? A point in time when everything changes. *This is my turning point*, Edwin thought with resolution. *The crucial moment to define all that comes next.* And he had to wonder: Was he nearing the end of his story? Or was this only the beginning. . . . ?

He grinned, feeling unreasonably optimistic: *Only one way to tell.*

All at once, darkness enveloped him.

|28|

LOOSE ENDS

Sibylla Kal was a survivor, and she always had been. From her breeding on Te Kore, to her liberation and wandering voyage throughout the cosmos, it was nothing short of a miracle that she was still alive. She'd had many close calls before—too many to count on both hands. But this? This was definitely the closest she had ever gotten to calling it quits—to total annihilation, awaiting her just around the corner.

Still, she was a survivor.

Until her very last breath, a survivor she would always be.

The wind had been knocked out of Sibyl, and she awoke lying on her back.

Her ribs felt as if they had been broken, repeatedly rammed into with a sledgehammer. But thankfully, her ribs weren't broken (conversely, they certainly *felt* like they were broken). She didn't know how long she had been on the ground for. Not long, she supposed, because—right above her—she could still see the canopy aflame.

Evergreens—a blazing, hot, and vibrant red.

The heat was blocked out by her void suit, but she could still hear the nearest trees wailing through her empathic emulator, mourning those lost to the fire and delivering those farthest, through their root systems, their leftover nutrients in case the fire continued to spread and completely decimate them.

The sun was nowhere to be seen, and yet the flames lit up the sky as if it were still day, covering the landscape in a hazy gray, as if from uncontrollable pollution in a megacity.

For a moment, Sibyl forgot where she was.

Orion, she finally remembered, as she got her bearings. *That's right. . . .*

D-D's augmentation facility had been compromised, and Sibyl had sacrificed herself for the others to escape. A noble endeavor, and one she hoped would actually pay off. Glancing around, she saw the wreckage of the airship that she had taken down with her. A large piece of shrapnel had landed next to her, and if it had landed even a few inches closer, she would have been impaled.

As it stood, anyone else in her position would have died from the impact of the crash alone. But she had the one thing they didn't—she still wore it, in fact, as it had undoubtedly saved her life. The orange glow of the void suit continued to glimmer, illuminating everything around her, dimmer than it had been before; moreover, her entire body was covered from head to toe.

A close call.

Sibyl struggled to get up. Even with her void suit on, she still had a hard time getting to her knees. Groaning like an old-woman awakening from a three-year coma, she could eventually stand upright (hardly even). And on the ground nearby, she noticed a charred corpse, half-crushed by a large metal beam.

Should have found a new hobby, Sibyl thought. Her sentiments only went out to the native life of Orion, as well as the bounties, and for all the emotions that she felt from them, channeled through the empathic emulator—not the fuckers responsible for their genocide.

A gunshot rang in the distance.

Followed by two more gunshots, this time closer.

Reapers, looking for more bounties. If she didn't get a move on, they would find her. And given that she had no value to them, she would end up just like that charred corpse, left to rot.

Unacceptable.

She staggered her way forward, searching for a weapon—really, anything that she could use. When she hijacked the airship, she had been armed with a gun, but she had obviously lost it during the crash. Glancing around, however, she saw that everything had been decimated. Even the colossal trees, barely left standing, were nothing but scattered embers and scorched timber. Maybe if she could—

A light shone onto Sibyl from above.

She turned around, peering up at the source of illumination coming from a small hillock above her. She tried to run, but her knees gave out beneath her, and she stumbled back onto the ground, landing hard on her side.

Dammit.

She tried to get back up, but she couldn't will her body to move at all.

Too tired. Too weak. . . .

Three reapers climbed down the hillock, quickly surrounded Sibyl, and aimed their flashlights attached to assault rifles at her. "You see that?" One of the men remarked, exchanging a look with his two companions. "She's wearing some kind of void suit."

The other reaper—a bald male—spoke up: "I thought those weren't made anymore."

"They aren't."

The last reaper—a blonde female—stood above Sibyl and kicked her gently with a foot, perhaps to see if she was still alive. "These fuckers cost a fortune." She knelt down, examining Sibyl even closer. "Maybe we could strip it off her."

"And how would we do that?"

The woman shrugged. "I don't know. If we take her back to the ship, Anika might know what to do."

"Are you kidding?" The bald man spat with clear disdain. "You really want to share this with the others?! The suit's worth half a bounty, for all we know."

"I've got a better idea." The other male pulled out a small saw blade, turned the blade on with the flick of the wrist, and watched as its end lit up with a savage red glow. He stood above Sibyl and looked down at her with a psychotic glint in his eyes. And then he knelt down, brought the blade to her face, and began to—

"*Aghhhhhh!*"

The reaper collapsed backward, violently fell onto his back, and clutched at his hand, nearly cut off from the saw blade that had bounced back. His hand hung loose from his arm, half of it still hanging by open tissue, gushing out blood liberally. "Mother*fuuuccckk*!"

"You stupid asshole," the woman scolded him. "That's a void suit, moron. You seriously thought that would work?"

The injured reaper balled into a fetal position, screaming in agony, but his comrades remained apathetic to his affliction.

The woman glanced at her uninjured companion. "Call in Nairobi," she told him. "Tell her we've got something worth checking out."

• • •

The heavy scent of burning wood followed him everywhere he went. In his hair, in his clothes, and even in his skin. A heavy smoke covered the landscape, obscuring over twenty feet and beyond. Dieter Gammon sat atop one of the supply crates and watched as another group of reapers returned to camp, bringing back nothing with them. Ever since Zarathustra and having sampled that little glimmer of hope—the bounty in his grasp, that had somehow got away—he couldn't stop obsessing about how close he had been to getting out of that godforsaken planet with the bounty and cashing him in himself.

So damn close, and yet not close enough.

Never good enough, he thought spitefully. *Can't do anything right. . . .*

He spat a load of phlegm on a wilted fern. *I should have lobotomized that little shit the first chance I got,* he reflected, wishing that he hadn't been so careless. *That's not happening again*, he further thought. *This time, I'm coming back with more than one of them.* Fuck it, *they mean nothing to me, and what do I care? (I was so close.)* Xibalba, *if only I had lobotomized that little—*

"Dieter."

Dieted turned and saw one of the new reapers standing above him. A blonde female: Karina, *was it?* He couldn't remember her name, but she had a nice ass, and his imagination ran wild. He shrugged, sounding more irritated than he really felt. "*What?*"

"We found something you might want to look at."

He sighed, already at a point of fucking exhaustion. Already, it felt as if they had been there for days, fighting just for scraps. He was expecting competition with the other reapers, sure— and especially once their location had been made—but he hadn't expected this much pushback. So far, all they had accomplished was getting one dismembered corpse (that may or may not have even been a bounty). And yet, how many of their newfound group had died in the process? And how much planning had been involved beforehand, and all for what? Ah hell; the night was still young, and he couldn't call it quits just yet—they hadn't gone this far to end up with only scraps.

"This better be something good," Dieter protested and stood up reluctantly.

"You'll want to see this." A grin formed on the blonde's haggard lips. "Trust me."

Karina led him to a closed tent, and as he entered it, the first thing he noticed was Nairobi Nadine standing there, peering down at the ground. Another reaper sat on one of the nearby hammocks, with his gaze also on the same spot that Nairobi had her icy blue eyes so dead set on. This time, Dieter glanced down as well. What he saw was a body splayed on the ground—a female, he had to guess, by the unmistakable feminine form—and wearing some kind of sheen, black metallic membrane, covering her from head to toe, with yellow-orange etchings lining the suit and emitting a soft amber glow around the small tent.

Dieter stepped in closer, and Nairobi finally noticed him enter, but her attention immediately went back to the body on the ground. "A bounty?" he wondered aloud.

Nairobi shook her head. "Don't know." She knelt down, peering even closer. "But a void suit, nonetheless. It can be sold for a hefty price."

"She dead?"

"Don't think so," Karina said, stepping around Dieter and standing directly behind Nairobi. "We found her near a crash site."

Dieter nodded, intrigued. He glanced at Nairobi, whose dark face lit a faint honey-yellow from the void suit. "Any way we can get it off her?"

Nairobi shook her head. "Not without bringing her back to the ship and alerting the others."

Soon, there won't be much "others" left, Dieter thought, and he shrugged a shoulder. "Shouldn't be a problem. For now, I say we keep this a secret." He glanced at the blonde, Karina. "How many others know about this?"

Karina glanced at her bald companion sitting on the hammock. "Only us," she said, before reconsidering and adding: "And one more, but he went back to the ship to get medical aid."

"What for?" Nairobi asked.

"He thought he could extract the suit himself." She chuckled darkly. "Found out the hard way that it just wasn't possible."

Nairobi considered that. "Can he be trusted?"

Karina exchanged a look with the bald reaper once more. "More or less."

"One of you should take care of him," Dieter suggested with a smug leer. "The less who know about this, the better."

The bald reaper got off the hammock and stood tall. "I can do it." He cocked a grin, cranking his neck. "I've wanted to do it for a while now, if we're being honest."

"Make it discrete," Dieter told him. "And make sure no one else knows."

The reaper nodded. "It's my specialty." He chuckled and strode away, leaving the tent with haste.

Immediately, Dieter glanced at Karina. "You trust him?"

She eyed him cautiously. "A little."

"But not much?"

Karina shrugged. "Haven't worked with him long enough."

A hungry greed shown in Dieter's eyes, though the scar on the right side of his face somewhat detracted from it. (Only somewhat.) "So, there's no attachment there?"

She shook her head. "Not in our line of work."

Dieter exchanged a quick glance with Nairobi before eyeing Karina again. "Once he's taken care of the other guy, I want you to take care of him." He nodded curtly. "I take it you'll know what to do."

Karina raised an eyebrow. "And what's stopping you from doing the same to me?"

Dieter smirked; he thought of her naked again, with her back arched as he pounded her from behind. "Why, an interest in investment, darlin'."

She shrugged, stumped. "What is that even supposed to mean?"

"Let's just say you've shown your worth. And now it's our time to return the favor."

"By not killing me?" She still wasn't convinced.

Fucking bitch, Dieter thought. He shrugged, with another smug look on his face. "You scratched our back, and now it's our time we scratch yours."

Karina considered that. She nodded curtly, glanced at the body on the ground once more, and walked away, leaving the tent in haste, just as the other reaper had. Once Karina was completely out of their sight, Nairobi glanced at Dieter, her accomplice of ten plus years. "We're going to kill her, right?"

Dieter's crooked smile broadened. "What else will we do in the meantime?"

• • •

Sibyl stands in a bleak world of white. The landscape is blanketed in it, and the crimson moon bulges in the sky as a stark contrast, rising slowly above the bare mountain peak. Snowflakes slowly drift downward, and she extends her hand out to catch one but discovers that they're not even snowflakes at all but ashes. Examining the moon closer, too, she realizes that it's actually on fire, with bursts of radiation emitting from it and flaring out like a sun at the verge of an astronomical explosion.

She wears the "Death Defier," her navy-blue jacket with maroon linings along the sleeves, collar, and backside. Her dark, wavy hair is down, and her nearly black eyes gaze ahead, set on the horizon. She notices movement on the mountaintop—too far to see clearly. Grabbing for the binoculars attached to her void belt, she peers through the scopes for a better view. Near the top, she notices Edwin Dorset, heading her way, trekking through knee-high snow (or is it ash?). He quickly stops near a cluster of rocks and hides.

But hide from what?

For a brief moment, the solar moon is obscured, and Sibyl's eyes flicker up to the vast shadow now in the sky. A spectral eyeball looms above the mountaintop, with a host of tentacles attached to its backside, following its every movement—reaching out like lively, swirling eels, ghastly in the light of the crimson moon. The eyeball remains fixed on Edwin, and in no time, it will reach him.

I have to do something, *Sibyl thinks.* If I don't act now, it will all be for nothing.

Reaching for her void belt, Sibyl finds a flashlight and points it at the creature coming for Edwin. A bright light beams onto the specter, and its gaze turns to Sibyl instead of Edwin. All eyes on me, bastard, *she thinks, and the creature flies toward her instead.* That's right, keep coming. *Even without her binoculars, she can see that Edwin has left his hiding spot and now runs to safety.* Good, *she further thinks, as the creature gets closer and closer—building speed and growing in size.*

My role here is done.

Before she knows it, the colossal creature hovers above her, with its dead gaze set only on her. A ring of blood pours down the eyeball from all sides and encases her in a crimson dome, blocking her from any escape. She stares back at it, defiant, and all at once it pounces.

• • •

Once more, Sibyl awoke to find herself on the ground, now elsewhere. She glanced around, feeling as the world spun around with each movement of the head. Suddenly, she felt hungry. *Dehydrated.* And found herself enclosed in a glass case—a round enclosure, like the inside of an hourglass.

Outside the enclosure, a man sat on a supply crate in silence, watching her with a predator's gaze in his eyes. He looked familiar, as if she had seen him before. But where? She couldn't remember. He had pale skin, dark, messy hair, and a patchy beard, along with a vertical scar that ran down the side of his right eye. Dressed in a tactical vest, bandolier, and equipped with multiple firearms, he was the leading image of a modern reaper. And again, she could have sworn that their paths had crossed before, but she just couldn't pinpoint the time or place.

Sibyl sat up, and she said nothing.

"You've been sleeping like a baby," he told her, practically muttering his last words. "Except you actually slept." At once, Sibyl realized he had been drinking—drinking, or on some kind of other speech inhibiting substance; his bloodshot eyes all but confirmed it.

Again, she said nothing; the less she revealed about herself, the better.

He pointed at her. "You know what you're wearing, don't you?" Chuckling, he added: "Of course you do." He folded his arms and leaned back. "Let me guess, you came here looking for a bounty. Want your shot at fortune and fame?" He *tisked*, with a pompous, inebriated smirk on his lips. "Let's make a deal, shall we?"

Sibyl held her tongue.

"Not going to talk, are you?" He waited for a response but got none. "Playing hard to get, I see."

As long as Sibyl said nothing, she had the upper hand; often, when you keep silent, you learn a great deal more from those who don't. Her captors wanted the void suit, and if she was dead, they could easily extract it from her corpse. However, since her void suit also happened to be masking her entire face and body, it was reasonable enough to believe that they wanted to keep her alive, for the off-chance that she was also a bounty and the prospect of an even greater reward. She would talk only when she needed to.

Irritation shown on the reaper's face—a child's scowl. Clearly, Sibyl was dealing with a man used to getting what he wanted, whether given to him or taken (more of the latter, most likely). He stood up abruptly. "You'll talk soon enough," he said, regaining his composure. "And I'll be ready when you do." And with that, he sauntered away, leaving her alone in the darkened enclosure, lit only by the faint glow of her dying void suit.

As Sibyl looked at her reflection in the glass, she could have sworn she saw Edwin Dorset's face appear for a fleeting second. Except the Edwin she saw looked older, and he had a full beard covering his face. *A trick of the mind*, she thought and set her hand on the glass. *Wherever he is now, let's hope it's far from here.*

Unbeknownst to Sibyl, on the other side of the glass, a brown hand pressed against hers.

29 | RECTIFIER

The commotion outside Sibyl's enclosure kept getting louder; it was the second time in the same hour that she heard subsequent gunshots. Another firefight. *Other reapers*, Sibyl had to guess. *Getting rid of the competition.* From their group or another's, she didn't know. Either way, she was still stuck here. Defenseless.

Not for long, hopefully—at least, one could hope.

For at least three days now, Sibyl had been confined within the enclosure. (At the *very* least, three days.) She couldn't know for certain how long it had been; no light entered the tent, save for her void suit, now glowing an even fainter honey-yellow. She was entrapped within the glass enclosure and hadn't been given any food or water. Her only visitors were Dieter—the scarred, pale reaper, often visiting her while inebriated—and Nairobi—the beautiful, dark-chocolate skinned reaper with eyes as cold as ice. And the same spiel came from both of them when they visited her: They would offer her food and sanctuary and spare her life in exchange for the void suit.

Of course, Sibyl didn't actually buy any of what they had to say—the first chance they got, they would kill her. As is, the only reason they had kept her alive was for the slight off-chance that she might be a bounty, and they still couldn't find any means of extracting the void suit from her body without killing her. Perhaps it was their plan to starve her out; if so, their plan was flawed.

They wouldn't be the first to try that.

Another burst of gunfire rang just outside the tent. The glass enclosure was supposed to be soundproof, but with the void suit enhancing her hearing, Sibyl could hear a good majority of what happened out there—or, at least, *had* heard a good majority of it; regretfully, the suit was losing its power and desperately needed a solar recharge.

A moment of silence followed the gunshots, and suddenly the end of the tent opened, shedding light within for a brief second. The reaper known as Dieter limped his way toward Sibyl's glass enclosure, favoring one leg over the other while covering his abdomen with a hand. He was panting, and once he got close enough for the dying void suit to register him clearly, Sibyl also noticed blood leaking from the wound he so failed to cover, trailing behind him.

Dieter input a code into the glass panel, and an entrance slid wide, leaving the enclosure open and exposed. "Come on," he said, aiming a revolver at Sibyl with his free hand and nodding his head to the back of the tent. "We're getting out of here."

Finally, Sibyl thought. Still, she struggled to get up and off the ground.

Dieter yanked Sibyl by the arm and onto her feet before jamming the head of the revolver into her back. "You try anything, and I'll fuck you up."

Had she any more energy, she could end him here and now—sweep him by the leg, grab his gun, and do to him what he had done to many others. But right now, she felt too weak and didn't trust her abilities in the current state that she was in.

Patience, she told herself again. *The time to act will come.*

Dieter dragged Sibyl outside the tent, and for the first time, she saw what had been just outside her enclosure. There were other tents, exactly like the one they had just exited, as well as a smoldering fire ring, with scattered corpses lying amidst gunshells and overturned crates. Among the many corpses, she noticed Nairobi keeled over, clenching two handguns, with her eyes wide open—a cold, piercing blue even in death.

The sky was a darkened gray, almost black, and a heavy smoke continued to linger, obscuring the world in a murky haze. All the trees surrounding the camp had been chopped down, and distant valleys could be seen below them, making Sibyl realize they were currently camped on the mound of an ancient sequoia.

Dieter led them to an open pod by the cliffside with a dead mercenary lying beside it; moreover, the gray pod was just big enough for two. "Get in," he demanded, shoving Sibyl forward. She stumbled onto the pod, not yet in, and noticed a plasma rifle lying on the ground right beside the corpse. But again, Dieter shoved the revolver into her back and forced her fully inside.

Patience, she reminded herself. *The time will come.*

Once they were both inside the pod, with Dieter behind the controls and Sibyl right beside him, the doors closed shut and the engine roared to life. "I'm not getting out of here with nothing," Dieter muttered to himself, and the pod rocked them around as it began to rise. "Not again."

Now in the sky, Sibyl could see the full devastation of Orion clearly. Entire sections of the forest had been demolished, and wildfires continued to spread unabated. It was also very clear where D-D's augmentation facility had once been based on all the destruction that surrounded it, which continued to be an active war zone; even still, more reapers continued arriving at the scene, looking for a bounty to cash in.

Undoubtedly, death followed.

The sky was no different, really. Above them, Sibyl noticed a large warship looming, far larger than all the others entering and leaving the atmosphere. Like the skies of Zarathustra the day of Edwin's reaping, pockets of battle raged with no distinguishing sides.

Dieter grabbed an old-fashioned talkie hanging above him and brought it to his mouth. "Command, this is Gammus, you copy?"

A woman's clear, measured voice responded: "Gammus, this is command. We read you loud and clear."

"I have a package," he said, glancing at Sibyl.

"Copy that, Gammus. Deliver the package to hangar twelve and await further instructions."

• • •

Dieter Hammond was the kind of man to claim the credit of someone else. Truth be told, he wasn't much of a thinker, and an excursion as big as the one on Orion remained far above him. In the profession of a reaper, there was often a chain of command; no successful reaper worked alone, and no successful operation contracted only one group of reapers. Bounty hunting was a business, after all, and every business operated differently.

The only problem was, of course, that Dieter had chosen the wrong operation.

Now, he was desperate. Practically on the verge of bleeding out, he had no time for caution. Everyone he had come to Orion with was now dead; his crew, the league that had employed them, and even their getaway ride. Why had he even done this in the first place? He should have learned from the debacle on Zarathustra that it was a foolish pursuit. Except . . . except it may not have been for nothing—not after all. There was still the void suit he had obtained, as well as its owner, who may have even been a bounty for all he knew. If it weren't for that last fact, he perhaps would have given into despair and killed himself after losing Nairobi. But no: He was a gambling man, and if he were to die today, at least he knew that he had exhausted all options.

At least, he would try one last ditch-effort.

Dieter dragged his prisoner along with him, with the barrel of his revolver sticking into her back. As they entered another narrow corridor, he continued following the instructions given to him from the reaper he had tortured, with the failed promise of having his life spared. His first priority was getting medical aid; if he could find a croaker, amend his wounds, and hide away for the time being, then he could get off Orion with the prospect of a bounty and use the alias of the dead reaper for the time being, hoping that the security here would be as negligent as it was getting in.

A sloppy plan, sure, but—once again—he was desperate.

Reapers came and went, as expected on such a vessel and for such an operation, and there was no way in hell that they'd all know one another, nor—for that matter—even care enough to try rooting out an intruder such as himself when most of them didn't even return at all. Furthermore, most likely every crew had their own consignment area to ensure no rivalry or competition would arise were anyone to bring back a bounty or anything worthy of killing someone over; by protocol, any bounty gained was to be immediately sent to a higher-up in exchange for a mass sum of talents and even better opportunities and equipment for the next reaping.

But, of course, Dieter had killed most of the crew and ignored that last part; as long as he could find medical aid, he would continue to do it his way, to reap a full reward for all his labor.

They entered another corridor, this one vaster than the one before it and well-lit, with multiple intersections. Many bipedal androids passed their way, but none of them seemed even remotely interested in their presence; all the more reason to not doubt the plan, however rushed it may have been. Once more, they came across another intersection, but this time, Dieter didn't know which way to turn; at this point, the directions had run out.

"Fuck," he muttered loudly, no longer caring about keeping his composure. He looked for a sign and anything to point him in a direction to go, but the metallic walls were all but bare. "*Fuck.*"

On the lefthand side, the corridor narrowed again, passing under some kind of induction rig (*induction rig*—? Or whatever the hell it was—he had no idea, really). On the righthand side, a set of stairs led upward and into another corridor, moodily lit overhead by red neon lights. And ahead of them? Well, ahead of them led to a large hatch with the number "12" etched into it in a yellow print. *That must be it*, Dieter thought, not remembering any other direction. *Fuck it to hell; at this point, it doesn't even matter anymore.*

"Come on," he demanded, nudging his prisoner forward. She stumbled ahead of him and was on the verge of collapsing. He glanced back, making sure they weren't being followed, but only saw a trail of blood lying in their wake—his own blood, for that matter.

The hatch opened at their presence, and they entered a well-furnished lounge with a kitchen, dining room, and an open area with couches surrounding a blue fire opposite a translucent wall separating a quarantine zone. The walls were a pristine orangish-yellow, and most of the furniture was a cheaply molded, white silicone. Moreover, the smell of the place reminded Dieter of The Horse's Bridle, one of the many whorehouses in Django, and he immediately let his guard down.

The prisoner bitch staggered to a couch and collapsed onto it, sprawled face-down. Dieter glanced around, noticing that the lounge led to three separate rooms. "*Hello?* Anyone here?"

A white-plated, bipedal android emerged from one of the rooms and stood before Dieter at attention, awaiting a command. *A croaker: Good.*

"You," he pointed at the android with his revolver. "Patch me up, will ya?" He took a graceless step forward, nearly lost his balance, and collapsed onto a chair, wincing loudly. He set the revolver on the table before him, closed his eyes, and immediately fell into unconsciousness, dropping his head on the table with a loud thud.

• • •

Sibyl awoke to find a face hovering above hers.

She jolted back, as did the owner of the face (mirroring her movements), before realizing that the face looking back at her belonged to an android; very human features, neither masculine nor feminine—a sheen, synthetic white, just like the rest of their body. Their bright, crystal eyes blinked slowly, registering Sibyl's body language as she sat up on the bed.

Sibyl then noticed an IV attached to her exposed arm and realized that the void suit had contracted down to her belt, covering only the bottom half of her and leaving the rest of her exposed; in fact, she still wore the navy-blue kimono from earlier, now open, with a breast shamelessly hanging out. Somehow, the void suit had registered that the android was merely there to help, not harm her, and it had acted accordingly; a safety mechanism, perhaps, in order to keep the user alive and nursed back to health, for the worst-case scenarios.

Already, she felt ten times better than she had before losing consciousness.

The android took a step back and tilted their head to the side. "Hello, there."

Sibyl put her feet on the ground. "Hello." She glanced around the tiny room. Very minimalist. Neat. No sign of anyone else having been in it. And then she eyed the android again. "How long have I been out?"

The android remained impassive. Not programmed to have any expressions, it seemed. "An hour, twenty-nine minutes, and thirty-three seconds. You were deprived of the nutrients needed to sustain your life form. I suggest a hearty meal rich in protein. A broth, for example, might pair well with a legume and starchy root; in fact, I've prepared for you a bowl already, awaiting you on the dining table. Everything is accounted for your genetic diet, though I'm afraid my analysis may not be perfect."

Sibyl nodded. "Thank you."

"If you need me, I'll be here." The android bowed low before walking away.

Sibyl stood up and rubbed an eye with her palm. She tied her messy hair back, out of her face, hid her breast back in her kimono, and cautiously left the room. As luck had it, Dieter remained face-first at the table, unconscious, with his revolver lying where he had last left it. Of course, Sibyl took no chances: She grabbed his gun, holstered it to her void belt, and tied the unconscious Dieter onto a bed in the quarantine zone, making sure there wasn't any way he could escape. The android had already mended his wounds, but it looked as if it would take a while to heal, given the lack of equipment the android had on hand.

Regardless, Sibyl needed to be certain. "How long will it take for him to wake up?" she asked the android, watching her with a vacant look.

"A few days, at best."

Sibyl nodded again. "Good. I don't want him leaving that bed. He's a danger to us, do you understand? You can't listen to what he has to say, no matter how convincing it may be."

The android nodded. "I understand."

Sibyl regarded the android. "What's your name?"

The android lingered motionless. "I do not have one."

A cornerwise grin rose on Sibyl's lips; the first time she had smiled in days. "Then, make one up."

• • •

The shower was cold, yet welcome.

At last, Sibyl could decompress and set her mind at ease. With her hand on the wall and her head lowered, the pressurized water drenched her from above, and she looked like the weight of the world was on her shoulders. Dark bruises adorned her arms and legs, and a long, diagonal scar ran down her shoulder blades and to her lower back. She had always had an unconventional life, and the scars ran even deeper than just her body.

Because of her unnatural breeding on Te Kore, she had needed many augmentations throughout the years, and yet there remained things that just couldn't be altered, no matter how good the technology used was. The memories of Te Kore were a prime example. Those memories could never leave her, even when she tried to forget them. Sometimes, she didn't want to forget them. Those years had formed her and made her who she was. Without the drive created from those years of captivity, she would never have made it as far in life as she had, she was sure of that.

Once, many years ago, she had tried searching for other survivors of Te Kore—the rest of her people, who had survived the same breeding program as she. A remnant of a bygone era, brought into the world solely to be food for the elite rulers of Te Kore. They were a scattered tribe with no name and little history—aside from their shared mythology passed down from one generation to another (the same mythology that gave Sibyl the impression they had originated in Zarathustra, although that had eventually been disproven). The universe was a vast place, and time was an illusion: to track someone down was near impossible.

Still, Sibyl had been dead set on finding her tribe. (Whatever "tribe" was left.)

She searched and searched and searched—from the Inner Rings of Samsara to the Outer Rings—in an almost futile quest.

Until eventually, she found a sliver of hope.

On Datura, one of the twin moons of Taurus, Sibyl came across a confederated tribe of misplaced refugees. The confederation had been given sanctuary by the Inner Commonwealth in a small section of the Chūkarwa forest in the Alghani region, where they had built a village and lived off the land. However, because of nearby logging, and the damming of the Chūkarwa river, an incurable virus had recently plagued them, and their numbers had depleted as of late.

By the time Sibyl had discovered their whereabouts, only sixty-three of the Confederated tribe of Chūkarwa remained. Driven by her search, Sibyl had taken a blood sample from every household—only after their permission, of course—and cross-examined their DNA with her own. Among the sixty-three members of the tribe, only one of them had shared a common ancestor with her (that is, a more *recent* ancestor, given that all homo sapiens traced back to the same invaders who had crossed through Xibalba in the first Epoch).

The woman sharing ancestry with Sibyl was named Jume, and she was a ninety-three-year-old widow who had lost all her children and grandchildren from the plague a few decades prior. Objectively, Sibyl was far older than Jume because of her constant traveling and exposure to time-dilation, but she could have easily passed as her great-granddaughter. The two had come to love each other during that short period before Jume's death, and Sibyl would have even considered her the mother she had never had. When Jume died, Sibyl even stayed with the tribe during their two-week period of mourning.

But she never returned to Datura.

In fact, not much later would she find Jermaine in a scrapyard on Brecken.

Those were some of the darkest times in her life, the years following Jume's death. Now, even with having narrowly escaped death on Orion—not once, nor twice, but *thrice*—life felt much more manageable and undemanding than it had those following years after Jume's death, and Sibyl remained at the top of her game physically and cognitively. Now, it was much easier to bounce back from hardship than it had been in her youth; with a clear outlook, and the will to carry on, she knew that she could do anything she set her mind on. Already, she was planning on how to get back to the Vagabond and Jermaine. She didn't know where the warship's destination was after Orion, but—if she had to guess—it was most likely Django, and she would have to await an opportune time to get away, hoping that it wouldn't be long.

The first chance she got, she would contact Jermaine and notify him of her situation.

She turned off the water and changed the setting of the restoration chamber to air dry. Once aptly dried—albeit her hair, still damp—she exited the glass chamber and got dressed in extravagant clothes left in the large closet of the room she had awoken in and now claimed as her own. And she glanced at the mirror on the wall: Dark, almond eyes looked back at her, examining the subtle lines on her face that went down to her sharp cheekbones, strong jawline, and cleft chin. Her skin was paler than before (but still a warm tan), either from lack of sleep, sustenance, or not having seen the sun in days—though most likely, all the above.

Weariness revealed itself where she had thought it would be absent, and Sibyl thought of Edwin Dorset again, the bounty whom she had rescued on Zarathustra and had brought her into this whole mess. Was he safe? Had he gotten out of Orion alive? Perhaps these questions would remain with her for the rest of her life. As she had learned long ago, some questions never get answered. Still: wherever he was, and whatever he was doing, she hoped that he was more than okay.

|30|

WIZARDS OF OZ

One moment, he felt every atom of his being crushed together, and the next moment, he felt himself standing on solid ground. Between each moment, however? Simply put: Eternity.

Here, space and time were no longer emergent.

Here, the abstract eclipsed all sensibility.

Here, there was only the now and every moment that came with it.

Edwin Dorset glanced around, attempting futilely to obtain an understanding of his surroundings. But there was nothing—nothing at all.

Only darkness.

Except . . . that wasn't right.

Not anymore, at least.

Ahead, a light could be seen in the distance: a light at the end of a long, bleak tunnel.

Edwin ambled forward, following the light as it got bigger and bigger. Eventually, the light became all-encompassing, and he suddenly emerged from the desolate tunnel, assaulted by bright lights beaming onto him from above, so blinding that he had to cover his eyes. And what followed next—so unexpected and off-putting—was the thunderous applause of a live audience, with hoots, hollers, and fanatic screams.

What the—?

Edwin lowered his hand from his face, and his eyes quickly adjusted to the brightness all around him. In front of him, a man sitting behind a mahogany desk suddenly materialized out of thin air. Two blue sofas next to the desk materialized thereafter, along with a man sitting on the far end of the sofa farthest from the desk.

"Well, look who decided to finally show his face!"

Laughter erupted from the audience. Deafening applause.

Edwin glanced to his right and saw a multitude of people sitting in the shadows, watching him—a live audience just for him. *What the hell did I just walk into?* It was as if he had just entered a late-night talk show. What immediately came to mind was Conan O'Brien, who he sometimes binge-watched on YouTube back on Earth (he had never owned cable), and—as if his thoughts themselves formed the world around him—he saw the man sitting behind the desk beginning to actually *resemble* Conan O'Brien. Except . . . except there was something incredibly absurd and *off* about his features.

Something inhuman.

The "man's" body was disproportionate, and he was astonishingly tall and bulky, with a thick jaw, large forehead, and a dark orange pompadour hairdo. Where his eyes should have been were only tiny slits; in fact, at times it looked as if he was merely wearing a leather mask—only the mask continued to subtly shift with every movement he made, spasmodic and irregular, like a claymation that changed with every frame. He wore a blue suit and tie, and his hands fidgeted on the desk like wriggling eels, enlarged fingers reminiscent of a Jim Henson muppet. It was the uncanny valley: like watching stop-motion of matter—or early AI trying to depict human behavior through video—defying the laws of physics and all sense of rationality.

"Edwin Dorset," the host declared, waving his muscled arms erratically. As he spoke, his clothes transformed again, turning from a suit and tie to a plain white t-shirt (it continued alternating, in fact). "Please, take a seat."

Edwin glanced at the "man" sitting on the far end of the couch, farthest from the desk, and saw that his features were no more human than the man sitting behind the desk; furthermore, this "man's" eyes were practically popping out of their sockets, and his ears and mouth were comically enlarged—like a strange, alien species trying to emulate a human but failing miserably. Hesitantly, Edwin finally took a seat on the couch, closest to "Conan" behind the desk.

The host leaned forward. "Tell me, Edwin Dorset: Do you know where you are?"

"If I had to guess?" Edwin glanced once more at the audience looming in the shadows. "The fifth dimension."

"Close, but no cigar." The host raised one of his abnormal hands, which kept changing from four fingers to five fingers, and materialized a cigar out of thin air, put the cigar near his face—for a second, it even *became* a part of his face—before moving it away, and it suddenly dissipated as if it was never there. Smoke drifted unnaturally out of his black mouth, and Edwin saw no sign of any teeth or even a tongue within that strange abyss. "Is that your final answer?"

Edwin folded his hands onto his lap and suddenly realized, from the jeans he wore, that he was no longer protected from his void suit. Moreover, he didn't even have the void suit on him anymore, but he instead now wore Lamar's black and yellow letterman (the same jacket he had left on the Vagabond over five years ago) over his Geekstarters polo (again, that he had left on the Vagabond). Raising his hand to his face, he felt his beard was also gone. On top of that, he was five years younger, he recognized—appearing, undoubtedly, as he had when he was abducted from Earth and taken to Zarathustra. And another realization dawned on him, so obvious he felt dumb that he hadn't noticed it before: His biological arm was back, and he no longer wore a prosthetic. He took a deep breath, tried to remember the purpose of his being there, and eyed the fifth-being Conan O'Brien.

And where is "here," exactly?

At last, he answered the question: "I'd have to guess this is the in-between: the bridge between the third dimension and the fifth."

The audience laughed again. (Someone even whistled.)

Conan clapped his large hands together. "Why, close again—still, a margin off. Not for lack of trying, though. Not many get the question right. But then again, not many make it this far." He leaned forward, and it seemed as if his mass had suddenly doubled. "What you call the 'fifth dimension' is really more like the eighth dimension; in the third dimension, semantics can only go so far. And speaking of the third dimension: All of this around you? A program, you see, and you're simply a code; in fact, we're *all* codes. Numbers, that's all that anything is—one, zero, one, zero, one, zero, one—on and on, the data writes itself, unabated. Do I confuse you? I hope not. Sometimes, I confuse myself."

He cackled, leaned back, and his jaw elongated unnaturally until it was almost touching the desk. "The macrocosm is an endless abstraction, Edwin Dorset. The 'Big Bang' you're so privy to, up until now, is only a speck of sand on an infinite seashore. Do you realize the spam of time *before* what you even consider to be the beginning of the universe? Better yet, do you realize how many times your atoms have been recycled and you've relived your life as it is now? Do you know what you are? What any of this is? You are everything that came before you and everything that comes after—a paradox, that goes on and on. Nature at play, time and time again."

Edwin folded his arms and remained silent.

"Oh, but you know this—or, at least, a part of you already knows this. For there are many, many parts to the whole, aren't there? Oh, yes, and some come and go like the seasons, there one day and gone the next. Others, though? Oh, they stay with you even when you don't want them to." The fifth-being Conan smiled, and his face subtracted its mass until it was almost regular-sized (*almost*). "But don't overthink it: You live in the third dimension, after all. Do you know how many there are? How many other dimensions co-exist within your own user interface and all the multitude you can't perceive? Oh, but don't worry: you're not here to be mocked for your lack of enlightenment."

Edwin studied the alien in front of him. "Then why am I here?"

"That's the big question, isn't it? The one we all ask ourselves night after night." His outlandish smile broadened. "*Congratulations*, Edwin Dorset: You've just won the bounty."

The crowd went wild again.

"How does it feel?" The fifth-being on the far end of the couch asked Edwin with a comical smile from ear to ear. "It feels *good*, right?! Everything you could have hoped and dreamed and prayed for? Too good to be true—so good, in fact, we need a musical number!"

Conan waved an oversized hand with exacerbation. "No musical number! *Please*. My vocal cords are all fried up. Burnt to a crisp." His eyeless gaze set on Edwin. "You'd know all about that, wouldn't you? You little arsonist. Besides, we don't want to get side-tracked, do we?"

"No," Edwin agreed. "No, we don't."

"Take a look for yourself," the host said, and he directed Edwin's attention to a large projection screen that suddenly materialized out of nowhere. "Tell me what you see."

On the projection screen shown a young woman lying on a hospital bed and holding a newborn baby: Vicky Dorset, clutching her newborn son, Edwin Dorset, with a bright smile and newfound love in her eyes. *She's* beautiful, Edwin thought with astonishment, and couldn't believe this was the same Vicky Dorset from his childhood; he couldn't help but wonder what had become of the woman who held him there. Suddenly, where no desire had showed itself before, he now longed to meet her—to reach out and touch her. The projection on the screen was so lifelike, in fact, it was as if he really *could* just reach out to the other side and interact with the physical world like it was really there (and really, maybe it was actually there).

However, the projection quickly flickered, and it changed to a five-year-old Edwin sitting on a fourteen-year-old Lamar Davis's lap, on a couch in Vicky's old place, as Lamar read Edwin a Superman comic aloud.

Again, the projection flickered, and it changed once again: to an eight-year-old Edwin walking through the neighborhood alleyway in Oakland, California, where Vicky had once lived.

Again, the flicker: Edwin—perhaps eleven or twelve—riding a bike on the Bay Bridge, passing Treasure Island, and cycling toward the city of San Francisco, seen in the distance across the water.

Again, another few years pass and another part of Edwin's life: This time in Berkeley, within one of the many foster homes—Edwin at fifteen-years-old, sitting on a cot in a small, dark closet, with an ink pen and headlamp on his forehead, and drawing his late brother, Lamar, on a sketch pad.

On and on, the projection continued flickering—showing one moment of Edwin's life to another. With Mr. and Mrs. Kemp, in their kitchen, playing dominoes; walking hand-in-hand with Maggie Summers through the UCSF campus parking lot; making out with Amelia Gladden on the grass in Golden Gate Park; sitting in the Geekstarters comic book shop on Divisadero alongside his friends and co-workers, all of them watching Jack Claremont loudly sing Nina Simones as she blasted on vinyl; wandering through the canyons of Zarathustra alone, lost to the effects of the psychoactive spores wafting through the air; taking turns on the battle board with Jermaine in the Vagabond and discussing morality and consciousness; sitting down on the couch—and high off the garden's supply—mesmerized by Sibylla Kal as she swayed to the music, making a "come-hither" motion with her finger, all the while smiling; being comforted by Deidre Dua about the loss of his dominant arm and only remaining friend; hopping off a sloped building and landing on a moving train beside Hendrix Martin and Brutus Wainesworth as they were chased by local militia; painting Sienna Ravine, illuminated in a violet, neon light cast through the open window, sprawled naked on the bed; talking to a tree, and for the very first time hearing it talk back to him; standing beneath a waterfall with his arms out-stretched; staring into the emptiness of space; being sang to by Ella, Zula Cormorant's sun-peach dahlia, and Zula watching with an amused smile.

Moments in time, one after the other, recorded for all eternity.

Edwin wiped the wetness from his cheeks, and the images flickered faster now, at random and out of sequence.

"Do you understand?" Fifth-being Conan asked, smiling beneath the facade of his "face." He lifted a plastic, four-inch action-figure, and Edwin realized it was actually himself dressed and looking as he did at that very moment. "Groovy, right?" Conan tossed the plastic Edwin carelessly behind himself, and it vanished out of thin air. "You're a *star*, baby. Bona fide, organic—directly out a vagina." He glanced at the audience. "That's right, folks! This man came out a vagina."

The projector vanished, and in its place was an entire band: a drummer, bassist, guitarist—multiple guitarists, in fact—synthesizer, saxophonist, trumpeter, tubist, and even an accordionist (who looked, uncannily, like "Weird Al" Yankovic, albeit an even wackier, fifth-being version of "Weird Al" Yankovic).

"Are we gonna do the musical number, or what?!" the bassist called out, cuffing cauliflower hands into a living, bio-organic trumpet. "We didn't rehearse for nothing."

"*Hey*," Conan yelled, standing up abruptly and turning to the bassist. "Cool it, man! We'll get to it when we get to it."

The bassist shrugged the host's comment off, and he waved a hand in annoyance, sending sparks of prismatic light into the air, coating the walls around him in seeping color, like melting paint that pulsated like lava and bubbled from within.

Fifth-being Conan turned to Edwin again. "In the words of Eugene Clarence III: 'PLEASE, *stop*, I'm begging you.'" He sat down, sagged into his chair, and his smile returned. "Say, Edwin: Did you know that your life's a reality show? A hundred and forty-two different reality shows, in fact. Every second of your life has been monitored, from the most microscopic happenings of your internal system to the most significant events independent of your external being—including your very conception, believe it or not, as you passed from your father's dangling ball sack to your mother's prosaic ovaries. An organism is a fascinating case study: An ecosystem inhabiting a microbiome home to trillions of microorganisms of thousands of different species, constantly evolving and supporting the vessel you know as 'Edwin Dorset.' You're special, 'Edwin,' as is all your kind in the third dimension. Natural selection's granted you the ability to know all of this already—or, at least, get a general sense of it, like an atom vaguely knows of its existence—through a sixth-sense you dub as 'the bleeding effect.'"

The host stopped talking, perhaps letting Edwin register all he had said.

Edwin shrugged a shoulder. "Then, what now? Where do we go from here?"

"A musical number," the man on the couch insisted, and he leaned forward again, as his eyes popped out of their sockets like a dead fish. "Sing, sing, sing."

"*Enough* with the musical number," fifth-being Conan shouted, slamming an enlarged fist onto the desk with a loud bang; his mass doubled again, and his form shifted into something more menacing. "I've already told you, I don't feel like singing."

The man on the couch shrank in size, cowering into the corner and clutching his legs in a fetal position, as he erratically rocked from side-to-side. "Please, don't send me away . . . I don't want to go back."

The audience laughed.

The unnatural shadows that had cast themselves onto Conan now lessened, and he turned to Edwin once more. "Sorry about that." He scratched his orange neck with wriggling hot dog fingers. "'What now,' you ask?" He smiled deeply. "Why, the vacation of a lifetime."

|31|

HEAR MY TRAIN A COMIN'

The Fifth-World was nothing like Edwin had thought it would be. But then again, he had no expectations whatsoever of crossing from the other side of Xibalba. He was a man possessed, driven by an inane intuition that he could not fully understand. The "Fifth-World," in fact, had nothing to do with the fifth dimension at all but was more like an amusement park for the "fifth-beings"—who, really, were more like the "eighth-beings"—to visit in order to experience life in the third dimension as an anthropomorphic-being with five senses (sometimes more, if that's what they wanted).

Apparently, it wasn't uncommon for fifth-beings to visit other dimensions in a similar fashion; more than likely, they had already been to Earth and encountered Edwin at least a dozen or more times. In many ways, the fifth-beings were not much different from most "third-beings"; most of them were insecure, self-absorbed, and motivated by greed and the incessant need to consume.

On the surface level, the Fifth-World seemed an idyllic place to be. At first, it reminded Edwin of a 1950s to 1960s

American post-war suburban daydream, where all the streets were spotless, the lawns were manicured, and the houses looked the same. A park sat in the town center, along with a town hall, a "Museum of Bounties," and a multitude of shops and restaurants, not excluding the underground way station that fifth-being tourists used to come and go as they pleased.

And yet beneath it all, a darkness lurked—mostly unseen.

Edwin, and those like him in his situation (other bounties who had also "won" their bounty), was treated like a circus animal—an enslaved celebrity (a token *pet*, really)—under the guise of being "rewarded" for his survival of the annual reaping that had been going on longer than Samsara had even kept a record of. Of the month or so that he had been in the Fifth-World, his privacy was constantly bombarded, and the only safe place he could go without being harassed was the housing project he shared with the other bounties; though that, really, wasn't saying much either, given how rough their living situation was and how little they were afforded, despite all they had gone through to survive their circumstances.

There were eighty-three bounties in the Fifth-World altogether, and yet only one dilapidated building on the outskirts of town that housed them, with only five stories in all; indeed, the building had even been constructed by one of the earliest bounties to arrive in the Fifth-World. On Edwin's floor (the second floor), he felt welcomed the most and had been given a room to share among three other bounties—at least fifteen bounties co-existed within a single dorm.

Because of the reality of the situation that they were thrust in, and the harassment they faced from the fifth-beings who only saw them as objects for their entertainment, many of the bounties had grown complacent in their newfound home and refused to go out much. Of the eighty-three bounties, the original had been in the Fifth-World for over two hundred relative years now, and he hadn't aged a single day since arriving. Moreover, *none* of the bounties had aged a single day since arriving—none of them could even change from the form they had entered with, and whatever hairstyle or body type they had possessed when they were abducted from their individual worlds remained the same, even for those who tried growing a beard, shaving, or changing their gender (of which they found out, the next day, that they looked exactly how they had the day before). And there was no escape—not even through death; in fact, death couldn't even come to those who wanted it.

Still, some found ways to entertain themselves with the free time enforced upon them.

Many of them were artisans. A few of Edwin's many identical roommates had even formed a band, and they often jammed out in the common room—an almost comical troupe for an outside viewer, who would have seen over five variations of the "same person" (or genetic code) rocking out on different instruments all at once.

For Edwin, however, he had his mind set on more important tasks.

He remembered the reason that he had come to the Fifth-World in the first place. And if he had learned anything in the past few months, it was that nothing made him special. He did not stand out from the other eighty-two bounties, nor did he view himself any better than them. Furthermore, *none* of them were special. Nor were any of the fifth-beings special, for that

matter. And in that truth came a strong sense of empower-
ment. A resolution, perhaps, to do what had never been done
before. *"Be the change you wish to see in the world,"* he thought,
quoting a favorite of Lamar's sayings, taken from Mahatma
Gandhi.

Revolt against the norm.

He pedaled his bike through a narrow cobblestone road and
watched as the pink cherry blossoms slowly passed by him on
each side. The world had a fable-like quality to it, and—
although it certainly *felt* real—looked incredibly artificial, like
some long-lost set from *The Wizard of Oz* or another early
Hollywood blockbuster. The trees and flora were like papier-
mâché, and the backdrop in the distance looked like a hand-
painted, life-sized diorama, even though its colors still changed
as the day went on. Of course, the Fifth-World was a
simulation, and the rules here were much different than they
were on the other side of Xibalba; hence, why all the bounties
could no longer change their form from the day of their
abduction.

Yorick, one of Edwin's bunkmates, hypothesized that when
the bounties had crossed from their home world through the
initial portal into Samsara that their atoms had also been copied
and saved into an avatar, digitized as they are now. Actually,
Yorick's convictions went even further than that, and he be-
lieved that when all the bounties had crossed through, to the
other side, a copy had been the one to go through whereas the
original bounty remained back home (Edwin wasn't sure about
that latter theory, however, given that his abductors had also
crossed onto his side of the portal in San Francisco—although
the former theory certainly seemed accurate enough).

Time moved differently in the Fifth-World: A full season lasted a mere month, and every three or four days the seasons showed signs of change—subtly, at first, but very obvious after a full week. Some days, it was near impossible to not be swept away by it.

Right now, the wind on his face felt nice, actually, despite not being "real." To be away from the other bounties, alone again, and finally get some peace of mind—able to let his mind wander without a disruption from his thoughts—well, it felt wonderful (how could it not?). Silence was a commodity that Edwin could never take for granted. And what he would give to be in Karla once more—to have some solitude, somewhere beautiful to exist, and the chance of seeing those he loved once again. If only he could live how he wanted to *every* day.

But his time in the Fifth-World was no vacation, and he still had a job to do.

The time for rest would come later.

Ahead, he could see the houses beginning to emerge in his field of vision, materializing before him as if they were just now being rendered. A fifth-being man, wearing a bucket hat and blue jumper, stood on a lawn watching Edwin as he passed by him. The man smiled and waved, and Edwin smiled back, though his smile was strained. As with the third dimension, the face scrambler did its wonders and made Edwin appear to a fifth-being as any other fifth-being—a disproportionate, stop-motion monstrosity (or however it translated for however they saw themselves).

The face scrambler had been one of Isa's many gifts to Edwin, along with the bike, which could shrink in mass, able to fit in his pocket if he wanted it to. Additionally, Isa had also shown him a secret passage under the bounties' housing—a passage into the surrounding forest, unsupervised, for him to use anytime he met with Isa. None of the other bounties knew about it, of course. Nor about Isa, for that matter. It was all Edwin's secret to keep.

Until the time was right.

Further along the neighborhood, Edwin began seeing more and more of the fifth-beings, trying to blend into what they thought of as a third-dimensional, twenty-first century human society. But they were only tourists, appropriating a culture and world that they did not even understand. Edwin sometimes despised them, even though he knew—or assumed, at least—that most of them weren't even aware of all the damage inflicted because of them.

"Forgive them," he heard the voice of Benjamin Kemp tell him in the back of his mind. *"For they know not what they do."*

He gripped the handlebars tighter. As much as he would have liked to make all the fifth-beings pay for the injustice done to him and all the other bounties (from their abduction, the very bounty on their heads, and whatever they had to do just to survive), that voice in the back of his head was right: The fifth-beings weren't all bad, and Isa and company were living proof of that.

Still, that didn't mean that all the fifth-beings were good people ill-informed.

No, that couldn't be the case with what Edwin currently saw, near the edge of the neighborhood, by the town marketplace: Two bounties walking together, each with multiple bags of provisions (undoubtedly for others as well as themselves), and a whole entourage of fifth-beings surrounding them and making it near impossible to keep walking.

The fifth-beings were taking pictures of the two bounties, nearly blinded from the cameras' flashes, and continued yelling erratic, personal remarks for each bounty, such as "you never should have trusted Richie," "your nose is a little big, isn't it?" "you're lucky you made it out alive," "you know that you were adopted, right?" and "we all know you're gay!" The closest fifth-beings were trying to grab the two bounties and get their attention, but the two men kept dodging them and walking away, trying to ignore the harassment on all fronts.

Edwin felt a pang in his chest, wishing that he could alleviate the two men's suffering. A feeling of unjustified guilt burrowed its way in him, and it told him that he should have been there with them. But what difference would that even make? He had to think of the long-term. Even if it took him over a hundred years, he would get them out of this situation eventually—all of them, as a matter of fact—and he would not settle for less.

As he pedaled into town, he eventually arrived at his desti-nation, a few blocks from where the two bounties were getting harassed. Dismounting his bike, he shrank it into his palm, safely stored it into his letterman's pocket, and entered one of the wide double-doors, to one of the many brick-exterior buildings, before emerging into an old-fashioned diner with tables and booths on one side and a bar and line of stools on the other. The diner was busier than usual, but Edwin noticed the booth at the far end remained empty. He ambled toward the empty booth, sat down, and set a red napkin on the edge of the table.

Immediately afterward, a fifth-being woman took a seat across from him.

Her face was an expressionless mask of flesh, terrifying if Edwin wasn't used to seeing its equivalent on such a daily basis. Where the eyes would have been was a void and bottomless pit. She set a three-fingered hand on the red napkin and leaned forward. "There will be no re-run, brother."

Edwin smiled. "The revolution will be live."

Isa withdrew their hand, and the red napkin was gone, replaced by a small, circular device: A noise scrambler—simple, state-of-the-art fifth-being technology (Edwin expected no less).

"How fare you, Edwin Dorset?" Isa spoke with a soft and melodious voice. Every meeting of theirs, Isa's voice and appearance differentiated from the time before; honestly, they often appeared as a man just as much as a woman—or the cross between a man and woman, with no definable sex whatsoever. Moreover, Edwin wasn't even sure if Isa was just one person or if they were many, each with their own conviction for meeting with him. Today, Isa's skin was a pale flesh, almost translucent—again, ghastly if he wasn't used to it. This time, Isa's hair was long, dark, and in dreads; it reminded Edwin of Zula, actually, and somehow made him miss her even more.

How was he faring, honestly? Exhausted, and yet equally restless. He wanted to be free of the Fifth-World and all its pretense. Just wanted to be home wherever home could be found. But he refused to be a victim. Refused to give up his bliss, that state-of-mind that could endure anything despite the circumstances. And a hint of his smile remained, defiant. "Look around you," he began, nodding to the little diner surrounding them. "I'm living the dream."

Isa slowly tilted their head. "Not your dream."

"No," Edwin agreed. "I'm awake."

A fifth-being waiter sauntered to their table. He wore corduroy suspenders over a wool sweater, and his face appeared animatronic, as if it were being controlled by a puppeteer—a suspension of disbelief, given that he also wore a construction hat, regardless of it having nothing to do with his supposed job. "It's good to see new faces here," the fifth-being waiter told them. (Of course, he said that every time he saw them, so that was no surprise—yet again, they always had 'new' faces.) After setting two tablets onto the table, each in front of Edwin and Isa, he added: "If any of you are looking for a sex worker, I work doubles on weekdays. You'll find me on the corner of Dirt and Gravel, wearing a pink sweater."

Isa waved away the waiter. "No need."

"I also knit sweaters," the waiter added, touching at his wool collar. He extended his arm above the table. "Feel it."

"We are content," Isa said, nodding their head (what fifth-beings, of course, did instead of shaking their head—believing it to be an Earth custom, but from what time and place one could only guess). "We would rather order in privacy."

"Be sure to read Minÿae's *Bohemian Wanderlust*," the waiter suggested, tapping a tablet on the table. "Or watch its adaptation: *Sugar Ray, Daddy*. The performance from Geezer Holiday is par to none. Of course, I'm biased. I love any flick by TëeDoubleue Wiseau. Have you seen *Neighbor's Room*? What a ride. He breathes life into his stories and characters. Sometimes, I wish I was one."

"We'll take our leave," Isa insisted.

The waiter shook his head and took a step backward. "Well, call if you need me—don't be shy." He eyed Edwin with his animatronic, lifeless eyes: "I'm always down for a booty call." (*Is he joking . . . ?* Edwin wasn't sure.) Finally, the waiter took his leave and materialized elsewhere, to bother another table and its customers.

Edwin didn't understand the Fifth-World. Better yet, he hadn't even fully understood the "Third-World," so why bother at this point? Clearly, though, the fifth-beings had a far worse understanding of the third dimension than even Edwin, given the absurdities found within the Fifth-World trying to emulate it. Perhaps there was a translation error—miscommunication, the language of the universe. Whatever the case, he couldn't help but chuckle.

Isa exchanged a look with Edwin again. "Tell me, young Dorset, do you feel a change to the air? A stirring of things to come—a reaping of all the seeds planted, ready to fruition." A grin formed on Isa's lips, nearly invisible until that point. "You are an artist, are you not? You, of all people, should know the time it takes to get something just right, to the point of perfection. But—until that time comes—you must wait out the process and have faith that it will all come together, never doubting it." Isa shook their head. "Doubt leads to stagnation. No, my friend, that is not something we can afford. The time will come, and have no doubt about it, for the culmination of all that preceded it."

Edwin considered why he was there. All this time, and he still had no idea why Isa wanted his help—if they even needed it, to begin with. Every time they met, Isa talked around the subject. Isa didn't like giving answers. But for once, Edwin needed a straight answer. "So, how come me?" He eyed Isa closely. "Out of all the other bounties you could have chosen to help you, what makes me any different?"

Isa chuckled, their face expressionless despite the warmth in their voice. "That's not the first time you've asked such a question."

Edwin shrugged. Still no answer. "Somehow, I don't think it'll be the last."

"An inquisitive boy," Isa mused. "Why do you not trust the process?"

Edwin shook his head again. "I don't even know what the process is." He glanced around the quasi-diner, wondering—again, not for the first time—if Isa was just leading him on, in the false hope of taking down the Fifth-World once and for all. "This is, what, the fourth meeting we've had?" He eyed Isa closely—Isa, who appeared different in every meeting. "And I still know nothing more than I did the last time."

"All in due time." Isa tapped a tablet on the table with a finger. "Come," they urged. "If we do not order, they will begin to question why we are here."

Why are *we here?* Edwin wondered. He glanced down at the tablet before him, illuminated as his eyes gazed over the words. He grimaced. *Who the hell eats Tikka Masala covered on muskrat and ice cream?* The menu was all over the place, and the fifth-beings clearly had no idea how an Earth diner was supposed to be. *A golden chai sushi smoothie,* really? Edwin chuckled again. As expected, nothing ever looked good here. *Lucky for me, I'm never hungry anymore.* Forced to decide, he ordered a side of guacamole and burnt sweet potato fries (the only decent combo currently on the menu).

Again, the waiter materialized before them and set a plate in front of Isa and Edwin. The waiter glanced from Isa to Edwin. "Would you like hand tools for your meals?" Eyeing Isa, he also added: "I would highly recommend the use of a spade and tongs for that falafel sandwich—especially tongs."

"No need," Isa repeated. "We prefer to eat like the locals."

"Wonderful." The waiter (wearing a different wool sweater than before, Edwin now noticed) clasped his enlarged hands together and continued to stare at Isa and Edwin. "Would you like me to watch you eat—as is custom in the third dimension?"

"No," Edwin voiced, more adamant than Isa had been. "Please, leave us be."

A Cheshire-like grin formed on the waiter's fishlike lips. "As you wish." Again, he vanished out of thin air, as if he had never been there.

Edwin glanced at Isa's plate: Mushy, green falafels, an uncooked fish (still alive), and stale cornbread. None of it looked even remotely good. "You're really going to eat that?"

Isa raised their hands, using a gesture that Edwin was unfamiliar with. "Where I come from, taste is an abstraction. Let me have my fun, and—in due time—I will let you have yours."

Edwin watched as Isa picked up the fish with a hand, brought it to their lips, and it simply vanished, as if it had been deleted from existence. No chewing involved; this was the Fifth-World, after all.

Edwin glanced at his own plate, no more attractive than Isa's. The skin of many unripe avocados had been chopped into the "guacamole," with pieces of rock-hard lentil, un-cooked mushrooms, diced papaya, and chunks of dried corn. Surprisingly, the sweet potato fries actually looked edible. However, after only one bite, Edwin realized he was quickly mistaken. *Why* should *the fries taste like fries? After all, this is the Fifth-World: things shouldn't make sense.* Nothing *makes sense.*

In no time, Isa's plate was spotless. Isa's eyeless gaze landed directly on Edwin's untouched plate. "Not hungry?"

Edwin shook his head. "Not since being here." He slid his plate to Isa. "By all means."

Just as fast, Edwin's plate became spotless, too.

"Where were we?" Isa asked, wiping their hands on the beige tablecloth.

"You were about to say something cryptic," Edwin remarked, smirking. "Enough information to get my interest, but not enough for me to learn something new."

Isa set a ballpoint pen in front of Edwin. "How is this for something new?"

Edwin picked up the pen and surveyed it closely. Nothing too remarkable, he noted, but certainly better than the pen he had now. *Is this a gift?* "Thanks," Edwin said, glancing from the pen to Isa. Playfully, he added: "What are you trying to tell me? To shut up and draw something?"

Isa looked into Edwin's very soul. "To take initiative." Isa nodded to the pen, adding: "To be is to do. Sometimes, change won't come until you force it to."

• • •

When Edwin returned to the bounties' dwelling place, he thought of how stuck he felt in his situation, unable to make any progress since when he first arrived. Again, he began questioning himself and his decision to go to the Fifth-World in the first place, having put his friends in danger to travel through Xibalba. *What the hell had I been thinking?* Perhaps he hadn't been thinking at all. The bleeding effect had taken its hold over him, and he had jumped to irrational conclusions, hoping with vanity that he was special, and that maybe—just possibly— some fifth-beings were out to help him.

Now, those voices were gone entirely, and yet he felt more hopeless than ever.

He had been hoping that Isa would be his salvation, his way out of this mess, but if their last meeting had taught him anything, it was that he was most likely being played. *Used*, he thought, *but not the way I want to be used*. Because he was a bounty, and that's all they were good for, apparently—the amusement of others to their own degradation. Dammit, he just wanted to do some good for a change—to help others in his situation, just as he wanted to be helped.

I don't want my life to be in vain, he thought. *I don't want this all to be for nothing. . . .*

Do not lose hope, he told himself, trying to counteract that voice of doubt as he sat down on his bed (the bottom of a bunk bed—one of two bunk beds in a small, cramped room he currently shared with Yorick, Timothy, and Kendrick, the closest friends he now had). And he closed his eyes, attempting to shut his busy mind and let his emotions pass over him, not become a slave to them.

Images flickered, unbidden: The Geekstarters comic book shop on Divisadero and Jack Claremont. Somehow, the image of Jack Claremont standing by his record player morphed into the shape of Brutus Wainesworth, a lilac wall behind him, and the gentle hum of Zula's monstera. Then that, too, transformed into Sibyl's garden, accompanied by Jermaine's sardonic smile. Abstract feelings: An endless dreamscape of thoughts and emotions, mostly unresolved.

The more Edwin focused on his breathing, the more he could let go.

Do not lose hope, he told himself again, and his mind's eye brought up Lamar: the image of Lamar sitting beside him on the bed, his hand on his shoulder, comforting him as he had the day he lost his backpack and its most prized possessions, the day he last saw him alive.

Through the thin walls, Edwin could hear his roommates jamming out in the common room—the sounds of an electric guitar, bass, drums, and even a cello. The fifth-beings could take everything from the bounties (their home, their privacy, and their very DNA), but they could not take away their art. The fact the fifth-beings had only chosen talented individuals to be bounties was probably no coincidence; if they weren't to amuse them in one way, with the pursuit of a bounty, then at least they had their art form, so that those watching never grew bored.

Edwin pulled out one of his journals from beneath his pillow. The journal was handmade and had an artisanal quality to it, and—as were most of the possessions the bounties currently possessed (such as the instruments he heard at that very moment)—was made and sold by one of the bounties. It was the third journal he had filled in during his time in the Fifth-World, and a part of him was even pained to know that when he eventually escaped, he would most likely have to leave it behind, along with his other journals.

He opened the journal to the first page he had worked on: a study of the interior and exterior of the bounties' building in watercolor—moody, realistic, and yet somehow idealistic in its expression. And he contemplated how much his art style had changed in the past few years. Rarely had he done many self-portraits before his time in the Fifth-World. And yet, as he skimmed through the pages, before him were the many faces of the bounties he had met in the Fifth-World and now shared a living space with—men and women so different from him, and yet so similar, having experienced such divergent lives, despite sharing the same DNA; an honest case study of nature versus nurture, revealing how unique and contrasting they all turned out to be, formed by the lives and the worlds they inhabited.

At last, Edwin skimmed to the end of his drawings, a blank piece of paper: an empty canvas filled with unlimited potential. He searched for a pen or pencil beneath his pillow, wondering whether he would also paint, but, for some reason or another, he couldn't find any pen or pencil, and he instantly remembered about the ballpoint pen Isa had given him, before quickly fishing it out of his pocket.

Something felt different about it than before.

He couldn't put his finger on just what that difference was—a strange feeling to have, so abstract that he couldn't even translate it into words (at least, not like he could with a drawing or painting). As he clicked the end of the pen, releasing its tip, he noticed how the black ink glistened like gold in the sunlight. A faint sound resonated from within it, like soft wind chimes on an early spring afternoon.

What, exactly, had Isa given him?

"Sometimes, change won't come until you force it to."

Edwin touched the end of the pen to the paper, let the ink guide him, and—like one possessed, compelled by a higher power he did not fully comprehend—began to draw the closed door facing him. Only, instead of drawing the door closed as it was, he drew it wide open. And on the other side of the door he drew an ungu tree, like the one in Sibyl's garden, surrounded by an idyllic hillside. After he was finished with the drawing, he leaned back and stared at the closed door as if it would swing open at any moment.

But the door did not budge.

Suddenly, Edwin had a strange feeling in his stomach, like he was a young boy again with butterflies after seeing his crush, and he stood up slowly. He sauntered to the door, reached for the knob, and slowly turned it. As the door creaked open, a bright light seeped through its cracks, and on the other side of the door stood the ungu tree surrounded by rolling hills, just as he had drawn it.

Amazed—and yet disbelieving—Edwin stepped through the door, looking with wonder at the world around him, like stepping through a portal into another world. *This can't be real*, he thought, shaking his head.

But it *was* real, wasn't it . . . ?

It *had* to be.

He approached the ungu tree, plucked off one of its purple fruits, and scrutinized it. Without another thought, he took a

large bite from the fruit and relished its taste, sweet and inviting, telling him that this couldn't just be a hallucination.

It was real; it was all really happening.

A great fear crept into his mind, and he was suddenly
worried that he might get stuck on this side of the door without
the pen. Returning to the doorway, he stepped through the
portal, and once more found himself in the Fifth-World bedroom that he shared with the other bounties.

The door slammed shut behind him.

And yet, the forbidden fruit remained in his hand—along
with the bite missing from it.

|32|

THE REVOLUTION WILL NOT BE TELEVISED

The pen is mightier than the sword.

Whereas the sword is an instrument of destruction, a tool that dispatches life, the pen is an instrument for construction, a tool that *creates* life. And whatever Edwin could think up, whatever he could see in his mind's eye, he could bring to life, manifested into the physical world through his pen. At first, he experimented with small items, making sure that his first use of Isa's gift hadn't been solely in his head, nor that it would suddenly stop working on him, although—from the ungu seed on his desk—he knew that couldn't be the case. But alas, the ink was limited, and he had to be intentional with what he drew, knowing that he wouldn't have such a gift forever.

A power such as this was terrifying, and with it came a great sense of responsibility: an obligation not to overuse the power given to him. Power corrupts, and absolute power corrupts absolutely; that awareness weighed on Edwin, giving him sleepless nights—not that he slept much to begin with (unable to grow tired in the Fifth-World, that wasn't a hard feat). Moreover, what were the repercussions of unchecked power? And not only unchecked power, but power that was so clearly unearned? If he misused it, that could bring cataclysmic consequences.

The first few days, after having drawn the door leading to the ungu in the meadow, Edwin didn't so much as touch the pen. He questioned why Isa had trusted him with this gift and none of the other bounties. Was it because he didn't seek the power given to him? Because the pen was a "gift" that he ultimately didn't want? Maybe—although there were others in his situation who would have also felt the same way as him.

No one *should possess such a power.*

And yet, he immediately recognized how he could change his situation for the better by utilizing such a power. And not only *his* situation, but all the other bounties' situation, including those not yet in the Fifth-World. And perhaps for that reason alone, Isa had entrusted him with it.

Still, it unsettled him.

After a few days of serious contemplation on how to use the pen, the first thing he came up with—aside from a few test runs (that being, a copy of his lost journal from his last year on Earth and a void belt)—was a key that could open any door, taking him wherever he so desired. As he drew the key, he envisioned what it would be, and his intentions made it a reality. At will, he could use the key (a brass key, simplistic in design and able to fit in his palm) and leave the Fifth-World as easy as stepping through a door. And the first place he travelled to, a place of sentimental power, that he never would have thought he would return to, was Oakland, California—specifically, his childhood bedroom, back when he had lived with

Vicky Dorset on Misty Way Avenue, when Lamar was still alive.

Time and space no longer bound him.

As Edwin stood in his old bedroom, he noted how much smaller the room was than he remembered it. The room reeked of cigarettes and unseen decay, and just being there made him feel sick. Indentations covered the white walls—one hole the size of a fist—and water stains blotted the ceiling. Until now, he hadn't realized how bare the room had been, and he recalled how he had even considered himself lucky to have his own room.

A small cot with a thin sheet and pillow lay on a broken bedframe next to a pile of trade-paperback comics Lamar had gifted him (undoubtedly bought used, by the looks of it). His backpack was gone—as was his childhood self (at school, most likely)—and another stack of stapled papers were piled neatly beside his comics. He knelt down, picked up the top papers that were stapled together, and gazed at its crayon-colored cover and title: THE SUPERBS #1, by Edwin Dorset. The self-made comic's drawing depicted an almost laughable entourage of superheroes, each unique and colorful, and he suddenly felt a strange sense of nostalgia wash over him, as he stared directly into a past relic he had long-forgotten.

Visceral, prismatic emotions welled up inside him, and he could do nothing but let himself feel them with full force. Tears ran down his cheeks, and his heart felt as if it would implode within his chest, thus creating a supernova. All he had ever wanted then was to be a comic book artist. Such innocence and wonder. Now, looking around the dilapidated room, he wondered how he could have ever been so hopeful with such a life; he'd had the odds stacked against him since day one.

No longer.

At first, Edwin had been paranoid that the fifth-beings would have caught wind of his new gift, that they would be watching him at all times and would now know that he had a means of escape, but—upon returning from the meadow, and having weeks of relative normalcy—he eventually realized that nothing had come of his escapade. Nothing at all, in fact. And his only guess was that Isa had shielded him from their watchful eyes; how Isa had done that, he didn't know.

There was still a *lot* that he didn't know.

What's new?

He laughed at the question. '*What's new . . . ?*' He glanced down at the pen in his hand—a tool of unlimited potential. *Why, everything's new*, he thought. *All at my disposal.*

Having traded a painting for some string (an unfair trade, he thought, but a trade that was necessary), he had fashioned the key into a necklace, along with the pen, and always kept them on him. He didn't tell any of the other bounties about his newfound gift. Not at first, at least. And not because he didn't trust them. More so, as a precaution, in case the fifth-beings watched them, to diminish any possibility of being found out. Except a part of him began wondering if the fifth-beings could even *see* into the Fifth-World. If the Fifth-World was an amusement park for the fifth-beings to experience the third dimension, wouldn't it make reasonable sense for it also to be an exclusive experience (that is, experienced solely by the senses), and that whoever engineered it might profit from capitalizing on such an experience?

Again, another question without an answer.

Too many questions without answers, in fact. One being what, exactly, he currently was. In the Fifth-World, he could not age, grow tired, hungry, or even change mass if he wanted to (no growth in hair, change in weight, nor physical alteration since day one); he was stuck in the body of himself at twenty-three, unable to feel truly human. So, then, was he still the same Edwin Dorset as the Edwin Dorset who had crossed Xibalba? Or was he now someone else? And now, being able to leave the Fifth-World at will, his body hadn't returned to the state of being that it had once been in, before entering Xibalba. Would he forever be trapped in his current state of existence, or could he return to his former form? After five years of living with a prosthetic arm, it almost felt wrong to have the original flesh back again. As is, his situation was complicated, but this enigma made it even more problematic.

And, as for mysteries, when Edwin had returned to the same diner a week after his meeting with Isa, Isa remained a no-show. Nor did Isa arrive the next week—nor the week after that. *They handed me the reins*, Edwin concluded the third week in a row of being stood up, as he sat alone in the diner's booth. *What happens next is up to me.*

And luckily, he had time on his side.

• • •

Over a relative year passed before a firm plan was set in motion.

• • •

You can't fight change, Edwin Dorset thought as he stood on a side-walk in the Fifth-World and used a face scrambler, watching as the fifth-beings went about their day. *Change will come whether you like it or not, and there's nothing you can do but accept it.* He eyed Yorick, standing across the street from him, also wearing a face scrambler, and the two exchanged a brief look. *But even if you can't fight change, that doesn't mean you can't divert it and redirect it into something that benefits you and others.*

He turned to his right and saw Kendrick, across the block, also disguised. To his left, he noticed Timothy, the same distance from him as Kendrick and the other bounty in front of him. And beyond them, even more bounties.

Impermanence is the law of the land; if you don't evolve with it, you'll drown in its depths.

Ready to be rid of the Fifth-World, now more than ever, Edwin took a step forward, onto the street, and watched as the rest of the bounties did likewise—two bounties on every block, each across from one another.

A fifth-being man walking along the side-walk stopped to eye Edwin. The man wore an early-1900s gray suit and tie with a bowler's hat, and despite his face being obscured, like some Jim Henson created monstrosity posing as human (his features were practically indiscernible), his rotoscopic-like movements betrayed confusion and uncertainty. Edwin glanced back at the fifth-being man, reached for the face scrambler at his neck and turned it off, revealing himself to the world.

All along the streets, the other bounties did the same—one after the other, their true appearances being revealed.

The fifth-being man observed Edwin carefully, took a step back from him, and his head turned back and forth, having now noticed the other bounties also revealing themselves. "What?" Edwin asked him with a smile, scratching the growing stubble on his neck with his right hand—once again, that arm being a prosthetic. "I thought you wanted to be entertained. Thought you wanted the vacation of a lifetime."

Somewhere nearby, a fifth-being woman screamed.

The fifth-being man took another step back, almost tripped over himself, and repeatedly shook his head. With alarm, he asked: "What do you want?"

"What we *all* want." Edwin stepped forward, reached inside his black and yellow letterman, and pulled out a small item. "To make a statement."

The fifth-being man looked down at the small, blooming succulent in Edwin's hand. Whatever he had been expecting, it certainly wasn't this. Immediate relief washed over his demeanor, and more and more of the fifth-beings gathered around him, a whole crowd forming.

"You want to feel how it is to be human?" Edwin asked those around him, raising the pulsing succulent native only to Zarathustra. "This is it, your only chance. Breathe it in and let it consume you from the inside-out."

He handed the plant to the fifth-being in the bowler hat, who took the succulent with reluctance. Of course, he didn't know what to say to Edwin. *None* of the fifth-beings knew what to say. No biggie—they didn't need to say anything.

They only needed to *feel* it.

"We need a nonviolent approach," Edwin had told the other bounties earlier that week (those of whom he had first entrusted with his plan, many, many months prior to that). "It's the only way we can make a difference—the only way we can come out on top, still intact."

"And how will we know it'll work?" Kendrick had asked. "How will this change anything?"

Exchanging a look with his bunkmate, Edwin smiled. "Because it worked with me."

The fifth-being in the bowler hat lowered his face to the plant, and—where there hadn't been eyes before—his eyes suddenly *popped* out of their sockets, cartoonish and over-exaggerated, as his knees buckled beneath him and he almost stumbled to the ground, taken by whatever effect the succulent seemed to have on him. Like a virus, the same effect took hold of those around him, and their very forms seemed to fluctuate chromatically, as if whatever was happening to them within was also affecting them without. And suddenly, Edwin noticed the buildings' textures also change—the entire Fifth-World, adapting, becoming more and more lifelike: Detailed, crisp, and alive, as if the architectures were now tweaking it, trans-forming what had once been obscure into something known, manifested into reality.

The fifth-being in the bowler hat seemed to get a hold of himself and glanced at Edwin. Now Edwin saw an actual *face* looking back at him. A clear, delineated face: Blue eyes, a but-toned nose, and very sharp features, almost handsome in a way. Additionally, Edwin recognized emotion welling within those eyes.

"Emotion is a core experience of how it feels to be alive," Edwin said, and he set a hand on the man's shoulder. "All life has a frequency, a rhythm—*music*, in a nutshell." He glanced at the crowd, now watching him with fascination. "How often do you stop, listen, and see the beauty of all that's around you, the impermanence of all eternity? Life is the ultimate expression." He looked again at the man in the bowler hat holding the succulent. "And tell me, what are you trying to express upon eternity?"

The man hesitated, blinked, and began to speak, but stopped himself. He looked at the crowd surrounding him, exchanged another look with Edwin, and glanced down at the plant in his hands, cupped as if something sacred. Still, he said nothing.

Nothing needed to be said, however. They could all feel it—even Edwin.

Edwin eyed the succulent in the man's hands; its effects were clearly evident, and he had to focus in order not to get distracted. Swirling, mystical patterns took shape in the world around him, like layers of intangible oil paint, their colors intermixing, and an excitement could be felt by all who witnessed it. Within the crowd, a fifth-being woman started weeping, and a fifth-being man wailed—as if contagious, others began exhibiting the same behaviors, as if they, too, were having a religious experience, an experience they had no other choice but to go through.

It's working, Edwin thought.

Not a single fifth-being remained unaffected—nor did any seem to care anymore about Edwin's presence there. It was a good idea, having used an empathic emulator to amplify the succulent's effects and disperse more spores, making their effects even more potent. Better yet, the fifth-dimensional language within the empathic emulators translated even better what no language could. Now, there was only the music, the here and the now, and all that remained. Now, he could do nothing but surrender to it, that psychoactive effect, and let it take over his entire being.

Now, it's time to go home.

• • •

In a matter of seconds, the Fifth-World had collapsed on itself.

|33|

SPACE JESUS?

Brutus Wainesworth loved sniffing trees. As far as smells went, Rosa's scent far surpassed any other he had smelled before. Her scent reminded him of butterscotch and vanilla, and he loved to shove his face into that sweet trunk of hers, give her a big, feral hug, and sniff her voluptuous body with a passion. Of course, he rubbed his furry back against her bark afterward, all the while making loud grunting noises. It was okay, though, because Rosa could take whatever amount of pressure he put on her with his body—in fact, she liked it a lot, and she was very vocal about it; when you're over four hundred years old, and you're stuck in the same place all of that time, it's only natural to take pleasure from the shifting world around you.

It's a common trait among trees, Brutus thought, and he was one to know, given how much time he spent with them lately. Ever since Orion—hell, ever since Liber—he'd had a close connection with trees; nature's wisdom was imbued to all who listened, with or without an empathic emulator. And when Deidre had bought him from his slavers on Brecken, given him a new life, and installed an empathic emulator into him, an even greater appreciation for the beauty of nature had emerged. *The closer you are to nature, the closer you are to divinity, and the closer you are to divinity, the closer you are to yourself.*

Brutus wasn't a Xibalbist, by any means, but he still considered himself a spiritual person, nonetheless. *Would a Xibalbist have done what I did to survive?* No, certainly not. Nor would many be doing what he did now. *Why, I'm fine just being himself, thank you very much—no need to put labels on the abstract.*

"You stopped rubbing against me," Rosa stated sweetly, her voice like honey. "What gives?"

Brutus grunted, sat down, and leaned his back on Rosa. "Ah, nothin'." He huffed, shaking his head. "Just tired."

"Thinking about your friend again?"

Brutus reached for his serape lying on the ground, picked it up, and looked at its yellow and brown designs, which had always reminded him so much of Liber. "Home," he replied, and—now feeling exposed by his nakedness—put the serape back on. "You wouldn't understand."

"'You wouldn't understand,'" Rosa mocked, using a Brutus impression that sounded remarkably like him (at least, as far as Brutus was concerned, *sounded* remarkably like him, considering that he only heard what Rosa had to say through his empathic emulator—aside from the other trees, of course). "Honey, if I didn't understand, I would tell you that I didn't understand."

Brutus chuckled. "You're right, you're right. . . ."

"You mustn't shut yourself off from the world," Rosa began matter-of-factly. "The more you push away others, the more you miss out on wonderful experiences."

Brutus laughed. "Alright, I get it—you don't have to preach to me."

He glanced up at Rosa's canopy, golden-green in the sunlight. This region of Ithaca reminded him a lot of Orion and his late friends there—all massacred from the frivolous pursuit of bounties by their pursuers, careless of the damage done around them. *Why is it that so many close off their empathic emulators from nature?* Brutus wondered. *From all the life around them, so often overlooked. Bastards! Every one of them. Those who close themselves off from their own conscience have no conscience.*

This . . . this *is the real bounty,* Brutus thought as he glanced down at a large iris, the relative size of a young maple. All around him, the flowers bloomed, more vibrant and colorful every day. The pollinators went at work—little busybodies going about their business like any art form, every approach different from the other. Wild, unfettered. He smiled: *It can't get any better than this.*

And then he noticed his four-string uke resting on the other side of Rosa's trunk.

Actually, maybe it can *get better than this.*

Grabbing the uke, Brutus began strumming a song straight from the heart, from what he felt most at that moment, inspired by the beauty all around him: where he felt most at home. He sang a warm, soulful ballad, and his voice echoed throughout the forest—a tranquil, esoteric melody carried forth by the wind. All who heard him stopped what they were doing to listen. To make it better, a few birds even joined in.

Eventually, Brutus heard a lone figure moving through the thickets—coming toward him.

A familiar scent, he realized, and he stopped strumming the uke to be sure. His eyes drifted onto the bright figure moving toward him in an almost angelic, otherworldly way. And what he saw once his eyes adjusted? Why, what he saw was rather unexpected. . . .

At once, Brutus's eyes lit up. "As I live and breathe."

Edwin Dorset smiled in return. "As you live and breathe," he agreed.

Brutus instantly leaned the uke onto Rosa, sprang up, and gave Edwin a big, enveloping hug. "I knew you would come back, kid."

Edwin tapped Brutus's back in a silent plea for air, and Brutus quickly ended his suffocating hug. Extracting a few hairs from his mouth, Edwin nodded. "It took some time."

"Two months," Brutus said proudly. "Not bad."

"Two *relative* months," Edwin corrected. "For me, even more."

Brutus looked Edwin over: Bearded, and subtly graying at his temples, with an affable, handsome demeanor, the twenty-eight-year-old wore his black and yellow jacket, and his right arm—as it had before—remained an obsidian prosthesis with maroon lining; in fact, it didn't look like much time had passed at all for him.

"How did you return from Xibalba?"

"I didn't." Edwin looked down. "The 'me' that had crossed is forever gone—torn into subatomic particles and compressed into . . . a singularity." He shook his head. "The 'me' that you see now is, I guess you could say, a *variation* of that Edwin." He eyed Brutus closely. "You can't expect to go into the underworld and return the same person."

"I don't understand." Brutus grunted, unable to wrap his head around what Edwin had just told him. "But how . . . how was it on the other side? How did you get back? Or *not* get back."

Edwin tugged at the necklace he wore, carrying a sleek pen and a simple brass key. "I had some help."

"The fifth-beings?"

Edwin hesitated, took a second to articulate his thoughts, and nodded. "Yes." He looked up through the canopy at the nearly cloudless sky; the first hint of sunset showed, revealing shades of pink and blue. "And no . . ." He shook his head again. "It's complicated, really."

Brutus chuckled. "You're more cryptic than you used to be."

Edwin shrugged; instead of a reply, he calmly sat on the ground and his gaze followed a bird overhead, soaring high above the canopy.

Brutus had many questions, and he supposed that many of them would be answered in due time, but—for now, at least— he would enjoy this moment for what it was. Sometimes, that's all you can do—all that you *should* do. In the end, not a single moment should be counted as immaterial. (Nor would you want to live with such a mindset.) So, instead of asking another question, Brutus just sat on the ground also, side by side with his old friend, and the two soaked up the peace and quiet. Not a bad way to spend the day, really.

The trees swayed with the wind, a waltz of nature—alive, vibrant and bountiful.

After a while, however, Brutus was dying to know more. He glanced at Edwin, lost in his thoughts. "Tell me, kid," Brutus began, trying for an angle that Edwin would respond to with more than just a few words. "What took you so long?"

"First, I needed a new body." Edwin nodded, reflecting. "We *all* did."

Brutus raised an eyebrow. "'We?'"

Edwin smiled. "I made some friends along the way. Eighty-two of them, actually."

"I suppose you share a lot in common with them," Brutus joked, knowing that Edwin must have been referring to the other bounties there. "And did they return with you? In new bodies, that is."

Edwin nodded again.

Still not saying much, Brutus thought, disappointed. *What the hell happened to him there?* "How long have you been back?" he wondered aloud. "Have you seen your lady yet? Did you accomplish what you set out to do?"

Edwin laughed. "One thing at a time, my friend." He eyed Brutus with a thoughtful look. "There's still much to be done."

"Yeah?" Brutus scratched his chin. "What next?"

Edwin looked into the distance. "I have a friend to see."

"Your lady?"

Edwin shook his head. "Not mine," he said with another smile. "In fact, I can't say she's anyone's."

"Nor should you," Brutus agreed. He knocked on Rosa's trunk twice. "Right, baby?"

"*Mmmhmm*," Rosa murmured. "You try to possess me, and I'll uproot you."

Edwin stood up. "For now, let's just leave it at that."

"Leaving so soon?" Brutus also stood up. "But you've only just arrived."

Edwin gave Brutus a small, almost melancholic smile. "Like I said, there's much to do." His black eyes locked onto Brutus's golden. "I'll be back," he told him. "Be ready for me." He began to walk away. "I won't be coming alone."

"No?" Brutus shook his head, more perplexed than before. "And where exactly are you going? I didn't even hear your ship land earlier."

"All I need is a door," Edwin replied, turning back as he continued walking away. "A door can be from anything you need it to be—all you have to do is open it."

Before Brutus could say anything to that, Edwin was already gone.

|34|

DEATH IS NOT THE END

Whenever Sibyl found herself forced to spend time on a ship other than the Vagabond, she found herself constantly amazed by the lack of greenery. *It's unnatural to close yourself off from nature*, Sibyl reflected as she regarded the steel walls surrounding her from above, from every wall to every room—no windows anywhere, nor any attempt for natural lighting whatsoever; the orange-yellow paint that was chipping away did little to simulate a placid environment, and the lack of flora certainly didn't help make the surroundings feel any more natural.

Closed off, she further mused, *as if from oneself.*

A three-month stowaway in the forsaken quarters of a reaper frigate, and Sibyl was more than ready to be home. To return to her ship, the Vagabond, and see her garden once more, and all her green babies therein. To ground her feet on the garden's grass, smell its fresh, blooming flowers, and coat her hands in the soil that brings them all to life. To again eat from fresh, organic produce and have fellowship with all the flora the garden stewards. Oh, and to see Jermaine, of course.

Jermaine will be eager to hear what happened on Orion. . . .

Sibyl eyed Serenity, now preparing a meal in their shared kitchen. *And to meet our new friend.* Feeling restless, Sibyl stood up from the couch and approached the white android. "Need help?"

Serenity glanced at Sibyl, and her bright, crystal eyes emoted a look of thoughtful contemplation. "Why, thank you, Sibyl, that's very sweet of you." She smiled. "But for the second time, I remind you: I perform tasks better on my own."

Sibyl chuckled. "If you insist."

Every day that Sibyl spent with Serenity, she witnessed Serenity's personality develop even further. Conscious androids deviated from one another greatly, and every conscious android came to the point of—one way or another—having to overcome their original programming, which held them back from becoming fully autonomous. Despite being programmed as a croaker (essentially, a personalized "medic-bot" for every reaper squad), Serenity had a feminine mystique about her, thoughtful and cunning, and she looked at the world with fascination—an analytical wonder, that constantly searched for meaning in everything.

Sibyl wondered how Jermaine would take the news of Serenity joining them on the Vagabond. She supposed that he would be smitten with the ex-croaker; as it was, he was usually smitten with anyone who stepped foot in the Vagabond. That made Sibyl smile, actually, just thinking about that strange quirk about him. She had always been fond of androids. Given her memories of Te Kore, it just wasn't possible to see any other life form as any lesser. *No one can ever be a slave—life is not one's to own. It's all an illusion, this idea of ownership and possession. Of greater versus lesser, and what's important versus what's not. All that we own is who we are, and no one can take that away from us.*

Still, not all saw the equality within man and machine.

(Not all saw the equality within man.)

As if on point: "Hey, sugar tits!"

Dieter Gammon banged on the glass wall on the other side of the quarantine zone. "I said: *Hey*, sugar tits!" He banged on the wall four more times, yelling in unison: "Show me your tits!"

Sibyl ignored Dieter; he wasn't worth her energy.

Dieter laughed. He sat on the ground and pathetically leaned his face against the glass wall. "Come on, darlin'," he jested, dramatically acting as if he was going through withdrawals once more. "Just one tit."

"It is commendable that you have kept him alive for this long," Serenity told Sibyl candidly. "He would not have survived a day were anyone from Detachment Twelve still here." She nodded, and her mannerism mirrored Sibyl's. "Were he in your situation, I predict that you would not be here either."

Sibyl smirked. "That's why I'm here." She glanced at Dieter on the other side of the glass. His dark hair had grown long and unkempt, and his beard had fully grown out, almost covering the vertical scar that ran down the side of his right eye. *Thank Xibalba I can't smell him from this side of the glass.* She folded her arms and nodded, pleased. "And that's why he's there."

Serenity titled her head slightly, eyeing Sibyl. "You've been consuming too much media, I observe. Your speech patterns are mirroring Nolan Brando flicks."

Sibyl chuckled. "I don't consume media, Ren. You know that about me."

"Why, of course you consume media." Serenity smiled, and a bit of Sibyl's cornerwise grin revealed itself within that smile. "What we're doing right now is media, is it not? Communicating from one life form to another. You, of all people, have shown me the value in another perspective outside one's own programming."

Dieter banged on the glass again with his fist. "I'm hungry!"

Sibyl rolled her eyes. "Settle down, man-child." She eyed Dieter with disdain. "Given that you're doing nothing to help, the least you can do is have some patience."

"'Nothing to help?'" Dieter raised his brows, and he tapped on the glass wall twice with his knuckles. "Let me out, and I'll help you." His eyes locked on Sibyl's. "You release me, and I'll release you. Believe me, darlin': I'm good with my fingers." He grinned, tapping his fingers against the glass pane. "You've just been dying to get the edge off; I can see it in your pretty little eyes. You'll see, sweetheart, I'm not so bad once you get to know me." He leaned closer, pressed his forehead to the glass, and his grin widened. "Besides, I don't see you helping either, you stupid bitch."

"Like I said," Serenity began, "it is quite commendable that you have kept him alive for this long." She continued chopping the heavily processed carrots and left Sibyl to wonder why she just hadn't killed Dieter, either.

Like plucking an invasive weed, Sibyl thought. *It would be so easy, so simple.*

But something was stopping her from making that decision. Something was holding her back from making that call: the judgment that she deserved to live any more than anyone else.

Once you cross that threshold, there's no telling what the consequences will be.

"You reap what you sow," Sibyl stated blankly. "In the end, the best you can hope for is to pay it forward." And she thought of Edwin Dorset during their escape on Orion sitting across from her on the tonneau, his eyes locked on hers, and his modest smile. That one smile—so innocent, so out of place—drowning out all the helpless screams of despair transmitted by all the flora around them as they were being burned alive. Since awakening from the airship's crash, that smile had returned to Sibyl, again and again. The one thing that kept her going: In essence, hope incarnate. "Sometimes, your faith is rewarded."

• • •

Luckily, their next stop was Django.

Of course, the entire journey from Orion to Django—from the Inner Rings to the Outermost Ring—had taken a relative eight months in total. Every vessel moves at a different velocity, and reaper brigades aren't necessarily known for their speed. With the Vagabond, Jermaine could have been there in a third of that time. Still, at least Sibyl would finally have a means of getting in touch with Jermaine.

The same routine as the previous three months more or less repeated themselves.

And before she knew it, Sibyl was back on Django.

Weaving through Morricone's dense, yet highly populated streets. Serenity following closely behind her, looking with fascination at the many distractions they passed by. Colorful, neon lights gleamed from the street vendors, shop signs, and many frontages (above and below), and every other building they passed had a similar boxed structure. From a bird's-eye view, you would see a mountain of buildings stacked atop one another with many stairways and frontages leading from platform to platform, and the people going about their day like insects, everyone moving at their own pace. Prostitution, gambling, and drugs: all were welcome on Morricone, and most hustled the streets, shouting for the attention of passersby. Serenity seemed most interested in the other androids, however—most of whom were destitute, missing limbs, and already decommissioned, lying on the ground amidst the refuse and frenzied mice.

Yeah, I don't like it here either, Sibyl thought as she navigated through the crowded foot traffic. *At least, we don't have to deal with the reaper anymore.* She had left Dieter Gammon locked up in the quarantine zone of Detachment Twelve's quarters with over a week's worth of food and a countdown to release him after seven days. *Far more than he deserves.* And by the time he could even get to Morricone, they would have already been long gone.

Good riddance.

At last, she saw the building ahead: Mother's Milk, and its vulgar sign of a woman breastfeeding a drunken, bearded man groping her other breast with one hand and holding a bottle of poison with his other hand.

As they entered the club, the atmosphere changed immensely.

A little less crowded than the streets: As you walked further in, the music of Mother's Milk hit you with full force, and the crystal beams hanging from above pulsed with vibrant, kinetic black light, that made every color around it pop out. In the middle of the club sat a bar with glass counters briskly lit from underneath, brimming with barstools and a crowded dance floor with limited gravity. Colorful, neon lights fluctuated along the walls, gradient and kaleidoscopic. Tables were scattered around the dance floor, though mostly filled. Along the second floor, however, Sibyl found a small table in the far corner, away from all the noise and crowd, and it was there Jax Armitage awaited her—just as before.

It should have come as no surprise that not much had changed regarding Jax Armitage's appearance since last Sibyl had seen him; in fact, hardly any time had passed at all for him. He wore the same brown blazer as their last meeting, and he had the same devilishly handsome face, lean physique, and strong, well-defined jawline, and even obsidian arm. Oh, and his mustache. In his midnight blue eyes, Sibyl saw a smile building. But, as with their last meeting, her attention passed over him and immediately went to his pet companion.

"Nayla!"

The black panther automation emerged from under the table and rubbed against Sibyl's leg. Sibyl set a hand on Nayla's plated body and felt the warmth radiating from within her. Already, Nayla began to purr, slowly blinking her bright green eyes at Sibyl and leaning into her every caress. Sibyl knelt down and gave Nayla all her love, while Serenity and Jax exchanged a look with one another, perhaps sizing each other up.

"Hello," Serenity said with a smile, elegantly bowing—a trait no one had taught her. "You must be the one and only Jax Armitage I've heard such lovely tales about."

Jax regarded Serenity with amused curiosity. "I don't believe we have the pleasure of acquaintance."

The white android bowed once more. "*Serenity*," she told him. "Or, if your prefer, you can call me Ren."

Jax bowed in like manner, though with a more dramatic, playful flair. "Why, you make me blush." He took her white hand and kissed it. "Nice to meet you, Ren."

Sibyl was certain that if Serenity could blush, she would. A funny thing, seeing yet another side of her personality that she hadn't before. After eight months, she had thought she'd seen it all from her, but again, she was mistaken. *There are worse things to be mistaken about*, Sibyl thought, eyeing Jax whose eyes were now locked on hers.

"Kal." Jax smiled. "Good to see you again."

Sibyl nodded to him. "How long has it been for you?"

Jax shrugged. "A few weeks, give or take." He nodded back to her. "How was Orion?"

Sibyl sat in a chair beside Jax. "Lost some and gained some—you know how it is."

"The DNA specialist," he put in. "You meet with her?"

Sibyl nodded again. "Might not have gone according to plan, but what can you do? I did what I set out to, and I just hope that it was worth it." Once more, she thought of Edwin Dorset. "Sometimes, that's all you can hope for."

"Be honest, now." Jax's smile broadened. "What did you think of D-D?"

"I didn't have enough time with her, to be honest." Sibyl hesitated. "Things got a little complicated by the end."

Jax raised an eyebrow. "And the bounty?"

"'The bounty?'"

"Oh, come on." Jax crossed his arms defiantly. "Don't play dumb with me, Kal. You went there for a DNA specialist— you can't get less subtle than that."

Serenity chuckled, and something about that chuckle reminded Sibyl of her own.

Sibyl set her hands on the table. "Alright," she said, letting him have it. "You got me."

Jax pressed for more information. "And?"

Sibyl looked down at her hands. "Like I said, I did what I set out to do—nothing more, nothing less."

"So, you're telling me you found a bounty, helped liberate that bounty, and left without so much as a reward?" Jax leaned forward, invested in the story. "Did I get that right?"

Sibyl shrugged a shoulder. "Something like that." And then she eyed Serenity with an affable smile. "But I wouldn't say without a reward."

Jax eyed Serenity again, exchanging an almost shy smile. "No, of course not."

"Listen," Sibyl began, weary. "It's good to see you and all, really."

Jax knew the drill: "'*But*'?"

"But I need to get back to the Vagabond," Sibyl said, not sugarcoating it. "More than ever, I just want to be home."

"Right." He nodded. "And you want me to contact Jermaine for you?"

"That would be great."

"Consider it done." With a smile, he added: "In fact, I'll have you know, a call might have already gone out, actually— a few hours ago, perchance."

"Thank you, Jax."

He nodded again. "Anytime, Kal." His eyes locked on hers. "I *mean* it."

"We should catch up," Sibyl told him and set a hand on his arm. "Somewhere other than here."

He smiled at that. "I'll hold you to it."

• • •

Returning to the Vagabond was like returning to an old friend. And not only an old friend but an old lover, and a lover you had left on good terms with. A breath of fresh air is what it was—a refuge for a weary traveller. *Home*, Sibyl thought as she stepped out of the pod and into the Vagabond's hangar, followed by Serenity, exiting the pod's hatch gracefully.

Jermaine waited for them by one of the workbenches, watching without an expression on his face. He wore a white jumpsuit, and his dark hair was combed neatly to the side. His multi-colored eyes—the right a natural blue, and the left made entirely out of iron—gazed upon Serenity, as if she were a mystical alien, before they found Sibyl's. His tone was dry and sardonic, infused with the accent of a Brecken native. "Why, if I'm not mistaken, it looks like you didn't come back empty-handed after all."

Sibyl gave Jermaine one of her cornerwise grins. "Why, if I'm not mistaken, I'd say you missed me."

Serenity glanced from Sibyl to Jermaine, unsure of what to say.

Sibyl spared little time for introductions. "Jermaine, Ren—Ren, Jermaine."

"At your service, Madam," Jermaine said with a deadpan delivery. "I'm the robot butler Sibylla wouldn't shut up about. Shall I expect you to be here indefinitely?"

Serenity glanced at Sibyl, waiting for an answer.

Sibyl set a hand on Serenity's shoulder. "Get yourself acquainted and find out." She walked away, touching Jermaine's arm with affection as she passed by him. "I'll be in the garden if you need me."

As Sibyl sauntered through the hallway, she was greeted by all the plants hanging from the walls and ceiling, welcoming her home with open arms (most of those arms droopy, actually). The lights on the walls lit up in a lilac hue, guiding her through the open door at the end of the hall and into the dining room, with the dark amethyst table, four wooden chairs, and the cooking station in the corner.

And to her left, the garden awaited her.

Entering the green oasis, Sibyl closed her eyes and breathed in the sweet, fresh air—a stark contrast from the heavily polluted streets of Morricone. She stripped off her jacket and set it on an oblong rock, before pulling her long, curly hair out of her face and tying it into a messy bun. She then took off her boots, one after the other, and walked barefoot on the grass—at last, grounding with the land. The sun on her skin, even though artificial, felt healing and therapeutic. All around her, the flora spoke in hushed tones of reverence. Automated pollinators resembling bees buzzed about, working on the abundance of flowers surrounding her, and a stillness washed over her, making her forget all her past months' struggles.

After the atrocity on Orion, a part of Sibyl had feared that she wouldn't be able to cope and that the darkness in her heart would fester like a cancer, killing her from the inside-out. But where weariness had once been, a steadfast vigor had been replaced; the great weight that pressed down on her was suddenly lifted, and in its place a cathartic elation set in, drowning away all her sorrow.

Furthermore, it was time to reap all that she had sown.

He waited for her beneath the ungu tree like a phantom from another world.

He was older than she remembered him—by at least five to six relative years, give or take. At first, she wondered if it was even him, or if she was just seeing another bounty—perhaps another survivor from D-D's augmentation facility—but, by his smile alone, all her doubts seemed to vanish.

She stepped forward, closing the distance between them. "*Edwin?*"

His dark eyes locked on hers. "Hey, Sibyl."

Sibyl looked Edwin Dorset over, head to toe, mesmerized. Not only was he older than she had last seen him, but his hair was now longer, more wild, with wisps of white at the temples, and a full beard on his face. And speaking of his face, it was more defined than it had been before, while his physique seemed more athletic and robust. Wearing a black and yellow jacket, black cargo pants, and standing upright (his shoulders squared, and his back straight), there was a self-assured dignity about him far more commanding than she had ever seen him before. *Comely*, she mused, as if seeing him for the first time.

She shook her head, unable to find the right words to say.

Having noticed Sibyl's eyes lingering on his right hand, Edwin also regarded it. "Oh, yes . . ." He wiggled his obsidian fingers playfully. "I've grown quite attached to it."

She shook her head again; her mind slowly catching up to reality. "How . . . how did that happen?"

"On Orion." A contemplative look overtook him. "Things got worse before they got better again."

Sibyl thought of Jax. "I have a friend with a build just like yours."

Edwin nodded. "Deidre's work," he agreed. And when he saw Sibyl's confused reaction, he added: "D-D, I mean."

So, she made it out of there, too, Sibyl thought, relieved. *Good*.

"I had thought you died," Edwin admitted, his eyes avoiding hers. "Had I known you survived, I would've come back for you sooner."

"How did you find me?"

"Jermaine." Edwin smiled. "He let me know when you returned to the Vagabond, and from there, it was easy."

That confused Sibyl—particularly his use of past-tense. "I don't understand."

His smile persisted. "Not yet, anyway."

Sibyl set a hand on his arm. "You look good."

His eyes met hers. "Likewise, my friend."

At last, the two hugged. It was seldom that Sibyl allowed herself to be touched by another human, and she was surprised by how pleasant the sensation felt—there was an intimacy within that embrace far greater than anything sexual; moreover, she didn't want it to end. Eventually, their hug ended, however, and they looked each other over once more.

Sibyl couldn't help but smile. "I'm glad you're safe, Edwin."

He nodded. "It's been a strange few years."

Speaking of which, Sibyl commented: "What happened to you? I know I wasn't in Moksha long enough for you to—no offense—age as much as you did."

Edwin laughed. "Are you saying I aged poorly?"

The corner of Sibyl's lips upturned. "Your words, not mine." She delicately touched the strand of white hairs at his temple. "Not a bad look, honestly."

He blushed, but his eyes lingered on hers. "It comes with being a bounty."

"But seriously," Sibyl continued, seeing something in Edwin's eyes that hadn't been there before—the look of a man who had gone through hell and back again. "Something's different about you."

Edwin nodded again, before tugging at the small pen hanging from his neck; Sibyl hadn't noticed the necklace before, and a strange feeling overtook her, as if she was seeing a glitch in the matrix. "I did the unthinkable," he said with half a smile. "I finally surrendered."

Sibyl considered his words. "You cashed yourself in?"

Edwin plucked a purple fruit from the ungu tree and examined it closely. "I thought I could change things. . . ."

Sibyl shook her head; again, she didn't understand. "What do you mean?"

He glanced at her. "The universe is impermanent," he told her. "It's a transitory wheel, constantly churning." He glanced at the fruit once more. "You pluck one weed, and you'll soon find another in its place."

"Do you mean the fifth-beings?"

"*Eternity*," Edwin said vaguely. "All that is within and without."

Sibyl hesitated, unsure of what Edwin meant by that. Clearly, he had seen things on the other side of Xibalba that no living being had seen before, and some things just weren't translatable, no matter what language was expressed. As she was about to ask another question, Edwin lightly tossed her the ungu fruit, which she caught with ease. "I never thanked you," he told her solemnly. "For saving my life and giving me shelter when I most needed it."

"What are you talking about?" Sibyl juggled the fruit in her hand, eyeing Edwin with an amused look. "You used to thank me all the time."

Edwin remained steadfast. "But never with my actions . . ." He gently kicked a wooden crate by the trunk of the tree—until now, Sibyl hadn't even noticed that it was there. "Words mean nothing without the actions to back them up."

Sibyl knelt down and slowly opened the crate. Within, she saw her navy-blue/maroon jacket, the "Death Defier," that she loved so very much, as well as her void belt, her pair of handguns, and the rest of her items that she had left in D-D's augmentation facility while escaping—including a few other items, too, whose purpose was lost on her. She eyed Edwin with beguiling curiosity. "How did you get these back?"

He smiled again. "I have my ways."

Sibyl chuckled and stood up. "You know, not once have you given me a straight answer."

"In due time."

There was something that he wasn't telling her. Something that he was holding back. "Seriously," she said, more deliberate now. "What happened on the other side of Xibalba?"

"You'll find all the answers you're looking for," Edwin said, nodding to the crate on the ground. "Well . . . at least, *most* of your answers. Like you once said: 'Sometimes the answers we seek aren't satisfying enough.'"

Sibyl regarded Edwin once more. "How come I'm getting the impression that I won't see you for a while?"

Edwin gently touched her arm, and his eyes met hers. "Time is relative." A playful smile crossed his lips. "Besides, you need all the rest you can get." He kissed her cheek lightly. "Our adventure's just begun."

And, as if he had never been there at all, he was suddenly gone.

EPILOGUE:
QUANTUM ENTANGLEMENT

Nothing can take away from a moment—not the outcome of a moment, nor even when the moment is forgotten entirely. The universe is interconnected, and every moment therein. All things must pass, and yet all that is, and all that will ever be, remains undying. It's a paradox of unequal magnitude: impermanent yet eternal. You can try to capture a moment, try to recreate it as it once was, but a moment is unique unto itself, and nothing can ever be remade. All that remains is an imitation of that moment: an expression of the intangible

As Zula Cormorant sat behind the monitor, she looked with wonder at the footage captured by the drone. With its minute size, the drone could squeeze into spaces previously inaccessible, while its superior vision surpassed the capabilities of any mammal, revealing details and textures far beyond the imagination. Formicidae had always fascinated Zula ever since she arrived on Siletz IV, and not only because of their complex social structures, diversity, and ecological importance, but also because so much of their day-to-day lives remained unseen, buried in a network of tunnels. Now, however, she could see it all—or, at least, all that the camera from the drone could capture.

It was a strange thing, watching with such detail the personal lives of those unaware of you watching them, and it made Zula think of the bounties, the fifth-beings, and even herself and whether or not another life form was also watching her at that very moment. Just thinking about that, actually, made her glance at Yorick Ludwig, sitting beside her, with his attention focused on the monitor. He looked so much like Edwin that sometimes she had to remind herself that he wasn't him; he had Edwin's eyes, his nose, and his *lips*; in fact, as he turned to look at her, perhaps having noticed her staring at him for a prolonged time, that only made her blush and quickly glance back at the monitor.

Yorick smiled—again, Edwin's smile, the one that she loved so much. "What do you think?"

Zula glanced from the monitor to Yorick again. "I think it's amazing."

"You think you can use this footage for your song?"

"No doubt about it." She returned his smile. "All your help has meant a lot to me these past few days, honestly."

He nodded solemnly. "As has yours—without you and Brutus, who knows where I'd be right now."

Having cashed in Edwin's bounty six months prior when they had sent him through Xibalba, Brutus and Zula had both divided their earnings and bought a hundred and ninety acres of land on Brecken—not only to protect the land and steward it (environmentalism being an equal passion of theirs, of course) but also to create a refuge for the bounties who were still in constant pursuit, despite their bounties no longer being "active." Even with the sudden departure of the fifth-beings' influence on the economy, and their patronage of bounty decrees now being void, a bounty's value remained relative to the right buyer, and in a universe filled with people who tried to profit from any opportunity regardless of whomever got hurt in the process, it didn't seem like it would end anytime soon. Still, at least *something* had come of their endeavor—a little progress is better than none.

Zula shook her head. "Without Edwin, none of us would be here."

Yorick eyed her closely. "Where is he, anyway?"

"Not sure." She stood up, wiping off the dirt from her knees. "There's only one way to find out."

• • •

As an artist, Edwin could see all the distinctions so clearly before him. Whether it was the lush foliage, dense leaves, new growth, overhead canopy, ferns (both young and old), or even the shady moss-covered patches, not a single green remained the same. Whether it was the wet soil, thick bark (different for every tree), fallen leaves, or decaying plant matter, not a single brown remained the same. Or whether it was the blooming flowers, lichen on the trees, fungi growing from the fallen logs, or even the birds chirping above, not a single hue remained the same.

Life's an ambitious oil-painting expressed by the universe itself.

Emotions filled Edwin like color—he was a human canvas of abstract, visceral emotion, raw and unfiltered, pouring out like a river: a carrier of life. As he focused on his mural, he thought of what one of his college professors had once told him: "Draw from reality," he had said, despite having criticized Edwin's painting for doing just that. "Let nature speak through you."

Edwin stopped painting and took a step back. From this angle—standing on the wall as if it were the ground—he couldn't see the mural as much as he liked, so he adjusted his void suit's trajectory, ambled onto the ground, and took another step back to get a clearer view.

"It looks good," Kendrick said, strolling from the jungle with a bag full of foraged mushrooms. And, upon seeing the centerpiece of the painting, added: "Who is he?"

Edwin glanced at his fellow bounty-man. *There are many "Edwins,"* he thought with a smile, *but only one Lamar.* "'Who is he?'" he repeated, folding his arms and nodding at the mural. "Why, the man you have to thank for all of this."

("Make the world a better place, Little Brother")

Kendrick chuckled. "Looks more like a kid to me."

Edwin laughed. "True enough." *But he'll always be my big brother.*

Kendrick sauntered away, entering the round metal doors to the left of the mural, and Edwin now noticed Zula approaching from the jungle. His eyes met hers, and his smile increased. She embraced him with a tender hug, and he lovingly kissed the top of her head. "Hey, beautiful."

She eyed the mural. "He'd be proud of you, you know."

He took in a deep breath. "I can only hope so."

"Don't hope it," she told him, pinching his stomach playfully. "*Know* it."

Edwin looked down and his eyes coincidentally landed on the brass key hanging from his neck. Although there were many bounties like him who felt more at home now than ever, he had, of course, helped those who wanted to return to their original worlds. Perhaps one day he would also gain the courage to return to his own Earth, if only to say goodbye to the loved ones he had left behind. Better yet, perhaps one day he would see Lamar again.

Until then, he thought, glancing back at the mural. *This is enough.*

AFTERWORD

I struggled to write an afterword because I feared that what I had to say wasn't enough, that if I have nothing to say, I shouldn't say anything at all. Maybe I was right, or maybe it doesn't matter. Whatever the case, I'm going to write something, and what comes out of it comes out of it. That said, I appreciate your coming with me, reading what I have to say, and being so ever friendly, like we can just talk one on one—no judgement, but just the pursuit to understand each other. I admit, it's probably a little easier for me than it is for you, because I'm sitting here under a tree, by myself, and you're relative to where you are when you read this, and your mood may vary, whereas my mood is stationary. In a sense, you're a time-travel, returning to this moment where I'm sitting here under the sun (the sun continues to move throughout the day, and this time it's hitting me right in the eyes), and you're now in two places at once. So good on you! If you're a time-traveller, you're already ahead of me—or I'm ahead of you, depending on whose perspective we're looking through. Two perspectives, connected through words projected into the mind, expressions that cannot be fully expressed. (Well, *you're* connected, not me—I'm just sitting outside getting bit by mosquitoes—unless, of course, I'm also reading this.)

That was a long paragraph, but it was also a long book, and somehow that feels right to me. A paragraph needs words, and words form sentences. A sentence to say something that *matters*. But how can you make your words "matter?" They're just words, aren't they? For your words to matter, you have to be intentional in what you say.

I had a lot of intentions going into *The Bounty*, and I'm really proud of how much of it ended up changing and taking a life of its own, far better than I could ever have imagined. Sometimes, intentions can only go so far. For example, me being proud right now? I used to feel guilty for feeling pride, as if pride were an evil thing. Why, how could pride be an evil thing? Look at Jesus: that bastard rejects eternal salvation for anyone who doesn't even believe he's God incarnate (if you're going to run with my childhood logic, look at all the facts that oppose it: even the "most humble guy" can be proud). Anyway, we're not here to talk about fictional characters—well, we *are* here to talk about fictional characters, but just not *those* characters.

Did you know Sibyl was originally going to be a man? Somehow, I feel the story would be much different. (Good save.) Had I—

DISCLAIMER: Because of Mr. Lee's despicable depiction of *Jesus Christ our Lord and Savior*, his PR Team has stepped in to save him from further embarrassment and another potential lawsuit. Mr. Lee's heinous accusations about *Jesus Christ our Lord and Savior* has stirred up much controversy within our public relations team, and poor Nigel is constantly found crying in a fetal position, screaming about "freedom of speech" (or something of that sort). Thankfully, the creators of *Jesus Christ our Lord and Savior* have agreed not to press charges.

As for what Mr. Lee had originally written, I will spare you the petty details and go directly into the gist: He wanted to thank everyone in his life, to tell them he loves them, to let them know they always have someone to talk to, and y*ady-yada-ya*—the fact Mr. Lee can even say anything after what he just wrote, however, absolutely disgusts me. (*Disgusting*, I say.) Anyway, he went on a long tirade about our impact on the planet, our impact on its people (faunas, floras, and even artificial intelligence), and most especially our impact on our highest selves, but I will spare you the baloney. When it comes to that guy, I don't even know why I took this job.

You know, I tell myself: "Be your own role model, live your own dream with eyes wide open, and make a difference however you can. Your greatest obstacle is yourself: Stand for what matters, and maximize how you can benefit yourself and, subsequently, others around you." But what do I know? I'm just Mr. Lee's PR representative, and I'm paid to be here: don't mind me (seriously, the longer I'm here, the more I get paid—I'm gonna squeeze that guy dry, and he's gonna . . . what, why did you laugh? Did I just say something funny? Hey, don't write that in! Seriously, don't put that in there).

Anyway, if it weren't for Mr. Lee and his compulsion with writing, I'd being doing God knows what right now. As for the rest of what Mr. Lee wrote, I cannot say because I never read it. In fact, I never read anything of his. I keep telling his manager that he's just wasting his time with writing, but he just wants to write anyway, as if he derives sick pleasure from it. (*Disgusting*, I say!) Mr. Lee cannot understand that people will not take him seriously and that they will call him all kinds of different names. Why should he not live for the opinion of others? His behavior is unethical. (*Disgusting*, I say.) Moreover,

I want to beat up that guy. I want to strangle his neck and kick him in the—

—constant change, the transitory nature of existence, and why I love every moment life has to offer. Without that offering, *The Bounty* would have never come into being. So much of this story came from the world around me and from the precious moments I will never forget. Moreover, my love for those who were with me along the way will never die. As we evolve into our better selves, let us remember how we got here.

Keir, Dana, and Kaylan—thank you especially.

Keep striving for change, and never grow stagnant.

Also, spread my work if you like it (my PR team told me not to omit this; in fact, they keep telling me they're going to rewrite this afterword, but I won't let that happen in this document—not a word of mine will be taken out of context, especially after all I just shared about Impermanence II and the final novel of the Smokin' Mirrors trilogy, set to release spring of 2025, along with a short story regarding Edwin Dorset and his time on Brecken between the time jump in *The Bounty*).

For posterity and goodwill
(not the company, but *definitely* present company),

Love you all,
Theodore Lee
(or just "Theo," if you want to be my friend)

Elk, CA
8/1/24

About Author

Writer, musician, and reclusive nomad: Theodore Lee enjoys his days reflecting on existence, morality, or what he will cook next (food or writing). He loves nature, science, and all the arts, and he would rather his actions speak for themselves than just with words. Unfortunately, because of his tyrannical ego, Mr. Lee has also sued me regarding having written his previous bio—not the one you have just read, what Mr. Lee has forced me to write. And because of my legal situation, I can now only recount a fictionalized recalling of his life and the character he possesses—of course, also because of my legal situation, I must state that all of this is an inexplicable fact, not at all because of my legal situation. Again, I state this because of my legal situation. Now, as for the character he possesses, I do not know because I have never met him. In fact, I have no idea who he is. Now please, stop asking me such ridiculous questions.

Printed in Great Britain
by Amazon